ALSO BY NANA KWAME ADJEI-BRENYAH

Friday Black

CHAIN-GANG ALL-STARS

CHAIN-GANG ALL-STARS

Nana Kwame Adjei-Brenyah

PANTHEON BOOKS

NEW YORK

All rights reserved. Published in the United States by Pantheon Books, a division of Penguin Random House LLC, New York, and distributed in Canada by Penguin Random House Canada Limited, Toronto.

Pantheon Books and colophon are registered trademarks of Penguin Random House LLC.

Library of Congress Cataloging-in-Publication Data
Name: Adjei-Brenyah, Nana Kwame, author.
Title: Chain-gang all-stars : a novel / Nana Kwame Adjei-Brenyah.
Description: First Edition. New York : Pantheon Books, 2023
Identifiers: LCCN 2022017029 (print) | LCCN 2022017030 (ebook) |
ISBN 9780593317334 (hardcover) | ISBN 9780593317341 (ebook) |
ISBN 9780375715402 (open-market)
Subjects: LCGFT: Novels.
Classification: LCC PS3601.D49 C48 2023 (print) | LCC PS3601.D49 (ebook) |
DDC 813/.6—dc23
LC record available at https://lccn.loc.gov/2022017029
LC ebook record available at https://lccn.loc.gov/2022017030

www.pantheonbooks.com

Jacket design and illustration by Kimberly Glyder

Printed in the United States of America

First Edition

6 8 9 7

For my dad, who said,

"There's nothing quite like helping someone in need,

nothing quite like it."

I hope the Universe love you today

—KENDRICK LAMAR

Contents

PART II

PART III

CHAIN-GANG ALL-STARS

The Freeing of Melancholia Bishop

S he felt their eyes, all those executioners.

"Welcome, young lady," said Micky Wright, the premier announcer for Chain-Gang All-Stars, the crown jewel in the Criminal Action Penal Entertainment program. "Why don't you tell us your name?" His high boots were planted in the turf of the BattleGround, which was long and green, stroked with cocaine-white hash marks, like a divergent football field. It was Super Bowl weekend, a fact that Wright was contractually obligated to mention between every match that evening.

"You know my name."

She noticed her own steadiness and felt a dim love for herself. Strange. She'd counted herself wretched for so long. But the crowd seemed to appreciate her boldness. They cheered, though their support was edged with a brutal irony. They looked down on this Black woman, dressed in the gray jumpsuit of the incarcerated. She was tall and strong, and they looked down on her and the tight coils of black hair on her head. They looked down gleefully. She was about to die. They believed this the way they believed in the sun and moon and the air they breathed.

"Feisty," Wright said with a grin. "Maybe that's what we should call you—Little Miss Feisty."

"My name is Loretta Thurwar," she said. She looked at the people all around her. There were so many of them, so many waves of humans who would never be the object of such cruel attention. Would never know how it made you feel, both tiny and all-powerful. How the thrum of thousands was so loud, so constant, it could disappear from your ears but continue to roar as something felt in the body. Thurwar gripped the weapon she'd been given: a thin spiraling corkscrew with a cherrywood handle. It was light and simple and weak.

"Not Little Miss Feisty, then?" Wright said, walking a wide orbit around her.

"No."

"That's probably for the best, Loretta." He stepped toward his box. "I hate wasting good names anyway." He laughed and the crowd echoed him. "Well, Loretta Thurwar"—he threw his playful condescension directly at her, chopping her first name into three hard syllables, using a singsong child's voice for her last—"welcome to the BattleGround, baby."

There was an electric cough in the air and Thurwar was pulled down so forcefully she feared for a moment her arm had been dislocated at the shoulder. Kneeling, not knowing what else to do, she started to laugh. Chuckling first, then deep laughter. The feeling of hold that came from the magnetic implants in her arms was actually one of gentle massage under the skin. She could wiggle her fingers freely, but her wrists were glued to the platform. The ridiculousness of it all. She laughed until she felt out of breath, then laughed some more.

The bells began to sound.

Wright screamed into the air, "Please rise for Her Majesty!" He ran the rest of the way to his announcer's box.

The crowd stood on their feet. They held themselves still and erect. For her.

She walked onto the faux football field. Aluminum alloy on her arms. Braids that stopped at the back of her neck. Exposed shoulders each tattooed with the WholeMarket™ logo. A series of rods jutted out from her chest guard and circled her muscled abdomen to form a sleek cage. It was a custom creation. Thurwar had watched, even cheered, the first time she'd seen that the metallic pieces, initially thought to be exclusively defensive, were more. She'd been watching, huddled with the others in her cell block around the streaming video feed, when the woman had removed two of the rods from her guard and pressed them into Slingshot Bob's eyes.

And now Thurwar was seeing them up close. This was Melancholia Bishop's final fight. Bishop had made it. She had done what no woman before her had done, survived three years on the Circuit. Three years of slamming down her hammer, Hass Omaha, and swiping her mace, Vega. Three years conquering souls.

"Drowned King County's very own Queen of the Damned!"

All she had in her hands was her helmet. Melody's Helm. Crusader-style, made of tin with a gold cross down its middle.

"The Annihilator, the Bad News Bitch, the Death Songstress herself!"

The seventh bell rang; the people screamed. For years this had been their sacred ritual. The seven bells of Melancholia Bishop. They'd seen her wipe scum off the earth. They'd seen her kill women and men whom they'd once claimed to love. Now she stood and looked out at them for the last time. Soon, she would be free.

Melancholia
Melancholia
Melancholia

The crowd chanted. Her brown eyes explored the bleachers. Then she raised the helm above her head. Once it was on, she was home.

Melancholia
Melancholia
Melancholia

"For the last time ever," Wright cheered, "please help me welcome the winningest woman ever to step on the BattleGround. The Mistress of the Murder Ballad. The Sacred Sweetheart. The Crusader. The baddest the planet has ever seen. Your very own Melody 'Melancholia Bishop' Price!"

Your very own, Thurwar thought, rattled by the force of the love that exploded out from the audience. They loved her so, and still, this woman, despite it all, belonged to none of them. She had an aura about her that made that clear. It was enough to push Thurwar's eyes down to the ground. As if the woman in front of her truly were royalty.

Thurwar watched, bowed in her Keep, an impossible power in front of her. The hammer and the mace. On one side of the field there was a knight in her armor. On the other, there was Thurwar in a jumpsuit, a corkscrew slick in her clammy hands.

Bishop!

Bishop!

"Any final words for us, Melancholia?" Wright asked.

"What's left to say?" she said, her voice echoing metallic but familiar through her helmet as she addressed the crowd. "I'm in the same place I started."

The crowd cheered wildly.

"When I got here, I had two Ms on my back. Two murders. When I leave, I'll still just have two. But I had to kill so many more people than that to get here."

"That's very true. You've cleaved through so many," Wright said. "But any of those stand out to you? So many highlights. And you've overcome more than your fair share of doubt. Here on the mountaintop, when you look back down, what are you proudest of?"

"Proud?" A metal face turned toward the sky. Her shoulders bounced and she laughed. The crowd followed awkwardly. Chuckling because this was their queen. As the crowd grew raucous with laughter, Melancholia fell silent. Then was a moment when the crowd seemed not to know what to do next.

"Lock-in!" Wright yelled. Again, a force sounded, this time locking Melancholia Bishop into the platform beneath her. The HMC* that she'd been speaking into flew up and behind her. The crowd let out a small gasp. To force-lock her, to silence her, on her freeing day. It was beneath them. A sudden force-lock was what you gave the despicable, the uninitiated, the unruly, the afraid. And so they turned their noses up at it, but turned them back down just as quickly to take in the history unfolding before them: the freeing of Melancholia Bishop.

"Let's deathmatch!" Wright yelled.

---

* Holo Microphone Camera (HMC) EyeBall™ is the primary video/sound recording device of all things action-sports. These intelligent, self-aero-propelling cameras can get in down and dirty, so you don't have to. A Kodex Product.

The loud, empty sound of unlock called through the arena. The women were released upon each other.

Thurwar stood up and she ran, ran directly at the unbreakable woman in front of her. Once she was close enough for it to matter, she leapt in the air and pulled back her fist, clenched around the corkscrew, and aimed to strike. She screamed, thrust down. The neck, the neck. Her body said the neck.

Melancholia snatched her by the wrist, dissolving her force to nothing, then punched her in the gut.

Melancholia

The people screamed to the beat of bass drums. Again and again, they'd seen her "catch and crash," had seen her drop Hass Omaha or Vega and grab her opponent with one hand before using whichever weapon she still held in the other to deal a death blow. But now she held this nothing by the wrist and threw a bare-knuckled punch. A blow anyone could survive. She was playing with her food. They laughed and cheered and cried. A show-woman to the end.

"Swing through, not at," Melancholia said. This the people could not know. In her helm, with no HMCs buzzing around—they might distract or affect the fight—the two women on the BattleGround were alone with their words.

Melancholia punched Thurwar again and threw her down to the grass.

Thurwar knew she'd been spared. She didn't know why. She swallowed the death she'd seen in the moment Bishop had held her. She looked up at the heroic, terrible woman standing above her.

"Can you hear me?" Melancholia asked.

Thurwar scrambled through the field, panting hard, sweeping over the green. She'd lost the corkscrew. She hated herself, an intense, familiar feeling. She was crying. She pitied the sad thing she'd become in that moment, hunched and searching. Frantic and soon dead. But her murderer was speaking to her. "Listen to me," she said. Then Thurwar felt a kick to the ribs. She rolled over in the grass, gasped air in, and scrambled to her feet again.

She gathered herself and looked at the Crusader. Thurwar wanted to win. She wanted it desperately. She had a furious desire to crush this woman in front of her. She wanted the crowd to weep. For the first time in so long, she wanted to live.

With no weapon at hand Thurwar ran at Melancholia. Before she could leap, she saw that both the hammer and mace were on the ground. The titan was making a game of her life. She sprinted and tackled the woman with the urgency of the dying. They tumbled together briefly, their bodies rushing over white hash marks. Then Thurwar felt a tightness at her scalp. She reached up in the tussle and felt a blow to the chest. She was dragged by her hair to her knees.

"Shave all of it," Melancholia said, her fist full of Thurwar's hair. This time Thurwar heard her, understood that she was being given a directive.

"Shave off your hair," Bishop repeated, her voice hard and low. She punched Thurwar in the face again. Thurwar tasted blood falling from her nose to her lips. Again she was thrown to the ground.

"It's right in front of you," Thurwar heard. "Choose now." Melancholia raised her arms in victory. The whole world screamed.

Thurwar saw it, the coil of metal stuck into the wood. She leapt at it like a snake and in her rush to grab it, she cut her own middle finger deeply. She ignored the blood, rose to her feet, and as she did, Melancholia Bishop turned to her, then reached down and grabbed the hammer.

Thurwar took long, careful steps as she moved in a wide perimeter around Melancholia. The noise had settled to an even roar, but the sound was just an echo now, as was the pain in her body.

"I played their game. You don't play it."

"I'm not dying here," Thurwar said. A long-smothered part of her emerged.

"Then swing through, not at." Thurwar watched Bishop. "I am very tired," the other woman said. "Do you understand?"

"I'm not dying here," Thurwar repeated, the words summoning themselves. She continued to circle Bishop, backing farther away, gathering space to charge. Bishop followed her in a smooth pivot.

"Then swing through, not at. And shave your fucking head. And make them love a version of you. That's the important part, whatever you do. Love, then get out."

Thurwar waited. Corkscrew clenched in fist.

Bishop's knees bent just enough for her stance to say, *Come at me*. She looked at Thurwar and spoke. "I'm not going to let you live. You are going to choose to live. I'm going to swing across my body. Once the hammer goes I can't stop it. Understand?"

Thurwar did and she didn't. She couldn't. Not then. Bishop reached for her helmet and pulled it off. Even against her dark skin the scars on her neck gleamed. Her black hair was in tight cornrows. Melancholia raised her arms and the crowd screamed anew in delight. Thurwar glanced up at the Jumbotron. It occurred to her then that this god was a woman like her.

Melancholia Bishop smiled briefly once more before her face became hard and murderous. Thurwar stepped forward toward her destiny.

Her left arm pumped into the air. Her hand was cupped loosely, and she shot her right leg up, planting it as hard as she could. She pushed forward, fully immersed in the freedom of building momentum. Her eyes were trained on Bishop's neck, as supple and human as anyone's. Her left arm careened back, scooping the air and hurtling it behind her as her left leg jutted up, her knee pulled forward, and her stride grew. She ran.

Mel—

Her left foot fell first, the midsole landed, and she rolled purposefully to her toes before pushing off again. Her body remembered, would always remember, how to run with purpose.

—an—

Again, her arms reversed themselves, slipping precisely past each other as her right leg rose and fell, her stride opening still. She was very close. She thought of nothing, put her trust in her body as it sped forward.

—cholia

Her arms switchbladed and her legs carried. She continued the push and switch of her arms and legs, forging speed. Her body told her, This speed, me, your body is your weapon.

When she was two paces away Melancholia's arm swung backward, a negative motion, a buildup. She pulled the hammer back, the picture of destructive potential.

Thurwar's foot came down again. Melancholia came forward, pushing first, then letting the hammer pull her. It swung across the air in a murder song. Thurwar dove toward the ground, tucked in her head and neck, and rolled as the hammer sowed fresh death into nothing. She crouched and then leapt, her right, corkscrewed fist leading. She screamed as she ripped open Melancholia's jaw.

The silence bore something new in Thurwar. Her body tingled as red fell into her fist. A spattering of blood burst from Melancholia's lips. The hammer rose briefly and crushed down, just grazing Thurwar's shoulder as she twisted out of its murderous path. Thurwar jumped onto Melancholia's back. She wrapped her legs around Bishop's waist and stabbed hard into the side of Bishop's neck, then pulled the corkscrew out and punched in again. This time as she tried to pull it out, the screw resisted, caught in the tangle of Bishop's flesh. Thurwar pulled harder, and when she did, the handle came out alone, the metal screw lost somewhere in Bishop's throat. With nothing with which to pierce, Thurwar punched Melancholia's head. She'd given three heavy blows before she felt the champion's knees buckle.

Bishop swatted weakly behind her at Thurwar, as if at a pesky fly. Her hammer was on the ground. Thurwar drank the sweet, rich silence of absolute awe.

She screamed a roar, and in that moment she was the only sound. She jumped from the woman's back and Melancholia stood sleepily, somehow, still. Seeing the woman on her feet, Thurwar scrambled to grab the hammer. Her fingers found the grip and Melancholia looked down at her. Suddenly afraid, Thurwar jumped back. Bishop swayed, holding her neck, then letting it go. Her eyes were brown, beautiful, tired, and yet they widened for a moment as she looked at Thurwar, her killer.

Come at me, those eyes said.

Thurwar obeyed. She ran. She brought the hammer like a bomb to the face of its first master, and the people, those people, were silent no more.

PART
I

Hurricane Staxxx

This was sacred.

The low roar of thousands waiting for her. An ocean of voices above, all around. She held her scythe in her hands. She told the guards to give her space and swayed left, then right. Warmed her spine. Energy flowed through her. She closed her eyes and entered her body. Her body didn't always make her feel safe, but there, underneath the ocean of voices, it felt immaculate.

The gate in front of her pulled open. There at the end of a tunnel that opened to light, Hamara "Hurricane Staxxx" Stacker was still a silhouette.

A floating ball of glowing metal appeared before her. She spoke into it: "Who makes the knife feel good?"

An electrosynth jumped on top of a swinging melody and a pitch-shifted vocal loop. The people's hearts beat harder.

STAXXX, they said together, definitively.

She sprinted onto the field. Show lights flashed down and golded her sandy-brown skin. Her locs fell free in thick ropes down her neck, past her shoulders, even past her lightweight reinforced carbon-fiber-polymer chest guard, branded with the WholeMarket™ insignia, a bountiful fruit basket. Her shins and left arm were mummied in white bolt leather, the style Thurwar had made popular. There was a sleeve of hard armor above the wrapped battle cloth on her left arm too. Her formerly white combat boots were splotched with browns and reds, a pale, grainy earth tone. Her thighs were compressed in elastic that stretched against her muscles, the tights also marked with the WholeMarket™ fruit basket, emblazoned near her hip, conspicuously not centered on her genitalia, as many other major brands might have opted for. WholeMarket™ was a family brand.

Her wrists glowed, perpetual proof of the forever hold of the mag-cuffs beneath her skin.

An additional floating camera moved around her, taking in the Xs inked all over her body. There was one on her tight abdomen, a few at her neck, several on her arms, and one on each eyelid. Every X was a story of her life's triumph over another's. She was a collection of death and vitality.

"That's the best you can do?" she called out to the stadium.

Her face collapsed into a frown that was magnified a hundred times on the Jumbotron above. Seeing their failure, the crowd screamed harder. Staxxx's mouth snapped to a wicked grin.

"Who's that beautiful bitch you bastards beat off to?" Staxxx sang into the HoloMicCam floating in front of her. She was propellering her scythe, LoveGuile, around her hands and forearms. The momentum accrued, the bladed head leading, speeding, and eating through the air as Staxxx charmed it around her body. This staff and blade, the world knew, were an extension of her person. They screamed her name.

STAXXX!

"Who's that heartbreaker you need to break you down?"

STAXXX!

"Who do you motherfuckers love so bad it hurts?"

STAXXX!

Hurricane Staxxx. They were her wind and thunder.

"Love is dead here. I'm trying to change that. Come on, call me to life!" Staxxx slammed LoveGuile's head into the ground so the blade's point was buried in the dirt and the rod, wrapped in black and gold bolt leather, sprouted at an angle from the arena's packed dirt, empty and flat but for a few mounds near the center and five cars positioned around them to give viewers optimal exposure to the models on display.

The outer rim of the grounds was made to look like a looping high-way, though the "asphalt" was just treated plastic. The white sedan opposite Staxxx had a cracked windshield from the previous fight. The passenger-side door of a blue Power truck not far from the center of the grounds was hanging from its frame like a loose tooth in bloody gums.

"Do you like the Hurricane, or do you love her so bad it hurts?"

Love. Love. LOVE. LOVE!

"Y'all don't even know what it means. How could you? You've never seen it. But we're gonna change that. I came to hand out some electric love tonight! Would y'all like that?"

The flood of sound created a kinship throughout the audience, from the people high in the nosebleeds to the ones sitting up front in the BloodBoxes, right behind the Links who had paid Blood Points to be there, like Thurwar.

Thurwar's bald head itched as she watched in reverent silence. To her right and left were two soldier-police; they'd locked her into the seat with her palms pointing up to the sky as if she were asking for grace from above. The three red glowing vertical lines on each of her wrists meant she couldn't move even if she wanted to. She looked down at her right arm, its middle line broken, a defect of a cosmetic nature only. She forced herself to forget the itch, focused instead on her awe for the performer out there captivating the crowd.

"How much?" Staxxx said, wrenching LoveGuile from the ground and stepping forward. As a signature of sorts, Staxxx would sometimes start her match with her weapon dropped somewhere far away from her person. She'd put herself at a disadvantage for the amusement of the crowd.

"Do you love me this much?" Staxxx spit into the HMC in front of her. It tracked her, just a split second behind each of her movements, as she used the staff end of the scythe to draw a line in the dirt. The crowd booed, wanting more.

"You greedy bastards," Staxxx laughed, jogging forward a few steps, dust clouds rising and falling beneath her boots.

"How 'bout this much?" She drew another line. Again, the crowd screamed hard in discontent. "All right, all right, you think I can handle him?" Staxxx said, pointing to the gate in front of her. She stepped out into the very middle of the arena, onto a mound of tightly packed dirt. The people erupted once more. LoveGuile rested on her shoulder for a moment, then she swung it off her body and bit the sharp blade into the ground. She let go, let her scythe stand like a planted flag. They'd never seen her leave it this far. They screamed, delighted.

She pulled a thick hair band from her wrist, gathered the cords of her hair together, and tied them so they went from loose whips to a single branch flowing from her head. Then she turned away from her weapon. She walked back as the people screamed. The spirit was something felt, not tamed. It flowed through her, made her buoyant, bright, alive, almost free. She went over to the black tile that was installed in front of the gate through which she'd entered the arena. The Magno-Keep platform glowed red at its rim as she got close.

Staxxx stood with her arms above her head. She let the sound of adoration wash over her, then pointed to a plain black X on the left side of her neck.

"Hit right here and you can be the one who stilled Hurricane Staxxx!"

The pulse came: the sound of the magnetic shackles initiating. For a moment that was a performance in itself as Staxxx stood against the incredible pressure pulling her down. Her wrists shot from orange to triple red as the cuffs beneath her skin, grafted to her bones, demanded she fall to the platform at her feet. She made a kissing face as the half second slipped away and the magcuffs in her wrists slammed into the black platform, her body forced into an irreverent kneel. Staxxx waited, knees to the platform, her wrists magnetically locked down. Her fingers spread open, ready to push off when the time came.

Micky Wright watched as he climbed on top of his BattleBox, which served as stage and announcer's booth. He was just a few feet from the gate Staxxx had emerged from. He checked his smile on the Jumbotron before taking a deep breath and yelling into an HMC, "One of our competitors is ready to savage. But who will survive? The grizzly or the storm?" *Grizzly in the Storm* was the tagline for the fight, and the stands were full of T-shirts depicting a great grizzly bear clawing at a cloud exploding with jagged lightning. "Seems like the Hurricane is at full gale," Micky said as he paced atop the BattleBox. "Let's see how the Bear is doing."

At the opposite end of the arena a metal gate churned open. A hulking mound of human emerged: Barry "Rave Bear" Harris.

Death metal blared from the speakers. Rave Bear was booed mercilessly. He trudged forward slowly under his armor, a slab of thick tin across his chest and back that looked like it had been salvaged from the hull of an old submarine. He had a similar slap of metal on one of his thighs. His exposed hands, arms, elbows, and knees were dirty and pink. He wore no shirt beneath his combination chest/back plate. Two metal bats hung off his back and hip, clanked off the plates, both marked with Horizon Wireless's famous winged H. He had an iron helmet over his face like a welder's mask, the open mouth of a salivating silvertip grizzly spray-painted on the front.

An HMC floated in front of Bear and he growled into it. His signature "Grizzly Growl" sounded like the collapse of a mountainside and garnered a few cheers from his most faithful fans. He'd crushed a few pretty good Links after all. Made Powell Angler's spear look like a bee's stinger. And Powell Angler hadn't been a slouch.

Bear took his bats off and set them on the ground beside his platform. He kneeled into his Keep, which pulsed and locked him in.

"All right, we have the Hurricane and one very hungry Bear locked in and ready," Micky Wright said happily. "Time for final words." He climbed down from his BattleBox and onto an electric scooter. He rode around the perimeter of the arena, smiling and waving. He drew out the moment, the wait for what people really wanted.

He found his way to the hulking Barry Harris. When he was close, he kicked off the scooter and sat cross-legged beside Rave Bear on the MagnoKeep platform, the two men so close to each other, it was an image Wright knew people would remember. The man-bear in rusted metal and him in a gray, tailored suit. Of course, Wright still kept far enough away that if Rave Bear's magcuffs were somehow to disengage he'd still be just out of reach.

"So, anything from you, Bear? Any last words before taking on thee Hurricane?"

Bowed, his cuffs glowing red, Bear looked up across the undulating field of dirt to Staxxx and the scythe she'd placed so far from herself, as close to him as it was to her.

"None for that bitch," Bear said. His heavy voice was muffled by his mask. *Kill this bitch, kill this bitch,* the Bear said to Barry. The Bear had kept him alive this long. *Kill this bitch.* He'd made it this far. He couldn't think anything else. He was ready. He roared. He was ready. The crowd screamed. They hated him. But if the match went his way he'd be an all-around favorite.

"Ohh, feisty!" said Wright as he popped up, got back on his power scooter, and headed toward Staxxx to repeat the same routine, but faster; the people were warmed up enough. They'd waited and soon they'd be given their treat. This time he stayed on his scooter, as if he were already late for some appointment. His voice boomed through the arena: "What about you, Ms. Staxxx, any last words?"

Staxxx looked up. Her head had been bowed for several minutes, as if she'd been deep in meditation or prayer. She smiled sincerely.

Thurwar could almost make out her chipped bottom front tooth. She didn't need to look up at the massive screen to see that Staxxx's eyes glowed with a kindness that made Thurwar feel something like fear.

"I love you," Staxxx whispered, looking over at Barry Harris. Her last words were the same last words she'd had for each and every one of her last ten BattleGround appearances, and so, as she said them, they were multiplied by the thousands in the stands, who repeated the mantra along with her.

I LOVE YOU, the whole world screamed. Staxxx heard the proclamation echo through the stadium and retreated into her body to feel the truth of her power. She was a vessel for it, love, and every death-match she preached it explicitly. Love, love, love. She forced love into this loveless space, made it the subject of her life. She showed them that she, the Hurricane, was capable of great love, and that if they'd look they'd see they were too. And maybe someday they would understand what they'd enabled, what they'd created.

"Well, all right," said Wright. "I can't wait any longer!" He drove himself to the announcer's room and secured himself and the scooter inside. He peered out through the floor-to-ceiling Plexiglas, leaned into a wired mic near his face. "Unlock!" he screamed. The sound of high-powered magnetic fields disengaging, as if the air itself let out a hard cough, shot through the stadium. And then it began.

Bear roared, offering his rage to the sky, as was his custom. Across the field Staxxx had pressed her palms off the platform and was up and walking. Her first few steps were precise and deliberate. Like she was stretching out.

Bear gathered his bats in his hands and began to run. His movement was lumbering, hungry, and obvious. He clanked his bats above his head as he went. The HMCs, which trailed a good distance away, picked up the sound of his iron plates, held together by leather straps on his shoulders, slapping and clapping against his moist skin and back.

Staxxx also began to run. Thurwar watched her dart forward, easily and unencumbered. Her hands unclenched and soft as her arms pumped faster and faster, her strides making a snack of the distance before her.

She was just grabbing LoveGuile's shaft when the two met.

Bear swung to crush.

With LoveGuile in hand, Staxxx twisted her body back as easily as if she were performing choreography. The two bats seared through the air inches from her left flank with the cold, vicious momentum of a slugger missing a breaking ball. Staxxx kept spinning, angling her blade down so that it reaped the world behind her in a flash so harsh it wasn't until Bear's heavy body bounced off the ground that he understood he'd been separated from his right leg.

The crowd was unified: stunned inhalation.

Then elation, honest, raw joy, swallowed the whole. They stood up from their seats. Thurwar, if she could, would have stood with them. A masterful work of violence. A legendary strike. And then Thurwar was standing, as the guards had shifted her cuffs to orange and asked her to follow them to prep. She watched Staxxx until her neck no longer allowed the twist. Then Thurwar disappeared into the stadium with the guards.

Bear's face was in the dirt, but his arms were still swinging, still holding his bats, up, down, up, down, as though he were trying to swim on solid earth. The nearest HMC floated down and picked up his yells, which turned into groans, into mumbles and whimpers. The years of life gathered in him flowed out in a volcanic rush from his thigh. The crowd was frenzied.

"Shit," Barry said.

"I love you, okay?" Staxxx said, then she pulled her secondary, a hunting knife called Kill, and cut the straps from Bear's helmet and body armor. His back showed a single blue letter M tattooed into his skin. She turned him over so he could see something besides the ground. When she pulled the iron helmet from his head, the crowd could see how the Bear looked in death. His brown eyes seemed incapable of focusing, as if he were trying to keep track of something floating this way and that. His hair was matted and greasy. His chubby cheeks were colorless. "Don't worry about them, baby," Staxxx said. "Don't worry about them. This is yours. Don't miss it." She kissed his face several times, then slit his throat.* Her theme music erupted from the speakers and the audience roared. She carved his body with Xs. Blood sprouted forth, and with each X, she kissed the weeping skin. She was grateful for how far she could be removed from herself. She knew what she had to do and why she was doing it, was watching herself just as if she were part of the screaming audience.

When she was done, Bear looked like he'd been pulled from a woodchipper. Staxxx looked like she'd showered in blood. "I love you!" she screamed as guards jerked and pulled her from the body, force-locked her back into the Keep.

"That's a closed-casket finish if I've ever seen one," Micky Wright said from his room as two guardsmen rolled the dead man up in plastic and dragged him back through the tunnel he'd come from, a third man trailing behind them with Barry's leg. "Which means some additional Blood Points added to Miss Stacker's already hefty stash." Wright

---

* Barry Harris had been drunk. Again. Officers found him passed out over the body of Harold Marcer, a man Barry claimed was his best friend. "Well, you sure have an interesting way of showing you like a guy," an officer joked, then punched him in the mouth and shoved a handcuffed Barry into the car. Barry and Harold had wrestled together in high school. They still wrestled sometimes. And Harold wasn't the type to back down, even though Barry had wrestled at 220 and Harold at 160. "Do you remember being upset about something?" Barry did remember being upset about something, but he couldn't imagine ever getting that angry. Harold was usually the one who kept him company when Tiff acted up, dumped him, or took him back just to dump him again. But they'd been drunk, and he'd woken up with Harold cold and asleep, his head resting on Barry's chest and Barry's arm tied around his friend's neck. Barrington Eli Harris.

poked his head out and skipped across the battle-worn earth toward Staxxx.

Staxxx raised her head and spat at the ground as he approached. Wright slowed but didn't stop. "What a show, what a show," he said, holding a smile in his voice. "How does it feel to be the Hurricane right now?"

"It feels like crushing a child in your hands. It feels like watching your own skin open up as you carve a message to the future in your arms," Staxxx said, her breath steadying. She was a spectator too. She was watching this. "Call me Colossal, 'cause I can see the future. You're welcome." One day they would understand.

The crowd clapped appreciatively. They were cultured, they liked it, Staxxx and her words. They wanted her to live and they loved that she continued to do so. The BattleGround was a shrine to harsh violence and Staxxx was as violent as any, but unlike the others, she offered something more after almost every match. A poem, a story, and of course more love. She insisted on it. Her violence, her warmth, the messages cryptic or clear: They accumulated to the character they called the Hurricane. And as they considered themselves good, learned people, they had long before decided they could appreciate the way she entertained them, even as it made their chests heavy, even as they wondered if— Well, no need to dwell on that. Mostly they were excited that she was that much closer to the rank Colossal, a plateau only the very greatest Links ever reached.

In the halls of the stadium, Thurwar smiled at the pang of uneasiness she felt as the newly minted Grand Colossal.* A kind of ownership. She was now almost three full years in, and she felt a proprietary hold over her new title. A title she'd earned after the recent death of one of the best friends she'd had in this part of her life. It was hers now, Grand Colossal. And while Staxxx may have just told the crowds to call her Colossal, the fact was, for now at least, Staxxx was still a Harsh Reaper.

---

* The title awarded to the Link closest, at any given time, to freedom. All Links exist as one of the following rankings: Rookie, Survivor, Cusp, Reaper, Harsh Reaper, Colossal, Grand Colossal, Freed.

"The bard has spoken," Wright said, motioning for the guardsmen to retrieve Staxxx.

"Any words of encouragement for lovey-dovey?" Wright grabbed a handful of Staxxx's blood-drenched hair before letting go and making a sour face as he flicked red from his hand. "This is a big night for her, you know. If she wins, she'll have reached a new plateau. Almost thirty-five months. What do you think about that?"

"I think we'll be celebrating out on the Circuit," Staxxx said. "And maybe guys like you will get something to hand grease to." The crowd laughed together. Wright put a hand over his mouth, feigning embarrassment.

"We can only hope," Wright said as one of the guardsmen standing behind Staxxx pressed a black Magrod™* to her wrists. The three red status lines merged into one as Staxxx's wrists adhered to the rod and she stood up. She looked like a shark on a fishing line as she rose.

"I love you," Staxxx said once more in parting. The crowd roared. She turned her head as they pulled her away to see if she could catch a glimpse of Thurwar. She found an empty seat, as expected. One of the guardsmen picked up Staxxx's scythe and her knife, and they all disappeared into the guts of the stadium as the crowd watched a commercial for the new FX-709 Electriko Power™ pickup truck.

The soldier-police's boots clapped against the gray floors and echoed off the walls, which were plastered with portraits of the Vroom Vroom City Rollers, a minor league baseball team. "So, nobody thought I might need a towel?" Staxxx said. The guard pulling her along stumbled back a little. She could tell he was embarrassed despite his eye shield. Like all soldier-police, his helmet had a black visor that hid his eyes completely.

"Shut up, convict," said the lead guard, a distinction marked by a gray band on his biceps. He nudged her in the back with his black rod.

"You don't mean to say that," Staxxx said, staring into the visor.

"Your trap needs to be shut, convict," the guard repeated. He motioned for the unit to proceed.

---

* ArcTech™ Magnetic Handle Baton Te-SIP 2.2 Magrod™ model 7 can engage with all series 7 products of the Magnetic security family as a control device, a carrying aid for transport, and a sturdy instrument of blunt defense and discipline. ArcTech™, the Coldest in Tactical Security.

Staxxx closed her eyes and kept walking. "I want a towel."

"You'll have one in your dressing room, and a shower. You know that, Stacker."

"Staxxx."

"Convict," the lead said.

"Colossal."

"Not quite."

Staxxx dropped to the floor. She fell on her back, her arms raised above her, still connected to the guard's Magrod™. She felt the blood on her skin, which was drying and flaking. She tried to absorb these moments, these few moments in her life when she was not being observed by hundreds of thousands, but instead was just under the watch of a few weak men. When there were no cameras floating up her ass, asking her to be the Hurricane. Here she could regret freely, she could hope openly, she could be herself. She tried to think of herself specifically. Not the Circuit, not Thurwar or Sunset or the poor man she'd just slaughtered.

One of the guards hit her in the ribs with his baton. Hard enough that she coughed, but gently enough that she knew he feared what would happen to him if he damaged her. "Come on, convict."

She wanted to enjoy this time with the self she hardly ever got to see. She could feel a deep dread, the adrenaline comedown, a headache, and a hard fear of the retribution that could come for her in one of so many ways. She told herself that she was Hamara Stacker. She told herself that she was Hurricane Staxxx. Then she told herself that she was also neither of those people. Her anxiety pressed her down and she tried to remember to breathe, tried to remember that this was her happy time. She was kicked again in the ribs and a rod came down hard on her hip. She took a breath and thought of what was there in front of her: Weak men who feared her. Fresh-spilled blood. The cool of concrete. The sound of more boots clapping closer.

Staxxx opened her eyes again and looked at the lead. His head swiveled around. The unit was focused on him.

"Mighty Miss Staxxx," the lead said, "please get your Colossal ass up." He pulled her up by the underarm. She allowed it and stood.

"That's all I'm asking for," she said sweetly.

She rolled her shoulders and stretched her neck to show that she wasn't hurt, couldn't be hurt by the soldier-police. A door opened a few yards ahead of them. Staxxx smiled and wiggled her fingers in a wave.

.   .   .

"Let me see her," Thurwar said quietly.

"Real quick," one of the soldier-police said back. She was Thurwar after all.

Thurwar could see that Staxxx had orchestrated whatever pause had allowed them to meet in the hall. Seeing her alive and smiling, even dressed in blood—especially dressed in blood—Thurwar felt she was seeing straight through to the real Staxxx. This person who had just killed and was fresh with all the feelings that came with bringing death. She tightened her grip around the war hammer in her hand and walked forward. The men around Staxxx knew to stand aside as Thurwar approached. The officer holding Staxxx on his rod looked at his superior, who nodded, then he released his prisoner. Her wrists displayed two red lines as they snapped together. The two warriors, one clean, one soaked in spent life, locked eyes.

"You did well," Thurwar said, her wrists kissed together just as Staxxx's were.

"Romantic," Staxxx said, twisting her face and projecting a disappointment too big to be real. Thurwar smiled. Then she turned and offered her shoulder, bound in a carbon-fiber guard branded with a hammer crushing a nail, the LifeDepot™ insignia. Staxxx turned in kind and offered her own shoulder. They rubbed together, blood smudging the home improvement company's logo as Thurwar closed her eyes. Staxxx kept hers open and watched Thurwar enjoy the moment. It was a battle hug between two true warriors, the kind the world hadn't seen for centuries.

Thurwar continued to rub until Staxxx pulled back, stood erect, and waited for Thurwar to open her eyes. "Focus now," Staxxx said. "I need you back to me so we can change things. Make it like Sun wanted." She stopped short of saying more; to suggest too much of a future outside the fight was dangerous. You had to be present in the now to kill. "It's me and you," she finished.

"You and me," Thurwar mouthed back.

And then Thurwar was thinking of Sunset, the former Grand Colossal. Like her, he'd understood what it was to choose this life and thrive in that decision. But earlier that same week, they'd woken up to find him dead. He was dead and no one had claimed it. He'd died during a BlackOut Night, when all the cameras were off. No one in the world had seen how he was killed but for the person who'd done it. They'd found he'd been sliced across the neck, as if someone had snuck behind him. Whoever had done it had used Sunset's own sword and been precise. Sunset had been so close to seeing the world. She'd let him slip through her hands. One of her own, one of the other members of the Angola-Hammond Chain-Gang, had killed Sunset Harkless, and she, Loretta Thurwar, who knew everything about A-Hamm, who was A-Hamm, had almost no idea who it was. And the small inklings that she did have she couldn't bring herself to think about.

A feeling rose within her and she pressed it down, as she so often had to. She breathed through her nose, held it, then released everything that wasn't her and her hammer. Until the fight was done nothing could exist beyond that. Finally Thurwar opened her eyes, looked at Staxxx. Thurwar had drawn a Question Match face-off; there was no telling who she was about to face or what they could do. But even that, Thurwar could not think of.

"There's nobody out there you should worry about," Staxxx said. "You're just lucky you're on my Chain," she added, smiling. It was a joke, but it was also true. Links on the same Chain never fought one another on the BattleGround. A Chain was not designed to be a team, but because of that rule, it could be one. They could share battle strats or help one another earn weapons, as Thurwar had for so many. Chain solidarity, that's what Sunset had preached. The Links on your Chain were some of the only people whom you could trust. Still, they destroyed one another so often. But Sunset was different, and he pushed others to be too. He'd been among them, a champion, not stressing his strength or how many he'd killed, but preaching the idea that every one of them was better than what the world thought, and they could use one another to show that.

"You're on my Chain," Thurwar said, implicitly emphasizing which one of them was a Colossal.

Staxxx tried to squeeze one more grin out of Thurwar, but Thurwar's face had eased back to flatness. She knew that Thurwar had already transformed into the warrior the world feared. She wished for a few more minutes, a few more warm seconds, with her one person. But it was done.

"All right, all right," the lead officer of Staxxx's party said. And for a moment everyone in the hall was grateful for him. Staxxx continued toward processing and a shower and a new X to ink on her skin.

Thurwar walked forward. She could hear Micky Wright preparing the people for her.

B3

B *Three is not for me. B Three is not for me. B Three is not for me.*[*]
The Coalition to End Neo-Slavery was just one of several groups of marchers outside the MotoKline Arena. Altogether they numbered in the—dozens? Were there a hundred people there? Nile didn't know, but he hoped that the reporters would say hundreds, not dozens, even though there were definitely not two hundred people at the demonstration. He was proud still, with his palms sweaty around the megaphone. The call to gather had gone out. They'd seen the news on their feeds. And the surprise death of Sunset Harkless meant they *had* to come.

Nile had driven his car from Saylesville, where his branch of the coalition was based. He'd packed snacks. He'd been disappointed that Mari hadn't ridden with him, had ridden instead with her mother, Kai, the chairwoman of the coalition's steering committee. But he'd come

---

[*] The Rightful Choice Act, commonly referred to as Bobby's Bloodsport Bridge, or BBB, B3, or B Three (passed under President Robert Bircher), states that under their own will and power, convicted wards of the state may elect to forgo a state-administered execution or a sentence totaling at least twenty-five (25) years' imprisonment, to instead participate in the CAPE program. After three (3) years of successful participation in said CAPE program, said ward may be granted clemency, commutation of sentence, or a full pardon.

dressed in black, as they all had, and was out here sweating, chanting, not watching Staxxx or Thurwar or Sai Eye Aye, but instead reminding everyone who passed them and entered the arena that they were consuming poison, no matter how savory the package. He was here with his friend to grieve. Plus, it was cool that the other members thought he'd do a good job with the megaphone, a vintage piece of slick plastic that felt like power in his hands.

"B Three is not for me!" His magnified voice led the dozens who followed. They'd marched around the arena more times than he could count. They made their voices heard with each step. They'd been here for over an hour before he'd felt confident enough to accept the megaphone. And now here he was.

"All right, switch it up," Mari said, gently elbowing him in the ribs. "You got the mic, so keep it going."

"B Three is not for me!" Nile chanted one last time. Mari's hair spiraled into an explosion of black curls around her head, and they were held back by a black band that covered her forehead and hairline. Her eyes held a knowing brown simmer, and if her lips curled just a bit, the dimples on either side of her face would come alive. This had not happened much at the protest, which, of course, Nile understood.

Nile listened to the crowd, heard how the words dragged rather than leapt from their throats. He pulled his face from the horn and whispered to Mari, "Okay, so?"

"This is evil can't you see, we don't want no BBB," she replied.

"This is evil can't you see, we don't want no BBB," Nile repeated into the megaphone. The small crowd roared approval as they continued their lap around the arena. With the soldier-police watching closely, they chanted with renewed vigor. Before he'd ever been brave enough to lead the call-and-response, Nile had watched others closely. It was an art form. Quickly, precisely, and honestly choosing words to carry the moment. If you did it wrong, it felt awkward, like running on a bad ankle. If you did it right, it was as if you'd sewn all the souls who had gathered together into a single powerful force, unified and invincible. And if you could gather enough people into one voice, then, Nile believed, you could do anything.

This is evil can't you see, we don't want no BBB
This is evil can't you see, we don't want no BBB

This is evil can't you see, we don't want no BBB

Nile took in the people around them. The soldier-police were their "escorts," there for their protection, as the permits promised. "Ask for permission and you're giving them power," Kai had said three meetings ago. But the local Vroom Vroom group that was leading the demonstration had opted for permits. They'd hoped for a good showing and wanted to make sure things didn't get too crazy. Now Nile agreed with Kai.

The soldier-police were uniformed in dark blue and rigid black, orbiting the group on their motorcycles or walking with their chests puffed out, their badges shining in the mild late-afternoon sun. And, as was the case for most major sporting events, concerts, and (especially) rallies and protests, a small black tank was parked across the street, the letters VVPD inscribed across the side in bright yellow, a single soldier-police officer's head poking out the top, an easy grin exposed under his helmet's visor.* When a car had driven by and screamed, "Bitches!" at the crowd, Nile had seen one of the officers chuckle and give the driver a thumbs-up.

Still, some bystanders did raise their fists in solidarity. Some clapped as they passed. Some laughed. But most of them acted as if the protestors weren't there at all. And of course, some weren't acting. Some truly didn't think about the fact that men and women were being murdered every day by the same government their children pledged allegiance to at school.

This is evil can't you see, we don't want no BBB
This is evil can't you see, we don't want no BBB

Nile's voice was growing hoarse. He pinched Mari on the shoulder and held out the megaphone for her.

"Nah, you got it," Mari said, taking the cap off her water bottle, making a show of how it refreshed her, almost choking on the water from laughing. Nile swallowed his spit and was about to return to yelling when the music came back. From outside they could hear it just fine—the theme music for one of the most lethal and beloved

---

* The Law Enforcement Support Office (LESO) operates the 1033 program, which arose during the administration of President George Herbert Walker Bush and transfers excess military equipment to civilian police departments. The surplus equipment, weapons, etc. are to be used to support drug enforcement.

hard action-sports stars, Hamara Stacker, famously known as Hurricane Staxxx.

"Shit," Nile said into the megaphone before he could think to pull it away from his lips. He had tried his best to avoid the actual Battle-Ground. But its brutality was everywhere. Supposedly, SportsViewNet was preparing for full coverage of the games. Thus far, they'd just shown still images of the Links with one person pumping their fists or flexing their biceps or beating their chests, the other dead in the dirt. Now even that small editorial decency was going to be abandoned for full coverage. Rather than the pay-per-stream model, Chain-Gang was about to be easily accessible on standard stream spaces.

Nile didn't watch SportsViewNet anymore.

The BattleGround made him feel like his organs were exposed. When he'd still been in school, in the few years after the inception of Chain-Gang All-Stars, he'd lost friends because he refused to talk about the deathmatches, except to engage in harsh criticism of the killing. He'd worked for a few years before enrolling. He'd been the age of a traditional senior as a freshman, and his refusal to be down with anything Chain-Gang further othered him on campus.

It's a sport.

They sign up for it.

This guy's a rapist, bro.

There are some white people on it too, it's fair.

These people are dangerous.

Don't be a pussy.

He'd rejected it all and it had made him a very particular person. But finally he'd found friends who felt what he felt, and then, because they knew they needed to do something, they'd become activists. Or they'd tried. Usually they'd partied and studied and lived young, foolish lives. But when they'd had time, they'd demonstrated and held meetings. They were called the Human League. Nile, who'd graduated three years earlier, was proud that there was still a chapter on campus.

"Boy, move," Mari said quickly, and pulled the megaphone from Nile's hands. She took a deep breath and called out louder, more clearly than Nile had, "A man was murdered today." The first time she spoke, it felt like she was asserting a fact, almost casual. "A man was murdered today," she said a second time, and lowered herself to her knees.

The group around them followed suit in a wave that didn't quite have the uniformity of falling dominoes. Eventually they were all on their backs or facedown in the South Plaza of the MotoKline Arena, as was their custom whenever a match ended while they were out marching.

"A man was killed today!" Mari said, screaming as if she were watching a family member in front of her. A father. Nile could see her chest rising and falling, could feel her raw energy, violent and true. She had not had an easy life. So much of it had been defined by people she did not know, people who had been taken away from her. When Nile tried to talk to Mari about how she'd grown up, she quickly shut him down. He didn't like to push, but he decided he'd ask her if she wanted to talk after the protest.

"A man was killed here today!" Mari screamed again, looking up at the sky, taking big breaths between calls. The marchers were with her. Nile was with her. He accidentally grazed the ground with his lips and did not care at all. They were a living memorial. They were together completely. The voices, led by Mari, came out of their mouths and brought their souls to a kind of synchronization. They repeated and chanted.

A man was killed here today.

A man was killed here today.

A man was killed here today.

And then: *We hope and pray for a different world. We ask that you see that we've lost our way. There is a better way. Please see us. You are afraid. We are afraid and there we are the same. Please hear us. A man was murdered. His name was—*

Nile scrambled for his phone, found the information.

"His name was Barry Harris," Nile said to Mari.

"His name was Barry Harris," Mari yelled, and the machine made her voice a choir of rage and worship unto itself.

His name was Barry Harris, the group screamed to the world.

His name was Barry Harris, they said, and together they meant so much more.

He was born and lived and loved and hated. We do not excuse him or the chaos and pain he thrust into the world, but because we see and know that what he did in a moment of confusion and rage was an assault on all that is sacred, we must remember and see that what we've done to him in retribution has prom-

ised him that he was right. Retribution of the same kind promises he was not wrong but rather that he was small. To punish this way is to water a seed. His name was Barry Harris. His name was Barry Harris. We've sacrificed him to feed our fear. To pamper our sloth.

His name was Barry—

"Fuck y'all!" From a sliver of a partially closed window. The car sped by without stopping but the words had punctured.

"Fuck you too," one of the marchers said, shooting up, tense with fury.

"Hey, it's all right, hey."

"No, fuck that guy!"

Kai and a few others went to calm the man now standing with his fists at his sides like little weapons. Nile watched as the soldier-police officer near the crosswalk chuckled, showing his white teeth. The officer dropped the smile for a moment when he realized Nile was staring, then laughed anew before settling back into a weak grin. Nile wiped gravel from his lips. He heard, suddenly and definitely, the thunk of a fist hitting a face. He was confused for a moment, as to how, who, but when he turned, he saw that a new group of men, all wearing shirts adorned with their favorite Links, one with an X tattoo under his right eye, had sprinted into the South Plaza. The brawl was already happening. Mari rushed toward the people flailing against one another.

Mari, who had just lost her father, the man known as Sunset Harkless, one of the most famous Links in the world, ran to fight.

And Nile ran after, feeling full of violence himself.

Teacup

Hass Omaha was alive in her hands as she swung at the air, using her shoulders and back to pull the hammer slowly, methodically. Its face was wide and blunt, its handle two feet long, ending in an angry point that could punch through bone, skin, and some metals, as Thurwar had proven in her matches against Kenny Da Doggone Demi-Demon Fletch and Sarah Go. The back of the hammer scorpioned to a point.

After wielding the hammer for a year, Thurwar had wrapped Hass's handle in treated bolt leather that kept it from growing slick with palm sweat. The hammer was a part of her, and she'd sung a March song she'd picked up from another Link, one who'd sing before each match, as she'd hugged the material around the rod.

There were six guards around Thurwar. While the guards treated most of the other Links like rag dolls or slaughterhouse cattle, they treated Thurwar like an aging parent, with careful distance and even, sometimes, glimpses of deference.

She looked at the young lips of the guard to her left. His hand fidgeted around his baton. She could tell he wanted to say something. Because the fear she felt was beginning to bore her, she spoke.

"How's your day going?" she asked him.

His mouth splintered into a nervous, toothy smile that quickly simmered to a detached smirk. "Very well, ma'am."

"Quit that, Rogers," the lead guard said. "She needs to focus," he added chivalrously.

"It's fine," Thurwar said, thinking about how lax the men were with her. She was completely unlocked from herself. A single green line on her wrists. This slim freedom was as untethered as any Link could be. She could move her arms and theoretically go up to four hundred yards away from one of the central Anchor points in the facility. In some sick irony, the deadlier she proved herself to be, the fewer precautions the men and women who shuffled her between performances took with her. Often it seemed that they wanted to align themselves with her. Her success, she knew, legitimized something in their minds. She killed, they loved her better, and she hated them more deeply. She took a breath. They were just people, and people were all the same. "Everybody just wants to be happy." This she'd heard from a brilliant woman she'd shared a cell with when she was in prison. Everybody was looking for the same thing in a lot of different ways.

"What do you wanna ask?" Thurwar said.

"Well," the guard began, "how do you feel right now? Like *right* now. What's it like?"

Thurwar took a moment to consider him. He was thin and young, not just her jailer but her executioner, and he didn't even realize it. She was relieved that she felt no urge of violence toward him. There was a time, a long time, before she'd met Staxxx, when she was regularly seized by sudden, deep urges to destroy others. She felt the urge to destroy herself, of course, more constantly.

"Have you—have you ever ridden a bike really fast down a hill?"

"Uh-huh," he said. She could see how he would frame this story to his friends.

"I mean as fast as you can." He'd explain her in superlatives. The most confident, the calmest, the smoothest skin, the strongest, the coolest, the coldest. The greatest, maybe second-greatest, Link of all time.

"And maybe while you're riding, you try to brake, and you realize the brakes are cut. Has that ever happened to you?" she asked, looking at each of the men around her. They took her words in, thinking about them, trying to appreciate the moment, her attention.

"No. But sure. I get it," he said.

"That's actually happened to me," another man said shyly. "Not on a super-big hill, but a kinda big hill. When I was a kid. Whatever. Yeah."

"That panic, that you can only know when you're going down at speed. You know what I'm talking about." All of the men nodded. She lowered her voice and watched them draw closer. "When any mistake might turn your insides to your outsides and it's almost like your soul knows in advance and starts peeling away. You know that feeling?"

When it was like this, when the stakes were low, when she didn't care, Thurwar remembered how to hold an audience. The men nodded so hard their helmets rattled around their heads.

"Well, it's nothing like that," Thurwar said, and looked away.

The young guard's chin dropped as though he was about to say something else, but it snapped back up as he thought better of it.

The gate in front of her disappeared. The people roared. There was no music; Thurwar had decided against the tradition, citing it as "a distraction of comfort in a comfortless world" to her corrections officer/ agent.

She was now officially the third-longest-lasting participant of the CAPE program ever, and since Sunset had died, she was the closest Link on the Circuit to that universal goal, freedom. Freedom, for Thurwar, was a ridiculous possibility. One that had been so far away for so long that she hadn't had to imagine it. Now it bore down on her like a train.

She was an icon in the hard action-sports world. She knew because Micky Wright regularly asked her how it felt to be an icon in the hard action-sports world. The question used to make her stomach lurch. She'd become something of a sex symbol. "What's it like to be the hottest fucking woman on the planet?" Micky Wright had asked after she'd crushed the skull of a woman from Tennessee, who'd cried the first half of a desperate request before the hammer fell: "Ple—" A pathetic final syllable. And Thurwar had been disgusted with herself for having enjoyed hearing it. It had been her third fight. And it had garnered the biggest crowd in the history of action-sports. A record held until her next fight. She'd gone from nobody to legend. She was the woman who'd won the hammer.

After her early success, Thurwar had shaved her head bald. She took the advice of Melody Bishop, thinking it would dim her celebrity, and also, hair was a liability on the grounds. But the shaved head, like the hammer, had only made her more iconic. In the crowds now, half the women had shaved heads. Among the fans, the "LT" cut was only legitimate if you did it yourself, as she had. It had to look like it was done with a knife, as Thurwar's was.

She couldn't escape it, her fame. She read less and less of her fan mail now, the vast majority of it from men telling her that her brown skin was delicious, that if she just removed the shoulder armor her strikes would be even deadlier, telling her how she should handle Staxxx when they were together in bed.

Thurwar had once loved the unfiltered adoration, loved pleasing her fans. If she was honest, she still did, even as she hated it. She loved not being the weak one. The person whom the world knew as "Thurwar" was all she'd known for so long. And so she continued. She was still continuing. Every day she woke up ashamed that she had continued for this long, but having Staxxx in her life, having something real to hold on to, made it easier to let go of her fans, her fame, all the pretty decorations that obscured the fact that the state was trying to kill her and that even though she was ashamed of her life and did not think she deserved to live, she would not let them.

It was all death, slow or fast. Painful or sudden. Nothing more. The culture of Chain-Gang was death.

And that was something she'd understood when she'd signed the papers. She had wanted to end her sad, wretched life. But now she had Staxxx, she had her Chain, and it felt as though she couldn't just leave. And so she continued in a world where death found everyone but her.

Four months before, out at Camp, a Link on her Chain, Gunny Puddles, had mutilated another Link, then whipped out his dick and urinated on the body while the HMCs circled him like fireflies. "Welcome to the big leagues, kid," Puddles had said after he zipped his pants back up. Thurwar had watched it happen. Puddles had killed a Rookie who'd tried to establish himself as someone not to be fucked with, but in doing so had fucked with the wrong Link. Thurwar had seen so much on the Circuit that she watched the murder with an ease, even a casual interest, as she spooned hot dinner into her mouth, Staxxx beside her.

Sunset had watched it happen too. He'd leveled a mild protest. Gunny had told him to fuck off. Sunset had laughed, but only because Staxxx and Thurwar had already picked up their weapons to defend him and he was tired and ready for his freedom.

Now Thurwar walked out to the light and a chorus of screams.

Thur-war

Thur-war

Thur-war

An orb floated in front of her mouth and she said nothing. It had been many months since she'd had any last words. For some time she had pretended, performed a character who maybe wanted this life. Wanted to exist and thrive. But now, even with Staxxx in her life, the shame of her existence made the BattleGround anything but jubilant. So she chose silence. She chose silence because she could not say to the people she was ashamed of her success, of the very fact of her continued existence.

"There she is, with thirty-two wins, twenty-three closed-casket finishes. The deadliest woman on the planet, Loreeeeettaaaaaaa," Micky Wright screamed, "Thurwar!"

Thurwar lowered herself to the dark platform. Her left knee, her problem knee, creaked and she breathed in the pain as she kneeled into the Keep. "Stoic as ever!" Micky Wright said from his broadcast space on the grounds. "Have you ever seen a more focused killing machine?"

The crowd bellowed in response.

Most humans never felt this, Thurwar knew. This electricity. This concentration of attention. This collective solidarity in the name of her perseverance. She let the energy run through her body. She let herself enjoy it despite all the shame. It was the now, and now was all there was on the grounds.

"And fighting today in her record fifth Question Match!" Wright continued. Her magcuffs engaged red beneath the skin as she waited.

"She's always been a woman of action!" Wright tried to make drama out of her absolute refusal to be dramatic. And, of course, he succeeded. Louder, louder.

Normally she'd have been going through some specific mental notes on her opponent, their weapon and temperament. But this was a Question Match. All she could do was consider her fundamentals, remember not to resist the pain in her knee. To move quickly, efficiently. To swing through and never at.

"Her opponent?" Wright asked the world, and the Jumbotron flashed to an image of a giant slot machine, the three reels spinning. Anticipation spilled over the arena.

No one had ever gone into the unknown as many times and walked back out. Maybe it was that Thurwar knew that so much of her power was in her preparation; she'd elected to be eligible for yet another Question Match because she wanted the person on the other side to have a chance. Or maybe she wanted to prove that she, not Bishop, not Sun, was the greatest Link of all time.

The first reel stalled and stopped on the letters CCNA.* The people were largely unimpressed. CCNA was one of the larger networks, so that alone told them nothing. They waited as the second reel slowed and froze on a large V with a snake slithering up one of its halves. This they loved.

The Velmont Vipers were a Chain that had originated in a corrections facility in Velmont, Indiana, and had, for a time, produced some incredibly beloved Links—Ray "Lefty" Peterson, Tito "Turnup" Marcon, and Jane Marshall, all deceased. They'd done well enough that fans tended to think of the Viper Chain as ripe with potential. Two of Thurwar's most memorable wins had been against Viper Links. Who could forget the marathon match against Udine "Ulcer" Potly or her mangling of Falcon Winston Eaton? This was a rare chance for vengeance in the name of Viper. The people hoarsed their throats waiting for the final reel to stop.

All this was for show, of course. Whoever was going to face Thur-

---

* Corrections Corporation of North America (CCNA) is the largest private prison corporation in the world. Cofounded by Tomas Wesplat, Berto Rants, and T. Ron Kutto, with multiple facilities across the country, CCNA consistently generates billions in annual revenue.

war and Hass Omaha was already waiting on the other side of the gated tunnel.

Thurwar looked up at the Jumbotron. Now, she thought.

The reel stopped and landed on the face of a boy Thurwar had never seen before. She frowned. The audience, the vehement patrons of hard action-sports, gasped, then laughed sheepishly and nervously, then roared anew.

"Well," Wright said, "what a way to get that cherry popped!" The gate opposite Thurwar ascended. A skinny pair of legs in jeans walked out. The boy wore no shirt, so the two Ms tattooed in blue on his back were plain for everyone to see. He held a cooking pot in his hands. Thurwar noticed, and briefly appreciated, the singed bottom of the pot. Had a producer grabbed it from his home, expecting to be reimbursed after the weaponing ceremony? Or had they taken the time to hold the pot over a burner until the dark rings on its bottom allowed for a perverse sense of authenticity?

The boy's eyes gave her nothing. He blinked as he stepped forward, looking out at the crowds, who cheered and cursed him. "Whoa, whoa, whoa, what a baby! Let's welcome him!" Micky Wright screamed from the box. "Please tell us your name, *sir*."

"Tim," he said. He visibly startled at the magnitude of his voice through the speakers. The orb he spoke into moved closer to his face. You could see a rash of pimples on his forehead on the Jumbotron.

"Full name, please," Wright said, rolling his eyes deliberately for the cameras.

"I'm Tim Jaret," the boy said.*

"Tim Jaret, Tim Jaret. Let's call you Teacup for now." Micky Wright brought his hand to his mouth and leaned to one side as if he were telling a secret and not booming over the speakers. "Because he looks like

---

* Murderer, murderer.

It didn't feel good. Or it did and it didn't. Always felt alone. Never not been alone. Finished the job, get all the way alone. Already no friends, now no parents.

I took a gun and pointed it. Mom and Pop. Popped and Popped. Dead and Dead. Thought it would feel better. But all the pain still the same.

Then they said, "He's an adult." He scares people. Well, everything scares him. Especially himself.

Maybe this will feel good. At least it's an end. The youngest Link ever.

he might break in half if you dropped him." The audience laughed. Wright continued. "But seriously, Teacup, why are you here today? How'd you get into so much trouble?"

"I killed my mom and pop," Teacup said. The crowd booed, screamed at him. They loved their mothers and fathers.

"A problem child. We've seen those before," Wright said. "But I've heard you're something of a special case."

"I ain't special," Teacup said. He didn't seem to know where to look while he spoke, so he stared across the field at Micky Wright's box. Wright stared back at him.

"But you are," Wright snapped. "At sixteen years and one hundred and twenty-two days old, you are officially the youngest Link ever! Congratulations!"

Teacup said nothing.

Wright continued. "And why did you—"

"Stop." Her voice carried and stilled the crowd. Wright smiled at her with hate in his eyes.

"Oh! Miss Thurwar has some—"

"Do not say anything else," Thurwar said, looking across at Teacup. "You kneel down and don't say a single other thing." Was it cruel to cut this boy's life even shorter? She had been Teacup. And with each word he spoke she was thinking of the past, which was even worse than thinking of the future there on the BattleGround.

Micky Wright pouted. "I guess if Mama says," he said, feigning amusement. "Why don't you head over to that pad there." Teacup looked at Thurwar and obeyed. She thought she saw a brief smile on his face but figured there was no reason for that. When she looked up at the Jumbotron, the camera had already shifted to her. She seemed stiff, angry. She took a breath and checked to see if she had relaxed. She hadn't. Finally, she turned away and focused on her opponent, the young man named Tim, whom she would soon kill.

The Bandwagon

This was competition. All other sport was just a metaphor for this. This was the real thing. There was nothing better. And still, Wil was not happy. His seats were solid. He was full of a hearty local IPA, a nice surprise to see on tap at the concession stand, and he was contemplating a third hot dog slathered in mustard and sauerkraut. He'd seen Staxxx kick ass. It was quick, but it had been beautiful. A crazy reverse slash. A strike that screamed Colossal. He couldn't wait to watch it again at home—he'd recorded the entire All-Stars broadcast even though he was there in the flesh. He'd splurged on the platinum package so he had access to all things Chain-Gang all the time. Even the archives.

He'd known the Staxxx match would be quick. Her matches averaged just under two minutes. She was one of a kind. He'd been thinking for a while that she was maybe even better than Thurwar. He'd been thinking that way before everybody else started thinking it too, and now he was annoyed that if he started telling other people that Staxxx was his overall favorite, he'd seem like a bandwagon jumper when he was, in fact, the bandwagon leader. He'd built the Staxxx bandwagon. He'd known she'd make Colossal back when she was a Cusp. He didn't have any Xs on his body—yet—but he had been known to take his two middle fingers and cross them in front of his neck when his boss left the room, to the approving chuckles and smirks of his coworkers.

The best thing about Staxxx's dismantling of Bear Harris was that it meant he'd lost to Kyla, who'd bet him Staxxx would beat Bear in under a minute. Wil had figured if she was gonna beat Rave Bear, she'd do it in under forty seconds, but he'd taken the over because he wanted to lose to Kyla; it was the more workable in. Into her life and into her pants. Now he could be all, "You got me," and she'd laugh and probably tell him what she wanted for lunch that day, which, as a result of losing, was on him, and he'd offer her the free upgrade to a dinner either that night or later that week. On him, of course. He was sure she'd be down for it. She'd been throwing him vibes ever since she'd found out that he was big into hard action-sports. And if he could do anything, he could catch vibes. So the Staxxx match was great for him. Which was good because Thurwar's matchup really pissed him off. He looked over at the parent-killing piece of shit at the east gate. A fucking piece of cannon fodder if he'd ever seen one. The sound of lock-in came and the boy, Teacup, almost had his arms ripped off as he dropped down to the MagnoKeep.

The beauty of action-sports, he'd often explained to anyone who didn't get it, was that everybody had a fighting chance. The games gave people who, let's face it, didn't deserve shit on a stick a chance to live, to compete, to see the country, to be a hero even. At their heart, they were an exercise in fairness. Women, men, gender-nonconforming individuals of all colors and religions and backgrounds, they all had a chance at one another. Almost a hundred percent of the time, Battle-Ground matches were mostly pretty fair. They tried to match fighters who had a similar number of fights under their belt. And they did a great job, considering losses were fatalities. There were some who were just in a class of their own, but then injuries and the weight of surviving the Circuit that long sort of leveled the playing field.

But a newbie versus the pound-for-pound champ: cannon fodder. And it was true, now that Sunset Harkless was gone, Thurwar was the top of the mountain. Thurwar was the mountain. And Wil had thrown a mountain of cash at celebrating her greatness. He considered himself a feminist, and she'd been his gateway into the awesomeness of feminine power. But somebody at GEOD* must have pulled some strings, made sure she had a guaranteed win as she approached the finish line. He wouldn't ever want to sully Thurwar's good name—she was his GOAT, M-Bishop aside, and Staxxx, certainly on her way to that status—but you just had to call a spade a spade. A sixteen-year-old kid.

"This really is bullshit," Wil said, loudly enough to invite conversation with the people sitting around him and his wife, Emily.

"She deserves an easy night," said a man in a hat that read *thurWAR*.

"Yeah, yeah," Wil said, smiling sheepishly. "What she needs is something to keep her on her game. Staxxx is on her heels already. Thurwar's just lucky they're on the same Chain." He was the goddamn conductor.

"Let's see if Staxxx can make Colossal. Then I'll compare her to Miss Loretta fucking Thurwar."

"He's probably a fucking virgin!" Wil yelled, and this garnered a fair number of laughs. The approval of the nearby strangers satisfied him in a robust, uncomplicated way. He sat back down for a moment to check up on Emily, who had been watching horrified and sitting through the entire thing. She really embarrassed him sometimes.

"You okay, baby?" he said, lowering himself to her level, disappearing into a sea of thigh gaps and back pockets. He could barely see the arena.

"I'm fine," Emily said, acting as though she were watching intently, not bothering to look at him, though she did glance up at the Jumbotron from time to time.

"You get why it's not fair, though? 'Cause Thurwar is a badass. The Grand Colossal. It means she's, like, more than thirty wins in. She's the top dog. There isn't any higher status. Well, except a Freed, but that doesn't matter right now. And this kid's a total Rookie. Even if he was a Cusp it wouldn't be fair. A Cusp—"

"I get it, Wil. She's going to kill him."

"Yeah, but usually it's not like this." He was being patient with her

---

* GEOD Group Correction Corporation. The father corporation of 20 percent of the Chains on the Circuit. The second-biggest participant in the CAPE program after CCNA.

because that was something he'd admitted he could work on and this was a teaching moment. "Usually they'd give Thurwar someone much more battle-savvy. A Reaper or better—someone who has a chance. You know?"

"I understand."

"And, I mean, they're probably compensating because she didn't know who to prepare for, since it was a Question Match. But I mean, damn, you know?"

"I know."

"You all right? You sure you don't wanna stand up?"

"Positive," Emily said.

"All right," Wil said. He got back up and it was like entering a whole new world. It was brighter and louder, and he was happier. The air was fresh with spilled beer and smoked meat and dirt and the breath of thousands of people who really understood what competition was. Who weren't afraid of the fact that everyone died at some point. That there was no point in running away from it.

"Are. You. Ready?" Micky Wright screamed in his singular way. Hearing it live made Wil feel like he was down there on the Battle-Ground himself.

"Fuck yeah!" he screamed, and all his brothers and sisters screamed with him. But he could sense unease. He was still screaming hot screams, and he wouldn't know how to say what he felt, or, if forced, he'd reduce the feeling to a gut reaction to this Teacup kid's being creepy or fucked up or strange. But what really bothered Wil, and he could tell it bothered others by the flavor of their yells, the spattering of boos, and the volume—extremely loud but could be louder—was that before them, down on the BattleGround, which he could take in fully because of the awesome seats he'd scored, he could so easily see how in jeans and sneakers, a cooking pot in his hands, Teacup appeared very much a lamb. And watching a lamb get slaughtered was not good sporting.

"Let's fight!" Micky Wright screamed. A flare gun shot in the air. Wil gulped as the sound of the magnetic release hit his ears. Thurwar ran. The weight of Hass Omaha should have made her a step slower than the other elite Links, but today, as she had shown before, even with the dense metal force in her hand, her stride was hard and smooth. Not like it was a year ago, when she was in her prime, but still incredible to see. You couldn't see her M because of her armor but her back looked strong as she moved. He checked out Teacup. The boy was standing, pointing the round pot in his hand toward Thurwar as if it were a magic wand, as though green light would explode from it and strike Thurwar forever dead. Thurwar advanced, her long legs evaporating the distance. What was that like? To have her run at you. Nobody alive knew. Then the pot fell. Wil saw it. It dropped from the boy's hands. His seats were that good. And Thurwar was upon him, a great force upon a lamb. The young boy pumped his arm forward as if to stab, but his hand was empty. His eyes were wide. Thurwar swung hard and fast, her legs and hip and back creating the momentum. Hass Omaha obeyed her movements and found the mark.

The entire stadium heard the boy's skull crack. Like a tree splitting in half.

Wil watched, taking in the carnage. What had happened? How could it be that just a moment before that body was a boy and a second later it was a husk? An empty cradle. A monument to something gone.

And yet.

"YEAH!" Wil screamed. That was probably even faster than Staxxx's match. He high-fived the man wearing the *thurWAR* hat, then looked down at his wife. She was covering her face with her hands, peeking at the Jumbotron through her fingers. He slinked down beside her amid the chaos of cheers and delight.

"How was that?" Wil asked, poking Emily in the side.

"You really enjoy this?"

"Don't tell me you didn't a little?" Wil said. "Not a teeny bit?"

"Maybe a little," she said, frowning at herself, then punching her husband in the arm.

Electric

Another win. An offering, perhaps, to the fallen Sunset, who would surely have been thrilled with this demolition," Wright said. And as if pulled by a cord, Thurwar stopped walking toward her Keep.

"No," Thurwar said.

The arena plunged to a hush.

Micky Wright smiled. "What's that, Blood Mama?"

"Don't," she said.

The people murmured, unsure what to expect, elated by Thurwar.

"You know I hate that word. But tell us, what's bothering you, Your Bloodness?"

"I'm saying, that isn't true. He would not have been thrilled." Thurwar looked at Micky Wright and allowed herself the small delight of watching the self-proclaimed "most electric voice in all of action-sports" as his face fell for just a moment before flashing back to that perfect smile. The blood of the boy was still warm. The stadium was as quiet as she could remember it post-fight. The HMC floated closer to her lips. She spoke.

"A few days ago, I woke up and found Sunset dead on the ground far enough away from Camp that I—I only had a few moments before the Anchor pulled him away. He'd been there, all night and morning, his throat slit." The crowd listened. "Dead for no reason. Dead and I didn't even realize until a few minutes before the March started. I barely got to look at him. Dead and I can't do anything about it. Don't even know who did it. And you're telling me he would have been happy today? Are you insane? Are you all insane?" She was screaming now. She had promised herself she would never let them hear her like this. She took a breath, found calm.

Micky Wright chuckled nervously.

"It's a kid. A dead kid. Sun was—he probably would have cried over this. That's all."

Each word echoed off itself before fading into the next. When she was done, she walked over to her platform, put her arms together, and kneeled down for lock-in. She was a champion, so they offered her the dignity of bringing herself down to the Keep. Her muscles tensed in anticipation, and soon her brown wrists showed their three red lines.

Thurwar put her head down, as she always did, for Micky's commentary. To herself she said, "Miss you, Sun. I'm sorry." So low even the HMC inches from her mouth heard only breath.

The stadium held the messy sound of many people collectively not knowing what to say. Micky Wright hated that sound. He kicked out of his BattleBox and stomped into the arena.

"Well, there you have it, people! As if that stunning Question Match weren't enough, now we see mourning, we see heartbreaking sadness from the Blood Mother herself." There were murmurs, but the crowd was still far quieter than he would have liked. He ran his hands through his slick blond hair and took a deep breath before yelling into the orb before him. "After slaughtering Teacup, who—and we'll have to get this checked—may be the youngest person ever executed as punishment by law,* the Queen of the Cuff, Loretta Thurwar, has shared her outrage at the killing of the man who had the title of Grand Colossal before her! Can she keep it together?"

---

* George Stinney, Jr., actually. Young, Black in South Carolina. Of course, of course. On June 16, 1944, fourteen-year-old George Stinney, Jr., became the youngest person ever executed by the United States. He was charged with the murder of two young white girls who'd been killed by a railroad spike to the head.

    Seventy years after electricity pulled his life apart, he was exonerated.

    Since 1973, at least 186 who were wrongly convicted have been sentenced to death.

More murmurs, but no uproar. Wright wanted uproar.

"You beautiful, sensitive, murderous bitch!" Wright said. That got them going. The T-Gang loved when he called her beautiful, and they loved just as much when he called her a bitch. Loretta Thurwar. Easily the biggest star on the Circuit. She was almost at her three years. The average life expectancy for today's Links was about three months, but many didn't make it past their third week. In less time than that, if she survived, Thurwar would be freed into the population, her crimes absolved in blood.

Micky Wright had loved Thurwar. Her rise was his. But now her smug, holier-than-thou attitude toward everything made him feel a sinking in his chest. He sniffed the entitlement in her. Just look at her name—or rather her staunch refusal to embrace any of the AKAs he'd assigned her. It had started as a playful game, his offering a name and her refusing it. But at this point, it was clear that she just thought she was above him. He'd given her so many monikers—Blood Mama, General T, Bald Jesus—but mostly everyone called her Thurwar. The one name that hadn't come from him.

Wright liked knowing that he was one of the few men in the world who could stand next to Thurwar and not feel even an ounce of fear, albeit only when she was bowed down and unable to move. Most men would have feared her even if she were dead at their feet. The beating in his heart was the pure exhilaration of being next to the star. And he was no fool—he knew she was the star, not him. That beautiful, heartless bitch. She'd caught him off guard on purpose to cause a stir.

Wright walked in short, precise steps. He reached down and patted Thurwar's bowed head. Smooth, just a little wet. She didn't flinch. "Who knows. She won here, but could losing Sunset Harkless be the loss that finally makes the mighty, mighty Thurwar crack?"

There was uproar again. Their screams made his cock twitch. He lay down on the Keep beside her. "Is that what's happening, Lori?" he said in his special baby voice, one of his many signatures. "Is Mama finally crack, crack, cracking?" He could smell her sweat. He looked at her. The bold shoulder guards. The thigh armor that poked down to her left knee. The pristine bolt-leather battle gear around her arms and neck. A recent survey had found that viewers of Chain-Gang programs were most attracted to Thurwar post-fight. Since then, production had told Wright to draw out that time with her. Three HMCs floated in the air; a trio of lights circled their bodies, giving viewers access to every angle they could ever want.

This was the first time in months that Thurwar had said anything after a battle. And if he was honest with himself, her reticence had hurt his feelings. He was her hype man. They'd become stars together. He'd shown her the best love a performer can show, brought his absolute A game to each and every one of her BattleGround appearances. And now she couldn't be bothered with him. It stung. But no matter. Soon she'd be gone, and he'd still be the voice of the fastest-growing program in the world.

Wright pointed and one of the holo orbs nudged its way underneath Thurwar's bowed head. Her heavy breathing echoed like a great wind through the amps. He let the subjects in the stands listen to their queen breathe. Wright could feel them getting off on it. They loved everything about her. Literally. During *LinkLyfe,* there was not a single part of Thurwar's day that viewers didn't tune in for. She was the brightest among so many supernovae, and somehow, her star was growing still.

When he couldn't take listening to her breathe anymore, Wright snapped back to his feet. "Talkative as ever," he said with a chuckle. He dusted his pants and patted Thurwar on the head one last time.

"Thanks to Wal-Stores, Sprivvy Wireless, and McFoods for sponsoring season thirty-two of Chain-Gang All-Stars. As always, all of this was made possible by CCNA, GEOD, Spigot Correctional Systems, and TotemWorks, the best in corrections. Also, major shout-out to ArcTech Security.* ArcTech, the coldest in tactical security systems. Tune in next week to see Mark Marks and his Pale Bruiser take on Levi Paul and his sword, Lickem-Splitem. And be sure to cast us your reactions to Queen Thurwar's big moment. See you at the next BattleGround!"

---

* The Coldest in Tactical Security. ArcTech™ is an American arms, defense, and carceral technologies company with multinational interests. CEO Rodger Wesplat is the son of Tomas Wesplat and Monica Teasley-Wesplat.

Before she was escorted to the transport van, where she would wait for her gang in enforced silence, Thurwar would greet the people who were, as they always were, waiting for her. The guards took her out of the arena through a freight exit, the heavy, pale doors pushed open with a metallic scrape.

Her eyes adjusted to the late sun; the people screamed. She stood in sweats, a crewneck.

They had signs with her likeness. They said they loved her. They screamed her name like they owned her. A mass of hundreds gathered behind a metal barricade.

The soldier-police led her toward the crowds and she breathed in slowly. The shame was setting in. They roared, and she was relieved. Relieved that the sound of their adoration could take her mind from the fact of her continuing.

Her hands were loose and easy, set to green. The guards looked at her. She nodded, and they followed. The metal barriers strained against the people's excitement. Their hands shot out like weeds. She walked along, letting them touch her. They rubbed her head, felt her arms. She let them, even leaned into them, extended her arms back toward them. She touched their skin, so impossibly soft. Their clothes, their hair. If it were possible to take a piece of her, they would have. They pinched her. Rubbed, pulled. Small men pretended it was an accident when their fingers grazed, then grabbed, her chest.

Thurwar. Thurwar. I love you. Fuck you. Thurwar. Cunt. Murderer. Queer bitch. Here. Here. A picture. Picture! Please. Thurwar. Right here.

They slapped her neck, pulled at her sweatshirt, and she rolled along, sometimes stopping to hold someone's hand. Really hold it. The guards watched but kept their attention lax. She was Thurwar after all. She stretched to touch a child sitting on their father's shoulders. She didn't know if the heat she felt was her hating herself as the people who paid to watch her imprisonment begged for a chance to touch her. It was as if they needed to feel her with their own hands to know that she was real. What did they think could be gleaned from her skin? She could get drunk on their wild want. They made her feel like she was someone else. Someone deserving.

She saw a man and a woman at the barricade. The woman's tan-brown skin was glowing soft purple around her eye. She had a black band on her head. The man she was with was tall and his T-shirt had been wrung around so that the neck dropped down, revealing his dark chest. They screamed too, and the woman's voice cut through the crowd; it spoke to her in a way that suggested she'd known her, before. She sounded desperate and familiar.

"Loretta!" the woman said. She was in her twenties, probably. Thurwar looked at the woman and the man, who was helping her clear space as they nudged closer. "Loretta!" She reached a hand out. "You are worthy, Loretta!" Thurwar felt herself reaching for the outstretched arm. "You are worthy!" The voice sounded desperate with energy that pierced through the rest. It was the voice of someone calling out even as their throat tightened, even as they fought for their own life.

A short man with a greasy face broke between them, reached up, and touched Thurwar's clavicle before letting his fingers find her nipples, which he pinched lightly, purposefully. Thurwar looked down at him. He grinned, then faded into the crowd. She said nothing. She searched for the woman with the bruised eye, was terrified that she'd lost her in the forest of humans. She knew that this woman was different. She knew it by the sound of her voice. The way she carried her name, her tears. A lot of people cried in her presence, but this was different. This woman seemed like her care could be true, something real, not a moment to consume. Thurwar slowed down so as to let the woman find her again.

"Loretta." This time from farther left than she had been. Thurwar whipped her head around and found the young woman still reaching out, her hand in a tight fist. She leaned forward and arms flooded over her shoulders, neck, chest, and back. The more she gave, the more aggressively they grabbed. Pulling on the cloth of her sweatshirt. *Thurwar, Thurwar.* Finally, her fingers found the woman's. As she reached, she felt the woman's hands, soft but not impossibly so; they opened into her, and the two women clasped each other.

"I'm a friend. I want you to know what's coming," the woman said, or Thurwar thought she said. There were so many voices all screaming for attention. And then she let go and watched as Thurwar continued down the long line of adoration, now with a small piece of card stock hidden in her hands.

"Sir?" one of the soldier-police said.

Thurwar's heart throbbed. She wondered if the men had seen the transaction. If the contraband would be taken from her before she'd even had a chance to look at it. She gripped tighter.

"Yes, Daniels," the leader of the troop said.

Thurwar set her jaw. She decided that this was a thing she would not let go of. She would rather be Influenced than release the gift in her hand.

"Was wondering if I could get a picture?" the officer called Daniels asked. "With Thurwar."

"Do you think that's appropriate on a work shift?"

"I understand, sir, it's just—Jakey is a huge fan and . . ."

Thurwar watched this interaction. This bartering over her body.

"Well shit, don't make me some kinda asshole, then. Take your helmet off at least. Give me your camera."

"Thank you, sir." Daniels took off his helmet, revealing his brown hair, matted in sweat to his head. He ran his fingers through the wet strands a few times.

"I look okay?" Daniels asked.

"For Christ's sake, Daniels," the lead said.

"Okay." Daniels turned to Thurwar. "Do you mind smiling?" He posed with his fists on his hips near his gun and baton and Influencer.

"I do mind," she said.

"Oh, of course," Daniels said, and he adjusted himself a little, allowing for an inch more of room between them as the lead took the picture. Thurwar, despite herself, smiled as a flash of light captured their images.

"Thanks," Daniels said.

"Anytime," Thurwar said.

The men unlocked the van and she walked inside. It was empty.

"I'm gonna set your lock to blue. You understand what that means?"

Thurwar resisted the urge to say something snide—of course she understood that blue lock meant silence. That if she spoke while her wrists were set to blue, she'd feel a crippling shock. It was hard to forget the things that hurt you. You didn't often forget the shape of your cage. Instead she nodded and said, "I understand." She wanted to be alone.

"All right," the lead said. "Good job today," he added, and pressed some buttons on the black Slate controller in his hands. A single blue line appeared on each of her wrists. The doors closed.

Thurwar sighed silent relief. She was alone. The rarest luxury in her life. Before she opened her hand she rested in herself, in this moment in which she was unseen, unwatched. She let herself come down from the high of the crowds. How had she, a person who, before any of this, had wrung the life out of a good woman, become this person whom people thought they loved? She deserved the M on her back. And because of what she'd done she didn't just believe that she didn't deserve adoration. She didn't believe that she deserved to exist at all. And yet she continued.

She opened her hand, stretched her leg out, let blood flow to her knee. The card stock was crumpled but the words on it were clear. On top of the paper it read "CHAIN-GANG Season 33." She scanned what was written beneath the heading, and any good she had left in her was ripped away. She felt as though her insides had liquefied and a galloping adrenaline seared through her chest. She heard the fanfare of a crowd outside. She wiped the tears from her eyes. She ripped the note in half and put both pieces in her mouth. The card stock tasted of dry earth.

But by the time the van doors opened to deposit another Link from the Chain, Thurwar was almost smiling.

Hendrix "Scorpion Singer" Young

Inside, I have no say.*

"I know you hear me, Eight Two Two," morning guard says.

He throws words around like he don't care for the treasure he has. I lie back in my cot. And by not moving I make him speak again.

"Eight Two Two, let's go," morning guard says. Voilà, look at this power I have.

"C'mon now." I look at him on the other side of the iron. I wave my arm and see his eyes follow it. We are here together, but not. A starving man knows the price of food best. A glutton spills his portion to the floor. He is in uniform, dark green on the bottom and gentler green on the shirt, and he has a gun on his waist, and a hot spray on his waist, and a baton on his waist, and an Influencer that can throw pain into your bones, make you crumble and cry and shit yourself because your body belongs to the pain and not to you.

Only some of the guards carry the Influencer, and those guards you

---

* New Auburn Re-experimental Facility, modeled after the Auburn System created in the nineteenth century. The Auburn System required that prisoners live silently. This was designed to strip prisoners of a sense of self, which was thought to help them perform their day-to-day tasks—building products and doing other work to be sold commercially—more efficiently.

only see when you done fucked up something serious. Besides all the hurt on morning guard's waist, he got a callbox to talk to other guards. They all got that. I look at my wrists. I look at the blue line sitting at the vein. Blue line means, you speak, you get the pain. Speak and get a good shock. Use your voice and feel the hard lightning. Blue line means shut the fuck up as long as it's there, which is forever. Blue line means here we are, still. In here it's always a blue line on our wrists.

I nod at morning guard, who moves on past my lonely cage to rustle the next man. I dress. And before too many moments I'm sitting sporking gray eggs into my mouth. It sounds like chews and scoop-carves and sometimes a crunch. Not a voice in the chow hall. I look around and see the men around me scooping, carving, just the way I do. Men at long gray tables with gray seats.

I am like them and they are like me. Our wrists. Our hands. Our eyes. Our skin. The horn sings and we all move from chow to the Square. We get dressed in a white jumpsuit to put over our gray jump-suit. Over that we wear orange or green aprons. They give us clear goggles for the eyes. Nets for the hair. Gloves to handle the slaughtered.

The Square what it sound like. A big room. Warehouse more. Four long sides. Meat hanging from hooks comes slowly through a space in the east wall. Carcasses of soon burger and steak. There's vertical saws on my side of the Square. Or better, our side. Our job: split the ani-mals in half. We pull down, lower the meat to the cutter. Saws, three rising out of the conveyor belt in front of us. After we split them the meat floats to the next table, where the men with knives trim the bod-ies further. Men with green aprons have knives and men with orange work the saws and the conveyor. A square of men all cutting. All we do is tear flesh. Imagine that, prison full of men holding and han-dling blades. They control so good they don't worry. That's the Square. That's the job. That's the day. We prepare meat.

There's blood all on the floor and also on us. In the Square, our wrists is blue plus one red line so we stuck in place.

Above us, the guards, watching.

Wrists look purple from a distance.

We work. My work is my life. I pray for work. I hate my work. I need my work. I pull/push meat for the buzzing saws.

I halve the body.

The saw eats gladly.

Two halves a body.

I have a body.

I halve a body.

I do the same. I do the same.

The saw goes like God told it not to stop. All us on the line work like this. The saw is strong and hot.

Do the job. Do it right.

Man beside me today. He cuts and pushes good. Man beside him, he don't. We work. Just four feet between us. Blue lines on all of us mean there is no say. It's always blue lines.

We cut and across from us they slice and push. Saw sings a *whirr* when it's air and a *scree* when it's meat and a *crrrr* when it's bone. The saw sings solo. On year five of twenty-nine. Five years I ain't heard my voice for more than a moment. But this I deserve. No excuse.

Press and hold so the saw eats the meat and not the hands. Blood is the same color. Lose half a hand and not realize till you try to make the peace sign and don't have the digits. Only a meaty L. Solo. The saw don't care what's in front of it.

Man beside me been beside me for not too long. A year, maybe two. Man beside him old now. We could be folk. Generations of Black plus Black plus Black. Man beside the man beside me, he old and wobbly. Can't cut right. He mess up, we all get the pain.

We cut in the morning, then chow.

Gray-water rice and who knows. The sound is slurp-chew and there's the smell of blood on my hands and every other thing in this place. Then back to the Square. It's tired work. I look at the man beside me and the man beside him and see myself, then myself even farther. Last man got gray hair and glasses and shakes when he tries to be still.

It ain't no happy place.

Late in the day we all tired, and late in the day last man is especially tired. Worse than tired. Wobbly and crooked. We work for nothing. We work and work for no money. We did wrong so now we slaves.*

---

* Ratified on December 6, 1865, the Thirteenth Amendment to the United States Constitution reads "Neither slavery nor involuntary servitude, *except* as a punishment for crime whereof the party shall have been duly convicted, shall exist within the United States, or any place subject to their jurisdiction" (emphasis added).

Work for nothing on the inside for people on the outside. Yes. Slaves in a mean box. That's all.

Last man been a slave. He wobbly now. Too wobbly. A thin branch in a silent wind song. I knock the man beside me with my elbow so he might knock the man beside him. Nudge him awake 'cause third man don't look right. I have to lean on one leg to reach him, but I do. I knock him so he can do the same to last man so last man don't kill his old self. Man next to me don't do nothing. Only thing I can do is I knock him again. Push my elbow into his shoulder. We all locked to where we stand. I look at him and tell him with my eyes to look at the old man next to him. Man beside me look at me with a mean face like I was the one that magnet-chained him to this line so he could cut meat forever. His eyes say, *Fuck you.* Then he look over at the last man in our line wobbling on his feet and man next to me shakes his head and doesn't do nothing else. I nudge him one more time 'cause all he got to do is nudge old last man awake. Last man's cuts discombobulated now. Meat gonna get trashed. We'll all feel the pain. He looking sick, like he might topple back to the floor, knock his head on a rail probably, or forward and split his whole self wide open. Man beside me looks over at the last man, struggling, looking crazy, then looks back at me and grins like this the part of the movie he been waiting to see.

I try for steps. Sometimes they don't set the magnet clutch hard enough. Not usually, but I always check and see. We can move inside an invisible box so we can cut our meat and nothing else, usually. I try to take a step back. I can. I try to take another and it's like a hand stronger than any man pulling me back in place. The invisible chain locks us all to the meat line. All we do is cut meat.

Last man letting his slabs run by uncut. He teetering. I clap my hands once. I clap again. Guard up top looks down at me. He doesn't see anything but some slaves so he looks back at whatever. I nudge that man beside me one more time. Hard in the ribs because last man isn't all right and won't be up much longer. Man beside me hits me back in the shoulder, not to tell me nothing 'cept if I mess with him one more time he gonna do more than nudge. I clap and look. I halve a body. I see the man over there, the man who been a slave for years, teetering back, then forward. Maybe he need to fall. Sometimes I think the same. Maybe we had enough. Maybe this a way out. I see him and look around at the meat getting cut and all the men wearing blue lines on their wrists, which mean they are work and nothing else.

I remember how to say. I remember and breathe deep because the blue line on my wrists mean there is no say except that which is pulled through hurt.

"Hey!" I say with my own voice. I haven't heard it in a long, sad time. It sounds stretched out and dried, like roadkill, but it's mine and I love it. Everybody is looking at me. Young, onstage, and then the electricity wrecks me up. It's a clench that squeezes all the muscles at once. I scream more and that's my voice letting them know they still have me and also they don't.

I fall to the floor. Farther than I should be able to. The shock gives some slack. The cuffs can only do so much at once.

"Hey," I say again from the floor, and again I feel the lightning bolt stab me up. But I can move some. I struggle from the ground. Crawl through the shallow seas of blood on the floor. Feeling possessed by the pain and a different kinda pull that can't be ignored. "Hey!" I scream again, and my body writhes so hard my tongue pokes out my mouth and stamps the bloodstained floor. If I taste anything I don't know. Pain is what I see, hear, taste, and feel. I press my knees on the bloody floor. I push and crawl. I move toward my last man as boots come stomping toward me.

Then I hear more voices, voices like mine, stomped on but there, still.

"Lionel!" somebody up top screams.

"Mary, I miss yo—"

A small riot, the kind that happens when they know ain't too much can be done about the chaos.

"Fuck them!" somebody screams, then he screams different when the shock come.

"Twenty-two years tomorrow and—"

More and more of them go. A slave chorus. Each note snuffed short by electric, but a chorus still. They'll take the shock just to hear themselves. Just to say something at least. Them like me keep screaming their names and whatever else they think of. In here your own voice is a kind of wish. A shooting star. You don't waste it on nothing. It's a magic show of quick voices, then hard grunts, screams. They get wrecked up, then stand back up, ready to cut.

I crawl 'cause it's hard. I crawl past the man who was beside me. I breathe heavy and I grab myself up at the last man and pull the old slave back and sit him down on the hard, bloody floor so he don't fall and split himself all the way open.

I get up. Stand on my feet.

And look down at last man, who don't look so good but is at least not cut open, and I feel my wrists pulling me and I'm almost moon-walking back to where I was. And then a body in green legs and a less green shirt swings a baton at my face and blows me back toward the sound of whirring.

It's a long John,
He's a long gone,

"How you know that song, son?" he asking me, and he want me to speak back. I keep on singing.

Like a turkey through the corn,
Through the long corn.

"If you sign these papers here, you understand what your life in CAPE will be like, Mr. Young? It's important that you understand." He a man in a suit talking like I can't read or think. I'm in a bed that's soft, so I'm singing. I'm in a bed. I'm eating food I can taste, food with color on it, so I'm singing. On my wrist is green, a color I ain't seen on them in a long, long time. So I sing.

Well, my John said,
In the chap ten,
"If a man die,
He will live again."

I left my arm in the factory, so I'm singing. I'm singing because even with some of me cut from the body, I am whole once more, listening to myself. It's hard and soft at the same damn time, my voice is, like a tree with tender meat under bark.

"You already had the Arc cuff installation procedure when you entered this facility, so that's one less thing you'll have to do now, in this transition. No new surgery will be needed except that which has already happened regarding your recent"—he pause like he don't know how to say you got your arm sawed off—"accident."

Well, they crucified Jesus
And they nailed him to the cross;
Sister Mary cried,
"My child is lost!"

"If this is your request can you please sign here indicating that this decision was made under your own will and power and that no one at the New Auburn facility has ever coerced you in any way to seek the CAPE program?"

Well, long John,
He's long gone,
He's long gone.

He talking 'bout Auburn now. Place I won't ever get back to. I'm singing a song that just fills me up. I sign his papers and he smiles and frowns at me and turns away, and I'm in the bed waiting to get healed enough to see the world outside if she'll have me.

The Van

All the Angola-Hammond Chain rode together in the van. It was all of them and then it was Jerry. And of course, the closed-circuit cameras perched in the four corners of the van's rear holding unit, which gave Jerry a good view of the Links at all times. While they sped away from Vroom Vroom, toward their next stop, Jerry made it a point to look, through his analog rearview and the series of screens embedded in the console, at his cargo of supervillains/heroes. He made a point of really watching them as they sat in silence. There they were, all eight of them, bound by their magnetic locks. In that moment, he guessed, he was their leader. The van was silent except for his whistling. He figured they probably liked to hear something from somebody, stuck in silence as they were.

Jerry considered himself an additional member of this bandit group, and in some ways, yes, he was definitely their leader. What else would you call the man driving the van—well, sitting in the driver's seat of the van as the hand of automation pulled them steadily down the highway toward the drop-off point? Jerry watched the console screens as he reclined in his chair. His promotion to assistant producer and head of inter-circuit transport of the Angola-Hammond Link System had been one of the few definitive wins in his life. And one of the perks was he got his own special episode of *LinkLyfe* that no one else would ever get to see. *LinkLyfe: The Van.* Maybe he would pitch it one of these days to the higher-ups.

Because no one but Jerry knew that after a brutal victory Staxxx wept silently on Thurwar's shoulder. It was Thurwar and always Thurwar whom Staxxx sought out in these moments. And no one else knew how Thurwar would gently massage Staxxx's scalp as the tears wet her sweatshirt. Though today Thurwar seemed to be staring into herself. Her arms were wrapped around Staxxx, but limply, as if she were surprised to be holding this woman whom she'd held so many times before.

So much happened there as they waited to be deposited at their next March location. A silent opera just for him. No one else knew how Gunny Puddles, that balding sicko, glared, jaw clenched, on the bench seat closest to the door for the duration of every van ride. Nobody saw Sai Eye Aye, the Thurwar-wannabe-turned-badass-in-their-own-right, as they tried to make the other Links laugh. If the laugh lasted more than half a second, Jerry would hear their screams as their wrists shocked electricity through them. If any of them got shocked the game would end for a while, then start again a few miles later. And there was Randy Mac, who tried his best to seem nonchalant, easygoing even. He tried especially hard to make it seem like he didn't care that it was Thurwar whom Staxxx chose for comfort and not him. Mac hid his jealousy by having Rock, Paper, Scissors tournaments with Rico Muerte or Sai or Ice. But Jerry could see from his screens how Randy peeked across at Staxxx even as he showed an open palm against Ice Ice the Elephant, the Samoan bruiser, who flashed a massive fist. And of course, the entire van felt the absence of Sunset Harkless, the only one of them Jerry had really, truly known . . . a little.

Randy Mac raised his two hands in victory. He clasped and shook them above his head. That Randy Mac, Jerry thought. What a sad man he is beneath it all. Jerry sighed as he reclined into his seat. Unrequited love. In this, Jerry and Randy were brothers of a kind. At least Staxxx lay with Randy sometimes. Randy was lucky for that. Jerry could only dream of being so lucky.

The A-Hamm Links knew Jerry well, though he'd hardly spoken a word to them. For the last year, he'd done most of their transports, dropped them off at fields in the middle of nowhere like he might drop stepchildren off at school. He was usually kind enough to share in their silence. In the entertainment business this time was called "being on ice." The idea was to keep the Links from speaking when the cameras weren't watching; if not they risked the juicy morsels' being spilled before the world could receive them. The van was one of the only places where a Chain could be together and not be directly monitored, outside of, of course, Jerry's watchful eye. There were the BlackOut Nights too, but those were unpredictable and rare.

If they hadn't been physiologically forced into silence, Jerry would have talked to them about his own life. Maybe the van, the show forming in his head, could be a talk show. He'd talk to them about his ex-wife, Meghan, and his kid, Kyle. But would talking about his family be like waving steak in front of hungry dogs? And to be honest, it had been months since he'd seen either his ex or his kid. He obviously couldn't talk to them about his job, and of course that was all he ever really wanted to talk about. He couldn't talk about his personal relationship with the late Sunset, which even his bosses knew nothing about. If they had, he certainly wouldn't have been given this new position, which was actually assistant assistant producer and co-head of inter-circuit transport of the Angola-Hammond Link System.

His new friends—all his old friends had chosen Meghan over him—loved to hear about his position as assistant assistant producer and co-head of inter-circuit transport of the Angola-Hammond Link System. And he'd actually reconnected with his niece over it too—or was she his ex-niece? She'd never liked him before. She'd even told him so on more than one occasion. But he'd called to check up on her after the divorce anyway, to tell her that he hoped they'd stay in touch.

Mari was one of those kids—well, she wasn't a kid anymore—but she was the kind of person who didn't like anything. She hated the government, hated most food that wasn't prepared in some kind of shrine of peace and happiness, hated most people on TV because they weren't doing enough about this or that. She was a tough one, always had been, and considering she didn't have her father in her life, that seemed fair. She'd been thrown some tough cards and now she played every hand the same: critically, without trust. But despite all her self-righteous protesting, she'd actually looked excited when he'd men-tioned his promotion. At first, she'd said she didn't believe him, didn't believe that he got to travel with Sunset, that he got to talk to, and sort of know, her dad. Then she'd asked him, timidly at first, then more insistently, to tell her about her father. What was he like up close? How did he seem in person? And Jerry told her the truth: The guy was always smiling. You wouldn't believe he'd done the things he'd done. He was always the first one on the van and the last one off. When he wasn't silenced he'd ask Jerry about his day, the both of them pretending their former partners weren't sisters.

Mari would listen, silent, on the holophone. Once Jerry had told her, "He's a much better man than he was when he went in. The program has some merit in—" but she'd hung up on him before he could finish.

Jerry had felt guilty that she'd reached out to him after her father had been murdered before he could get in touch with her. He'd told her the truth, he didn't know what had happened. And because he didn't know what else to say—he couldn't say "He was a good man"—he'd just started talking about the show, letting slip some rule changes he'd discovered in an email he'd accidently been cc'd on. It wasn't until she'd said bye and ended the call that he'd realized that he'd divulged confidential information. He sent her a message asking her never to mention it. She replied, *For sure.*

Both his ex-niece and his ex-sister-in-law had made clear long before he'd had this job that they did not vibe with Chain-Gang. But hard action-sports were how he supported himself and his family. And though it was not his place to have a feeling about whether or not the lives of the Links were fair, or to make judgments on the ways these criminals were serving the community via entertainment, he made it a point not to watch the show at home. It could be pretty grim.

And yet, somehow, because he was an assistant assistant producer and co-head of inter-circuit transport of the Angola-Hammond Link System and managing officer of human activity and security, entrusted with the responsibility of making sure that the Angola-Hammond Chain got where they needed to go, he cared for the convicts. They were the most popular Chain of all time, many of them celebrities in their own right. And in those moments on the road when no one was watching, he was their leader, kind of.

Jerry felt a fatherly flavor of affection for them. When he'd return for the Links after the BattleGround, or pick them up from a Hub City stop, or drop them off for the March, he'd do his head count and he'd feel a small pinch of shame if even one of them was missing. Whether it'd been on the BattleGround or some internal A-Hamm conflict, it made it hard to look any of them in the eye. Just a few days before, when Thurwar had stepped into the van followed by Staxxx and the entire Chain was seated and there was no sign of Sunset, he'd almost cried right then and there. As he drove the Sunset-less A-Hamm he felt desperately that he wanted to be a part of his actual child's life again. Sunset's child would never see him again, but Jerry and Kyle didn't have to be that way. Except Meghan was still making it hard and Kyle was suffering. For now, Jerry pretended there were a bunch of Kyles riding in the back.

A black-and-white puff jumped into the road, many yards off. More than enough time for it to get outta there. The truck didn't slow and the puff did not move. A skunk? A skunk. Standing in the road like a martyr. Jerry leaned forward but touched nothing. The van charged on its wheels. There was no reason not to speed through these empty hills. Except now. The thing sat there, looking at Jerry as though it had been waiting for them and was relieved to see they had finally arrived. Jerry peered out through the windshield, watched the steering wheel ebbing one way and then the other, correcting and remaining constant in an autonomous calm.

"Bitch," Jerry said, grabbing the wheel and pushing down on the brakes as he honked the horn. They slowed, harshly enough that he felt his body creep forward. Beneath them he could hear the sounds of weapons scraping against the van's undercarriage. But it was the horn, it seemed, that did it. Made the thing almost leap into the air before scampering off to the other side of the road, beneath a guardrail and into long grass.

Jerry looked into the rearview. He met eyes with Randy Mac, who stared back, hungry and tired. Randy Mac smiled and held his arms up, showing Jerry his palms, the blue glow at his wrists. Then he lifted what remained of his middle fingers—his left middle finger, and ring finger for that matter, had been partially removed some months prior—and flipped Jerry one full bird and the nub of another.

Really, it was a thankless job.

Jerry stopped whistling. They rode in complete silence, it seemed, for the last several miles until, from his reclined position, he felt the car slow and stop.

"Good luck, huh?" Jerry said loudly enough so that the Links could hear him, even though they were still locked inside. He'd parked on an empty road. Jerry opened up the van's undercarriage and pulled out a long black metal rod that spread out into an almost perfect flat disk at its top before pointing back into a cone at the head. Jerry pulled the black screen from his pocket and pressed its face. The ArcTech Anchor, which had been sleeping below them on the drive as it always was, became erect, then rose, suspended in the air, and waited there. Jerry pulled the small armory of equipment from beneath the van and set it down on the ground for each of them to grab. He laid down the hammer, trying not to hurt his back as he did so, plus the scythe, several knives, a trident, a golf club, and the rest of the destructive freight, dropped them onto the brittle grass at the road's edge.

Then he opened up the back of the truck so that the Links could get out, and sprinted back to his front seat and locked the door while they shuffled outside. All their wrists flashed a warning of blinking red as their cuffs synced to the Anchor. The same red flashed on the edges of the five-foot-long metallic ringleader, like a miniature Space Needle, like a floating black body.

As they settled into their open containment, they looked at the nothing all around them, at one another. Thurwar closed the van's doors. They'd been dropped on the outskirts of a long-dead farm. No cars passed as they waited and the only lights to be seen came from the waning glow of the sky and its astral bodies and the convicts' wrists. Five of them had seen the BattleGround that day: Thurwar, Staxxx, Randy Mac, Ice Ice the Elephant, and a man called Bad Water. Each had won their bout, keeping the A-Hamm Chain at eight Links strong.

They hadn't been out for even a minute before the van they'd arrived in began to pull away. And they stood in the small sliver of unseen and unsilenced time together. Thurwar, Staxxx, Randy Mac, Sai Eye Aye, Ice Ice the Elephant, Gunny Puddles, Bad Water, and Rico Muerte: the Angola-Hammond Chain.

"Nice to see everybody," Staxxx said, smiling widely. The corner of a white patch peeked up from the hem of her shirt. Beneath it her latest X tattoo, which she'd received from her post-fight tattooist, was healing on her skin. Tattoos had become such an ingrained post-match tradition that they were offered, free of Blood Points, in every arena.

A chime like tin falling against concrete sounded. Their wrists eased to orange. Staxxx picked up her scythe as Thurwar went for the hammer. Once Staxxx had her scythe, she seemed to brighten, as if a piece of her had been painfully removed and only now was she whole again. Scythe in hand, Staxxx rushed toward Thurwar and gathered her in her arms. She kissed her on top of the head and squeezed her midsection. Thurwar looked at Randy Mac, who smiled out the side of his mouth as Staxxx squeezed and quickly hugged her back before pushing her away. Sai Eye Aye approached Thurwar and pulled her in for a deep hug.

Thurwar breathed in this short window before the HMCs were deployed and the show began. This was what they did, and it was not lost on her that this was different from what other Chains did. When they got out of the van they re-greeted one another. That was a habit that she and Sun had instilled in the group. She felt she should say that whoever killed Sunset should come forward and at least explain why. She wanted to reestablish the hierarchy that even when Sun was around had started with her. She wanted to know who had killed her friend.

"Blood Mama," Sai Eye said through a sparsely toothed grin. A rock to the jaw had rid them of two upper premolars and a lower canine. Their skin was sandy and clear and their head was as bald as Thurwar's. "That was an interesting evening," Sai finished. "You're the Grand, carry it well. We're with you till High Freedom." Sai smiled the way a real comrade did.

After the silent ride, speech felt like water in a dry mouth. "Hey," Thurwar replied. "Yeah. You did well."

Thurwar and Staxxx both acknowledged Ice Ice the Elephant by touching his shoulder. He nodded in response. He was a few inches shorter than Thurwar, though he probably doubled her weight, with his arms, legs, and torso all thick as tree trunks.

"Well fought," Ice said.

"Ditto," Staxxx said. Then she continued. "Which one of you wants another good squeeze before we start rolling?" Staxxx asked. Her eyes stopped at Randy Mac. "I think I see somebody who does right here."

"It depends on where you're squeezing," Mac said. Staxxx approached him.

Feed will begin in sixty-five seconds, said the airy, light voice of the Anchor. It sounded human, yet it was distinctly soulless, its only concern directing their action.

A panel in the Anchor's head slid open and three HMC orbs floated out.

"I know you need this. I bet you were worried about me, you big pussybear." Staxxx was careful hugging Randy, so as not to decapitate him with her scythe. He took it warmly. Melted into her. Everyone watched them closely. It was hard to do what Staxxx did. To allow herself to be a relief to others in a sport designed very specifically for them never to relieve anyone of anything.

Gunny Puddles spit on the ground.

"I need a little of that too," said Sai Eye Aye.

"I'll take some, matter of fact," Rico Muerte added.

Feed will begin in thirty seconds. Report to line.

"All right, this is gonna have to be a double team," Staxxx said with an evil laugh.

Sai shrugged and Staxxx wrapped them up in her left arm as Rico Muerte stepped forward and let her pull him into her with her right. "Don't be shy, y'all. It's been a long day."

For the last couple of months this had been Staxxx's procedure. The touch of another human was like love on the skin. Sunset had encouraged Staxxx when she'd made a tradition out of starting each March with some love. In a way he had mentored Staxxx into the star she'd become.

Holoview initiating.

It was over. They separated, pulled apart by the force of their master, the Anchor; they stood in a line, shoulder to shoulder, some three feet apart. The three HMCs floated and rested at Rico Muerte's feet. He was already posed, crouched with his six-iron club on the ground as though he were assessing the lay on a tricky green. The HMCs flew and circled around him.

The most popular hard action-sports program in North America had begun.

Personhood Link

"There are some things I need to explain."

Ain't that seven kinds of true.

"I need you to confirm that you understand the nature of the Criminal Action Penal Entertainment program, which will henceforth be denoted 'CAPE,' that it is an extension of your thirty-six-year sentence for the murder of Keyan Thurber and in no way grants you clemency for your crimes against Keyan Thurber.[*] However, through your participation in the CAPE program you may earn your exoneration and be released into the public, but that is unlikely. To do so, you must successfully participate in the CAPE program for a period of three years, starting from the moment you sign the document I'm about to read to you. You have your own copy, so you can read along with me as I go through the terms aloud. Are you able to read?"

He speaks like a machine, says the names so easily. It hurts. It don't

---

[*] A man murdered. Shot right down. When you shooting a problem you see the problem, not the life they lived, not their happiness and sadness. Most of the time you shoot hot in rage, is what Hendrix Young imagined. When he killed Keyan Thurber, he was perfectly aware the man was a person capable of great feeling, great love. That was the problem. They call it cold blood. But when the trigger pulled, it all heat. Chest fire.

make me less a monster to say so. And me knowing that don't make me less one either. It hurts still.

It's three white men in this office space. I can turn my head and see myself in a mirror in the room. Every mirror a door. In this one I see my face, the dark skin, eyes brown, bright. Hair wild black on my head and across my jaw. I need a shave. A good shave is a kind of love. Love I have not felt for some time.

Man talking is a representative of the program, wearing a government-looking tie. Man on my side of the table is Dan, called director of personnel here at New Auburn. It burns the skin to be back here. A place that held me silent. A place I was a slave.

I'm signing these papers no matter what kind of death they speak.

Or rather, where I was enslaved. Just 'cause you enslaved don't make you a slave. You can't ever be that.

Dan, the director, slave master extraordinaire. Dan I didn't see much of on the inside, and when I did see him, he say it's good I don't see him much.

First meeting with Dan he asked me a question. I looked at my wrists. Surgery fresh, but the blue shined through the stitches. Dan had said, "You can nod yes or shake your head no to what I say." Then he talked at me. I said, "My name—" and the electricity shocked me to the floor. I wept there for some time. Dan said, "Please return to your seat, Mr. Young."

That was the beginning of my time at Auburn.

Across from Dan now is another man with black hair combed back and a tie the color of a goldfish. To start, he told me his name was Sawyer. "I'll be like your agent," he said. "I'm your new CO too. We're gonna have a good time, brother." He smiled and tried not to look at the bandaged stump coming out of my shoulder.

We in Dan's office. A tight room with blank walls and an old-style television flat against the blank. It's hotter than it needs to be. We in Dan's office, but it don't feel like it's his right now.

"He can read," Dan says, looking over at me, then at both the men across from us before he continues. "We practice the silence protocol as a re-experimental behavior initiative, and we maintain it at all times while on—"

"We know it's quiet in here. Just like we know it smells like shit,"

Sawyer says, then he looks at me. Winks at me. I'm with you, pal, I hear him think, even though he must know I see the guillotine in him. "I'd like my client to be able to speak. This is kinda important, Dan. We heard him speak a little bit ago when he was hospitalized, so why insist now?"

"Here on facility we enforce the policy strictly. In the infirmary we allow disengagement for obvious reasons." The reason being everybody screams when they hurt. Can't have screaming and electricity for more screaming. Man in here broke his leg, almost fried his brain from screaming so much. Sometimes you can cry if you do it quiet enough and the shock don't pick it up. We all get good at crying quiet in New Auburn.

Government Man speaks: "Again, we already have the preliminary confirmation, but I need Mr. Young to be able to speak for himself. It is the precedent moving forward, Officer Rottermith, that incoming CAPE participants must show compliance via signatory and verbal confirmation unless physically incapable. And if you'd like to have a standing opportunity to have your population opt into the program, as other facilities do, this will be the standard."

And I'm almost sad to see Dan lose his collar on me. I can see how much it hurts him to have to hear my voice, to hear me use my voice, even to use it to choose death. There's always more wicked if you dig deep enough. "It's part of—"

"This is not a negotiable issue. Your company president agreed to this a long time ago. Please disengage Mr. Young's SILENCE."

Dan blinks, then without looking to his left, to me, he pulls a small black screen out of the desk. He presses and slides his finger, presses and slides his finger again. The lines on my wrist go green.

"Thank you," Government Man says. "So again, I'd like you to read along as I go through the CAPE rules and conditions with you, Mr. Young. Can you confirm that you can read?"

I look at Dan, see how sad he is. Sawyer is smiling at Government Man and Government Man is bored. A bored executioner. A white shirt and black tie. His face seems squeezed of life.

"You can speak now, Hendrix," he says. "Are you able to read?"

"He can read," Dan says.

"We're talking to champ here," Sawyer says.

"We need you to confirm you are able to follow and comprehend what we are saying. And we need you to confirm that you are doing this without coercion."

One thing I give 'em, I think as I begin to laugh, they take pain and make it something brand-new every chance. They got every flavor and they keep making more.

Government Man frowns. Sawyer laughs with me, 'cause that's the kinda man he is. Haha.

"Are you able to—" And I can't stand him asking me again. I'll double over on the floor. It's surprising I can do it still. We don't laugh in New Auburn and still the spirit is right there waiting for this moment here.

"I can read," I say, laughing still.

"Thank you," Government Man says, back to blank slate. Sawyer nods. Dan, I can feel, would have preferred never to hear my voice. Like my sound will stain his walls with something he can't scrub out.

"I'll continue." Government Man so sewn into his language, but all it means is murder. It tries to paint all that nothing over death. He is nothing too. That's the only way he could. A shell, a cipher for a thing so great he'd be destroyed looking in the mirror if he weren't already dead on the inside. Like me.

I ask myself, Can I even hate a man like this?

"Please listen carefully and if you have any questions, please ask them after I've gone through all of the terms."

Of course I can.

"You, one Hendrix Young, by signing this document confirm and acknowledge that you have elected to forgo the remaining tenure of twenty-four years and thirty-nine days of a total twenty-nine years at New Auburn Re-experimental Facility to participate in the CAPE program, a hyper-athletic hard action-sports entertainment platform formed primarily by the association of the Corrections Corporation of North America, which will henceforth be denoted as CCNA, and GEOD and understand that Chain-Gang Unlimited and all its subsidiary series are part of the CAPE program and as such are in line with many Program-Initiated and Conducted Corporal Punishment models."

They paint the walls with words. They build walls with their words.

"As a participant in the program you agree to the following irreversible conditions:

"As a Link, the catchall name for participants in the Chain-Gang Unlimited branch of the CAPE program, you will travel with associate Links as part of the Sing-Auburn-Attica-Sing Chain, formally known as the Sing-Attica-Sing Chain. This Chain consists of inmates from the Attica Correctional Facility, Attica, New York; Sing Sing Correctional Facility, Ossining, New York; and the New Auburn Re-experimental Facility, Auburn, New York, all of which are owned by the GEOD correction corporation, or operated for the purposes of CAPE programming by GEOD. The Chain will also consist of Links who have been reassigned or 'traded' to the Chain, as is sometimes deemed logistically or financially necessary and beneficial. The CAPE program retains the utmost right to reassign any Link, so long as the directors of the Chains can reach an agreement.

"As a member of Sing-Auburn-Attica-Sing it will be your primary duty to defend yourself at all times and absolutely no liability for your person will fall to the CAPE program, any of the business affiliates of the program, or the government of the United States of America.

"As a Link you agree to have any and all aspects of your life recorded for public/private view, and consent to have your likeness used as a marketing tool at the discretion of the CAPE program from the moment of signing, in perpetuity.

"By signing the document herein, you agree to forfeit your right to any and all possessions, except those earned through successful participation in the CAPE program and outlined, in part, in this document.

"By signing this document, you forfeit any and all rights not formally distinguished and outlined by the CAPE program.

"As a Link you will be assigned a numeric economic value. This value is quantified in points colloquially known as 'Blood Points,' which are earned through successful participation in the program. These Blood Points will allow you to purchase goods such as food, weapons, certain levels of medical care, armor, and clothes, among other amenities. Outside sponsors may also support your participation. Blood Points may only be used to attain new weapons or armor after a Link has had one successful BattleGround appearance.

"Upon signing this document, you will be awarded fifteen Blood

Points. The value of each Blood Point is one one-thousandth of one cent.

"All Links begin at rank one-R, or Rookie. Upon three successful BattleGround bouts Links rise to the level of Survivor.

"The current sequence of rankings is as follows: Rookie, Survivor, Cusp, Reaper, Harsh Reaper, Colossal, Grand Colossal. You will receive a more complete listing of what opportunities, armor, and amenities are available via Blood Points to each ranking level as new regulations are released every season."

I listen to him talk his way up this ladder they've made. All the rungs, the different names you might earn as you become a death dealer. All the currency I might earn by killing the best of 'em.

"Do you follow thus far?"

I look at him straight and nod.

"Is that a confirmation?" Government Man asks.

"Yes," I say.

He continues.

"Once assigned the personhood Link, you, one Hendrix Young, agree to spend the entirety of your tenure bound by ArcTech equipment. You also agree that any attempt to flee the custody of the program will result in an immediate termination via injection, detonation, electrocution, or any other method deemed suitable.

"In agreeing to participate in the CAPE program's Chain-Gang Unlimited programming, you are also agreeing to participation in the standard Marches, each of indeterminate time (though usually spanning four to sixteen days). During said Marches, Links will be bound to a remote Prison Anchorage at all times. Any attempt to flee will result in forcible persuasion or termination.

"Each March session's end will be immediately followed by a stay in a 'Hub City,' where Links will participate in civic community activities to enrich and support host communities. Any failure to comply with those activities will result in immediate termination.

"During Hub City stays, which will last no more than four days, Links will live in assigned dormitory spaces, which can be upgraded via Blood Points.

"Following Hub City sessions, Links will be escorted via CAPE program transport to a stadium site for BattleGround bouts, which will have been determined during March sessions and communicated to Links via electronic message. Advance information regarding Battle-Ground bouts can also be purchased via Blood Points.

"During BattleGround bouts Links must defend themselves at all times. A Link can be deemed a winner only if all opponents have been terminated. As of the current season of Chain-Gang Unlimited, Links cannot be assigned a Link from their own Chain as their BattleGround opponent.

"Failure to defend oneself and failure to attempt to terminate the opposing Link/Links will result in immediate termination for all parties."

He goes on and on. It's impossible to follow everything he says and at the same time it's obvious: All he saying over and over is, You already dead.

"Do you understand?"

"I do," I say. Another kind of altar.

"Now, having understood these irreversible terms and conditions, do you, Hendrix Young, agree to enroll in the CAPE program?"

I look at Dan. I can see it's still hurting him. I look at Government Man, trying to feel nothing and succeeding in that. I can see Sawyer, licking his teeth.

"Yes," I say.

Sawyer hands me a pen.

"Awesome. Now that the boring stuff is over, let's go get you ready for this. You spin for your weapon tomorrow. And you'll get your marks and some basic threads."

I look at the men and my one wrist. I'm here with them because to love a voice is a painful thing. And now that I've traded my arm to get it back, my whole inside knows I can't return to the silence, 'less I throw myself against the saw again, more precisely.

I sign.

Circuit

Emily stared into an 8K display lodged in the back of their new Ufridge to watch a show she hated publicly but now watched religiously. With the money her grandma had left her she'd completely synced their apartment appliances, so there was hardly a single device that wasn't fully U'd. She looked past too-old grapes and saw Rico Muerte squatting like an absurd golfer, wearing a bandana on his head and camouflage cargo pants that tapered at his ankles. He pointed to the upside-down cross tattoo just below his left eye as he crouched. Muerte didn't have a true primary weapon, let alone a secondary weapon, since he was still just a Rook—or was Muerte a Survivor? Emily wasn't sure. Muerte was still fresh meat, though. So it was fitting to be watching him there in the fridge. Eww, Emily thought, one of Wil's jokes, leaking into her mind.

Of all the U-nification, the fridge had been the most ridiculous part. Wil loved it all, had spurred her to use some of her inheritance that way. And though she had trouble watching *Chain-Gang All-Stars BattleGrounds,* its sister show, *LinkLyfe,* was a study in humanity that she'd decided any intellectual, socially aware person at least had to peruse. It was part of the cultural conversation; even if she was ambivalent about its ethics, she couldn't pretend it wasn't an interesting part of the world and, because of Wil, her life. She watched both programs, but *LinkLyfe* was the far more interesting bit for Emily. Everything mattered on *LinkLyfe*.

Each new March started with the Lineup. It was a reminder of who was alive and who wasn't. It was epic. You could tell how the Links felt, having just watched their Chain-mates' triumph or death. You could see who it was they hoped to project into the hearts and minds of America and you could see their potential. Like Rico Muerte, the new kid on this powerhouse Chain, who had something of a sense of humor about him. He wasn't shying away from the enormity of his Chain-mates. He said, *I'm here, look at me, I'm not scared,* with every move.

Wil had explained over and over the nuance of the opening Lineup. He'd gone back into the archives and he'd teared up showing her an A-Hamm Lineup from four months prior, one following Madam Lulu Watts's* fall. Each member of A-Hamm had mimed her signature pinky-out drinking from an invisible teacup as the cameras panned through the group. Staxxx still sometimes held up a pinky in memory of her dead sister-in-arms, Emily had noticed.

Now the screen displayed Ice Ice the Elephant, whose solid build and eye for smart armor distribution had kept him alive for the last four bouts. He wore simple construction boots and a gray pair of sweat-pants on the road. He also had on a T-shirt and a light jacket that read *Mike's Autobody* in letters so small they probably wouldn't be around too much longer. Ice was growing more and more popular and *Mike's Autobody* would be replaced by some larger company soon. The spiked ball of his ball and chain was tucked inside a pouch, the chain wrapped around his thick waist like a belt. When the cameras rose to Ice's face, he snarled a playful snarl.

Next the camera scanned the blue cowboy boots that had become Gunny Puddles's signature, the golden MF of McFoods near his heels. He had no visible weapons, but he was known for having four secondary-tier weapons, his throwing knives, and no primary weapon. A unique load out that thus far had proven effective. His thinning hair looked greasy, slid back on his head. As his pale face came into focus he spat on the ground.

* Low Freed. Reaper. They called her the Class Act Killer. Her family called her Lucy.

But Emily's back was already hurting.

She straightened up with a ginger ale in hand after popping some sweet grapes in her mouth and closing the fridge door. "Worth it," she said aloud to herself, and walked the short journey to her couch, where she waved the main display on.

A Teleflex Infinity Viewcaster totally ready for full 3D Viewcasting with the awareness upgrades to register all gestures. How many times had she asked guests if they wanted to see the view, just so she could say, "U engage," while bringing her fingers together and pulling them apart as if opening curtains. It was magic.

"*LinkLyfe,*" Emily said, and the wall opposite the couch became the show. They were still doing Lineups. The camera was on Staxxx, her hiking boots planted into the ground. Then on to the sweatpants that Staxxx had ripped at the thighs, three cuts on each thigh. The Whole-Market™ logo was stamped on the chest of her sweatshirt.

When Staxxx wasn't in the BattleGround she wore a roll of bolt leather around her left arm, and you could see that portion climb up toward her palm.

"U engage and Immerse," Emily said, and she was basically out there with them. She could see the open field, grass rendered beneath her feet and superimposed against the hardwood floor. She could admire the Xs on Staxxx's abs and neck anew, and what a prize they were to watch. Staxxx's hoodie was cut so you could see her abs and the mosaic of Xs on her brown skin. Her hair fell behind her to midback.

The view was also perfect. When the cameras moved up to Staxxx's face, she was playful as usual: She held her right forearm over her eyes so that the two Xs inked across her ulna were covering them. She stuck her tongue out and dropped her head to the side, a knocked-out cartoon. With her other arm she held an invisible noose over her head. Emily watched, a little surprised Staxxx hadn't done something in memory of Sunset Harkless. She felt a pang. Sunset had been a good guy on the Chain for sure. She'd seen clips of his choosing to joke where others might have killed, and she'd been surprised by how the news of his death, a man she'd only known in archived clips, had brought a cloud over her that still had not passed.

Shit, she thought.

Staxxx held her pose until it was Thurwar on the screen. Thurwar and her perfect body were mostly hidden underneath loose-fitting black pants tucked into high socks. Both her arms were wrapped in bolt leather covered with the sleeves of a thick crewneck bearing the LifeDepot™ logo. Thurwar stared at nothing, gave nothing, stoic as she had been for the last several months. Then, at the last second, she shaded her eyes with her hand, Sunset's classic pose. Emily felt her own eyes growing hot.

March initiating in twenty-five seconds.

"Okay," Emily said as she wiped her tears and settled into the pleasure of another world's adventure.

March, the Anchor said. It began to pull.

The Anchor only had a few commands, all of them absolute: Line Up, March, Melee, Resume March, Halt, Rest, BlackOut. It would drag you before you could ever drag it, and its magnetic pull against your body was the surest thing in any Link's life. It rose farther into the air until it was fifteen feet above A-Hamm's heads and casually began to float north.

The Links were used to this, and so they stepped, stretched their arms, and tried not to wonder what would come next. They followed the Anchor and spread themselves out in a circle spaced evenly around the machine.

"Somebody important must like you, I guess," Gunny Puddles said, looking ahead at Thurwar. Gunny Puddles, who was southeast on their human compass, hated the bitch, too good to be called anything but her real name. But without question she was their leader now. A Black bitch, his alpha—imagine that. He walked, curious to see how she'd take his calling out the affirmative action masquerading as a Battle-Ground match she'd just been blessed with. Gunny spat on the ground and stepped through the grass.

Thurwar, their north, said, "Uh-huh." She was trying not to get angry at the way everyone was avoiding talking about Sunset. As she took steps the muscle memory of walking by the pull of the Anchor brought her attention to the now. How would she lead in her last few weeks? How would she deal with Gunny Puddles, a rapist/murderer, who'd wanted her dead for the better part of the last two years? How was she going to do that without Sun there to make everything seem easier than it was? And now that she'd learned what she'd learned from the girl in Vroom Vroom, did she care about any of it?

Staxxx was their south pole, had been for some time. She walked a little faster than everyone else because she was directly behind the Anchor; if she didn't keep constantly in step she'd end up getting dragged along. Sometimes she'd stop walking and watch as her arms were pulled forward, and then she'd run, catching up to the pull so her arms dropped again, then pause as her wrists floated up in obedience to the Anchor once more. Today she did none of that. Today she smiled and watched closely. Everybody on the Chain knew that Staxxx's position at six o'clock was a promise: If anyone attacked Thurwar—if anyone had attacked Sunset Harkless—who was relatively vulnerable walking with so many people behind her, Staxxx would be on them immediately. Staxxx took pride in being an enforcer. She hadn't enjoyed splitting Whittaker "Cha-Ching" Ames in half, but when he'd tried to stab Thurwar a few months ago on the March, he'd ended up in pieces. She hated what she was, but she loved what she could do.

Walter Bad Water walked to Staxxx's left, just in front of her. He watched quietly as he always did, in awe of his own survival, of the innocence that he still held in his heart like a dying thing cradled to the grave. He'd done nothing, and here he was, punished. He had a hunting knife that had been gifted to him by Gunny Puddles. He'd accepted it before he knew that taking a gift from Gunny would put him on the outs with Sunset, Thurwar, even Staxxx. Again, his innocence meant nothing.

"It's a smooth-looking night out here. Hopefully the mosquitoes don't fuck us to death," Ice Ice the Elephant said. He would make it through today and try to make it through all the days to come. Just before this he'd killed a man. He'd killed a man and now he was talking about mosquitoes. But that's how it went out here. One day at a time. That's what he'd told himself before and after every March. His metal chain rattled around his waist, a sound that always brought him comfort.

"I hear that," Sai Eye Aye said, echoing their friend. Just in front of them, off to the right, was Thurwar, LT, thee Grand Colossal. Sai still felt a lingering rush of pleasure, a euphoria that had set in as soon as they'd finished their own bout, quickly and easily, and continued through to when Thurwar's Question Match opponent had been revealed and the boy had appeared—an easy target. They'd watched from the changing station. Still cleaning blood off their own body. They felt sick for feeling that delight. But the kid had no chance anyway, and all they'd wanted as they watched was for their leader to survive her last two weeks. LT was LT after all. It was true too that thinking about LT made it easier not to think of Rolade Qurriculum, the warrior they'd killed on the grounds. They would think about him, process that death, but for now they would focus on LT and making sure the same thing that happened to Sun didn't happen to her.

"Deadass, those mosquitoes a few nights back were wild," Rico said, just to say something. "Fucking winged vampires." He laughed. No one else did. He was walking behind Gunny Puddles, near Staxxx, and was grateful for that because being near her made him feel safe. No one on the Chain had challenged him and he was grateful for that too. Being in the wrong place got people murked; he'd seen it himself. As his boots crunched over the dry grass he felt the usual terror washing over him. *Lord, you know my heart in all things,* he prayed. *I know I been prone to fuck shit and I'm not saying I didn't do things to deserve punishment, but you know my heart, Lord, and I pray you give me a shred of your grace through this trial before me.*

Randy Mac was a Reaper, and he walked with his trident, Holy Holy, in hand, using it as a walking stick. He kept quiet, was lost in thought considering the fact that now, after Staxxx and Thurwar, he was the highest-ranked Link on the Chain. As they walked, the ground seemed to grow softer. He didn't like the idea of that responsibility and grimaced as he pressed the rod to the mudground. This was the post-Sunset era.

The Chain walked 4.4 miles. They walked until dark was true across the sky. And except for Gunny's comment, they did not discuss the BattleGround. They moved easily. Their bodies had trained for much worse than this; Thurwar had made sure of that.

Randy Mac spoke. "Y'all know these parts? We're not far from Vroom Vroom, but I don't know anything more than that."

"I'm from Old Taperville. It's not so far," Staxxx said, brightening for a moment. The Chain listened.

"They make people like you in that piece of shit?" Randy Mac said, not looking back, trusting his words would find their mark even as he spoke with the softness that he reserved only for Staxxx.

"They don't make people like me anywhere 'round here. I meant that's where I landed," Staxxx said.

"You an alien now?" Mac asked.

"I'm from the other side of Uranus," Staxxx said.

"I think that changes how I feel about you some."

"I knew you were a racist," Staxxx said, laughing.

"My brother-in-law is an alien. I have a bunch of alien friends. I can't be racist," Randy Mac continued. The Chain laughed. Randy had a kind of lazy charm that entertained Staxxx. He was strong enough, handsome, and aside from some scratches at his neck and of course his missing finger pieces, his light brown skin carried few blemishes from battle or otherwise. Worse than that, he wasn't a dumbass—not mostly. Randy Mac was the kind of guy who let you know how many books he'd read. And, Thurwar begrudgingly admitted, he was instrumental in the project of keeping Staxxx happy enough to function and March with the Chain.

Finally they arrived at a large fire in the middle of a Camp that had been set up by assistant producers before their arrival. Beside the fire was GoFlame™ firewood stacked and ready to burn. The Anchor found a spot high above the flame and spoke: *Camp Phase initiation. March resumes in eleven hours.*

Their wrists softened to green. During Camp, green allowed them three hundred yards in any direction, although most would stay right there, near the fire. There were five stumps around the flame; they looked real in the low light but were actually BackYardPro™ seats made of treated plastic. Scattered beside them were several boxes of various sizes and colors.

This was how it had been since season 17. Eventually audiences had gotten tired of seeing the weary Links struggling to survive in the wilderness, and so the Camp had been developed, a curated location that mimicked camping but was actually vetted and commercially staged every night for each of the Chain-Gangs on the Circuit. The sites had been cleared by crews and inspected for particularly dangerous wildlife, hazardous plants, or anything that could compromise the safety of the Links. People wanted to see people killed by other people, not snake bites. There were tents and cots that Links could buy with their Blood Points, with different sets available for each of the different ranks. The food was professionally sourced and catered.

The last touch of real was the glowing fire at the center of each Camp, although there were also a few lanterns and some heat lamps available when temperatures dipped. Fire meant home. Fire meant something closer to freedom. They were not meant to use the fire for anything other than its light, which was supplemented by torches scattered about the Camp in a way that seemed random but was actually meticulously designed to provide a good balance of light and darkness everywhere within the free range of the area.

There was an assortment of backpacks and rucksacks waiting for them, leaning against "stumps" that were situated around a well-manicured bonfire. As usual, the first part of the March was the journey to the things that the Links carried with them, besides their weapons. Their worldly possessions stuffed into branded bags. Thurwar was first to step up and pull a black rucksack. Golden hammer emblems were pressed into each of the thick shoulder straps. She took it and disappeared into the largest tent—the Queen's Tent, the only one of its kind on the Circuit. Now that Thurwar was the pound-for-pound top champion across all Circuits, the Queen's Tent was hers.

Staxxx grabbed her own green-and-gold rucksack and pulled it to her body. "No place like home," she said as she took a seat on one of the logs.

The other Links grabbed their packs. In less stable Chains, this was a time as dangerous as any. Links lost hands for touching someone else's pack. Staxxx, LoveGuile resting against her body, watched over the process now. There was a sense of forced calm among the group today. Staxxx took a breath and looked into the fire.

"Suck my dick, America." Randy Mac sighed as he pulled his denim pack off the ground. His catchphrase, spoken without a smile.

There were eight Links on the Chain and six tents. Rico and Bad Water hadn't earned that luxury yet, so they had sleeping bags and the great cover of sky, unless someone on the Chain opened their space in offering. The Queen's Tent had, most recently, belonged to Sunset, though its name would forever refer to the great Melancholia Bishop, who had made dominance a lifestyle. It was large enough to stand in and came with additional rations—pita chips and hummus and some sparkling waters as well as pads, tampons, cocoa butter, and toilet paper on a small table—and was solidly fastened to the ground it stood on. The other tents were more traditional camping units, although Staxxx and Randy Mac and Gunny had spaces that were large enough to stand in easily too, with more than one section. In all the tents, what mattered most was the cot. Hers, created by SleepRoyal™, was the most comfortable place one could sleep in the wild.

Thurwar plopped onto the soft. She'd actually been sleeping in the SleepRoyal™ since she'd been a Harsh Reaper, thanks to her unprecedented success. In the world of Chain-Gang, Loretta Thurwar had been rich from day one.

And in turn, images of Thurwar in the bed had made SleepRoyal™ one of the most profitable mattress companies in the world.

An HMC floated her way. She dropped her rucksack to the floor by her feet. She pulled an AquaHGente™ water bottle out of it and gulped. There was also a warm set of clothes in there, including underwear (a new set always ready for her) and a poncho, as well as a notebook and two pens and her secondary weapon, an army knife called Jack. This moment of being reacquainted with possessions was both intimate and violent. Thurwar massaged her sore knee. She pressed into it, felt the good hurt.

Staxxx walked into the tent. "I know what's wrong with you," Staxxx said. She threw her own rucksack to the ground, dropped her scythe to the floor by the cot.

Thurwar put Hass Omaha down beside her rucksack. "What? Nothing's wrong." She regretted it immediately. Something was always wrong. Thurwar, in her heart, was a pessimist. But since Vroom Vroom and what she'd learned, years of pessimism seemed validated.

Staxxx kicked off her boots, curled herself onto the cot.

"It's okay," Staxxx said, and suddenly she was weeping. She pulled herself into Thurwar. This was exactly how they'd been after Staxxx's matches for months now. Staxxx would ritualistically take the time after she'd killed on the grounds and release into Thurwar.

"Crybaby," Thurwar said, rubbing the most prominent notch on Staxxx's neck.

"Fuck you," Staxxx said, sucking snot back into her nose, only to have it slide back down onto her upper lip as she heaved. Staxxx squirmed out of her sweatshirt, leaving on her beater. Then she began unraveling the bolt leather from her arm. Thurwar pulled her close, kissed her neck. The X on Staxxx's neck, "the target," was the first she'd gotten. It had become the ultimate symbol of this fighter whom the people had come to love.

Thurwar wrapped her arm around Staxxx's waist and held her as she cried. She kissed her snotty nose and felt Staxxx's abs as they expanded and contracted through her heavy breathing.

"I know you don't like it either. But today has to be the day," Staxxx said.

Thurwar stiffened for a moment before a look of understanding settled on her face.

"We'll do it soon. I have to figure out this Sun stuff first. Get my mind right. Don't worry. I know it's hard with me only having so little time left." Thurwar thought about the card and the information it had given her and how close she was to Freed. She almost joined Staxxx in weeping.

"Today," Staxxx said again. Thurwar felt a resistance to being told what to do. So few could for so long, but Staxxx continued. "There's something I have to tell you. But you have to do it first."

Her crying slowed as if to allow for the depth of her conviction to be unmissable.

"You do it then," Thurwar said.

"It has to be you. Just like he would have done," Staxxx said.

A flash of resentment came and went. Thurwar looked up with scorn at the HMC floating above them. She stared into the eyes of the country. Thurwar was the Grand Colossal, and so when things had to be done it fell to her.

"We can wait until our next double match. I don't want to—"

"Then I'm going to Randy's tonight," Staxxx said. "And if I go there tonight, I don't know if I'll come back. Like you said, you only have a few weeks. Maybe I start the process of letting go now?"

Thurwar paused in consideration. She wanted to say that no matter where Staxxx slept, she was hers, but she waited and let the words sit only in her mind. In many ways jealousy had shaped her life. It was part of why she'd been in prison and now it was yet another thing that the country loved her for. Her relationship with Staxxx, how it was opened up enough for Staxxx to periodically sleep with Randy Mac, and how she controlled her jealousy enough to let that happen peacefully.

"You think I care about that?" Thurwar said. She tried to sound bored, though she was anything but. The two HMCs rotated around them.

"Copy," Staxxx said. She pulled LoveGuile up from the ground and in her other hand grabbed her own rucksack. She stood, and immediately Thurwar stood as well.

"Please," Thurwar said. She moved quickly enough that her knee protested, but she ignored the pain. She stood in front of the tent opening, Hass Omaha in her own hand. It seemed she'd grabbed the hammer without even realizing. A great shame swelled in Thurwar's heart.

"Today," Staxxx said. "Sun's gone. It's you and me."

"This Chain is already fine. Why should we do anything that might take us—take me—off my game?" Thurwar asked. But how could they be "fine" if Sun had just been taken?

"It won't. I promise you," Staxxx said. Staxxx was putting her boots back on. "We can do it now. It will make you feel better after today. The kid."

"I feel fine about that," Thurwar said, and her voice stank of truth.

"Sure you do," Staxxx said. "Even more reason to do this right now." Staxxx wiped her eyes a final time and stepped out into the evening. It still smelled of an earlier drizzle, which had wet the earth and the dry, dying grass.

"Yo," Thurwar heard Staxxx say. She could hear the Chain. "Gather up, everyone. Big announcement for y'all." The HMCs whizzed past Thurwar, out of the tent, to find Staxxx.

Thurwar followed. She was hungry and saw a large black box with a hot portion of her dinner inside. Most of A-Hamm was eating already.

She cleared her throat. It was the feeblest sound she'd made in a long while. She stepped toward the fire, her shadow giant behind her. The Links were there, more or less paying attention. Thurwar looked at Staxxx, who smiled a knowing smile. Then Thurwar began.

"I'm going to say this now because I've been waiting for someone to come forward." Staxxx was smiling less now. "Sunset Harkless was killed last week and I want to know what happened. I want to know who and why and I want to know tonight. I want to know what happened to my friend. And when you hear what I'm about to say next, you'll see that you don't have to be scared to own up." She looked each of her Links in the eyes for a moment as she spoke, lingering, then moving on, lingering, then moving on. She tried to mask her truth: Whoever had done it was right to be afraid. "You can come tell me later. But I want to know tonight."

She spoke with her chest, addressing the group the way she did when they did battle drills or ran with their weapons on the days before the BattleGround. She was used to speaking to the whole. Gunny stared at her coldly. Bad Water looked to the ground. Mac and Sai watched her in earnest. She continued. "We've lost somebody important to A-Hamm. And to honor Sun, this is what we're saying. Going forward, we officially will not be harming one another on this Chain. That is our new policy. Just as real as any other part of the games. We do no harm to our fellow Links on our Angola-Hammond. That's done now. We don't do that to each other."

The Links looked confused, mildly amused even.

Thurwar cleared her throat again. She summoned her voice from her gut. "What I'm saying is, from now on, unless you're in a Battle-Ground match, there isn't gonna be violence among us. Sun preached that shit. Now we'll live it."

They responded with even less interest. As if she'd told an only okay joke a second time. Thurwar gripped Hass Omaha, moved him from her left hand to her right. She knew that, on some level, what she was saying didn't make sense. Her power, her ability to kill, was why she was who she was. Death, and the potential for it, was Thurwar's superpower.

"You know, when me and Sun came in, it was open season on everybody all the time. And that was kind of the point. Somebody like Rico would have been gone already just for being new." She looked at Rico and saw terror seize him before he could try to hide it. "It was the point because all this was a way out.

"I'm not telling y'all anything new. You know this. Most don't

expect to see High Freed. But still, most of y'all know that we're something different than the rest of the Chains. Here there's real chances.
If not for what happened last week, two of this Chain might have
seen High Freed within two weeks of each other. That's never happened before. But it almost did because we'd grown together. That
was only possible because me and Sun weren't always worried about
a knife coming down when we were on the Circuit. I have an M like
many of you." The Chain seemed to grow more attentive as she used
herself as an example. She did not talk of her own past. Not to all of
them, not like this. "I was with a woman. She was"—Thurwar already
regretted this path she'd taken, grimaced as the cameras circled around
her—"she was special and I treated her like I owned her. When she
wanted to leave—I—I'm saying, I know what it feels like to crush the
windpipe of someone you love. And for that I hate myself. When I first
met Sun, all I wanted was an exit. He helped me and I helped him and
we helped others and now we're all here talking. Sun was how he was
on the Chain because he thought people could change. He talked about
it all the damn time."

At this Randy said, "That's for sure." Thurwar was grateful.

"And what he was trying to get at was this. Making the Chain a
family. So, from now on, in honor of Sunset, no killing. Don't even
beat on anybody, unless it's to save your own life. Not during March,
not during Camp, not during chow, not when anybody is asleep. Keep
that stuff in the arena. Here, we're family, all right? Angola-Hammond
is family. Not just for Sun, but for us. We've played the game like they
want for a long time and now we're gonna change it up."

Thurwar watched and noted faint smiles and confusion on the faces
around her. She took a step forward toward the light of the fire, felt
its heat. Was what she was asking symbolic? No, she would enforce it.
This would be true. And yes, she hadn't been healed of her own guilt.
Yes, if not for Staxxx she would almost certainly no longer be alive.
But she was Loretta Thurwar and this was her Chain, and whether
it worked or not, they would try to be something someone could be
proud of.

"I'm not asking for a big change. We're already mostly solid. What
I want now is everyone here to accept those terms. That if you are on

this Chain, you vow to view your fellow Links as family and do no harm."

Ice Ice the Elephant said, "And if I'm trying not to smash somebody and then they stab me up, then what?" He looked at Thurwar in earnest. He was loyal to her and would do what she wanted. Within reason. She'd offered him the protection and weapons that had saved him thus far. "I'm just saying, it's not saints out here."

"First off, you could be a saint or whatever if you wanted to be," Thurwar said. "What's on your back, double MS? Plus one M." Ice Ice the Elephant nodded and then looked down at his boots. "That's not so bad, so you had some issues with drink, a manslaughter, and maybe you offed a guy along the way."

"One was my mother," Ice Ice the Elephant said.*

"That's a lot, and I'm sorry that happened," Thurwar said. "But I know you and you could be a saint." She tried to keep her momentum.

"And you"—all of the Links who made up the Chain were more attentive as she pointed to Rico Muerte—"you're a one-A, one-M, right? So one fire killed one person. You could be the next saint too, if you want. And you too, Sai." Sai Eye Aye stiffened but nodded.

"It was a church I burned, but I feel you," Rico Muerte said through a weak smile.

"Christ," Staxxx said, "still loves you, I'm sure." She got to her feet, dragging LoveGuile along her side. "The point is we're not gonna do bad stuff to each other anymore. Sunset's Rule."

"That's not what this game is," Gunny Puddles said.

"That's what it is now," Staxxx replied without looking his way.

"Yeah. Exactly," Thurwar said. She dropped Hass Omaha onto the earth. "We're gonna try for better. These marks don't mean we aren't people. These chains don't mean we have to do it like they want."

---

* Lany Vines, now known as Ice Ice the Elephant, was in a car. Drunk at the wheel. His mother, an alcoholic herself, asked him to speed faster. There was so much to see in the world and what were they doing, stuck in Wisconsin, seeing exactly nothing. They'd see it all now. But they'd need liquor for the sudden road trip. "Oh" was the last thing Opal Vines said. That he could hear anyway. He had no idea what the eighteen-year-old in the other car said as the headlights bloomed a last light across his face.

Then, once he was inside, he'd killed a man because the man wanted to kill him.

"Fuck that," Gunny Puddles said. He had his box meal in his hands and two knives on his lap. He was sitting on a stump. "I didn't come here to be no snowflake. Sunset was on that goody shit and he died face-down, and nobody will even admit to cutting the sonofabitch's throat. I know why I came here. And it wasn't to be friends with nobody. I'm here to eat until they let me go."

"You can still do all that," Thurwar said. "You're still gonna fight, you're still gonna get the serious Blood Points from your head-to-heads. But what there's not gonna be is any cheap stuff out here on the road. Chain-Gang is family from now on."

Puddles was a vet. Two years on the Circuit. Luck and a real knack for throwing sharp things had gotten him a pretty big following. "I know who I am," Gunny Puddles said.*

He was a man whose life had been taken from him after his vicious contempt of women had exploded out of him in terrifying ways. And Thurwar, a woman, was at the top of the underworld he inhabited. Gunny looked hard into the fire.

"It's convenient timing," he finally said. "The magic woman, neck-deep in bodies of her own, decides that we should all let our guard down and be lovey-dovey, just before she goes out to see the world without us."

This was it. The expected power struggle. And already Walter Bad Water had stepped back, as had Rico Muerte.

"I'm a lot closer to Freed than you and I'm trying to tell you all this is the best way to do it. It's better quality of life and better strat."

"So that's that all right. We're going to be one big family. The only people we know we ain't going to have to face out here are us. No raping, no killing, no stealing, no nothing," Staxxx said.

Thurwar felt heat in her chest. She waited a moment and her eyes settled on Puddles and she spoke slowly: "No raping, no killing, no nothing."

---

* And even if we weren't the worst thing we'd ever done, well shit. Gunny Puddles had seen their eyes, their fear, and taken something from their bodies. He knew who and what he was and, well shit, if he got a chance to see the country before he died then that was something. Winning in the BattleGround gave him that same feeling. They called him a monster. He did not deny it.

"I heard you, but fuck that," Puddles said through a mouthful of gravy-rice. "You know, that fucker you're claiming was a prophet of good killed and raped and that's the reason he was here in the first place. No matter what kind of nice-guy act he put on, it don't change that. Everybody here deserves to be here." Thurwar wondered if she agreed. She knew that regarding herself, the Circuit, the constant threat of death, the pain and suffering, even this was better than she deserved.

"It's done," she said. The horror you made was yours forever.

"I don't give a fuck what kinda—"

Staxxx whipped LoveGuile forward like a scorpion's tail. It moved with lethal speed toward Gunny Puddles, but somehow she was able to—midswing—rotate the blade so the blunt side was moving toward the man, then slowed its force so LoveGuile's back gave Puddles's neck a hard kiss. There was nothing Staxxx couldn't do with her scythe and every movement she made was intentional, precise. With LoveGuile, she made no mistakes. All the HMCs swirled around the action. A cough of gravy-rice fell out of his mouth. The Links watched.

"Gotcha," Staxxx said. "You were scared for a second. And wouldn't that have been a sad, pointless end to your life?"

Gunny didn't move. He looked at Staxxx, fire in his eyes. "You try and do it if you want. I deserve it just like you do, and Sun did. You all know that man was a murdering rapist fucker and deserved to die how he did. Just like every one of us here deserve the ground that's coming to take us."

"Damn, Puddles, shut the fuck up," Mac said.

"End him if he wants. The rest of us can be cool, do the family thing," Sai Eye Aye said.

"Starting now," Staxxx said, pulling the blade back, leaving Gunny Puddles alive and whole. Staxxx touched his shoulder, then walked to Thurwar. She pinched Thurwar's side with her thumb and the knuckle of her forefinger. "Aren't you glad we have this new rule?"

Gunny Puddles brought his hand to the gentle bruise at his neck. He got up and headed toward his tent. "Like I said." Gunny turned. "It's pretty fucking convenient timing. One of the motherfuckers trying to kumbaya here killed the very man you all are praying to not even a week ago."

"About that," Staxxx began. Staxxx had stepped forward, spotlighting herself with the fire.

"I have something to say," Staxxx said. And she seemed not to know where to look as she spoke. "I killed Sunset Harkless."

.   .   .

Emily stood up in her apartment and said, "Oh shit."

Sports Central

Tracy Lasser sits at a desk ready to speak to the world.

"Opal opted to exit Oxenfurt with only an optometer." She looked at the camera once, then practiced slowly shifting to camera two, a move Lee, the set director, had pushed her to do more often in the weeks leading up to this moment. The weeks leading up to the day her dream would come true.

"Peter Piper picked a peck of pickled peppers. Opal opted to exit Oxenfurt with only an optometer." She measured her words, tried to snap each of them just enough. She tugged on the dress she was wearing. It snagged a little around the hips, but she agreed with her in-studio stylist, Tom, that it would shine on-screen, a tan body-contouring piece with maroon accents. Her hair looked good too. She'd known this wig, a custom that cost north of a month's rent, would be part of her debut, her partner. She'd named the wig Stella.

She turned her head back to camera one, Stella following her movements magnificently.

"Peter Piper picked a peck of—"

"Don't worry, you're gonna do fine," Elton Vashteir, her other debut partner, said, smiling at her in his way. A smile that said, *Most of my problems can be solved by looking at people with this face.*

"Thanks, Elton," Tracy said.

She closed her eyes and imagined her parents gathered around the cast screen projector in Old Taperville. The same parents who'd asked the school to make a copy of the morning broadcasts she'd done in the sixth grade. The ones who'd thrown a party the first time she'd reported on a sideline for a local network. And now they'd get to see her on SportsViewNet anchoring *Sports Central,* America's number one sports program, or so it said on all the hoodies and sweatshirts she'd sent back home. She'd wanted to make them proud for so long, and this moment's arriving as it was about to made her feel sick to her stomach.

Just before getting to work she'd felt a panic so harsh she could hear the thrum of blood in her ears like raging river waters. As a reflex she'd grabbed her phone, and when she picked it up, she saw there was a cast from her dad. Just seeing the notification eased the sound of pumping blood. She'd set her phone on the table and said, "Establish holoview link," and then there was her father's face.

"You ready? I'm calling," she'd watched him yell to no one she could see, but she knew who would be there with him.

"Wait a second." Her mother's voice came through clearly although she still couldn't see her.

"Well, I started it already. Oh, what in the hell is that?"

Her father squinted into his caster, trying to make sure he could see and be seen.

"Who told you to go and do that?" her mother said as her face appeared beside her father's.

"I was just trying to set it up so we wouldn't be late. It's running now, I think, so don't mess me up."

"You already messed up enough," her mom finished, and then the two of them were staring at their daughter.

"Hey, baby," her mom said.

"Hey, Quickness," her father said, a big grin on his face.

Quickness first had become her nickname because she'd been quick to anger, quick to fight as a kid. Nobody from her little nowhere town messed with Tracy because everybody knew she'd swing on you with the quickness. It worked out that she'd taken a liking to the two-hundred-meter and four-hundred-meter sprints in high school.

Back when she was the one being interviewed by reporters for breaking records with her relay team.

"Hey, Mama, hey, Daddy," she said.

"What's wrong, baby?" Her father's voice came through the cast so clearly.

"It's nothing. I'm just excited," she said, and carefully dabbed the wet under her eyes away so no dark tears would stain her face.

"Well, we know it's a lot. But we love you. We know you'll do beautifully," her mother said.

"Thanks, Mama," Tracy said. She was now fully weeping. She had time to go back to makeup and reset. She covered her face from her parents. "I don't know," she said. And it was wild to think. This dream she'd had for so long, one she'd had since she busted her MCL at the South New Florida Relays and her own athletic career had ended. It was finally happening.

"Listen, Quickness, you're too good ever to have any kind of worry. We're already so proud of you." When her father spoke, Tracy always felt better. But today his words made her feel worse.

"No matter what, we got you, baby. You're gonna do great."

"Thanks, Mama."

"What about me!"

"You too, Daddy."

"I'm just messing with you. We love you, okay?"

"I know. I love you too." They looked at one another. Tracy forced a smile. "I was just nervous, I think. I'm gonna go to makeup again. All right?"

"Okay!" her parents said in tandem, making it clear that they were nervous too.

"We'll talk after you broadcast all over the world," her father said.

"Now, why would you say that, the girl just told you sh—"

"Bye, guys."

"Love you," her parents had said again together. She'd made a wiping-away gesture with her hands and the holo link had ended.

Then she'd gone to makeup and gotten reset.

She had worked a very long time to be there. She was going to look good for it.

———

Sitting at the *Sports Central* main desk with cameras one, two, and three looking at her and Elton, Tracy tried her best not to retch. "Peter Piper picked a peck of pickled p—"

"I promise, you'll be fine. Don't stress. You know how to read. You've done great already. The only difference is that this time the world is watching. But calm down." Elton rolled his chair over her way. "I'm here with you." He touched her thigh and rubbed up and down the cloth of her dress. "Love this on you, by the way. You look great."

Tracy looked at Elton and felt her fear turn to heat. "I'm calm," she said, and straightened up, pushing his hand away. She'd made it clear the first time he'd rubbed her shoulders in a "friendly way" that she did not want to be touched. And her making that clear had done almost nothing to change his behavior. In fact, over the last several months that she'd been in studio training, he'd made it perfectly clear that as long as he was thee Elton Vashteir he was going to do exactly as he wanted. For now, it was glancing brushes, friendly rubs, but it was clear what came next.

"We're live in forty seconds," the director said in her ear. Tracy nodded as Elton rolled back to his spot three feet away, in front of his notes. She had her notes, her own stylus. She was an anchor on *Sports Central*. Only the second Black woman in the decades-long history of the show.

She scanned the notes in front of her. It wasn't a surprise to see an old friend's name on the breaking-news report. An old teammate. She blinked quickly. She would not cry, though she wanted to break down completely.

"Twenty seconds."

She thought, as they counted down, about what it was to love sports, what it was like to accept a baton and sprint. To be part of a team. She'd loved what it meant to want something that badly. She'd loved running as fast as she could. The feeling of finding the finish line and looking back, knowing that what was left on the track was all you had. And she loved how in triumph or in loss you could discover avenues toward growth. Who was better? Me or you? Us or them? Me yesterday or me today?

The four hundred relay was the pinnacle of most meets. She'd wanted to be anchor her senior year and instead she'd been the third leg.

"Live in ten."

The anchor, the person whom she'd passed the baton to, was a superhuman athlete. A girl who was so strange and so herself even in high school that she was beloved by most everyone she met. Her talent made her the gem of the district.

At the South New Florida Relays, her senior year, Tracy had received a good baton pass. A blind exchange. She put her hand out and trusted her teammate. She felt the smooth metal in her palm, then she flew. Hard and heavy. Leave everything on the track. But at about three hundred meters: a pop in her right leg. Her speed melted to a limp. She begged her body to move but it did not. She saw the backs of the other girls bolt past her. She'd torn a ligament but wouldn't know that for some time. All she knew then was that she wasn't going to be the person she'd hoped, not anymore. But even as all those girls flew away, her teammate, her anchor, Hamara Stacker, was running toward her, then pulling her through, carrying her on her shoulders, supporting most of Tracy's weight. She laid Tracy down when she'd finished the leg and said, "Damn, girl, you ain't have to go that fast. Lemme see what I can do." And then took off. And somehow, she'd made Tracy smile, even as the pain in her leg grew to a real thing, even though of course they'd lost and been disqualified. Even though there was nothing left to win, Hammy finished out. The medics were upon Tracy before Hammy had crossed the line, but still Hamara had found a way to make it to the ambulance to wave goodbye before the doors closed and Tracy was alone with an assistant coach and the medics.

"Live in five, four, three, two—"

"Hello and welcome, good people, to *Sports Central*," Elton started. "It's been a busy weekend in the world of athletics, and as you might have guessed there're a couple of dominant women right at today's lead. But before we get into that, I hope you'll welcome another incredible woman to the *Sports Central* team."

"Thank you, Elton," Tracy said. She had two sentences of intro before jumping into a recap of the latest deathmatches.

"What a dream it is to talk sports on this stage. It's an honor to be here." She looked over at Elton, and he smiled for her, for the country. She turned to the teleprompter. "And as Elton said, today we're going to kick things off with the exploits of Loretta Thurwar and the woman you know as Hurricane Staxxx."

On monitor two there was a clip of Staxxx speaking to the crowds. Here Tracy was meant to give an overdub as the recapped clips continued over the television.

"Funny thing is," Tracy said, and immediately she felt the energy in the room shift, "I know Hurricane Staxxx very well. She was a great friend of mine. We called her Hammy. She was one of the best athletes I've ever known. But what she's doing now, what this program is telling you is sports—it's not sports.

"I wanted to be a part of this program to talk about achievement, not murder, not lynching, not death. But in the past few months this program I've dreamed of being a part of for years has adopted the practice of airing exactly that: murder, lynching, death. I hoped it would be a phase that would quickly pass. I was wrong. Shame on you, *Sports Central*. My name is Tracy Lasser"—and now the clips were over, and the camera had no choice but to blink back to her—"and I stand in solidarity with those around the country who have demonstrated against so-called hard action-sports. I support the repeal of B3 and all so-called hard action-sports just as I support ending the death penalty. We are fighting for a more humane society. Thank you for your time."

She got up. Elton's mouth hinged open. Then he turned back to the camera.

"Well, that's one way to make your debut. Always something interesting here at the *Central*."

"Fuck off, Elton," Tracy said, and then she walked off the set toward her dressing room. Toward the rest of her life. She waited for the sound of cutting to commercial.

"What the fuck just happened?" Elton screamed once they were off-air. "What in the fuck just happened here?"

She went to collect her things. And when she walked off the set with tears in her eyes, she was smiling, because when it came down to it, she was exactly who she'd hoped she'd be.

Salt Bath

A-Hamm looked at Thurwar, waiting for her to tell them what to do. Thurwar looked at Staxxx, the truth of Sunset Harkless's murder in the air between them.

"Well, Miss Peace-and-Reconciliation didn't have that in her heart last week it seems," Gunny said, laughing. "But listen, I ain't mad at ya. Like I said, he was a son of a bitch. Just like most here talking about it."

Thurwar thought of Sunset. She'd seen him cry over the life he'd lost, over his daughter, whom he'd held in his arms and was sure no longer remembered anything about him. She'd seen him become beloved by the country, clearing a path in blood with a sword. The night Sunset Harkless was murdered, Staxxx had told her that she'd spent the evening with Randy Mac.

Thurwar stood, her face revealing nothing. "Why?" she asked.

Staxxx's eyes found Thurwar, though it seemed they struggled to do so.

"I'm not proud." Staxxx dropped LoveGuile to the ground and stepped closer to the Links. "I loved Sun too. I was out chatting with him about High Freedom." Thurwar moved closer to the fire. She wanted to see Staxxx's face as she told the story of killing Thurwar's closest friend. The air was dry and warm. The fire danced shadows around Staxxx's jawline. Thurwar held Hass Omaha in her grip; it helped her move through her feelings. On some level, this wasn't a surprise. She hadn't wanted to think about it directly, but she hadn't been sure who besides Staxxx could have taken advantage of Sunset.

"Y'all know that was my guy. So yeah, I went out to him and was talking to him about the end of all this and the next world. And . . ." Staxxx looked around the group. Her eyes were brilliant with tears. "I'm so sorry. But I had to do what I did. I hope you all can understand that."

Thurwar knew it was her place to speak first, and she knew that what she said would carry them through this night.

"Un-fucking-believable," Gunny Puddles said. "The love lady kills a pal and surprise surprise, she can't even—"

"You feel . . . you had to?" Thurwar asked.

"You know I loved him, Lo," Staxxx said.

"And now what?" Puddles asked. "What happens now that we're all a big happy family with a daughter who killed Daddy?"

Staxxx looked at Gunny. She picked LoveGuile up off the ground and in the same motion wiped her eyes with her bolt-leathered forearm.

"There it is. The truth will set us free," Gunny said. He pulled three throwing knives from his jacket. He put one in his mouth, held the blade with his teeth, the other two ready to throw, one in each hand. "Do what you do. And I'll do what I do," he said through clenched teeth.

"You throw a knife at her, you die today," Thurwar said. She looked at Ice Ice the Elephant and Randy Mac, and they were up. Randy held his trident at Gunny, and Ice let his fingers graze the chain around his waist; both of their bodies were angled toward the other man.

Staxxx shook her head. "We just agreed. If he throws a knife into my eye right now what you're going to do is not kill him. That's not what we do anymore. Starting now. I'm sorry for Sunset. I swear it." And then Staxxx turned away from them and walked into the Queen's Tent, dragging her scythe behind her.

Sai had stood up, positioning themselves between Gunny and Thurwar, and now they looked at Thurwar as if to say, *Give us the signal and we'll disappear Gunny Puddles from this earth.* Thurwar looked at all the eyes on her, tried not to imagine the eyes looking at her all over the world.

"Don't touch him," she said. Her Links did not move. They stood at the ready, waiting for Gunny to do something they could respond to.

"I said do not," Thurwar repeated, and her Links remained watching Gunny, but they eased their bodies to show they had heard her and would only move if Gunny did.

"Fucking sheep," Gunny Puddles said. He dropped a knife from his mouth and caught it before tucking all three into his long coat and turning for his own tent.

Everyone but Thurwar sat down.

"Damn," Rico said, trying to laugh away his panic.

"Shut up," Randy Mac said.

"Okay. But don't talk to me like that," Rico said, puffing out his chest.

"Shut up, Rico," Thurwar said.

"Okay," Rico said, deflating as he bit into a peanut butter and jelly sandwich.

What did she do now? Now that they were all looking to her?

"Well," Sai said after a while. "Good work to you both in the arena today."

"He was a child," Thurwar said.

"Every BG counts," Sai said. It was a thing Thurwar had told Sai a long time ago after they had been forced to destroy someone who could barely walk, they were so afraid.

Thurwar nodded.

"Staxxx fucking killed it," Rico said, brightening a little, his mouth sticky in chewing.

"Staxxx does what she does," Randy Mac said.

"It comes from preparation," Thurwar said. She could feel her Chain giving her and Staxxx an out. She could feel the pleasures of loyalty and power and how they were going to make it so she didn't have to do anything at all.

Still, even the word "preparation" reminded her of Sunset, who had studied each and every one of his opponents so well before his matches that he called them his family. Thurwar helped him dissect the footage that he bought of their fighting with his Blood Points. And he did it for others too. She, Sunset, and Randy Mac had just watched tapes of Randy's last opponent, Glacier Reme, and Sunset had told him to wait until Glacier tired himself out before going for the kill. And indeed, when Randy had stuck his trident through Glacier's side, the man was panting from exhaustion after chasing him around with his scimitars for whole minutes.

And now there Randy was, acting as if he was going to let bygones be bygones. And maybe it was because he loved Staxxx, but so did she. And she felt none of the ease Randy seemed to present as he rested on his elbows near the fire.

She wanted to do something. But all the ways she knew to honor death, all the ways anyone knew to honor death, meant more death, and that wasn't an option.

She turned to her tent.

Staxxx soaked in warm water and Epsom salt. She let her eyes fall closed. She could hear Thurwar stirring and smashing the air as she guided Hass through her drills, careful not to swipe the walls of the large tent, but deadly even in practice. Staxxx didn't think it was the right time for strike drills.

"You're upset," Staxxx said, letting her body belong to the warm. She tried to breathe in the feeling of doing something good and right and difficult that no one could understand. She didn't wonder if she was right; she wondered why it was her destiny to do so many good, hard things. The floating cameras watched her.

Thurwar turned into a backhand swipe and Staxxx felt the breeze she'd made graze the edges of her skin.

"I'm always worried," Thurwar said. Her breath was constant, controlled, though she continued to crush the nothing around her.

Staxxx tried and failed to swallow a smatter of laughter.

"You are not always worried," Staxxx said. "That's just something we say to get you to relax more." She watched Thurwar.

"Why didn't you tell me?"

"I did. Just now."

"Why didn't you tell me when it happened?"

"BlackOut had ended, so we couldn't talk on our own. And I didn't want to distract you before your Question Match," Staxxx said, breathing in and out with her eyes closed. All of those things were true.

Thurwar stopped her drills and kneeled down slowly. Staxxx kept her eyes closed, though she could feel Thurwar's face hovering over the basin's edge. Thurwar exerted a kind of pressure just by being. Staxxx had grown to love the feeling, like a heavy coat, a thick gravity.

"You didn't think finding my best friend dead would distract me? It doesn't make sense. Why didn't you come to me?"

"I thought I was your best friend," Staxxx said.

"You should have told me."

"I made a decision."

Two HMCs floated above them. Their light shimmered in the water.

"It was not a good decision."

Staxxx frowned. She understood Thurwar's frustration and yet she hated having to explain her heart to the woman who knew her best.

"I know it seems like I'm being difficult."

"Seems like?" Thurwar said. Then, "I'm sorry."

Staxxx opened her eyes. Just as impressive as the pressure Thurwar typically exuded were the moments when she pulled it back. When she let herself be light for the people she loved.

"I'm asking you to trust me," Staxxx said.

"I do. I want to. But don't keep me out of something like this. I want to be on the inside," Thurwar said.

Staxxx rose from the tub. The HMCs spiraled her naked body.

"You're right. It's me and you. I should have let you in sooner," Staxxx said. She wrapped Thurwar into a hug. Thurwar protested briefly because of the wet, then began to unravel from her own clothes. "You do worry too much," Staxxx said as she helped her undress. Light, unarmored, just her body.

They went to the cot, pretending they were alone. Though they never were. But even though HMCs floated inches off their skin, they moved with ease around each other, the humans and the cameras all used to one another. Thurwar moved her hands from Staxxx's hip slowly up and down her thigh. Staxxx relaxed into the moment as they kissed. They were together outside of thought, feeling meeting feeling. Staxxx let her hands grace Thurwar's curves, her muscles, her body forged for death but capable of such softness. Thurwar's fingers moved between Staxxx's legs and Staxxx hoped, before she fell completely into the moment, that Thurwar understood. That Thurwar trusted Staxxx the way Staxxx trusted her.

.　　　　.　　　　.

Thurwar looked into Staxxx's brown eyes, kissed her mouth. And then shifted. She went from looking deep into Staxxx, searching her face, savoring the details, to somewhere far away, already thinking about what she had to do next, after not even thirty minutes of lying together. Staxxx wanted to say, "Wait," call her back before Thurwar got up, but she knew that the other woman was already gone. Thurwar didn't allow herself much joy. Staxxx took pleasure in being one of the great exceptions to this. She loved making people feel what they would otherwise not have access to. It was what she loved; she had no problem admitting it, as she did to the crowd before her matches. She knew she was changing the world there, even if it was in the worst possible context. Speaking to all those hurt people from the truest part of herself. It was all in service of her message. When she'd spun and won LoveGuile as her primary, when she'd eviscerated the first half-dozen of her opponents, she'd finally understood. Chain-Gang All-Stars was her purpose on earth. It was a place to remind the world of something it had forgotten. And to fulfill that purpose, she needed Thurwar. That had been obvious from the beginning.

But Staxxx, besides her purpose, was also a person. A person who needed to be poured into. A person who needed to be cared for, loved. And Thurwar did this, but only for as long as it took to make sure Staxxx was not empty; never long enough for her to be full.

Staxxx watched as Thurwar got up and picked up a roll of bolt leather. She slowly, lovingly wrapped her left forearm. Feeling the gray alloy-cloth pressed to your skin helped you focus. It was a reminder that you didn't have the luxury of getting ready. "Ready" had to live inside you. The bolt leather was breathable, but not so breathable that it was especially comfortable. And still, the Links who could afford it wore it most of the time they were out on the Circuit. You could only have a few yards at once, so most wrapped just one arm, maybe both, turned their forearms into shields.

Staxxx caught herself. This was one of Thurwar's powers. One moment you could be spiraling through the feeling of loving and being loved, and the next you'd be with her, thinking about the game. Thinking about how your body had to survive. Thurwar wore her bolt leather over one arm and one thigh, and at the waist. It was one of many things that she did that were widely copied by Links throughout the Chains.

Thurwar was obsessive about her training. Everyone knew that. It was why she'd become who she was. The Blood Mother. The Colossal. Staxxx understood that well. But to have her dressed, swinging her hammer around so soon—it hurt. The body was just a part of what had to survive the games.

Staxxx got up and found her way back into the tub. Her first soak had been cut short.

She turned a knob and water rushed into the basin from a tank a few yards away from the Camp. Its water flowed to three other basins outside and two communal hoses. The same hygiene stations existed at every Camp, as well as three or four sinks for drinking water.

Staxxx closed her eyes and let the heat take her body until she heard a rush of water spill to the ground. Wasteful, she thought. Then she opened her eyes to look at the glowing green on her wrists. A constant reminder that she owed them nothing. She laughed with her whole body, and more water bunched and spilled over the basin's edge. She watched the HMC slowly orbiting her like a moon. A second one oscillated between her and Thurwar.

"I don't owe you people anything," Staxxx said. The HMC flew in closer. "Anything but love," she finished. She closed her eyes again and let the fizzing water hold her. She heard Thurwar approach. The smooth steps on nylon.

"I worry because someone has to," Thurwar said.

Staxxx felt Thurwar's brown eyes on her before she opened her own. Thurwar stood above her, breathing deeply, sweat beading at her temple.

Staxxx felt a chill run through her, even in the warm water. She loved how Thurwar could make her feel something with just a look.

"We did the right thing. And we'll see how it goes," Staxxx said. She could feel herself grinning. "I don't want to feel like this is . . . this isn't some extra burden on your homestretch."

Thurwar walked the two steps to the cot and put Hass Omaha down on the ground. They didn't talk about the end. They were warriors on a ride that kept going until they were Freed. One way or the other. High or Low. But somehow here it was. Two weeks away.

"If anything"—Staxxx tried to keep her voice sleepy and relaxed— "this new way is a guarantee. There's a standard now. And if we're good here, we're good everywhere."

"I know," Thurwar said. "There are only five of us left."

"You giants." And though it shouldn't have bothered her, Staxxx felt a pebble of hurt in her chest at not being included in the group Thurwar was thinking of. Yet. On the active Chains currently on the Circuit there were only four Colossal-ranked Links besides Thurwar. After her next win, Staxxx would join that esteemed class.

"Us giants," Thurwar said.

"It's better for all of us," Staxxx said, and closed her eyes.

Thurwar started to pull off her clothes again. Once she was naked she used the showerhead attached to the basin to wash herself. She dried off and moved toward the freshly washed clothes that had been left for her. Clothes bearing both the hammer and the bountiful basket. As a kindness, the producers left sets of clothes for Staxxx in both Thurwar's and Randy Mac's tents as well as her own so she would never be tempted to wear the branded paraphernalia of a company that had not yet sponsored her.

Staxxx kept her face the same. She looked at her arms and saw names. Kitty Ruthless was the X on her biceps; Higgs "Landslide" Letupe on her forearm; a thick black bar crossed against another in honor of the massive man the Bear was above her knee. They'd all done so much. This was her purpose, making something of these horrors. And was there a difference between the Bear she'd mauled that morning and Gunny Puddles, whom she'd come so close to splitting open just an hour earlier? Was she a killer or had the world made her one?

"Yes," Staxxx muttered to herself.

"What?"

"Legit self-defense is a different thing," Staxxx said loud and hard.

"That's what I'm saying," Thurwar said. "We're already good."

"Well, this will make what is and isn't clearer. It shouldn't be that hard." Staxxx looked at Thurwar and then the HMC, which was Link code for *Don't let them see you like this*—or, in this case, *Don't let them make you something you're not.*

"Don't make it a huge deal. We're just trying something. We're reminding everyone they're something important, diamonds, better than diamonds."

Thurwar tried not to roll her eyes.

"I'm saying we can show that we're all, I don't know, pristine, deep down. We're just covered in varying degrees of shit. At our core we're gleaming. That's what we can tell them. And they'll listen 'cause it's you. You're the mom of this family. I'm just the crazy aunt–slash–mistress. You decide how we move."

Thurwar thought, If everyone is so pristine, then where did all this horror come from? They were quiet and Staxxx saw Thurwar blink against what she'd said.

"And I'm sorry, by the way. Sorry for today, the kid," Staxxx said. "How are you feeling?" They protected each other in a myriad of ways. This was one of them.

Thurwar slipped into a robe with the LifeDepot™ hammer insignia stitched into the chest. The HMC bouncing between them moved closer to her to get an optimal angle of the logo before easing back and bobbing between the two again.

"I felt good, physically. I was ready."

"Uh-huh." Staxxx sat up in the water. An HMC watched her drip.

"And that's why—" Thurwar turned to the HMC, deciding. She took a breath, then spoke as if to say, *This truth I'll share.* "I was angry. I felt cheated. I am—"

Staxxx got out of the tub, dried, and wrapped herself in a towel.

"I don't need help."

"That makes sense," Staxxx said. "Nobody wants to hit a little kid over the head with a hammer." She sat beside Thurwar on the cot.

"Yeah, and especially not me, because I don't need that. But also—" Thurwar stopped short.

"But also, of course you were relieved and kind of happy not to have to worry about winning."

"I didn't even let him finish saying whatever he was gonna say," Thurwar said. She leaned into Staxxx and laughed. Her dry and full laugh that Staxxx knew came out in the moments when other people would have cried. "Why didn't I? Why didn't I let him speak? Why did they give me some kid like that?"

"I guess they wanted to see if the kid could pull a Thurwar on Thurwar."

"I guess," Thurwar said. "It's dumb." And that was that. Staxxx wanted more; she knew what every BattleGround match was for Thurwar. She knew that every time, a part of Thurwar hoped to fail. And every failure to fail was a wound reopened.

"Okay," Staxxx said. "Us," she said, and closed her eyes again.

Simon

Es, eye, em, oh, en.

I'm going away. I don't think I'm coming back.* I've seen men go away for half a year for contraband.† I ain't get stuck with contraband.‡

I might come out.

I don't think I'm coming back.

---

* America locks more people in isolation than any other democratic country.

† Albert Woodfox spent forty-three years and ten months in isolation. Robert King spent twenty-nine years in solitary before he was released. Herman Wallace. Herman Wallace. Herman Wallace. Herman Wallace. He died of liver cancer two days after they killed him for forty-two years.

　　Albert Woodfox, Herman Wallace, and Robert King, Albert Woodfox, Herman Wallace, and Robert King, Robert and Herman and Albert. Herman and Robert and Albert. Wallace, Woodfox, King.

‡ The incarcerated can be placed in solitary confinement for nonviolent offenses such as possessing contraband or insubordination. Segregated housing is also sometimes used for the "protection" of the incarcerated individual.

The New

Two more, was the first thing she thought upon waking. At least two more people she'd have to kill. Two more times she'd have to defend her life on the BattleGround.

Thurwar was a collection of numbers and statistics. Numbers and statistics that she, a Grand Colossal, defined and defied. A great part of her lethality was her ability to understand them.

In the beginning, when she was still more civilian than Link, she'd relish the moments when she could almost forget her situation. Those seconds in the morning when, if the HMCs weren't floating above her to start her day, she could enjoy a sweet silence and pretend that her life was something other than a brutal entertainment.

She looked at Staxxx, who clenched her jaw in her sleep, and kissed her on the forehead once. The tense muscles on the sides of Staxxx's face settled. Then she rolled out of the cot onto the ground and dropped into the first fifty push-ups of her day. Each press of the earth was a kind of self-inventory. She observed any resistance in her elbows, the hold of her shoulders. She kept her core tight through each push and maintained a gradual energy against gravity through the drop. Her chest pressed nylon each time. She was still tired, but her body was what she needed it to be. She stretched, arched her back up, then pushed her core to the ground, cat, camel, several times to warm and loosen her spine.

She picked Hass Omaha up from the ground and did her squats. Hass had a shaft that was three and a half feet long, an alloy blend that kept it light enough. His head, ahistorical though it might have been, was shaped like any hammerhead you'd find at a LifeDepot™ store, except it was eight times the size. Blunted hard with an iron face and sharpened out into a gold-coated spike. She paid additional Blood Points every day to keep her primary weapon with her on the road; most Links who could did the same.

In total, Thurwar had amassed enough BP that, as far as people completely deprived of basic freedom went, she lived well. She ate two incredible meals a day, the first of which would be dropped to her in about—she looked at the WaYTime™ piece that holographically floated 7:08 A.M. in the air—twenty-two minutes. No surprise. She woke up at basically the same time every day. She tried not to feel annoyed with herself for being a few minutes off her regular schedule. She held Hass with her arms out, held the base of his neck with her dominant hand, the end of his shaft with her left.

She continued her squats. Again, a collection of data. One that grew grimmer and grimmer. A year ago, she could do her fifty hammer squats and her left knee would only begin to ache dully as she'd lowered through her fortieth. Her legs, in her life before and after prison and the Circuit, were her saving grace. You swung a hammer with your legs and back. You ran toward demons, sprinting. That was how you made it to Grand Colossal. But now, from the very first squat, she felt some pain. A spark of ache that grew and then relaxed a bit as she warmed up, then grew again until it hummed consistently. But she continued. As far as any of the millions tuned into the stream could tell, she felt no pain at all.

She would stretch more thoroughly, then take a quick shower. She would smile her best smile when Staxxx woke up at around seven-thirty. She'd try to maintain everything as it was even though Staxxx had killed Sunset, even though they'd forced a new way of life on the Chain, even though she'd learned about a devastating rule change coming in season 33 from the woman in Vroom Vroom.

She stepped into the basin. Staxxx's eyes fluttered, then she moved her arms over frantically, trying to find Thurwar. "There you are," she said, and she squeezed the REMington™ Sleep Cannon™ memory foam pillow that had cradled Thurwar's head through the night. She opened her eyes. "Oh, you thought I was looking for you?" Staxxx throttled the pillow still more, wrapping it up with her arms and legs in the same way she'd wrapped Pincer Goreten when she'd finished him off with four quick knife stabs through his neck and eye. Pincer's X was on Staxxx's left eyelid.

"You're great," Staxxx said. "But I just love how this feels."

Thurwar laughed despite it all. It was hard to imagine someone better or worse suited for this life than Staxxx. Besides her obvious ability to dismantle humans, she was funny and always thinking. She knew that if a particularly good sound bite or moment from the March really caught on with viewers, the Link behind it would be granted a meeting with the company they'd highlighted and that would likely lead to an offer of sponsorship. Sponsorship meant more and sometimes exclusive access to things that had to be bought with BP. And often at a discount, which meant you could save the points. More BP meant more life. Staxxx understood the game. Almost certainly REMington™ would be calling her when they made it to their next Hub City.

"Stupid," Thurwar said.

She turned the water on so it would come from the tall showerhead. She used a washcloth that was fresh and dry and took the opportunity to continue her daily assessment. She pressed against her shoulders, her biceps and triceps, the sides and back of her neck, searching for any undocumented pain. She continued her light stretches. She moved slowly, avoiding the HMCs that followed her movements like shadows.

"Fuck bitches, get money," Staxxx said. "Also, I love you."

"Yeah, whatever," Thurwar said, and again she was jarred by how easily Staxxx could bring her out of her head and into the world.

Staxxx rolled over to her pack. She tied her hair using a thick loc and then sheathed it with a shower cap that had been made with her in mind. She brushed her teeth and rinsed with bottled water. When Sun was around, he'd often traded tents with Thurwar or Staxxx, leaving the Queen's Tent to them, so it wasn't particularly novel to have so much of everything now, though there was a nagging strangeness in its all being Thurwar's.

"Don't forget those molars, kids," Staxxx said.

Staxxx played the game as if it were a natural and expected part of her life. She addressed the audience directly, made jokes that only made sense if you were the subject of a never-ending show, charmed her way into popularity, which garnered sponsorship, which ultimately made her a more lethal Link.

And then the two HMCs zipped away. They were alone, no cameras in sight. It had been a long time since Thurwar had felt what it was to be unseen on the Circuit. Her first thought: happiness at being alone with Staxxx, without the eyes of the world watching them. An opportunity to tell Staxxx what she'd learned from the woman in Vroom Vroom. This was a moment she could use. The truth sat on her lips, but she knew that once she spoke it, they would never be the same again. She swallowed the words, and as she did, it occurred to her that something significant had to be happening outside the tent, significant enough to pull the HMCs from her, naked as she was, and Staxxx, who was pulling on her robe already, clearly having come to the same realization a moment faster.

"Shit," Staxxx said, and she ran for LoveGuile. And the moment, Thurwar's chance to tell Staxxx, flew away.

Thurwar jumped from the basin, grabbed a towel, and wrapped it around her body. She rushed after Staxxx. Outside the tent, grass hugged her wet soles and collected against her skin as she ran, hammer in hand.

Rico Muerte was standing near the smallest tent, two hands on his six-iron. Sai Eye Aye was sitting a few paces in front of him on one of the Camp stumps. In one hand Sai held Knockberri and in the other, Tusk. Knockberri was a hard club made of bone with a round stone at its head, and Tusk was a thinner piece of wood fashioned with a rubber grip. Sai had killgraded Tusk several weeks earlier so that now it had jagged nails poking out of its top like sharp teeth.

"I don't give a fuck-all 'bout none of that shit," Muerte said.

He was standing with his chest out, his club in his hands, his eyes hot and darting to the eyes staring at him and then settling back on Sai.

"Hi, everyone, what seems to be the problem?" Staxxx broke in. Thurwar watched closely. Already there was a fight. Of course. It was foolish to think that they could curb all human instinct and history by asking everyone to chill.

"Sai needs to know I'm not for the play play."

Staxxx looked at Rico. She spoke as if it were the two of them alone in a room, though the rest of the Chain had gathered around.

"So why don't you tell me what the problem is, and we'll figure it out."

"They know what it is. I—"

"Because you aren't going to fight." Thurwar took a small step closer because she knew what Staxxx would say next. "Just the thought of anybody here going against what we established so clearly only yesterday. It's kind of a slap in the face. Ya know?" Staxxx slowly rotated LoveGuile so its blade pointed briefly in every direction. She kept it rotating, moving along a compass's path above their heads in the moist morning air.

"I got no problems with you and LT, but I'm not gonna let anybody herb me like I'm some kid. All due respect, but on my mama, that's not gonna happen."

As if suddenly boiling over, Sai stood up, their energy shifting darkly.

"We don't need to get the chitchatting. I'll take the points for your head, tiger." Sai spoke directly, almost bored, but with the bloodlust of a soon-to-be Reaper. It was an apt title for anyone who'd lasted that long in the games. The title before it was Cusp, and it was true that at that moment, you were on the cusp of becoming a different kind of killer. On the cusp of desiring it, of seeing death as a tool that might be used anytime, anyplace. "I like what y'all are trying to do, but if he wants me to kill 'im, Imma kill 'im," Sai said.

Randy Mac peeked out of his tent. Thurwar noted his taking in Staxxx's robed body. Farther beyond Sai and Rico, Ice Ice was lying on the ground, his pack a pillow. Walter Bad Water was near the community shower, his pinkish skin slick with wet.

"I'm not scared of shit," Muerte said.

"The next thing anybody says will be a clear explanation." Love-Guile stopped spinning. Staxxx dropped it so its blade poked into the earth between Rico and Sai.

Thurwar watched the three of them, and she knew that the one thing they all wanted was not to fight. As a Link, regardless of rank, the opportunity cost of a fight was huge. Even if you won, you'd almost certainly end up injured, and that meant a far greater chance of not surviving your next BattleGround match. It was much better to kill quickly than to fight. And yet, from Rico seeped a plague that ruined the lives of men and all they touched: He needed to be seen as strong, menacing, powerful. He struggled against it constantly.

"I was minding my own fucking business," Rico began, and gripped his six-iron tightly, "talking 'bout how I'm 'bout done being Peanut now and I'll probably never eat a peanut butter and jelly again."

"Okay," Staxxx said.

"So then even though I'm minding my own fucking business talking to Ice, Sai wants to chime in." Rico summoned an intense frown before mimicking Sai's low voice. "'Better worry more about what you hold than what you eat,' so I told them, 'I'm not fucking talking to you,' and they go, 'You won't be talking to anybody if you don't check yourself,' like really pressing me. I'm not the one!" Rico said; he was exciting himself. He stabbed down into the grass with his club. Staxxx looked at the tight, violent motion, then into Rico's eyes. He stopped doing it.

"On God that's what happened, Ice saw!" Rico said.

Ice Ice the Elephant was reading a book; reading was a habit he'd recently picked up from Sai Eye Aye. Surely, Rico understood Ice Ice and Sai Eye had become good friends. They were at about the same tier and had even fought in doubles matches together. Maybe on some level Rico was calling out the fact that he felt like no one was on his team? Thurwar considered this and watched.

Staxxx looked over at Ice, who said, "Yup, basically." A confirmation demonstrating very little interest in the whole affair.

"Anything you want to add, Sai?" Staxxx asked.

"No. That's exactly what happened," Sai Eye Aye said.

"Well, look at that, they're agreeing already," Mac laughed from near his tent.

"You shut up." Staxxx whipped her head at him for a moment.

"Yes, ma'am," Randy Mac said.

"So what you're saying is—" Staxxx started.

"What I'm saying is I'm not no bitch. I'm a Rook but everybody starts somewhere. I can say I don't wanna eat no damn peanut butter and jelly for the rest of my life and I don't give a fuck what anybody wants to say about it," Rico spat out.

Gunny Puddles had emerged from wherever he'd been and now stood only an arm's length from Thurwar. He shot a toothy smile her way and took a few steps toward the rest of the group.

As it was in civilian life, the loud, boisterous stuff was usually less of a concern. But the quiet ones were to be watched precisely.

"It's simple," Staxxx announced.

"Yeah, what's simple is I ain't soft and I'll prove it if I have to. Believe me."

"What I was going to say," Staxxx continued, "is that you're probably about tired of being the young blood, not having a real primary and all."

"Kid doesn't even have a real primary," Sai echoed.

"Four motherfuckers thought my shit was primary enough to Low out to it," Rico said, sticking his chest out farther.

Staxxx went on as if she had not heard either Sai or Rico. "And it rubbed you the wrong way to have someone rub that fact in your face."

"I ain't no bitch."

"And I don't think anybody is trying to dispute that. This feels like a misunderstanding." Staxxx pointed her scythe at Sai Eye Aye. This was a thing you only did when threatening another Link. Pointing your primary at another meant you were ready and willing to kill them. As it was, under their new rules, the gesture was benign, and yet the echo of its old meaning was felt.

"Sai, do you think our friend Rico here is, as he says, a bitch?"

Sai suddenly seemed amused by the theater they had made.

"Anybody that come in and out that BattleGround is tougher than most. Do it a few times and, well, that's something."

Staxxx beamed. Thurwar frowned. She did the math. None of this—the quick explosion, the easy resolution—seemed to add up.

"Well, that's that," Staxxx said. "Everybody cool?"

The group watched Rico.

"I wasn't pressed in the first place. I was just letting it be known once and for all." Staxxx put a hand on Rico's shoulder. He regarded it and softened. "Yeah, I'm chillin'."

"And what about you?" Staxxx asked.

"Ice," said Sai, unleashing Ice Ice's obvious but catchy catchphrase.

"See, that wasn't so hard."

The HMCs focused on Sai and Rico to see if the conflict would reignite. Thurwar took the chance to speak quickly to Staxxx as she walked past her back to the tent.

"When?" is all she asked. She kept her face straight, didn't even let her eyes move. Almost immediately one of the HMCs began to pull toward her.

"Don't know what you're talking about," Staxxx said, and she disappeared into the tent. When the HMC reasserted a position near Thurwar's temple, she was wearing a plastered smile, watching the resolution settle through her Chain.

This is day one of the new way, Thurwar thought. The game as it was had rewarded her so consistently that such a dramatic shift away from the violence that she knew worried her. You're scared, she thought in a clear, direct way that would have been voiced aloud were she not always being watched, had she not needed some things to be for her and only her. You're scared of what's new. You're scared of hidden intentions. You're scared of surprises. Thurwar scanned through her consciousness, breathed slowly, let the feelings of her body make her thoughts clear. You're scared and you hate that maybe something was planned without you, again. That Staxxx planned a fake fight without you.

The heat in her chest pulled inward. Thurwar played out the scene between Rico and Sai again, because a scene was obviously what it was. To erupt and settle so quickly. That wasn't how these things worked. Staxxx had to have orchestrated the charade, an attempt to reinforce the idea of the Chain as family. But she'd done it so obviously, so sloppily. That was unlike her.

The morning after they'd announced it. How convenient was it that suddenly two well-enough-liked Links would suddenly have beef that could easily have left either dead? And how convenient was it that

Staxxx should be able to settle the dispute in moments? They had to have planned it. But when? Thurwar thought through their last Hub City stay, tried to piece together Staxxx's itinerary.

You're wondering why she didn't trust you to help, Thurwar thought. You don't like that she only let you in on part of the plan.

Also, maybe you're paranoid.

Maybe you're paranoid because you're also keeping a secret.

Maybe it was real.

Maybe it's best to imagine it was real.

She had two more weeks.

Two more fights.

She tried to focus on the coming matches and not what Staxxx had or had not planned. Thinking of that place, those killing grounds, brought her an explosive, messy kind of calm.

From the very first time Thurwar had stepped on the BattleGround she had felt something erupt in her. Like a curse. Something that not only made her fight, despite how unworthy of life she felt, but made her prepare meticulously and obsessively. She'd wanted to be the best.

She blinked and looked up at the sky. She wiped her eyes. A flock of drones flew above the tree line and began to drop toward them. Two more fights, the first a doubles match with Staxxx, after which Staxxx would become a Colossal. Season 32 would end. And once season 33 began, the rules would change.

You're afraid of Staxxx keeping secrets from you because you're keeping a secret from her.

And that secret was that, once the new season began, it would no longer be allowed for two Colossal-ranked Links to be on the same Chain. Once season 33 began, Thurwar would be forced to fight the person she loved, the woman called thee Hurricane Staxxx, on her Freeing day.

Thurwar watched the drones descend, and her mouth began to water.

Food

Food floated to the ground around her. The drone that held the crate of curated meals was anti-grav, magnetically engineered. It flew with the same technology that kept the Anchor and the HMCs afloat. It made no noise as it slid through the air, part of a small flock of dark, smooth triangles, each dangling wire-net cargo holds carrying crates of food.

She could hear Staxxx in the shower as she watched them descend, dropping from the sky, then settling to an easy hover before releasing their loads in a circle around the Anchor, which floated above the ashes of last night's fire. Randy Mac jumped to his basket, grinning wildly. He had paid his Blood Points to ensure his daily meal package reflected his status as a Reaper: hot food, prepared by an actual chef. Things that usually tasted fine, sometimes even very good.

Ice Ice and Sai and Randy huddled together around the Anchor, hardly moving from the spot where the food had been left. They, Thurwar knew, were the core of the Chain. Those three had made it through some real shit together. She was grateful for them and how completely they let her lead them. Even if Randy wanted Staxxx exclusively. Even if Sai had secretly, maybe, orchestrated some quarrel with Rico to put a stamp on Thurwar and Staxxx's new decree.

"Eating time. Always a good time," Mac said, pulling his portion toward a stump to sit down. Randy Mac had gone from using a thread of copper wire, strangling other Peanuts for dear life, to the confident, trident-wielding Reaper he was now. She had more than seen it. She had midwifed his survival, just as she had with so many of the others.

She looked at Rico, watched him snatch a peanut butter and jelly sandwich, a "vitamin" juice box, and a banana. He glanced at Randy, Ice, and Sai, then began to walk off toward the second faction of the Chain: Gunny Puddles and Walter Bad Water. Gunny preferred to eat away from the core group, and Bad Water, a weak man who probably wasn't going to last very long on this Chain or any other, had never been pulled in by the rest of the group. Bad Water had just recently been able to afford more than his standard PB & J sandwich and had even more recently taken to spending time with Gunny. They'd bonded after surviving their last deathmatch as a tag team. Few things brought people closer together than killing as a pair.

Bad Water had explained to Thurwar that he "thought Black people were swell," but that it had seemed to him that Gunny was a lonely man who could use some company. Bad Water scratched at his purple headband and smiled as he opened his basket of food. As a Survivor, he probably had cheesy eggs and toast. After a few weeks of only peanut butter and jelly, the eggs and cheese tasted like life.

"You decent?" Thurwar called to Staxxx, her eyes still on Rico as he walked slowly toward Gunny and Bad Water.

"Never," Staxxx said.

"I think it's time to have breakfast with Rico," Thurwar said. "I'm calling him in." This was her job. She and Sun had figured out how to control a Chain together.

"Oh?" Staxxx sounded surprised, but happily so.

Was she in control? She was, and bringing Rico in would be a reminder to herself and everyone else of who she was.

"Yeah," Thurwar said. "Why not?"

"Okay." Thurwar heard the water's flow cease. "Call him in."

"Rico," Thurwar called. He was just a few paces from Gunny and Bad Water. "Come have breakfast with me."

Rico probably felt like he'd passed some sort of test. Thurwar looked over at Randy and Sai and Ice Ice. Each of them had been on the Chain much longer than Rico had when she'd called them in to come speak with her. Sai nodded. Ice chuckled to himself but nodded as well. Randy frowned, then shrugged and nodded too. She did not need their permission, but that moment of acknowledgment as Rico beamed and tried to collect himself was her way of showing that she still cared about their opinions. A-Hamm was not just Thurwar and Staxxx, but a collection of Links who were good and smart enough to protect one another. Rico hadn't proven he deserved to be brought in this way. Not yet. But Thurwar viewed this as a piece of her parting duties. Housekeeping for what would be left after her.

Thurwar moved toward the case that held her own breakfast, then stopped. "Grab these two for me." She pointed to the large, heat-insulated black box, which had her name embossed in gold letters on the side, and Staxxx's crate, next to it, red and painted with black and white Xs all over. Rico picked them both up, throwing his own meal on top of Staxxx's crate so he could hold it all in a stack.

Rico walked to just outside the tent, smiling stupidly at Thurwar.

Thurwar turned back inside. "We're coming in," she called.

Then she turned back to Rico, looked at the pride in his face and the food in his hands. "Come on," she said. She tightened the long towel she was wearing and walked in. Rico followed her gleefully.

By the time Sai Eye Aye had joined the Chain, maybe even before that, most of the Links who found themselves drafted to A-Hamm knew well of Thurwar. They'd seen her highlights and been amazed by her body's unwillingness to fold. Some had followed her before the merger of the Angola-Smith and Hammond Penitentiary Chains. By now she was the sole reason that a lot of the newbies joined CAPE at all. And Rico was the newest of the newbies. She and Sunset had meant something like hope for people like him. She resented it, but she also loved it, knowing that her name and life represented an entire avenue of possibility to people like Rico. Her survival made the impossible game seem possible. Of course they were foolish and misguided and would end up dead. But in her weaker moments she enjoyed being a beacon. When she was strong she knew she was a flame to moths.

"This crazy," Muerte said as he took the space in. Staxxx had just re-robed. She had a foot on the basin, her back to them as she massaged cocoa butter into her leg.

"It's a hard road to this," Thurwar said.

"But also, you're right, it is crazy," Staxxx said as she turned.

Thurwar let him take in the space and put a dark robe on over her towel as he did. She let him feel welcomed in the luxury that only she could provide.

Rico turned slowly, as if it required the support of his entire body for his eyes to absorb the Queen's Tent.

"Shit's wild," he said, finally.

"Have a seat," Thurwar said.

Two HMCs zipped back and forth between her and Staxxx while the other floated above the plush armchair opposite the bed, as if high-lighting where he was supposed to move next. Rico took the three steps quickly, then fell into the armchair. Small things like this were important. When Thurwar said sit, people sat. It was a part of being who she was to tell men and women who killed in order to live what to do easily and comfortably. They'd all already broken sacred law, and still her word meant something.

"Thanks," Thurwar said as she moved to one of the crates Rico had set down.

She pulled a latch and the sides of the box fell away, revealing a plate of eggs Benedict and a side of asparagus, as well as a cup of fresh fruit, all on a tray.

"Damn," Rico said. He chuckled sadly. He gripped the plastic bag in his hands tighter.

Staxxx walked to the bedside and picked up her own box, the Staxxx Pack.

Today there was a bowl with an over-easy egg on quinoa with assorted vegetables. It steamed when she released it from its plas-tic cover. As a civilian, Thurwar had never been in a nice hotel. And unlike her time at Angola, where she lived off the commissary when she could because the chow hall food was more mold than anything else, on the Circuit, Thurwar ate well.* She ate beautifully. She ate

---

* Incarcerated people suffer a disproportionate number of foodborne illnesses.

foods that she'd never heard of before she'd been imprisoned, the kinds of things most Links would never even get a sniff of. She looked at her plate of food. Took the fruit bowl for herself, placing the small dish of bright, plastic-wrapped pieces of pineapple, watermelon, and grapes on her bed. Then she lifted the tray with the rest of the food and pulled it from the larger black crate.

"It's hot, be careful," Thurwar said as she leaned over and laid the food in Rico's lap. She removed the plastic covering.

"You like eggs Benny?" Staxxx asked.

Rico looked down at what was before him. The hollandaise sauce gleaming as it draped the poached eggs, then pooled, yellow and creamy, in and around the crevices of an English muffin. A thick slice of Canadian bacon with delicately charred edges just poking out from under the eggs. Asparagus striped with fresh grill marks. And a cold sealed thermos of what Thurwar knew was either apple or guava juice. Three bottles of water also sat in the crate; Thurwar would pour those into her canteen. But now she watched Rico watch the food. It had been almost four years, she knew, since he'd had real food. And here he was, suddenly plunged into what, for him, must have been the finest dining.

His shaking knees rattled the fork on the tray.

"Please, Rico," Thurwar said softly. "Go for it." Her voice was calculated in its softness. She wanted him to feel with the deepest part of himself that he was finally safe with her.

Thurwar popped a piece of pineapple into her mouth and glanced at Staxxx. She had done this same thing many times, and Rico was not the first to cry, but it still made her feel something she didn't like to miss. A pouring that seemed to fall from her chest, through her body, a pride in what she had become. An oasis in hell. An unlikely power that had been forged by force of will. In these moments she understood intimately and precisely what the crowds who cheered her name felt in their hearts. She didn't perform in the loud, boisterous ways she used to. But she still performed. This was method. She let it feel real. This was her job and she let herself enjoy it.

She watched Rico until he turned back to meet her gaze.

"I'm not—" He took a breath and wiped his eyes. "I haven't had anything to eat for so long. You know?"

"I know," Thurwar said. "Can I have that? Can we trade?"

She pointed to the plastic bag that was still in his hands.

"This?"

"Trade me," Thurwar said. He looked at her as if she were insane and she looked at him in a way that made it clear she wasn't going to repeat herself.

One hour till March initiates. The Anchor's voice settled around them.

Rico handed the bag over. The sandwich was on wheat bread and clearly had been slapped together hastily before being thrown into a too-large eco-plastic biodegradable zip bag.

"Eat," Thurwar said.

"I am," Staxxx joked, piling quinoa into her mouth.

"Thank you," Rico said.

"And thank you," Thurwar said.

"Eat a little, then we'll talk more," Staxxx said.

"Go ahead," Thurwar said. She bit into the sandwich, its grating sweetness, its simple familiarity. Rico finally dove into the food. Thurwar watched with amusement as he slurped a stalk of asparagus down first, which surprised her, then used his hands with the eggs Benedict. She thought of reminding him that there was a plastic knife and fork tucked into the corner of the tray, but it was clear he had decided how he'd enjoy this. He chewed hard and quickly, then slowed down, savoring for a moment, and then continued at speed. To hell with reverie.

Thurwar still had a corner of the sandwich left by the time he'd finished. In a world where murder was everywhere, every meal might be your last. And when you felt that powerfully, something as plain as a peanut butter and jelly sandwich tasted like another kind of death. To her palate, though, it actually wasn't that bad. She said so.

"When I started on the Circuit, they had just made two meals mandatory," she said. "Our sandwiches were stale, and they didn't even have jelly on them." She finished it, swallowed. Then swallowed again to empty her mouth of the stick. "But that was a long time ago."

Rico looked at her, his fingers coated with hollandaise. Staxxx got up and pulled a hand towel from a rack near the water basin. She wet it for a moment, then handed the rag to Rico, who cleaned each of his fingers one by one before wiping his face.

"Damn," he said, slumping back in his seat. "A different life."

"It's something, right?" Thurwar said.

"It's everything." Rico smiled. It made him younger to smile. He was barely old enough to drink.

They were quiet for a moment. Thurwar let the food settle and then she looked at Staxxx.

"Why did you leave?" Staxxx said.

"I knew I couldn't live inside. Decided I'd rather die out."

"Where were you?" Thurwar asked.

"Jersey, one of the regular prisons. Not the experimental shit. General population."

"Didn't make any friends?" Staxxx said.

"I had a little group, but then I didn't. Shit got weird off some dumb shit. Tried to sell me out. Four times people that was supposed to be my brothers tried to stick me. So, I signed the papers."

"What changed? Why'd they turn?" Thurwar asked. She leaned in.

"Does it matter?" Rico put his tray down so it rested on the nylon beneath them.

"Fair," Staxxx said.

Rico said nothing.

"What did you think when you were sent to Angola-Hammond Chain?"

"I thought, Somebody loves me."

"Aww," Staxxx said, "that's so sweet."

Thurwar smiled a genuine smile. "Why did you think that?"

"You know why."

"I want to hear you explain."

"Being on y'all's team is a vibe. Everybody knows."

"What does everybody know?"

Rico looked at Staxxx, who Thurwar knew would be nodding reassuringly.

"Once the two of y'all connected, I mean, you and Sunset changed the vibe. And of course, thee Hurricane made it even better. Made it like people could get strong together. Helped each other out."

"Sunset Harkless was killed recently, as you remember," Thurwar said. "What do you think about that?" She hadn't planned on this part.

But she made it a point not to second-guess herself when she could avoid it. She turned her head just enough to see Staxxx, who had flattened a bit, though she still smiled at Rico.

Rico bit his lip. Thurwar looked hard at him. She could feel him struggling to keep eye contact with her. "I was sad as shit, to be honest—at first, I mean. But Staxxx is valid, so it's valid. So all good on my end. I just didn't know if you'd still be on your Blood Mother Angel shit without him."

"What do you mean by that?" Thurwar pressed.

"You're like the angel of this shit. Giving everybody a boost and whatnot. You give people a chance. Reaper-maker they called you in my cell block. And like, you was asking people not to try dumb shit with you like that, and your Chain been the least wild for a min. I seen on the cast how people don't try to murk each other like that here. Excluding last week, respectfully. And stuff like y'all just did last night made it even more official. Mad decent. I'm honored to be down."

"You mention last night," Thurwar said. She picked up Hass Omaha, which had been sleeping near Thurwar's slippered foot the entire time they'd been in the tent. Suddenly, the hammer's presence filled the space. Rico Muerte sat up a little straighter. "Last night I made it an official stance of this Chain to avoid violence against your fellow Links at all costs. You remember that?" Thurwar watched carefully to see if Rico would look to Staxxx for help. Maybe he'd flat-out admit that his "fight" with Sai had been a ruse.

"Of course."

"And now I'm sitting here, getting ashy, 'cause the very next morning you threatened another one of my Links. One of my core. How long have you been on the Circuit?"

Rico didn't run from her stare and she respected him for it.

"One and a half months. I seen the BattleGround three times. Next week I'll fight again."

"What's your rank?" Thurwar asked.

"Peanut—I mean Rookie. But I'll be a Cusp—"

"You're saying you're the lowest rank possible."

"Yeah, bu—"

"And what rank is Sai Eye Aye?"

"Iono even know, but my point with them was that—"

Thurwar stood up. There were Chains where this would be the last moments of Rico Muerte's life.

"They're almost a Reaper," Thurwar said. "On the Circuit for over a year. A solid Link for over a year, and you, the day after I make it clear that all the bullshit is to stop, the day after I do something for all of us, you tried to pick a fight with them."

"It was, I mean—" And here he looked to Staxxx. Just past Thurwar's right side. Thurwar crouched down, ignored her knee's whine, and took Rico's chin in her hand. She pulled his face back to her.

Ten months earlier a Link named Refar Nichs had been in the same position Rico was in now. It had been Thurwar and Sunset and Staxxx in the space. Refar had panicked under the pressure and tried to grab LoveGuile as they spoke to him. What he wanted to do with it, the world would never know. Thurwar crushed his skull before his hand had wrapped around the scythe's shaft. They'd dragged his body out of a tent in the morning light and no one on A-Hamm had said a word about the corpse.

"It was what?" Thurwar asked. She imagined crushing his skull here and now. She wanted him to feel her imagining it. How easy and complete it would be. "It was kind of like you wanted to spit in my face?"

Rico tried to look down at the meal he'd just devoured. The almost-clean plates.

"Eyes on me," Thurwar said. She felt the patchy stubble on his face.

"They got me hot. I'm sorry."

"You're sorry. And what else?"

"And I—I don't know. It won't happen again?"

"Are you asking me?"

"It won't happen again. It's my bad, Blood Mama. My fault."

She released him.

"Thank you, I appreciate it. Now we can talk about what I wanted to talk about."

Thurwar said nothing but watched recognition dawn on Rico. He tried not to smile but failed, grinning wide.

"What are you so happy about?"

"This," Rico said, "this moment. I was thinking if I'm gonna really be out here I wanna rock with some big shit, maybe something like Mac man got. Big-ass ax, maybe."

Staxxx laughed a little; Thurwar did not.

"You know what I want to talk to you about then."

Rico reeled himself in a bit. "Everybody knows. You held it down for like half the people here."

"I'm glad you're so well-informed."

"I'm not gonna cap, I'm a fan. I'm honored."

Thurwar thought of all the weapons she'd shepherded into the games. The rules had changed in season 24, allowing Links to spend Blood Points on other Links, and just like that, the games were different forever. Early on, Thurwar had realized that you could leverage your wealth and the promise of power into survival. From the beginning, because of how she'd entered, the mountain she'd toppled, she'd never wanted for a weapon or Blood Points.

"I've given and I don't do it for free. You know what I expect from my generosity."

"Till High or Low Freed, I got you," Rico said. He stood up. Put a fist to his chest and took deep breaths through his nose.

"Thank you. I also want you to extend that pledge to Staxxx." Thurwar had been thinking of doing this for some time. She'd wanted to go over the details with Staxxx ahead of time, but in that moment she decided to make clear what most already assumed.

"I'm two weeks, two fights, from Freed and I intend to take that journey." Rico nodded. "After that I want you to give the same loyalty you have to me to Staxxx. The position I have here will be hers when I leave. Do you understand?"

"For sure. I'm ready to pledge to whoever."

"Not whoever. Me, and when I'm Freed, to the woman to my right."

Thurwar guessed that Staxxx was upset before turning and seeing the hard smile on her face.

"Copy, for sure," Rico said. "I swear, I pledge, all that."

"Another thing. From now on you won't be eating those sandwiches."

Rico looked at her, confused.

"Now that we're family, everybody eats. We'll work out the system, but everybody is going to have a decent meal from now on."

Thurwar had not done this math. She wasn't sure how much of

this she could ensure once she was out of the Circuit. But she knew it would make him happy. And the math she had done said it was better for Gunny to have only one real friend on the Circuit than two. So it was good to have Rico there, happy to receive the blessings of Loretta Thurwar, the character he'd thought of when he'd signed the papers. She was the flame his wings would melt against.

"I appreciate it and it means a lot to me, but I wanna carry my weight like all y'all have. I just need a badass prime so I can do something out there."

"Preparation is how you win fights. That includes what you take in." She felt a power flowing through her. She watched the flying cameras dance around her face.

"I don't know what to say," Rico said. "Thank you."

"Let's get back to the reason this guy is so excited, yeah?" Staxxx said.

Thurwar turned to her and smiled. They both could do surprising things.

"Yeah, that's a good idea," Thurwar said.

"Right, so I was thinking I want something that really rings bells. Some heavy shit."

"Okay," Thurwar said. She raised her arm and held Hass Omaha in front of her. "Imagine carrying something like this in the deathmatch."

"Oh shit," Rico said.

"Don't get too excited," Thurwar added before letting him hold the handle. "This is the last time you'll hold this hammer. I just want to see what you can handle."

"Copy," Rico said.

Thurwar let go of the hammer. Even for this demonstration it felt like a sin.

Almost immediately, in Rico's hands, the hammer drooped and dropped to the floor. He strained and picked it back up.

"Let's keep brainstorming this," Staxxx said. And though he was embarrassed, Rico Muerte let another smile slip.

Door Four

You might be owned by a man, like I been. You might be owned by the state, like I was. Maybe the holding is your own voice taken and stripped from you. Your own body living under the eye of electric sizzle. Maybe that's what owns you. Not wanting to be more owned. When I went in, the killing games was debated, they were not to happen. Too cruel, too mean, too everything bad. They said. Then they said less. Now the killing games the new football. They'll say that what owns me now. My chains made of far freedom. I been silent. I ain't ever been blind. What owns me is my own wrong and nothing else.

No more, my lord
No more, my lord

"That singing thing you do, keep doing it, they freaking love it," Sawyer says. Sawyer my CO. Slick-smile man. Liar in a suit that sometimes tells the truth. He tells me people like how I been surviving. How I been killing. How I been using my voice since I got it back. My voice keeps me company.

"Scorpion Singer," that's what they calling me. I win, Auburn, whole system wins. They happy all the time I'm breathing. We sit in a room, before I leave to go in front of the cheering people. "You know

you've already revolutionized the culture for the limb-different. You're
an icon in that community. You're an icon before your sixth match,
and that means you can keep on building up. We need to get you some
better armor. It was nice at first, this free, open look, but it's gonna get
you killed."

He been saying this a month now.

Lord I'll never, turn back

No more.

"But this singing shit. Keep that shit. People love it. Scorpion
Singer. Excellent. You gonna have a real chance."

I'm missing my spear. I like it in my hands, I admit. It wasn't an
accident. Hard to say anything an accident if it happens. A spear. I had
it a few months and know it well. The spear opens me up just like it
opens up the others. It chose me. I admit that too. Didn't even have to
earn. God, Higher Power, whoever, put it right in my hands. Spin the
wheel, get a chance at life. Spin the wheel and eat of the tree. Spin the
wheel. Spinifer. Two months back I spun it free.

At the show a man spins the wheel with fear in his heart. He gets a
wrench, black with oil like it came from the shop just before. He'll
take it gladly. Holy, how he feels. Forgive me for I have.

Woman spins next. Gets a pair of scissors. Two sharp ones that
might be kept in a kitchen. She jumps up in the air, excited, happy
for herself. Happy for her chances. The crowd claps and cheers for her.
Happy for scissor's chances, happy, she happy like they all on the same
team.

Then a man come up to the wheel. Excited. Like the goodwill the
gods just blessed the woman before him with is still in the air for him.

"You ready?" blond host man says. We, those who chose death over
confinement, sit on a wooden bench off stage left.

"Fuck yeah," he says, shaking.

No more, my lord

Whole body shaking. Excited. The crowd feels it too. The crowd
wild for him. "Born ready, Micky!"

This part a game show. It's all a game show. *Chain-Gang Initiation
Special: Wonder Wheel.* Mean show. Same thing behind doors one, two,
and three.

"Spin away."

Clickety, clickety, clickety, click, click, cli—and the crowd gasps. The man stares. Makes to spin again.

"Wouldn't that be nice? One spin per Link, unfortunately," host says.

A spoon. Shining silver spoon.

This one the joke of the group. The wheel got pictures all flavors of silliness. No help in a fight at all. But the spoon we all see is cruelest. The spoon is so people can remember what this all is. But the crowd doesn't see it that way. They gasp, then boo. Like they all on the same team. Like they shocked.

Door number two slides away, then the man sees his own dead body. Jackpot, triple seven, somebody wins, just definitely not him. He stops shaking. I watch him close. Workers hand him a purple pillow with a spoon resting on top of it. More salt for new wounds. He holds the spoon in his hand. Looks at it. Sees himself stretched against the curve. I watch him close. It's a show I've seen before. When a man sees he has been forsaken. Discovers he might be unblessed. Thinking he understood. All at once he see the gods he kept don't keep him the same way. Not how he hoped. He see he had it all wrong the whole time.

Can you tell me where he's gone?

Go down, go down

Next man spins a bowling ball.

Then I walk forward. Singing, humming, making my own noise, even though they gasp at the sight of me. They feel sorry. They paid to be here. They didn't know there would be a man with just the one arm vying for a life. I walk up. Sometimes I feel my left though ain't a trace of it left. Shoulder, then air. I can feel the space in that air, sometime better than when there was flesh. Here in the spinning room, it's hot. Still got goose bumps on an arm that ain't there.

"Name?"

I look at the host and the crowd. Spoon is somewhere in the back, I can hear him hollering. Screaming his good heart out. We all hear it. Door one has opened in front of Spoon and he don't like that one either. He hanging from a tree in that one.

And perhaps you may find

Find him there

"That's a very nice voice you got there, what shall we call you then? Elvis maybe?" I stare at him, a blond Elvis himself. "It looks like you've already had a couple of tough matches." I make to choke him with the arm I don't got. The arm that's gone finds his neck and squeezes.

He pauses, seeing his funny ain't land. He clears his throat. "All right, all right, that was insensitive. What's your name, sir?"

"Hendrix Young," I say. I grab a handle on a purple slice of wheel and pull down. Fate spins. It spins and spins and spins and spins. I hear spoon man screaming. Fate spins us all. He don't stop crying out.

Behind door number three it's just a mirror.

And my arm that ain't touches the wheel, slows it just enough. And when the spinning stops, the arrow pointing to the one golden panel. For me the people scream. They party in the small studio. It's something I can use. The opposite of a spoon. A jackpot.

Door four. There is no door four. But I see it in front of me.

A long black rod with a black blade at the tip. The rod is strong and ridged with dark gold. It is a precious thing. The people screaming. They happy. Same team. Well look at this.

I use it to kill, my spear. Called Spinifer Black, named after the scorpion. The scorpion.

Stable

"The reason people love Thurwar is she gives everybody weapons?" Emily asked as a recorded stream played in the background, muted.

Rico Muerte, a skinny Link from Jersey, was swinging an imaginary sword through the air as Thurwar and Staxxx watched. Emily wanted to watch the rest of their assessment of Rico but her husband, Wil, had been muting the show intermittently so he could explain things to her.

"Basically," Wil said. He touched his dimpled chin, deep in contemplation. "But she's also earned every bit of respect she's got. It's not some bullshit. She's not a plant like Nova Kane Walker."

Wil said the name "Nova Kane Walker" with such disdain you would have thought that the crimes he'd been absolved of through participation in the CAPE program were against members of Wil's own family.

"He's the one that does the television shows now as an analyst or whatever."

"Yeah, that guy. Fuck that guy. He was a plant for sure. The only one ever to make it out all the way," Wil said. "Thurwar has a group that's more or less loyal to her. Even when Sunset Harkless was alive Thurwar had a group that followed her specifically." When Wil men-tioned Sunset, he tapped his own chest twice in memory of the fallen legend. "Staxxx obviously is Thurwar's right hand, and it's fucked that she did that to Sun. And to be honest if it was anybody else, I think A-Hamm would be fucked. But it was Staxxx, so I know she has a reason. It hurts, though. I've been sitting with it." Wil laughed sheepishly. "Sunset was supposed to see Freed."

Emily listened to Wil and thought, This is what is interesting about this game. Wil, who was a little basic but usually kind enough, this man who had come to feel like home to her, was negotiating a complicated forgiveness in real time as prompted by this, this show. Almost as if by accident, he'd become generally much more open-minded about what it meant to be a good or bad person. Someone he'd respected had done the worst thing possible to another person he'd respected and because of the way A-Hamm was, he was thinking about it in a way that Emily herself resisted but also quietly admired.

"But yeah, Staxxx was considered as loyal as they come. Now I don't know, though." Wil paused to make sure Emily was registering the gravity of his consideration, then continued. "Either way, Staxxx and Ice Ice the Elephant and Tracer McLaren and Sadboy Blusie and Sai Eye Aye all got fronted a stupid amount of BP for their primaries. It starts with the weapons, but it goes deeper than that. Some of them got Low Freed pretty soon after, but still." He looked at her and she saw that he assumed she'd missed something. "Low Freed means—"

"It means they're dead," Emily said quickly. She knew it made her husband happy to teach her, but he'd told her this same fact so many times over the last few days she couldn't stomach hearing it again. She'd been bingeing stream highlights. She'd moved through an alarming span of seasons by just watching the most explosive moments.

"Exactly, babe."

Emily smiled.

"But the weapons were really a quid pro quo, and those only last so long. She's more than what she gives out. So much more. It's kind of, well, you know a leader when you're around one. Like that book I told you to check out."

Emily had flipped through the first few pages of *Lead with Your Head: The Alpha Man's Guide to Understanding and Leading the Everyman* and quickly put it down.

"Right."

"So even though earlier I said the Chain was less interesting because it was so stable, I think there's a lot worth checking the stream for now." Here he literally rubbed his palms together.

"Yeah, there's a lot going on."

"I know you love the Sing Chain best, though," Wil said. He crossed his right leg over his left and leaned back into the plush, smiling a dreamy smile. "A woman after my own heart."

"I thought you liked Angola-Hammond best," Emily said.

"I mean, it's the most viewed, and of course there's Thurwar and Staxxx, but at the same time you're kinda right."

"Does it even make sense to have Chains if it's such an everybody-for-themselves game? Why aren't more Chains like A-Hamm?" This was what Emily had been wondering. It was part of why she was drawn to the drama. It was almost like the program and these characters that made up A-Hamm were adjusting to her relatively low tolerance for gore.

"The beauty of Chain-Gang"—a phrase Wil dispatched several times a week—"is that it's both a team sport and a solo game. The tension between both is the key to the whole thing. In a Melee you have to act as a team, and same in doubles matches, but you get rewarded for offing your own teammates too."

"But are they really a team if all they do is walk together from point A to point B?" She angled her body to look away from the screen and into Wil's eyes.

"Em, Em, Em." He shook his head in disappointment. "It's so much more than walking. But you'll see when they get to the Hub City. The March is where so many bonds are formed. Like right now, Thurwar just brought Rico Muerte into her core. She's basically adopting him. And she gave him a pass for disrespecting her NoWar Law—that's what they're calling it on the threads. So much happens between the Hub Cities and the Circuit March. The March is where the more cerebral parts of the game happen."

Emily blinked and turned her attention back to the television. Rico was still fighting an imaginary opponent. There were smaller feeds in the right and left corners that showed what the other two HMCs were focused on. The one on the left was in the Queen's Tent too, mostly filming Thurwar, though it made a point to flash toward Staxxx every now and again, definitely whenever she spoke. The display in the right corner of the screen hovered above the middle of the Camp and rotated in the sunlight. It showed Randy Mac and Ice Ice eating and talking. The feeling Emily had been getting less and less while watching Chain-Gang grew in her gut.

She hadn't even voted for Robert Bircher, the president who had paved the way for hard action-sports, and she believed that it was no accident that people of color, and particularly people from the African diaspora, made up so many of the characters on this show. She knew that Black people and other minorities were disproportionately imprisoned.* Thurwar, Staxxx, and Sai Eye Aye were all Black Americans, as was Randy Mac, though he was also half-Filipino. Plus there was Rico Muerte, who was Dominican, which, she'd learned from a documentary, also counted as Black.

And yet she was genuinely interested in the lives of these criminals on her U-enabled stream console. They were playing out some rich asshole's fantasy and it drew her eyes like an accident on the road. Somehow the promise and potential of carnage made you crane your neck, and if the strain resulted in some bloody prize, you'd have what? A story to tell. Trauma for yourself.

Once she'd seen a man thrown from his motorcycle on the highway. She'd been speeding along, manually attentive to the roads; her car was old enough that it was just as safe to control it with your body. Suddenly she'd noticed a wiggle, a wheel squirming left and right. A movement that was unnatural during the straight speed of the parkway. The next thing she knew, the man was flying forward from his bike. She slowed down to take in the scene. His body tumbled with terrible momentum across the road's shoulder. The last thing she saw as she passed was slick red against his neon-yellow long-sleeve shirt. She gripped the wheel harder. Was she supposed to do something? No,

---

* As of 2018: 2,272 out of every 100,000 Black men are incarcerated at a state or federal level, compared to just 392 out of every 100,000 white men. Eighty-eight out of 100,000 Black women are incarcerated at a state or federal level, compared to 49 out of every 100,000 white women.

she was already a quarter mile from the scene. But she'd felt the strange surge of witness. The electric awareness of the stakes of life. She was a half mile away. There was nothing she could do. Hopefully he was okay. The skin on his shoulder and back scarred away, but maybe that was all. Finally, she'd accepted that she was rolling, safe, and he was not. She'd closed her eyes and voice-commanded her vehicle to drive autonomously. She hadn't had the stomach for manual anything anymore.

Now Wil was explaining the concept of "Chain stability" to her for the fourth time. It seemed pretty intuitive that when a Chain wasn't in turmoil, when there wasn't any obvious tension between the Links, that was called "stability." When every Link on the Chain could make the day's March without much trouble. She had known this actually before Wil had told her. She, on her own, had watched enough of the streams and commentary on her computer at work. She'd watched several hours, coming to understand that the game's complexities were as infinite as its jargon.

"Right, okay," Emily said. She could fill any of Wil's pauses with general agreement and he would continue, undisturbed and unaware that she'd tuned him out. She wondered what it was like to be a woman like Thurwar. To command that kind of power, to be worshipped by legions. She looked into Thurwar's eyes and saw her vague amusement with Rico Muerte.

"But are they really stable right now?" Emily said, turning to Wil.

"What do you mean? You mean the Sunset stuff?"

"Yeah, I mean Thurwar just made some big changes, but Staxxx literally just killed a leader of the Chain, so it seems like the whole group might be in flux for a while."

From the backlog she'd taken in, to have a Chain that was overtly committed to non-harm among all members was unheard of. She'd also observed that for most Chains in stability, the status was a misnomer. Nothing was ever stable in anyone's life, Emily thought, let alone the lives of these people on the Circuit.

"Like in that archive stream I watched last night with that other Chain," Emily began. "Even though there wasn't any beef between the Eraser boys and that blond one, they still murdered him." The shame, that feeling, rose in her again. Yesterday she'd sat by and watched as a man was murdered. Yes, technically and legally it was the state and not the Eraser triplets that had sanctioned and administered the execution of whatever that blond dude's name was, but she was the one who had actually watched the men beat him to death before bed last night. She'd felt that surge and watched with the world as they felt it too. Then she'd watched it again.

"Yeah, but there was beef, babe." He spoke to her as one would a child. "It was just undercover. The Erasers never fucked with Phil the Pill because they thought he was a race traitor for being so cool with Razor and Bells and that side of the Chain."

"But just having separate crews within the Chain suggests that the Chain is unstable."

"Every Chain has people that are tight. Just like any job. But sometimes crews like the Erasers secretly want to kill the others. That's real instability. A-Hamm is technically never going to be stable as long as Gunny Puddles is alive, but with A-Hamm, Thurwar's so epic she kind of settles things over. The Staxxx stuff—I feel you, though. But I think they're gonna be fine, probably."

"I don't know," Emily said.

"Trust me, babe. Thurwar has them in line. They're fine."

"You really, really like Thurwar, huh?"

"I don't *like* Thurwar, I love Thurwar. She's arguably the greatest athlete of her generation."

"I've heard." Emily smiled coyly. A final delightful shame for her was that her husband's obvious infatuation with Thurwar piqued her interest more than anything else about the show. His infatuation with this woman who couldn't have been more different from her. Who was unlike anyone she'd ever known Wil to be with. And not just because she was Black, though that difference was bright in her mind, but because she was so even-keeled, so full of violence, yet almost perpetually calm in a way that was inspiring and also irritating.

"Don't tell me you're a Thurwar-hater, babe," Wil said, a huge grin stretching his cheeks. He suddenly was on top of her, half tackling her into their couch.

"I'm not sold on her yet. We'll see. Last time I saw her she killed some kid," Emily laughed as Wil peppered her with kisses.

"I need you to be very careful with what you say. Don't blaspheme the GOAT. Literally imagine if that kid won his first fight. That's how she came into Chain-Gang."

"I don't know. I'm not convinced. Convince me." Wil had her pinned on the couch by the wrists. "Convince me," she said again.

Wil looked at her and she looked up at him. There was no denying for them, for their marriage, it was an incredible thing that she'd taken up hard action-sports. Certainly, it made her husband love her more fully, more richly.

"Okay, I will. You haven't seen her first fight. That's why you take the queen's name in vain." Wil got off her, taking all the energy they'd built and tossing it aside. "I'll stream it now. You ready?" Wil asked, his voice drenched with glee. She didn't answer but Wil's fingers were already tapping his desires into the control tablet. "This was a couple of seasons ago, so some things are different."

"How many seasons ago?" Emily said. She could do the math, or search herself, but even though it made her feel almost sticky, it also made her life so much easier to give Wil what he wanted: to let him be an expert, a bastion of knowledge.

"Well, for the last couple of years there's been about three Chain-Gang seasons per year."

"Why are they so short?"

"They seem short compared to other sports," Wil said, again dropping to a thoughtfulness that maybe wasn't a lie. He was thinking about this stuff constantly. "It's such a young sport, hard action-sports in general. Every season there's new rankings, and the rankings change so often 'cause, you know."

"Because people die."

"Yeah, exactly. That and the game is always evolving, so rule changes come into play when the seasons change. As it matures the changes get less dramatic, but each season there's something different. When Chain-Gang started, they were really in the wild and had to hunt for food."

"How'd that work out?"

"They changed it by like season nine," Will said.

"Right."

"And during the season we're about to watch, it was a brand-new thing to be able to take a weapon from someone you've defeated. They had to be at least two ranks higher than you, though."

"Bishoping," Emily said knowingly.

"Yes! Exactly, babe. I'm about to show you why it's called that." He'd finished with the tablet. The screen flicked to the past.

PART
II

Simon Craft

"ongratulations, Craft. You made it to the century mark," Officer Lawrence says like there's a cake in his hands. "One hundred days in paradise."

See, are, ey, eff, tee. Craft. That's the first thing I do. No. First thing I do is wake before the buzzer. I don't get to hear much outside the sounds of men screaming. If it's not Lawrence, it's the buzzer. The sound shakes you. High and jagged.

There's a bed and a shit tin. Dark in here most of the day. But they glow in my brain. The hole is black. I only see when the door opens. The door opens one time a day. I sit, sleep, sing, flex, breathe, stretch, shake, cough, shit here. Here is where I come apart.*

One hundred days ago they started to kill me again. I've died so many times now I must be unkillable. I am the undying. It's a hard, wonderful life.

One hundred and seventeen days ago a man didn't like me. I killed a man one hundred and seventeen days ago.

---

* Solitary confinement has been consistently found, nationally and internationally, to induce anxiety, paranoia, hallucinations, depression, panic attacks, memory loss, and other cognitive defects.

There's blood on every piece of here.[*] Especially on the floors. Especially on the walls. That ain't poetry. It's an observation. Anyone can see. The rats drink the blood off the floor. Their blood exposed to the air. Makes people sick. It doesn't make me sick. I'm the unkillable. I don't get sick. Twenty days in the hole I licked the floor to see if I could maybe catch a little dying. Not even a fever. That's when I knew what I was. That I was meant to be forever. I am Job. No. Job pities me. I live beneath the fist of God. I've had my eyes taken from me twenty-three hours a day. The one hour I'm out the hole is the worst of them all. I spend the fifty-nine minutes afraid to go back in.

---

[*] 18 U.S. Code § 2340A—Torture
(a) Offense.—
Whoever outside the United States commits or attempts to commit torture shall be fined under this title or imprisoned not more than 20 years, or both, and if death results to any person from conduct prohibited by this subsection, shall be punished by death or imprisoned for any term of years or for life.
(b) Jurisdiction.—There is jurisdiction over the activity prohibited in subsection (a) if—
  (1) the alleged offender is a national of the United States; or
  (2) the alleged offender is present in the United States, irrespective of the nationality of the victim or alleged offender.
(c) Conspiracy.—
A person who conspires to commit an offense under this section shall be subject to the same penalties (other than the penalty of death) as the penalties prescribed for the offense, the commission of which was the object of the conspiracy.

18 U.S. Code § 2340A—Definitions
(1) "torture" means an act committed by a person acting under the color of law specifically intended to inflict severe physical or mental pain or suffering (other than pain or suffering incidental to lawful sanctions) upon another person within his custody or physical control;
(2) "severe mental pain or suffering" means the prolonged mental harm caused by or resulting from—
  (A) the intentional infliction or threatened infliction of severe physical pain or suffering;
  (B) the administration or application, or threatened administration or application, of mind-altering substances or other procedures calculated to disrupt profoundly the senses or the personality;
  (C) the threat of imminent death; or
  (D) the threat that another person will imminently be subjected to death, severe physical pain or suffering, or the administration or application of mind-altering substances or other procedures calculated to disrupt profoundly the senses or personality; and
(3) "United States" means the several States of the United States, the District of Columbia, and the commonwealths, territories, and possessions of the United States.

He came at me with the sharp end of toothbrush he'd worked to a shiv. He ran but I saw him. I see things sometimes. I've had plenty sharp things rushed at me. He came at me out near C-showers. A bald little man from down here. He was country like most of these guys. I'm not from down here. I don't speak slow or in roundabouts. I speak in silence. And with knuckle on bone on flesh on your muthafucking face. That's the only way out here. That's why he attacked. 'Cause I ain't lost one yet. To prove he was somebody he thought he'd try the quiet Yankee who ain't to be fucked with. Then the shank in his hand dropped when his wrist popped. Then that sharp tooth of a toothbrush was in his eye, and his eye and his neck and his neck. Then I spat on him and took a deep breath. Then I spat on him again and felt bad for it 'cause the part of him that had tried me was already sailing over my head. I sat easy so they wouldn't beat on me too bad before they sent me to the hole. They beat me bad. The last days before I died again the only thing I could see was the swell of my own face.

Then they threw me in.

Don't ever count. But you have to count. Nothing lasts in the hole. In the hell. But to pass the time before whatever is next I lick the floor and taste my own sweat. This body can't be killed. This body is stronger than it was before. I press the earth down every morning. I press it down first two hundred times. Now I press it down more times than I can count. I can't do many numbers anymore. I count to twenty-four and it's hard for me to remember what comes next. So I start again at one. Do it again and again. Do it again and again. It's hard for me to think of words that start with the letter J; you never know what will leave first. "Justice." I'm still here. "Jelly."

"Got any plans for today, Craft?" Lawrence says four times a week. He laughs and bangs his club against the iron door.

"Same old same old," I'll say. I'll laugh.

"Don't fucking laugh at me," Lawrence'll say.

Jungle.

This is what I do when I don't use my legs and arms to push my body up and down. I trace letters into the wall, and I imagine they glow in the dark against the nothing I see. I trace a letter with my finger. With my finger I can feel the rippling of poor paint against hard concrete. A paint that serves nothing. It is dark in my isolation. The hole is without light. I don't have eyes for twenty-three hours a day. That other hour, it is something I can't understand or know or tell you about. I eat a meal outside and my body shakes. But I trace the wall and my finger can make the wall glow. I draw a letter, then I draw a picture with my finger, and I might use only things that begin with the letter I've branded into the wall with my light. My index finger on my right hand and my pinky finger on my left hand can make the light on the walls. I went to hell and became an artist. That's what I do. I punch the air and the walls and push the earth down and my body up and feel the heat in my chest and breathe through my nose and out through my mouth and feel my body gathering. Gathering. Jump. Gathering the hell around me so that when they get me out of this I'll be not only an artist but a grim, great demon. They think I don't know what's happening. I know better than them. Simon J. Craft. I'm still here. I won't be later. I know that. They think I don't.

"Ey, Craft," Lawrence says from the other side of my door.

"Yeah."

"You're a disgusting motherfucker. You know that."

"I've heard before."

"You're lucky you're in here. You know that, right? Out there they'd tear you apart. Fucking rapist bitch."

"I been out there. My parts on me still."

"We'll see," Lawrence says.

"I guess."

He laughs a little. This was the time I thought there was nothing to lose. There is always, always a bottom you can't imagine. I didn't know that then.

Then one day he asked: "You know about the Influence Rods?" And from there hell erupted and I saw its true face.

Children of Incarcerated People

Dust and cinnamon.

The meeting included fifteen of the core organizers. There was water and tea and also a tin of tamales. Marta's aunt sold tamales to support workers who were being mistreated by local dairy farmers. They ate first. Mari took her time peeling the steaming banana leaf away and looked at the mound of love on her plate. It glistened tan and she poked a small hole with her knife to let some heat out. She resolved to enjoy the food that was there even though the reason they were there made her sick. Even though she was afraid of what she was thinking about doing.

This was the first meeting of the Coalition to End Neo-Slavery since Tracy Lasser had publicly stood up against the CAPE program. Their meeting today was about a protest that was planned for Thurwar's upcoming fight, which would be sixty miles away at the Renshire Stadium outside of Old Taperville. And now that Tracy Lasser, an Old Taperville native, had made national news, the protest was expected to be one of the biggest actions against CAPE ever. The Coalition to End Neo-Slavery had been invited to demonstrate alongside a growing number of anti–hard action-sports groups and abolitionists. Tracy's incredibly human display had injected new life into the fight; the world had been reminded of just how fucked it was for the state to murder its citizens in this or any other way. As such, the soldier-police were predictably increasing their presence around all Chain-Gang All-Stars events and many politicians had already appeared before holo-streams to implore nonviolence. An absurd thing for the murderous state to plead for, but, as always, the massive violence of the state was "justice," was "law and order," and resistance to perpetual violence was an act of terror. It would have been funny if there weren't so much blood everywhere.

But Mari was trying to focus. It felt especially important to see through what she had started. She was the one who had given Thur-war the note telling her what was to come. She had touched a woman who had not only known her father but who had killed with him. All she remembered of the man they called Sunset Harkless was that he smelled like dust and cinnamon. That and that he'd sometimes throw her high up in the air before catching her when she was too young to tie her own shoes. Her father, a man she hardly knew, had commit-ted murder. He had committed sexual assault. She was ashamed to have come from him. And the hard truth was, despite the work she did, the work she believed in, she had not been sure she wanted to see her father free in the world. She had not wanted to have him appear in her life. She had not wanted the world to know she was his daughter.

And then he'd died and all she'd had left was dust and cinnamon and the feeling of flying, then falling.

She had seen Thurwar's eyes and felt so clearly that she had been seen too. She had been seen by a woman who had loved and cared for her father, a man who had done incredible harm. And now she wanted to help that woman, a woman who had also done great harm, just not to her, as much as she'd ever wanted anything.

Her stomach churned and she poked another stab into her tamale just as Nile found her. He smiled weakly and took his seat on the floor near her legs; the couch had already been filled by Kendra and Pracee. They'd start soon. She watched Nile open his own tamale and put a bite in his mouth too quickly. She laughed loudly enough for him to hear as he tried to suck in cool to ease the hot he'd eaten. Nile could be funny sometimes, even if he was constantly a few moments away from annoying her. But more important, he was earnest, and she didn't know many earnest men.

Kai leaned over Jess, who was also on the couch, and tapped Mari on the knee. "You ready?" The coalition was explicitly leaderless and was run instead by several committees and their chairpeople. There was an overall steering committee, though, and Kai, it was understood, was their unofficial leader. Other people's fear and grief often kept them from doing the hard things, and Kai seemed always to swallow hers, to move in ways that could make change. She'd brought community library partnerships to the local schools and had worked for years to sever the relationships between schools and police departments. She was a professor on and off, but she'd been doing advocacy work for the past three decades.

Kai was also Mari's aunt, although she'd been the one who'd raised her for almost all her life. Mari's biological mother, Sandra, was serving the sixth year of a ten-year sentence. A mandatory sentence. The arbitrary nature of the law, the way weight had decided her mother's life, kept Mari up at night. She grew well versed in the statistics regarding the children of the incarcerated. She'd become an expert on the criminal-justice system and the long-term effects it had on families. She remembered, with a particular resentment, a study titled "Nowhere Near as Bad." The author's thesis was that the children of incarcerated people were six times more likely to become "justice involved," a euphemism she'd languished over. But now look at her. She wasn't justice involved. She was involved with justice. Better than that, she was ready to involve a lot more people in as much justice as they could handle.

Sandra, who had been in and out of prison before her current sentence, avoided Mari as if doing her a favor. But when they had been together Mari had been short with her. Polite and distant. They'd hugged each other deeply, though, imagining what could have been for those moments of embrace before Sandra disappeared once again.

It took six hours to drive to the prison to visit her mother. She tried to get up there twice a season. Mari had graduated with a bachelor's in political science just three years earlier. At her graduation, Kai had been there holding a bouquet of congratulations. The keynote speaker, a virtual reality startup billionaire, gave a speech about how if they just "stayed the course" they'd become *leaders* of something. As if leadership were the end-all, be-all of human existence. As he spoke all she could think of was her mother, locked for years in a facility, and how, as a result of people like her mother being perpetually tortured—as a result of her justice-involved life—some CEOs, some leaders, were millionaires. Many of these private facilities had government contracts that were determined by the number of inmates incarcerated—more prisoners, bigger contracts.

But her mother would eventually get out. Her father was forever gone.

They'd had a funeral that was impossibly well attended. All of those people who had come to pay their respects to Sunset Harkless. They'd had posters. They'd wept. Thousands of them.

The speaker at her graduation had ended by pumping his arm in the air. "Be the CEO of you, then of the world!" he'd said breathlessly. He'd inspired himself as much as he had the crowd, you could tell. Mari had watched. She listened to the cheers without moving. Her classmates, overcome with the possibility that they too could be leaders, leapt into the air.

"Thank you! Congratulations!" There was an explosion of green and blue confetti. Tasseled caps shot into the air, then rained down. Mari had stayed seated, taken her cap off, flicked it gently so it rose just to the level of her nose before dropping back into her lap.

.   .   .

Now Mari looked back at Kai and nodded through a mouthful. She swallowed. "Yeah, go for it."

Kai always seemed ready for whatever came next. Mari loved but sometimes almost resented her for how much she was not her mother. Kai wasn't addicted to anything easily observable. She was in control of herself always. She trusted herself above anyone else. Her brown skin was creaseless, and although she was over twenty years older than Mari, people often asked if they were sisters. Not as a way to compliment

Kai, but as a genuine inquiry. Kai was Mari's emergency contact on everything. She was Mari's mother as much as anyone.

"All right, everyone." The room quieted with a quickness that made Mari feel a heat in her throat. She sipped some of her water from the glass. "Today we're going to talk about the direct action we're planning for the upcoming entertainment lynching.

"Before that, I'm sure we all saw how sister Tracy Lasser stepped up and used her platform to amplify our cause." The room broke into a quick, honest applause.

Mari watched Nile slap his hands together.

"The fight against entertainment lynching has returned to the center of our national conversation and it presents a great opportunity to show solidarity with folx both inside and out of the system. We want to take the chance to show them not only that this is unacceptable, but that we will not allow it to continue.

"I want to acknowledge too what happened in Vroom Vroom. Clearly there are people who believe they deserve to watch murder and they hate us for fighting against that. I understand how frustrating it is to see that. I was there with all of you. I'm just now walking without a limp again," she said with a laugh as she made a fist and slammed it playfully against her hip. She'd strained it somehow in the brawl.

"As we've said over and over again, that kind of thing is not what we are about. I know that defense is not violence, but I want to make that clear in all of our minds just in case there's any question. We aren't any more effective because some idiots wanted to fight us. In fact a lot of the work we meant to do that day got lost in the fighting. And it was a difficult day to be sure. Especially considering the recent loss of Shareef, who was my sister's husband and Marissa's father. But what is essential to remember is we are fighting to support a movement. We are in opposition to institutional slavery, torture, and murder.

"Now we have another massive action ahead of us, this time led by Tracy Lasser herself and some organizers out of Los Cielos. I have here a short holo that Tracy's sent widely, an open invitation. Many of you will have already seen it—it's gone viral in the past few days. Nile, could you turn it on now?"

Nile opened his laptop and pressed a button on the metal projector ring he sat next to the computer. Kai moved to turn off the lights, and then Tracy Lasser was there in the room with them.

"My name is Tracy Lasser and I'm here in front of you now because enough is enough. I come not as a sports analyst today but as a concerned citizen and as an abolitionist. We are at an impasse. America has the highest incarceration rate of any country in the world. We cling to the archaic and destructive practice of using death as a penalty for crime, when most countries have abolished the death penalty altogether. But rather than follow the lead of the rest of the world, we've gone in the exact opposite direction. Under the guise of economic stimulus and punitive prevention, we've allowed the state to administer public executions as entertainment. We've lost our way, but we lost it long before hard action-sports like Chain-Gang All-Stars.

"I'm ashamed it took me this long to stand up against this system. Hard action-sports are just one piece of what must be changed. I know sports, and murder is not sport. Murder is not justice. Confinement is not justice. Our system is evil. All hard action-sports have only exacerbated that fact. I said I'm an abolitionist. I'm going to call on the great Ruth Wilson Gilmore to remind us exactly what abolition is. 'It is meant to undo the way of thinking and doing things that sees prison and punishment as solutions for all kinds of social, economic, political, behavioral, and interpersonal problems.' Chain-Gang All-Stars and the CAPE program must end. But our entire system needs to be reimagined as well. That is what we're fighting for. That is what must be undone so that we might create new systems, new ways of organizing that don't facilitate the death of our people.

"If you are tired of sitting by while your people are killed, join me. Join us for the first of many actions Project Undoing will be taking in Old Taperville. We will show up en masse and let them know that there will be an undoing."

Tracy's voice was clear and precise. Clearly she was drawing from her broadcast training, but there was a human edge to her voice that Mari had generally found to be absent from news shows.

"For specific dates and times regarding the coming protests, please visit the Project Undoing website and join us in making the world a better place."

Kai turned the light back on. Tracy was there for a moment longer, more a ghost than before, and then she disappeared entirely.

"I'd like to make a motion to open the floor to discuss the Coalition to End Neo-Slavery's potential participation in the Old Taperville protest," Kai said.

"Seconded," Mari said.

"Those in favor," Kai called. And all the hands in the room shot up.

Vega

Three days of Marching and restful evenings behind them, and Thurwar's knee ached. She thought of the time when she wasn't quietly holding this soreness, back before the world knew she was one of the greatest Links of all time. Hardly anyone had made it as far as she had, and even fewer had done so without any help—everyone knew that Nova Kane Walker had been shepherded to High Freedom by the producers, so that fans could see that the promise of freedom was real.

Yes, Sunset had almost done it the real way. His second stroke of great luck had been the Chain merger that had brought him and Thurwar together. From then on, they'd led together, kept each other alive. He'd been an honest man and had asked that they work together. But he'd slipped through her fingers.

So now Thurwar was alone at the top. A lot of people still thought Bishop had been better than her, she knew, even though she'd killed Bishop. And Bishop wasn't even the kill that had cemented Thurwar's legacy. That had been Lady ReckLass, the second Colossal Link she'd taken down.

ReckLass[*] was also the reason that Thurwar's knee ached. When she'd swung to finish ReckLass off, the other woman had been kneel-

---

[*] Low Freed Link. Rachel "Lady ReckLass" Nape. Ranked Colossal.

ing and gasping on the ground. But somehow, in that moment, she'd mustered the life force to ram her mace, Vega—formerly Bishop's weapon—into Thurwar's left knee. The blow had been strong because ReckLass was strong, only a handful of fights from High Freed, and unlike Bishop, ReckLass had wanted to live, very badly. Thurwar knew that. Before the match had begun, Thurwar had looked at Lady Reck-Lass in her Keep. The other woman had been staring at her with a kindness and a fury. She wasn't appraising her, or judging her, but accepting her for who she was, wholly. It was a kind of love. It surprised Thurwar because she had decided she hated ReckLass. Leading up to the fight, she had focused on the mace, on Vega, which Reck-Lass had acquired after Thurwar had killed Bishop. When the most popular Links were Low Freed, their weapons would go onto the Blood Points market. And when Lady ReckLass had chosen Vega, Thurwar had taken it personally, as if Melancholia weren't satisfied with haunting Thurwar's dreams, she wanted to strike out again in the real.

After that match, Thurwar was thee rising star among a small group of rising stars. But still, for a long while, people screamed "Fluke" at her from the stadium, from the nosebleeds all the way down to the seats that cost as much as a few car payments. Thurwar missed those days. When she'd let the people's words lift her. She'd used their animosity to keep herself tethered to the world. Their anger was an enemy she could focus her hatred on, that allowed her, briefly, to forget her guilt.

She'd wanted to prove them wrong. And she had. Then they became her soldiers; she was the general of an army she despised. But for a long time, she'd played the game, played the part they expected of her. She'd given braggadocious speeches, she'd crushed skulls with flair. They'd come long ways to see her and, sometimes, she'd truly felt like she couldn't let them down. And it was a fact that their support, their overwhelming energy, translated into something, an advantage of spirit on the grounds. And that kept her playing the games, made her believe at times that she was who the people thought she was.

Staxxx had broken that cycle of deception. Staxxx was real and gave Thurwar something true to focus on. Once Staxxx had settled into her life, Thurwar found it easier to shed the persona she'd created. She spoke less and less before fights. She stopped engaging with fan mail. She stopped giving them anything other than the carnage that was keeping her, and by extension, her Chain, alive. Staxxx gave her a new reason to live.

Thurwar turned now to check on the Links. Rico still beamed with excitement from their meeting. Sai and Ice and Randy Mac were chatting about sports they used to play, when they were athletes of a different kind. Gunny was brooding and Walter Bad Water looked as lost and afraid as always. And Staxxx was there speaking to him, trying to make him laugh. Staxxx was there, beautiful. The woman she loved. The woman who had killed her best friend.

They Marched.

The Chain continued with Thurwar at the head of their great circle, the Anchor trailing slowly behind her. They began playing one of their Marching games, as they had been doing on Marches for a long time, but there was a new kind of ease between them now.

Then Thurwar saw the Anchor rush past her and all the Links were forced to run to keep up.

"Fuck," Randy Mac said.

"Everybody get ready," Thurwar said. She felt the adrenaline rising up, masking her pain. "If you can, watch whoever is by your side. But protect you first. Rush them when we release." They ran past splintered wood and pressed and pushed out of any damp earth. It was important to watch the ground you stepped on.

They were being pulled to a Melee, toward violence, and she was ready.

The Board

It was a room of men and women. Twelve of them, all white, except for the vice president and director of public relations at ArcTech, who was also one of only three people in the room under the age of forty. His name was Kyrean and he was Forest's Black friend, a fact that they joked about when they'd link up for drinks or throw parties on Forest's yacht. The only other relatively young person was Lucas Wesplat, one of Forest's oldest friends and the ArcTech heir.

Forest sipped from his cup at the table. His father, George Woley, sat to his left laughing about something with the brownnosing broadcast director. Henry, one of the other Wesplat sons, was chairman, and so he did the chairman thing:

"I'd like to make a motion to approve the agenda."

The agenda hung in the air in front of them, projected from the boardroom table.

Forest scanned through it, trying to look engaged enough that he wouldn't embarrass his father but bored enough to convey to Kyrean that he knew this whole thing was bullshit.

Board of Directors of Chain-Gang Unlimited Agenda

Debrief on current trends and engagement

Revenue breakdown
Season 33 Chain-Gang All-Stars rule change review
Announcements

"Seconded," Forest's father said.

"Okay, so those in favor," Henry said. Forest had once seen Henry sniff/lick cocaine off the sweat-damp skin of three different people in a minute-long rush.

Several hands shot up, including George's. And what his father did, so did Forest. Though he noticed with interest and a jolt of embarrassment that Kyrean had not raised his hand.

"I think we need to throw the Tracy Lasser situation on the agenda," Kyrean said. Ky had been friends with Forest since their time together at university. It was pretty safe to say that their friendship was a large contributor to Ky's professional ascent.

Forest watched as Lucas frowned in Ky's direction. Lucas was Ky's boss. Forest called Lucas's father Uncle Rodge.

"We definitely plan to speak about that. Just didn't give it its own agenda item since it's not really as big a thing as some of the others that we're working on," said Mitchell Germin, the broadcast director. "We've been hard at work planning out A-Hamm's upcoming Hub City stay in Old Taperville, you know. Figuring out logistics for the farmers market event."

Henry looked around the room, saw that Kyrean's hand was now in the air above his head. "The ayes have it," he declared.

"But I'm glad Kyrean brought up the Lasser stuff," Germin continued. "We've been tracking the situation closely and based on our initial inquiries across most demographics, whatever she thought she was doing has only marginally affected viewership and potential viewership. In fact, we've seen some evidence that across our already engaged viewers, her outburst has deepened interest and willingness to participate in hard action-sports networks. Many survey participants who identify as regular viewers feel strongly that Tracy Lasser was significantly biased in her views due to her personal friendship with Hamara Stacker and . . ."

Forest looked over at his father, who was staring at Germin. It was extremely rare, Forest thought, for them to acknowledge in this room that there were people who hated them and what they were doing. They spoke about trends and outcomes. They rarely talked about the actual matches or said the names of the Links who made the whole thing go.

In this way, at least, Forest was not like his father. He knew what was happening. He knew the Links had names. He knew there was a reason Tracy Lasser had done what she'd done. And he knew that there were reasons he was doing what he was doing too. She believed punitive entertainment with rehabilitative potential was wrong, she believed in being soft on murderers and rapists. He believed justice couldn't be pretty for everyone. He believed the law always got blood on its hands.

"I told Gerald not to let that girl anchor," George Woley said. Gerald Haskinson, the CEO of SportsViewNet, was one of George's golf buddies.

Forest looked at Kyrean, hoping to commiserate, but Kyrean's eyes were locked on George with a clenched jaw and a look that made Forest feel hot. Lucas, he saw, was staring at the agenda.

"Regardless of what the focus groups say," Kyrean started, a new seriousness in his words, "we should put some real consideration into changing up the season thirty-three launch. So much focus on Staxxx and Thurwar. A match between the two of them—it's just not a good look right now." He seemed to be settling down a bit, appealing to logic rather than anything else.

"I actually agree, it's . . . it's not tasteful. I think we should reconsider the new rules too." Forest was surprised to hear this from the self-proclaimed most electric voice in hard action-sports, Micky Wright. A man who more than any of the others in the room was, to the world, associated with Chain-Gang and all that came with it. They were still moving through waters they rarely trod. Forest's father spoke about hard action-sports as the natural and obvious extension of his own work, corrections, which was what the family had built its fortune on. And when George Woley spoke about corrections, he spoke about a God-given responsibility to keep the public safe. He spoke about absorbing the world's negativity so that the good could shine through. At his last company speech he'd said, "A knife is always only so far from your neck. A man of ill intent is always only so far from your children, your daughters or sons." And that was the way George Woley thought of the games too.

"Tasteful?" George asked, confused.

"Yes, tasteful. You should get acquainted," Wright said easily and casually.

The room looked at George, and because he was sitting so close to his father, Forest felt their eyes calling for an adequate response.

"We aren't changing our plans because one bitch on SportsViewNet told me so. She can kiss my ass," George said.

Micky Wright shook his head and laughed. Kyrean stared hard at Forest.

"Maybe we can compromise somehow," Forest said weakly. His father seemed disappointed. "Compromise" was one of George Woley's least favorite words.

"Right," Lucas said.

Forest knew his father wanted to say something but saw him think better of it. This board of directors, together they decided the direction of the Chain-Gang universe. And while that universe was growing, made millions, for George Woley, it was just a small extension of a larger industry. But Forest was not his father; he understood that they ran what could be the biggest entertainment product in the world. That's what he was in it for. He wanted to be a part of something big, something new, something he could grow. An industry for him. He would worry about taste after he'd gotten out of his father's shadow. But for now he was grateful his father was there. This board was his incubator and George was there to groom Forest for the future.

"Well, if you mean perhaps there are opportunities for eliminations prior to the Season Launch, certainly there are ways we could potentially make things more"—he paused, searching—"add potential obstruction regarding Thurwar, given the current climate."

Forest smiled. At least this way, they'd have tried. He looked to Kyrean for affirmation of his success, but the other man's brown, clear skin and frowning fat lip were a portrait of disgust.

Forest looked away, toward his father. George Woley nodded.

This was the incubator. Forest would grow. Kyrean was his friend, yes. But was he really? No, he was an associate. A classmate. A person he worked with, who could always be replaced.

Melee

Don't be worried, baby, I won't let them touch a hair on your head," Staxxx said, running alongside Thurwar. The circle had become a single line, each Link beside another, shoulder to shoulder. What if Thurwar lost Staxxx, somehow, before she had a chance to tell her what she'd learned? The thought made her mind leap into focus. She tried to return to her body. The waking ache in her knee as she pressed off the ground, the weight of the hammer in her hands. She would not lose Staxxx. She would let anything happen before that.

"What the hell?" Rico Muerte said.

Thurwar looked over to see Mac was on it. Rico had, of course, already seen this sort of thing on the casts he'd watched, but it was a different thing entirely when you lived it. When suddenly the calm, steady hike becomes a run. When at the end of the run is a death, for you or for them.

"We went over this, now it's here," Thurwar said in Muerte's direction.

She looked at Rico and his golf club. Even he was hers. He didn't show any real potential, didn't seem to have much spark, but he was honest enough. He was hers, just like almost everyone running through the trees alongside her, suddenly, again, faced with the possibility of death. She would not let even Rico Muerte find Low Freedom.

"It ends when somebody does," Mac said to Muerte.

She knew what he would say next. That this was Melee, that they were about to come face-to-face with another Chain. That they would get to see everybody they would be Meleeing against before it started, that they would each call out somebody they wanted to rush. That probably Thurwar and Staxxx would rush the same person to guarantee a kill and end the Melee. That if you tried to run away you would be dragged back to within inches of the two Anchors in the center of the makeshift battlefield. Mac would tell him that whatever he did, if he ran he would definitely be killed, if not by the opposing Chain, then by Randy Mac himself.

"Remember our first time?" Staxxx said, running just ahead of Thurwar. Thurwar was aware of the pain in her knee, but as her body prepared her to create death, it was a shadow. A memory that was present and forgotten at once.

Thurwar said nothing, trying to see ahead of her, but smiled.

"No? Shame. Either way, happy anniversary," Staxxx muttered through a long frown, then a smooth grin.

"Hm," Thurwar said. "Did something important happen our first Melee?" She played along though she wanted to conserve herself. Even this run toward the Melee could tire a good Link out. It was one thing to run, and another thing to run with the tense, adrenalized force of battle.

"See," Staxxx said. Big grin. "You don't care about me."

During their first Melee as the Angola-Hammond Chain, Thurwar had whiffed a killing blow into the skull of a man carrying a huge wrench. Before the wrench could crack Thurwar's left orbital bone, both it and the hand holding it were on the ground. The scythe head had found the man's neck. Thurwar thought back to the time and considered how many of her best memories were dressed in blood.

In that first Melee, only six days after she'd joined, Thurwar had fallen in love with Staxxx. She loved her strength, how her body spurred survival.

Staxxx had appeared and suddenly she owed her life to another. She resented it. But it kept her alive. First it was the desire to repay that debt, which she had many times over, and then it was that she knew she had to stay alive to keep Staxxx alive and well enough to be who she was for the world. That was at least part of why Thurwar believed she was on the earth.

"I don't care about you," Thurwar said. "I love you."

Staxxx stumbled briefly, using LoveGuile to push herself off the ground.

Thurwar leaned into the giddy satisfaction of having caught Staxxx off guard. Thurwar rarely said the words, and she hoped she hadn't just said them now because she was afraid she wouldn't have another chance.

Staxxx smiled and Thurwar wondered if she could read her mind. She wished Staxxx could so she could tell her what had been rattling in her brain since Vroom Vroom.

It was Thurwar's twentieth Melee. For the last two months since her nineteenth, she'd felt a pang of guilt about the twentieth approaching. The GameMasters, the humans behind their chained lives, those people who sewed together story lines through matches and choreographed serendipity, they loved the obvious. They loved big numbers. Her milestones meant more danger for everyone on her Chain.

She also knew that some people thought those same GameMasters favored her. Were coddling her with easy matchups, like the boy she'd last crushed. As if anything about her life on the Circuit could be easy. Twenty fucking times she'd suddenly been forced to free-for-all for her life. Nineteen times she'd seen and survived. When they'd talked stats, when she'd cared to argue in her favor, she'd reminded them of all the times she'd Low Freed Links from other Chains so that no one on her Chain had to be. Eight times it had been her hammer that had ended the Melee. Eight Melee ends. Eight. Bishop had only seen ten Melees her entire tenure.

She kept her breath even as she ran. She had seen people pant their way to death. She had taught the Links of A-Hamm how to follow the Anchor with purpose. She had shown them how important it was to breathe deeply, to see the ground and the world ahead of you. Sprained ankles got people killed. She was the one. She was the one who had done the most difficult thing in the world: survived. And still people challenged her. But was she greater than—yes. The answer was always yes, she was. Thurwar believed it was part of her purpose to be the greatest ever in a new hell. She was still trying to understand why.

They moved at the pace Thurwar allowed Staxxx to set and finally they were able to see the other Chain in the distance. In the moment of seeing those whom you must either kill or be killed by, you had to dismiss the innate appreciation you had for them as your fellow human beings. After so long on the Circuit, it was almost automatic for Thurwar. She and her Chain were people; these others were a problem to be solved.

They were nine by her count. She opened her stride. She wanted to be the one they saw first. She wanted them to imagine their skulls crushed by Hass Omaha. She knew they'd seen her highlights. She knew they, whoever they were, knew all the many ways she could destroy a body. She matched Staxxx and soon felt the Anchor repelling her. She was forced to stop. They stood in a part of the woods that had recently been deforested. Green on the grounds, fresh light all around them, no leaves or branches to hide it, or their opponents. They were standing right across from the U-Blockers Chain. From the look of them, U-Block could see her well.

The wide-open eyes. Then the visible smothering of surprise. Faint smiles she could almost make out. They were thirty yards apart.

Thurwar settled on a young woman who had to be under twenty. So far as Thurwar could see, she didn't have any primary, probably was holding a pair of scissors or something small and sharp somewhere in the pockets of her jean jacket.

"Denim," Thurwar said to Staxxx.

"Poor baby," Staxxx said back. As simple as that. Thurwar and Staxxx consigned this weak-looking woman to death.

"We're taking the denim jacket," Thurwar said. Mac and Gunny Puddles made eye contact and nodded. Sai gave a thumbs-up. Ice grunted that he wanted the blond man in the middle of their Lineup.

"Check," Thurwar said.

Sixty seconds until Melee.

Before Thurwar had taken charge of A-Hamm, Chains had wasted the seconds of stillness before the start of the Melee. Links had greedily kept their targets to themselves, hoping for the glory and Blood Points of a Melee finish. But organization was life.

"Green sweat," Sai said, pointing to a man with a gut and what appeared to be a police baton.

"Igloo, check."

They ran through their matchups and Thurwar scanned each one before she gave her approval. If she thought a matchup looked tough, she'd deny it and say go for someone else.

She herself kept her focus on the woman in the denim coat. After she was dead, it wouldn't matter who her Links had marked. And denim was going to die very soon. Thurwar could see that she wanted to put her hands in her pockets. She was barely a Survivor, Thurwar was sure. She knew four of the Links from the U-Block Chain. They were Logan Igloo, a Cusp; Killian Stills, a Reaper; and Qiesha Howler, who, last Thurwar had heard, was a Cusp but had gotten there in such a way that she'd made it to Thurwar's radar.

The final Link was the only one whom Thurwar considered a real contender: Raven Ways. Raven Ways was a Colossal too. As of last month he weighed 198 pounds. He kept his hair cut to a dark Caesar and wore a bandana with a pyramid on it. And tatted on his neck was the pyramid of Triangle Keep Bank. He, like Thurwar, used bolt leather. She thought she saw some of the material looping around his clavicle and creeping up toward his neck. He was left-handed, though he was working toward weapon ambidexterity, which Thurwar had already mastered. His halberd was named Chi-Chi. He held it in his right hand and the gold head of its blade pointed right at the A-Hamm Links. At her. They had never spoken, but she knew him as if he were a brother.

"Yo." She knew the sound of his voice from the battle cries he'd made after his wins on the grounds. "Thurwar," he said.

"Focus, everybody," Thurwar said to A-Hamm. It was not uncommon for Chains to yell things prior to the release into the Melee.

"Nah, for real, Thurwar," Raven said. "I think we got something you wanna hear, Blood Mama." Thurwar looked at Staxxx, who didn't take her eyes off Raven. "How far are you from getting to it?" he asked.

The Anchor announced that in seconds they'd be loosed upon one another.

"Just two weeks, birdie," Staxxx said.

"That's a beautiful thing," Raven said.

Thurwar didn't like the pleasantry. This was not how Melee began. Melee began with threats and ironic jokes that were also threats.

"It is," Thurwar said.

"I guess this is another present for you then." He moved his head to indicate he was relinquishing the floor to a man Thurwar would have picked had she not settled on the denim girl who didn't even know what to do with her hands.

"All you," Raven said.

Fifteen seconds, the Anchors warned. They spoke in absolute unison.

The man Ways had summoned to the front had a black bubble vest that covered his tan skin. He wore shorts and slip-on sneakers. He clearly was no better than a Survivor. His eyes. Anyone who'd been on a Chain as long as Thurwar knew what eyes like those meant.

"I know you," he said. "Thurwar, I've watched you for so long. I thought I could do this. You helped me. You showed me I could get out. You showed me it could be okay out here."

"You have ten seconds before one of you dies," Thurwar screamed across the field, parroting the Anchors.

"I didn't wanna die. But I didn't wanna be there. I couldn't stay in the cages. Now I don't wanna die, but I don't—I can't live like this."

Thurwar breathed in through her nose and out through her mouth, evenly.

"You don't have to do this!" the U-Blocker in the denim jacket screamed. She looked at bubble vest and Thurwar thought from the sound of her voice she'd maybe started to cry.

"I don't wanna die. But now I don't want to live," Vest said.

Melee, the Anchors said together.

"Wait, Thurwar," Raven Ways yelled. He dropped Chi-Chi and raised both his hands in the air. It made a soft thud into the ground. Two of the six HMCs in the air danced around him. "Listen. Please." Thurwar raised her arm to her side to keep her Links waiting.

"I don't want to die. But I can't live like this. I want you to live, Thurwar. The fact that you're in front of me right now, it's a sign. It has to be. I'm grateful to you, even though you lied to me. You made me think it was okay. But it's hell. Again." Thurwar saw that bubble vest was holding a knife. He took several steps forward. Thurwar gripped her hammer tighter. She watched him, thought about how every day she choked down the part of her that lived in her head and said the same things that he was saying aloud now.

"I can't live like this. And you can. I see that now." He cried heavy tears and heaved heavy breaths. He kneeled on the dead leaves and cut a quick deep frown into his neck. The wound dribbled, then slobbered blood. He fell over and writhed until Raven stepped forward to finish the deed. But Raven was pushed aside by the girl in denim, who was weeping now. She, more completely, slit the man's neck.

Melee complete, the Anchors said as they floated back to their respective Links. Thurwar looked at the dead man, at the Chain in front of her. Denim had red spots splattered on her skin and coat.

"What the fuck?" Muerte said.

"Jeez," Bad Water muttered.

Thurwar considered this man, too weak for this world, who thought he had gifted her something; in his final moments, this man had called her a liar.

"It is an honor," Raven said with a wave. He looked at Randy Mac. "Sorry 'bout it, my guy."

"We'll see," Mac said. Raven Ways was Mac's next matchup.

"We will. But we can't all see High Freedom," Raven said. He picked Chi-Chi off the ground and he and his Chain followed their Anchor away.

"What was his name?" Thurwar called after him.

"Alley Bye-Bye," Raven called.

"What was his real name, Raven?" Thurwar asked.

"Albin or some shit like that. I can't even tell you, LT," Raven said.* "He was gonna off himself sooner or later, he just decided once we started running for Melee he would take the fall. I ain't know he was gonna have a whole speech."

Thurwar considered this. The way the man had spent his last words on her, how many times she had been the last thing a person thought about.

---

* Albin "Alley Bye-Bye" Lofgren. Albin was what they called half-smart. Smart enough to know how to flip a little bit of this or that to a lot of money. Good enough to try to get his mom a house with that money, not good enough to ever see her live in it. He wanted a lot from this world; it disappointed him. Then disappointed him again. Then again. Low Freed. Age twenty-two.

Raven continued. "He was a fan. Glad he got to see you. I'm a fan too."

"Likewise," Thurwar said, stepping backward. "Learn everybody on your Chain's real name, Marquis."

Raven slowed, and both Chains grew tense. Raven was not someone who was told what to do.

"You right, LT," Raven said. "When you right you right." And then he turned around.

The A-Hamm Anchor continued to pull away toward the lowering sun while the U-Blockers retreated in the direction Thurwar and her Chain had just come from.

Thurwar said nothing. She tried to keep her breath easy though she felt ravaged with adrenaline. And so she said nothing and walked, and her Chain followed. She walked and was grateful and terrified. She walked and looked at her Chain, intact, because of her. She thought of all the misery and hurt that flowed from her. She felt heavy with burden though she showed none of it.

To Be Influenced

"The J stands for Jeremiah."

"What?"

"The J stands for—"

"Shut the fuck up, Craft," Officer Lawrence says.

"Please."

"Please what?"

"Please do not Influence me, sir." I have never meant a request so purely. There's fools that think the Influencer is some Taser. It ain't. To be Influenced is to be made to feel the most pain your brain can produce at once. To be Influenced is to have your neural pathways rewritten so that you can become a better vessel for physical hurt. It allows your brain to take more than it should ever. It changes you in ways I don't want to disco—

The black rod sticks into my neck and—

Then he punches me in the shoulder.

And my shoulder explodes.

I can feel the bone shatter, my tendons firing into the air. I—I—*

"I'm sorry!" I scream.

---

* Don't look down. Help me. Please. Help me.

I scream.

I look, terrified, at my shoulder. It's still there. And it is bloodless. Somehow, some way. The black dart is still in my neck. The Influencer. This thing in my neck is the lord of all. That I know clearly.

This is the black rod's hell. I'm in hell. Hell full of ugly angels.

"You don't think that's enough, Lawrence?" Angel 1 says from outside the door. The black rod, needle at the end, is still in my neck promising everything will never be well.

"What the fuck you care?" Angel 2 says. Angel 2 is what I know Lawrence is truly called. I see it now. He holds the black dart. Angel 2 is who I must serve not to die each day. I tell him all he wants to know so that he might spare me some kind light. But today he has chosen not to spare any.

"He's had enough today."

"You really love these rapist motherfuckers, don't you?" Angel 2 says.

"Rapist motherfucker" is one of my names. My other is Simon J. Craft, the J is for—

"Jump up in the air, Craft," Angel 2 says.

And I try to fly. I can't. My wrists are locked to the bed with metal cuffs. When I try to jump the cuffs pull on my wrists and my wrists know all the pain this universe has. I scream and it doesn't make anything better. If my screams could heal anything there'd be no sickness or strife in this world. Here, the Angels love to hear you scream.

"What's your name, muthafucker?" Angel 2 says.

"Rapist muthafucker," I say, lava pouring from my wrists it feels like. The spittle crawling down my lips is like claws tearing at my face.

"You shut the fuck up or I swear I'll knock your head off."

And sometimes they don't want you to scream at all.

I try to scream more quietly. The room smells like piss and my own wild pain. Angel 2 laughs.

"She probably screamed too and that still didn't stop you, right? Right?"

"I'm sorry," I say.

My name is Simon J. Craft.

"Why the fuck you always saying your name? You think that's funny?"

The rod sticking into my neck is tied to a cord that is connected to a shooter on Angel 2's waist. I don't know what parts of what I'm thinking come out to my tongue. Or if maybe the Angels can hear my thoughts. I try to think quietly for their destruction.

"What the fuck are you talking about?"

"No. Not funny."

"That's what I thought," Angel 2 says, and pulls the Influencer out of my neck.

"Thank you." Thank you. "Thank you." Thank you. "Thank you." Thank you. "Thank you."

"All right, muthafucker, don't try and suck my dick now."

"Thank you." Thank you. "Thank you." Thank you. My body is no longer glass. For this I am only gratitude. In the moments after Influence I don't remember who I am, or why I'm here, or what I did to find hell. But I am grateful for its end. So grateful. So grateful.

"You better be grateful, for all I'm helping you."

"Thank you, thank you."

Angel 1 watches from just beyond the door.

"Nothing Ruiz throws at you will ever feel half as bad as what you just felt," Angel 2 says. "You understand that?"

"Thank you, thank you."

"Imma have you so ready for these fights you have coming. You're gonna be thanking me the rest of your life."

The black rod is in his hands. He presses a button. The rod retracts into its shooter.

"Thank you." Thank you.

"Last week Ruiz whooped your ass. In two weeks we'll have the rematch. Then we'll complete the trilogy. If you win in two weeks, though—well, you better win."

Angel 2 pats me on my shoulder. I start to scream, but when the hand touches me it feels like a dull regular touch, not hell. Angel 2 squeezes.

"You have good strong traps. Make sure you're working out every day. I want you to do your push-ups, crunches, shadowbox for a couple of hours. If you win in two weeks we'll make sure you have at least four hours out of the hole."

"Thank you."

"You need to be thanking me every day of your damn life, bitch." He smiles.

"Thank you," I say. Smiling, not because I want to, but because after the Influence the face muscles do what they want for some time.

"That's what I like to hear, you sick muthafucker." And then Angel 2, Lawrence, leaves. I hear his laugh as it slides down the hall.

Angel 1, Officer Greggs, stands still beyond the door. He disappears, then he returns. I feel him there. He comes in. He unlocks me from the bed end. I can move, do anything I want.

I've already started to feel myself returning. This is how it goes. The last couple months, as they've put me in the prison fight league they've set up. It's not exactly an opt-in-or-out program.

Greggs looks at me. I roll my shoulders, my body returning to me. Mine again. He hands me a towel. I sit it by the bed, afraid to have anything touch me for the moment.

"There's people that rip their own eyes out after being Influenced one time," Greggs says. "You know that?"

"I understand it." And I do, very well.

"You know how many times he's done this to you?"

I shake my head. It's hard to say because even now as the pain is gone and I am forever grateful to not have that rod in my neck, once you've been Influenced it never really stops. Once you've been Influenced, you are always being Influenced. Some of us anyways. That's how it's been for me. Always waiting for it to come again.

"That was your sixth time," he says. "You have a legitimate cause to file a complaint. Do you know who you file complaints with?"

Sometimes I'm sure I can't be killed. Sometimes I'm not sure if I've already died.

"Lawrence," I say.

"Exactly," Greggs says. "What that means is that this is your life now. I don't know what else to say about it." He's also holding a new set of gray clothes in his hands. I always know what the angels are hiding in their hands. "It also means that if he tells you to win that match in two weeks, you better win that match. 'Cause it's getting stomach-turning watching this shit every couple of days. You understand what I'm saying?"

"Thank you," I say.

"Don't thank me. I'm not doing anything for you. I'm letting you know what is."

I don't say anything.

"I will say, though. The fact that you can still respond and shit after all that . . ." He raises a fist to me, and I raise my arm to hit knuckles against his.

"Your name is Simon Craft," he says. "You remember your name, I think you'll be okay." He drops the fresh clothes on my bed.

"Simon J. Craft," I say. He nods.

When he leaves I write "Simon J. Craft" into the walls. Over and over. I lie down and write it out into my eyelids. I have nightmares where my body explodes over and over in different ways. I feel all of it. When I wake up my jaw aches from smiling and frowning and all the ways the pain shapes my face.

There is no ring. Just a hall on the F block. Lawrence leads me there and we have to walk through half of general pop it seems. All those bodies just walking around, it's easy to forget what freedom looks like. Compared to where I stay, this is freedom. A lighter layer of hell.

"White bro look crazy," I hear them say as Lawrence leads me to where I'm to kill a man called Ruiz.

It smells like stink and iron, like something is dead and rotting.

Lawrence leans back to me and speaks into my ear so I can hear him. He isn't holding the black wand, so even as I walk toward a man that's waiting to kill, I know that the pain I feel will be of the earth and not of hell, and so I worry not at all. No worry in me. Joy even.

"If you win tonight, that's a week I promise you there won't be any Influencer. If you lose, I don't care what kind of shape you're in, you're gonna have a long night, you understand me?"

"Thank you," I say.

"I want you to try to hurt him, okay? Don't worry about him. That's what he's gonna be thinking too. And if you don't win today, you understand, don't you?"

"Thank you. I understand."

He looks forward and I know as well as anything in this world that I will not allow myself to go back to the black wand.

"You better."

"Why the fuck he smiling so much?" one of the men, a gray shirt and pants, says.

"That's not a smile," another says. "That's that shit."

"Oh shit," says a man so short he looks like a child. "Sorry, bro," he says to me, to the idea of me.

I look at them and they look down to the ground, or they stare as if I'm the animal they've always hoped to see. They stare like they want a reminder of what never to become.

"That's that Cheese Rash shit. They be cheesing like that after the Influence. That's fucked up," says a voice that comes from a face I can't see.

"You're next if you don't shut the fuck up," Angel 2 says, and the voice disappears. In the far end of the block they've put four orange cones on the ground. The bodies are arranged into a square. The ring is made of men of different colors, all wearing the same color. And then, next to each cone, there are the guards in tan and black and shining badges on their chests and weapons wrapped around their waists.

In the "ring," sitting on an orange bucket turned upside down, is Ruiz. In our first match a month and a half ago, Ruiz made it so my nose won't ever look the same. I woke up to Lawrence telling me the next day I really was about to feel the pain. And he was right. Whoever holds the black rod is always right. Remember this above all things you'll ever know. Remember this before you remember your own name.

The bodies move aside and then close like a door behind me. There's a bucket turned upside down there in front of me too. It's green. Lawrence presses my shoulder and all it feels like is a hand on a shoulder. With the black wand it would feel like molten power licking its way through the muscle. When it's gone everything is so easy. And so never to feel that again I am certain that Ruiz is a man I will kill.

"Three rounds. You win," Lawrence says in my ear, "and this week, no stimulation. Fuck him up, champ."

"Sorry," I say to him, and also to Ruiz, and also to all the demons here and in the world and in me that brought me here.

"Don't be sorry. I want him to be sorry. Get up, you're on."

A man who used to be in a cell across from me before they threw me into the hole is standing near the cone over Ruiz's left shoulder. He gives me a nod of recognition. I stand up and so does Ruiz.

A guard steps in the middle of the ring of bodies.

"Don't nobody move an inch from how y'all are now. That's a good eight feet either way. I want them to have room to work." At the word "work" the crowd of men cheers. It's an inexplicable *yeahhhhh* that comes because something they have been anticipating is quickly approaching.

Lawrence helps me take my shirt off. Ruiz does the same. He hasn't stopped looking at me. I'm probably smiling at him.

"Shut the fuck up," the guard in the center of the ring says. He's bald and small. Beads of sweat grow above his eyebrows.

"This is gonna be three rounds, three minutes each. We don't got all day to be down here and I know you dumb muthafuckers ain't great at math, but that's just nine minutes of fighting. Y'all will have a minute and a half between each round to catch your breath.

"All moves allowed. You can box or do that karate shit if that's what you want. If you wanna tap out you can't just tap out, you also have to scream, 'I'm a bitch!'"

The crowd hoots with laughter. Big laughter. The bald guard smiles at his own brilliance. Even in hell angels love to think themselves funny.

"That's a joke. Ain't no tapping out. This not even ten minutes, ain't no reason to tap.

"Y'all ready?" he says, looking at me and Ruiz.

"Remember, don't put your fists down," Lawrence says.

I nod and raise my fists.

"Let's do this," the bald guard says. He disappears into the ring of people. It's hot and the air is made mostly of the breath of these hungry men.

"Go," Lawrence says. And I go.

One step in.

Ruiz shuffles forward and throws a jab to test my guard. He throws another quick flash of bare left knuckles. I don't move at all for it. It's short. He throws a straight as he moves forward and I can almost read the word "CAPO" he has on his right hand. The same kind of punch broke my nose our last fight. This time it seems as though Ruiz is moving through some invisible bind. Everything seems slower than before.

I slip the punch and load to punch Ruiz hard in the liver. I pull back and try to rip my fist all the way through his body.

He makes a sound as if some small animal jumped from somewhere he didn't expect and surprised him.

His body feels solid but completely breakable. I try to punch through.

He gasps, stumbles back. There is a sound of cheering and movement and it seems the crowd too is a slowed-down film.

There is fear in Ruiz's eyes. It's a look that everyone understands even if they've never seen it before. The look makes me feel very briefly as though this is all there is. I almost forget what the black rod can do to a body. I love the forgetting. The right-here of Ruiz breathing quick breaths. He throws a big hook. This one is even slower than the straight, it feels like. I duck it and load up everything into an upper that I know will break Ruiz's jaw.

The crowd choruses his pain. A collective *Ohhh*.

Then I punch him again with a hook in the newly broken jaw. He looks dizzy, confused. His body acting on its own, he throws another quick straight. I see it coming and let it hit my face. I close my eyes and take in the feeling, which I know is pain but is so far from what the black rod does it's almost hard to tell.

Ruiz's punch feels like only a suggestion of pain, not anything like the real thing. The look on his face as he connects fills me again with what I quickly know is my new favorite thing in the world. His terror makes me forget the fear I always feel. And this delight is what I think about as I wrestle Ruiz to the ground, straddle him, and punch and break his face until Lawrence and the others pull me off him, and I am disappointed because as they pull me Ruiz's face is such that I can't see fear or anything else on it at all.

"Fuck, Craft," Lawrence says. "If I lose my fucking job for this . . . What the fuck."

"I'm sorry," I say. Back in my hell I leap down to his feet. Bowing.

Head on the floor. Hoping with all I am that he'll stomp me with his boots until I'm just a smear on the floor and not go for the black rod.

"No, you're gonna be sorry. If he's dead I promise you'll be sorry for the rest of your life."*

I know Ruiz is dead.†

Greggs says, "Your shift almost through, Lawrence, let's leave it." I run to my small hell's corner. Praying to slip through the concrete.

"Fuck that," Lawrence says. And I press farther and farther into the corner's marked scratches, lines of time. I cry into that wall, begging.

Lawrence leaves and the waiting is almost as sickening as what's to come. Almost but also definitely not. While he's gone, Greggs steps into my hell, through the door, and sits on my sleep space. He rubs his eyes as if he is very tired. As if he is the one who will be ripped apart soon.

"There's a way out, you know."

I look at him. Every inch of me thirsty for whatever freedom he might be speaking of. I cry into the corner.

"It's fucked up to have a grown man become what he's making out of you. There's a way for people like you to at least be somewhere else."

"Please," I beg.

Every second is a second that Angel 2 is not there, and so I try to stretch them. I try to pull time slow, the way it felt as I smashed the life out of Ruiz.

"There's a place you can go. You'll die, but it will be easier than this," Angel 1 says.

"Please. Anything," I say.

"Can you act right? You have to be right enough in the head to sign a paper. Say yes to some questions. You have to know your name and be able to sign it. You think you can do that?"

"My name is Simon J. Craft," I say.

I hear the stomps of Angel 2 at the hall's end. Men howl and bang as they always do, but I hear his boots perfectly.

---

* He was right.

† His name was Angelo Ruiz, his family were those who kept him fed, safe, who raised him; they made him tough, taught him to fight, they made money. They had opps, they defended their territory. He could have walked, but you don't sell out family.

"Tell me again," Angel 1 says.

"Simon J. Craft," I say.

"If you can remember that past today you'll have a way out."

"No," I say. Past today means living through Angel 2 again. Please, I think. "Don't let it—"

"Fuck you doing?" Angel 2 says as Angel 1 places his hands on his thighs and stands up.

"Just making sure he don't bash his head open waiting on you."

"Don't even worry about that," Angel 2 says, spit shining on his lips. "This one's a fighter."

And then for the next three hours everything I am becomes was—

The Art of Influence

They broke their little legs. They bloodied their little hearts past the point of exhaustion. The rats. The rats ran themselves dead. This happened, and then it happened again, and then Dr. Patricia St. Jean found herself feeling a pressure she'd never felt before. Feeling was her specialty, the science of sensation was her whole bag, but this was not what she'd imagined, and she knew, as she looked down at the rats who'd felt such pain that they'd ended their own lives to avoid its ever happening again, that she had stumbled onto something powerful and precisely evil. It was a long way from where she'd started.

When she was eleven and still in Trinidad she'd watched her father wither away. He'd been struck by a cancer of the bone. Deep inside his hard parts something had begun to eat him. During the panels she would chair many years in the future, she'd warm the crowd by saying, "Running and fetching his water, listening to him groan, I developed a pretty good bedside manner for an eleven-year-old." And the crowds would do something between laughing and *aww*ing and she'd know she had their attention.

But as a child, she had watched him wither. And she had fetched glasses of water and taken note of the exact day he could no longer bring the glass to his own lips.

"Patty, Patty-Girl, I've dropped the damn thing," he'd said.

She cleared the glass from the wooden floor with a broom. The shards were still slick with water as she dropped them into the bin. She kept the largest shard for herself and wrapped it in a dishrag. Then she returned to her father, who was propped up by pillows on the bed. She held her hands around his and helped feed him fresh water that quenched his thirst, yes, but did nothing for the pain he felt constantly.

"Thank you, Patty-Girl," he said. He took two gulps, then vomited on her and his hands and his chest. She wiped him off, helped him get another two gulps down, then he told her to go so he could rest.

She washed her hands, then went to her room, where the glass dressed in a dirty rag was lying on her bed like an invitation. It said, Pain for pain. It asked her to join in a communion of feeling. Her father groaned anew, and she pulled her right foot up and let it rest on her left knee. She chose her leg because her father, in the state he was in, the two things he could survey well were the hands and arms that fed, clothed, and bathed him. She'd already begun doing push-ups daily to better shoulder the burden of carrying her father to and from the bathroom for each of his four weekly bowel movements.

He made another low sound, then finally released into a full "Ah aye," loud even in its breathlessness. She preferred when he didn't hold back his hurt for her. To know that he was trying to keep anything at all from her made the depth of his pain too unimaginable. That is, he already seemed to be suffering as much as a human might; to know that even a small fraction was mitigated so that his daughter might feel as though he were okay—

"Ahhh, fuck," she heard her father say. And that was when she made the first cut. She cut along her right calf with her glass in a straight line. Surgical and simple. She fought to watch it happen, refused to close her eyes as her father's pain sang through the hall. Pain, she knew from a young age, had echoes. Pain was in the body, but pain also seeped into the walls. Pain started in the body, but it latched to a soul and tried to take it. Pain could disappear people; her father's pain, for example, had disappeared her mother. She drank the feeling in, pressed deeper. Pain for pain. His pain needed something to bounce off of. Her father's pain alone was swallowing them both.

As she dragged the glass the few inches across her calf she watched as the skin opened and saw the pink beneath before it flooded with red. She did not panic. She took her shard, her cutting glass, and placed it back in the rag, then she put the suddenly sacred parcel under the bed. She palmed the blood coming out of her and went to find a fresh towel to cover the new wound. She paid attention to the feeling she had with each step. The stretch and hurt as she flexed her foot. She passed by the living room, the place that had become her father's, as she went to grab a new towel. She felt the tickle of blood spilling down past her ankle as she peeked in to check on her father.

"Need anything, Daddy?" And it hurt to ask this, because of course he needed a new body, a new mind, a new soul, one not so tarnished by the pain he'd been drowning in for so long. He needed everything.

"Thank you, Patty-Girl," he said behind gritted teeth. "I'm okay."

She looked down. There was a shallow smearing of blood. She pressed her toes just a bit, hiding her leg, only her head peeking in, and felt the pull, the re-tearing of the cut she'd made.

"You don't have to say that, Daddy," she said.

He didn't look back at her. His eyes were closed. But he took a breath that felt like a deep interrogative glare.

"Okay," he said.

And then she walked off, her footprints pressed and dried behind her. She got a towel for herself, then cleaned the floor as her father approximated sleep. He continued to groan and even weep until many hours later he fell asleep for real.

They said he was in remission.

She understood that was something to celebrate but when she looked at her father his pain was still everywhere. It stuffed the air completely, leaving no room for jubilee. Patricia, her aunt Lottie, and her father had been waiting for the new nurse. They had twenty-six hours of home care to spread through the week. They needed, of course, far more, but the insurance companies had made it clear that was not going to happen. She was thirteen and it was her job to manage her father's health.

"Allyuh doing well?" the nurse asked.

Patricia sat in a chair beside her father, who was whimpering. She imagined the glass in her room and took a breath.

"Ogosh," Patricia said under her breath, then louder again. "Does he look well?"

Her aunt, who checked in on them twice a week, pinched her arm and then nodded as the nurse explained that the treatments had done the job of killing the bone cancer, but unfortunately, they'd left him in this terrible state of health, an unintended side effect.

"It's a neuropathy," the nurse said. As the nurse spoke she looked at Patricia's father with a kindness that made Patricia want to strangle her. "The damage to his nerves is what causes the discomfort."

There was such a wide chasm between words and all that they held. This nurse was calm, a new face to a continuing issue. She had heard these terms before, but something about that day, the ease of the woman's words, the fact that she seemed completely unbothered by her father's dying right there beside them. She felt a searing happening. She didn't know then that she was being handed the keys to her life.

"Thank you, Doctor," Auntie Lottie said.

Patricia had wanted to say, *No, this woman is not a doctor,* but she needed Lottie to give her money for groceries, to keep visiting her twice a week.

"He says it's like fire," Patricia said instead. "I know it's the neuropathy, but what can we do?"

The nurse looked at Patricia, and her aunt told her to go to her room. She almost ran there, grateful because she knew the answer to her question was a simple one. There was nothing that could be done. All the science and doctors in the world had no idea how to help her father. She opened a box full of long-abandoned dolls and took out her glass. She pulled her leg free of the stockings she wore as part of her school uniform. Underneath them her leg was lined like a zebra. She was deliberate and immediate as she cut herself. She sucked the feeling in. Felt it and knew it and let it flow through her. The feeling of being cut open was what she knew best. The feeling of being cut open was her best friend. The feeling of being cut open was the feeling of her life. The feeling of being cut open was—

When her father died she was, of course, the first to see it. And after the heat and the terror and the cutting open, she felt relief. She felt a surge of relief that she'd feel guilty about, she knew, forever.

In her first meeting of her anatomy lab class, before they had the cadavers in front of them, the leader of the lab class asked them a question that many doctors would ask them over the years they'd spend in school. This was the icebreaker, and because she was not afraid Patricia learned early on that she was often the one who would cleave through first.

"Because I want to end suffering. I want to change how we feel. I don't want people to feel pain."

The professor was a white man in his sixties. He smiled warmly. Condescendingly, yes, but a warm fatherly condescension.

"One thing I can promise you is there will always be pain. There will always be suffering. But we will try our best to mitigate it. We try our best to help. How does that sound?"

Patricia blinked at him.

"I liked what you said" were the first words she heard out of his mouth.

He was a year or two older than her and his greenish eyes seemed honest. "My name is Lucas," he finished, and offered a hand. "Lucas Wesplat."

They were both just starting down paths that everyone had told them were necessary. Still human essential. Real doctoring was a work of creativity. They'd make someone proud. They'd save.

"Hello," she said.

"Where are you from?" he asked, still smiling, still trying to be friendly. "I love your accent."

She had perfected her American accent long ago and regarded him closely.

"I'm Trini," she said. Short 'n' sweet was her way. "Short 'n' bitter" was how her auntie called it.

"I love the islands. I've been with my family a few times."

"'Ave you?" she said with a smile. She was human too.

After they were done Lucas ran his fingers over her body. He worshipped her skin with his hands and lips, and she took it in. When he caressed her thigh down past her knee she was so consumed in the reverie of herself as presented by this man that she didn't stop his hand from traveling down her tibia.

"What happened?" he said. And the smoother pace of his fingers became staccato and clinical, even as he tried to be sensitive. It sounded as though he was genuinely concerned, and that made her furious.

"Please leave," she said.

"What? Why? What is it? I'm sorry?"

She said nothing. She remained perfectly still in the room and imagined all she'd had to be to get there. To be in the exact same spot that Lucas had been carried to.

"It's a lot of life," she said.

She meant that her leg was a reminder that she was still working on. A reminder that pain was still rampant in the world and despite how far she'd come, she'd done nothing to change that.

"That doesn't mean anything," he said. He didn't chuckle but he smiled, she could tell, even though her eyes were still closed.

She'd graduated at the top of her class. Lucas had graduated. And yet this was the conversation being had.

"We have a chance to do something beautiful," Lucas said. They met for lunch in an E-diner. A rolling contraption that looked older than her brought them trays of American breakfast foods. Eggs and pancakes and strips of bacon. They had dated on and off during medical school and had residencies in different states. He rode jets back and forth from his residency to hers. He didn't mind that his carbon footprint was more than ten times that of an average person. He'd hold her close and say, "It's worth it for you." And they'd joke about it the way people joke about a coming cataclysm, right until the point when it swallows their own and suddenly it isn't as funny in the same way but is also, in some ways, funnier.

"Just think about it," he continued with a face full of pancake. "You'll have your own lab, resources up the asshole. You won't have to ask for anything."

"I won't have to ask anyone except you," she said. She didn't touch her food but could already imagine the floor plan of station one. She could already see how she'd model the axon stimulation process so that the rest of the lab could re-create it. She could see herself changing the world.

"You already know you don't have to ask me for anything." He reached past his orange juice and touched her hand. "You know me."

Patricia sipped her water.

And though she understood the body so well, she had learned to accept her brain's tendency to turn against itself. She decided to go to therapy finally, because one of her lab techs had said it had changed her life. She went to the first session smiling, and three sessions later she had told this stranger things she'd never told anyone else in the world. "What are you punishing yourself for?" the woman had asked calmly. And Patricia had unraveled there in the soft chair. She stopped cutting herself for some time. Then she cut herself again. And then she stopped for a longer time.

As she looked at the bloodied rats, she let the feeling of creating something so far from what she wanted settle over her. She had been able to isolate the complete peripheral nervous system of the mammals. She could influence the small fibers, the body's pain receptors, while simultaneously increasing the brain's ability to receive signals. She had known this for some time, and in the sterile white and gray of her sprawling lab she often rested in the knowledge that she understood those fiber sensory nerves in ways no other human had before, or even could. The lab had all but eliminated Parkinson's, she'd found courses that quelled violent Tourette's, but those weren't her project. Those were not her purpose, and every honor she was awarded felt like a growing hole that could only be filled by her cutting glass.

Without lab coats and only covering their faces with masks, completely eschewing lab protocol, Lucas and his father, Rodger Wesplat, walked in. She took a breath and summoned a smile for them so that even though her face was covered, her eyes would lie the feeling.

"Hi, Rodger," she said.

"Heya, Patty." Even at his age, Rodger was a bulkier, broader man than Lucas. Though they had the same strong jaw and moved with the same air of ease, the product of many generations of familial wealth.

"Hi, Patricia," Lucas said, and he seemed almost to struggle to look at her as he did. "How's it going?"

Given the circumstances, she did not bother answering his question. The thrum of her machines whetted her silence further.

Finally, Rodger spoke. He wore a suit that cost several months' rent for the apartment she'd slept in during her residency those years before. "Patty, you've been doing some groundbreaking work, I hear."

"We've worked hard. Yes."

"And it shows. If I'm understanding correctly, you've already made some breakthroughs that can be used out in the world."

She smiled at this. "Oh no, Rodger. If you think anything I'm doing right now can be used out in the world you are not understanding correctly at all."

She pulled her goggles so they sat on her forehead.

"Is that right? Why don't you help me understand? And don't sell yourself short. I think you've done some important work here. From what I understand you have a powerful nonlethal deterrent. A new kind of behavioral fixer. There's a huge market for that kind of thing."

She wanted to say there was no way he would ever understand.

"What we've done with the canvas project is try to mimic the peripheral nervous system, the nerves that connect the brain and the spine to the rest of the body, and in doing so, we've been able to study the extent to which we can stimulate feeling and sensory responses. We've only just scratched the surface with live testing and we know for certain that we can get coordinated neuron responses of some kind, but at the moment we lack the facility to be"—she paused for the word that would fit best—"selective regarding the exact nature of the response."

"What she's saying, Dad, is we've been trying to think of the body as a canvas for feeling and we understand the borders of that canvas but can't control the paint yet. We can't control what happens. Not yet anyways."

"I understand what she's saying. It's an incredible thing already is what I'm saying. Having limited control thus far has led to repeatable responses, no?"

"Right now it isn't ready."

"No great problem is solved on the plane of its original conception. You've created something powerful and useful already."

"It isn't ready."

"Well, we'll let the board see and we'll talk it through."

"There's nothing to see. It can only destroy the nervous system. Make pain you couldn't imagine. You aren't understanding what I'm saying. It is the opposite of what we are trying to do and to not push farther—I won't allow it. When you force things, pain comes first. The worst you can imagine. Ease, pleasure, those take nuance and time and understanding. I will not allow you to disrupt this process." Her composure had escaped her, and she was yelling now. She regretted how clearly she'd said the truth.

"Patty, you've done beautiful work here," Rodger said, and began to turn around, "but remember, it's ArcTech that decides when and how what you do here will see the world." He turned and left. She thought of pulling a scalpel from one of the motorized dissection arms and planting it into Rodger's neck.

"Don't worry, Pat," Lucas said, then disappeared, trailing his father as he had for his entire life. Don't worry, he said. As her life's work was being stolen from her. As she was being used to do the exact opposite of ending pain.

When the soldier-police came to her door she was ready for them. She sat in a comfortable outfit, sweatpants and a crewneck. She was barefaced and had braided her hair. They knocked hard, then broke through her door, and she was sitting on a chair waiting for them.

"Are you Patricia St. Jean?" the man screamed at her, pointing a rifle in her face. Three more men flooded into the apartment.

"I am," she said.

"You are wanted for arson and attempted murder regarding the lab located at One Hundred Olier Way. You're coming with us."

Yes, she had done it. She'd burned the seeds of the most astonishing work of her career. She hoped she'd destroyed enough.

She paid attention to the feeling. The sinking and more sinking. The dread. The knowing she'd done her best to do what was right.

She stood up. They rushed her into clanging metal handcuffs.

"Miss," one of the officers said, "is your leg bleeding?"

Sing-Attica-Sing

I be so glad . . .
  When this sun goes down . . .
I be so glad . . .
When this—

"Aye, nigga, ain't nobody tryna hear your slave-chorus ass today, my boy. Gah-damn."

Sun goes down . . .

"I'm forreal, my nigga, you on some slave-ship, crazy shit and that shit is tired, bro. You here now. That shit old, cut that shit out, my nigga. Nigga got one arm and think he Kunta Kinte, gah-damn."

It the young one they call Razor Edgerrin. Young and tough and smart, but he got something to prove to everybody 'cause he got something to prove to himself. I ain't got nothing to prove, and I been silent so long, sometimes I don't recognize it's me making the noise I'm hearing 'cause I'm listening more than anything else.

We are Marching. The Anchor, the Big Warden, the rising all-powerful stick of you-not-going-nowhere in front of us pulling the way.

We side by side making a frown or a smile depending on how you look, a mouth of bodies. A frown or smile, and the eyes of this great face we make is the miles and miles we must walk.

I'm used to being side by side with somebody but also used to having work to do to cut the closeness. On the March, after the food flies in from the sky, we get up and walk side by side by side though grass and dirt and mud and rock. I pick the clothes I want to take with me. I got a few now. They send them. Hardly got to spend my death coins. And what I leave is waiting for me at the next Camp. I think of how every day they pick up and drop, pick up and drop, and we walk the miles between. The killing games something else.

"Thank you," Eraser Ed One says. The Erasers a triplet of skinheads. An actual brother, brother, brother, brought on the same crime. They don't talk much to anybody not white, but their skin screams their feelings loud. They got swastikas on them like some God, the chef of all, meant to sprinkle a pinch of hate and the cap fell open and they got stuck with a bucketload.

"You shut that mouth up too," Razor says to him. He Black as me. "Damn."

He looks at me with a smile trying to say even though he screamed on me, he not an asshole, and he not. He trying to say he on my side, but angry 'cause he walked so many miles and he tired. He trying to say I remind him of something not good that he's come from.

This the Sing-Attica-Sing Chain. Supposedly Sing-Auburn-Attica-Sing now, but that don't have the same ring.

Sing right there in the name, a fit for sure.

I got to them some months ago, waited for them at the evening Camp. An actual fire waited with me in a dry land not far from the ocean. The faraway sound of the waves made me feel calm even as the floating eye in the air near my forehead searched for fear on my face.

They'd driven me in a dying sun to a campsite and I waited for the rest of the Sing-Attica-Sing Chain to find me. My new family was how Sawyer said it. When them white boys seen me—and they was the first to see me—they were disappointed. Another nigger, they thought. I seen them, and had to look again, make sure it was three bodies with the same faces. Only the placement of the hate marks on their bodies tell them apart. I still don't know this one from that, they might all as well be called Ed.

In our smile below the Anchor, Ku, Klux, and Klan March on the far-right side. Here we walk in a line 'cause everybody might kill somebody all the time. When I have the space in me, I sorrow for them.

"Fuck up," Eraser Two says back to Razor.

I seen them kill for less than this out here. On God, they've lost their way. Three nights back a man called Smiley Ruff woke up in heaven. Strangled. Nobody said a word about it. Razor told me it was the Erasers. They ain't like dead man's perpetual grin. Smiley was as white as they is.

I hold my spear loose but ready. "Stay ready so you don't have to get ready," the Book of Mother Young, chapter 1, verse 1.

Razor stands beside me and to his right there's Bells. Kind enough, Bells shouldn't be in a place like this. Then again, she killed and keeps killing, so maybe this place is just the right place for her. She Black and white, so she Black. Bells got a machete that ain't a joke. She found herself a Reaper like Razor. Like me soon enough. To her right it's Eighty, who been through two double matches with Razor so they tight. Eighty older than me but he's strong. Big shoulders, big-ass smile. Seen so much he skips right over the bad and laughs at whatever. He carries a heavy flail, a spiked ball on a chain. Heavy flail he named Heavy Flail. And I smiled when he told me so. They call him Eighty because he been inside longer than Bells been alive, according to how he tell it. He old for the games. But some say it's Eighty because that's how many men he knocked out back inside and the name stuck. Everybody got a name: a story of truths and lies.

On the end of the line to my left it's LouBob. LouBob they call him. He won't last long. You get a sense about these things pretty quick.

We March in a valley of grit and grass between mountains that tear up into the sky so high the weather at the peak is something different entirely than that at our feet. I don't know where in the world we are. The air is cool and fresh. It's a long way from cutting meat, but at some times it's not. Chapter 1, verse 1.

"You know what, Singer?" Razor says. "My headache gone. Sing that shit if you need to let it out."

"I'm good." I sing when I need to.

"I just want you to know you good to do that shit. I love that shit. That's my ancestors' shit, and I fuck with it. Cool?" Razor says.

"You got that Holiday in your voice," Eighty adds. "What's that other one you sing?"

"Bee-ba-boom-be-bap-type shit," Bells sings, and laughs. "What you know about Lady Day? Those the work songs. That's my people's songs."

I smile. Damn.

"Singer laughing, y'all," Razor says. "Look at that."

"I laugh regular," I say.

"Where?" Bells says, breaking forward to see me in my eyes.

I smile and don't say nothing else.

"How you quiet and loud at the same time, Singer?" Razor asks.

"You got a voice just for one thing, huh? Just singing."

"Everybody voice just for one thing," I say.

"What does that mean, Singer?" Eighty asks.

"Deadass," Bells chimes.

"It means what it means," I say. And they let me have that.

All walking. It's quiet for a little, then LouBob says, "Sometimes esotericism is a way of hiding."

Bells looks at him and says, "Shut the fuck up, LuLu."

And LouBob looks out at the miles ahead of us.

"I'm playing with you, Lou, damn."

The way it is it's us and the Erasers. Two tribes in the Chain. LouBob belongs to nobody because he won't last long. Everybody that makes it to see the Anchor has killed someone. And anybody that's killed someone can kill again. Anybody that hasn't might too.

After they first gave me this black spear I had a night's rest in a real bed in a real hotel. The huge M on my back still peeling. A new painting on my skin. In the hotel I got to have a meal of my choosing. Let my legs hang over the bedside and felt sheet silk tickle my ankles as the night took the day. I ate beef Wellington and roasted vegetable medley cooked in duck fat. This death row, make no mistake. I knew most don't make it past the first fight. It was four days since I left Auburn's medical facility. Some months since my arm got offered to the saw. I looked at the plate, the meat cooked right, its juice licking out onto the pastry it was dressed in. It's a food made for somebody that has a lot.

I thought to pray over the food, then laughed at the idea of it, then decided to pray anyways. I prayed for the food and for a voice and to always feel that I am a different person than that which would destroy. I am not somebody else. I am Hendrix Young, worst of man. A taker of life. A jealous human. A wretched coward. Soon more of a killer. I used my knife to cut into the meat. One hand is an inconvenience. Meat slid. I tried not to weep into my vegetables. A funny thought came to me. I dropped the weak knife on the soft carpet floor. I took hold of the black spear. I brought it to the flame-scored meat. I stood above the plate and cut. This would be her first meal. One of joy. One of pleasure. She cut through the meat with ease. Sharper than sharp. Spinifer Black cuts fine. I stabbed into the pieces with the fork after laying my spear onto the floor. I ate it all. I ate it all, the shine on the plate my tongue's own wet, not no oil nor grease. Just me. Then I closed my eyes to wait for the sun.

The next day I arrived on the BattleGround. A door opened and a guard pushed my back. "Go for it," he said.

I stood hearing all those voices screaming for whoever. I felt just about pulled up into the air when I came out into the BattleGround, the way the collective took in a breath. The ground was asphalt, with traffic lines that meant nothing drawn onto it. The way those people screamed, you'd think they never seen a Black man with one arm and a spear before.

The man opposite me held a four-way tire iron. Tire Iron didn't have too many bodies on him. Just the one fight before this one. Just the one M on his back. But they say two a big deal in the killing games. And if you make it to three, you serious, they say.

When he ran with his metal in hand, was not the first time I seen someone coming at me with death in their eyes. It's a look you can't miss. It's something special: eyes almost beating like a heart they so focused. That's the rage they summoning. When you been in chains it's easy to have that rage on you. It's everywhere. It's in everything. For me, singing is the way to push that rage out of my head some. So with my voice back, I sang. I sang even in the arena. As they announced me I heard "I be so glad" in the speakers meant for the masses. From silence to the biggest voice in the world. Mama, I made it, I almost laughed. Then I remembered my mother might've been watching for real and the shame was drowning. The tattoo they pressed on my back, giant M in case I ever forget how I got here, probably almost visible since I was just in a tank top and some pants.

That man jumped in the air to get more momentum to crush my skull. Then, I discovered to my surprise that I was built for these killing games. I flashed the spear out across. I held it at the middle and the clang of metal on metal clanged as the sharp tip hit against his mechanic crucifix. The rush and cheer came. He swung again, and again I slapped the piece away.

"Motherfucker, I'm not scared of you!" he screamed. I wondered why he did, but also I knew why he did. 'Cause you say anything when you're as scared as you is in the eye of the killing games. I relinquished my body to its instinct to survive. While me and the man who aimed to kill me clanged our lives against each other we were also sprinting toward something together. As if we both could see the precise details of what was coming and reacted accordingly, immediately. He was already two bodies in. Two bodies is enough.

After his third swing, which I didn't have to block 'cause it was too short, I took a step back and ran to the right. Me and him fighting on the big stage, a journey in violent flashes.

Us two been inside. To be inside don't mean you did wrong, but many of us did. I killed a man my woman loved because he wasn't me. I didn't know what Tire Iron did, but I imagined him a sorry soul. And so the promise of the games is fulfilled in our joining. Does each evil cancel the other out? Does disappearing one person from the earth clean it some? I seen men I knew were a danger to the world and they too deserve better than this. A shame for me to hope for better, but I know it's better that can be done. Ain't no magic potions for these bleeding human hearts. Ain't no building full of hurt gonna save the masses.

Still, maybe they right. Maybe this what we deserve.

I ran up on a hill. Didn't know why then, but looking back, your body can know a whole lot. There was a Yield sign sticking out up there. Each BattleGround has its own strange I. What surprised me best was the heave of my breath. How tired you can become, how quickly.

With the Yield sign at my back, Tire Iron sprints toward me. He screams something, but everybody is screaming something so I can't hear it well. I hear my body say, "The high ground." The new angle.

I sway; there's a clang. The metal of his hand hits the Yield. I'm already pulling back. The spear, the black sharp in my hand, knows what to do. His eyes go wide. And for the second time in my life I take a life. It makes the heart quake. To know immediately you have done the unholy. The masses are jubilee.

No more, my lord

We March more and it's the afternoon when we stop. The stop comes suddenly; the Anchor does not announce it's rest, but you can feel it's coming. After three or four hours of trek it's rest. To relieve yourself and prepare for the next push. Men turn, if they're so inclined, while Bells squats. Either way Razor stands out in front of her in case anybody's eyes slide toward indecency.

The rest stop is a time to love and hate, as its coming means that what's passed has passed but also what's to come is to come. During today's rest Razor and Eighty and Bells gather after their relief. They come back near the Anchor and stretch into the grass to wait. Most folks carry as little on them as possible, their things left in the Camps. But I feel more comfortable with something on my back, so I keep my sack slung over my shoulder. In it are warmer clothes and a canteen like everybody got, and a notebook and a pen.

At midday rest, the Anchor provides us a slack maybe two hundred yards. Less than we get in the mornings and evenings. Far enough to squat behind a tree. Not far enough to feel alone from anything. It usually gives about an hour. *Forty-five minutes until reconvene,* it says. Its voice too human to be human. We are in a valley in nowhere like always, except this time there's a road just a few miles from us.

Being a civilian, not belonging to the Chains, it's easy to forget how much of the world isn't yours. How much is not your city or your town. How much is the in-between. If you don't live there, aren't forced to March, and know intimately what some might call nothing. The March goes through high grass and grass worked and cleared. Dry and dead lands. Through scattered trees. Up clearings on mountainsides.

We walk through all these. Learn them all. See them to be something different. *LinkLyfe* might be a nature show if people cared more for the canvas and less for the blood painted all over it. But out in the fields, the fields of the growing and unspeaking, we spend most of our time. We killers, one with the land.

As usual, we group ourselves. The Hitler-loving threesome together out east, near the echo of the sound of the road. Razor puts his katana and its sheath down and does a couple of sit-ups before lying down himself, using Bells's stomach as a pillow to rest his head. I stand near the Anchor, looking at this stick of might, black and metal, its head wider than its body. An alien thing if I didn't know we were on Earth. I'm starting to sit when Razor, without moving but a finger, tells me to come closer to them. His invitation has quietly been unraveling toward me. Had to see me as somebody worth extending a hand. Somebody unafraid.

My first test came when, on my first day, everyone on the Chain, everyone besides the Erasers, saw me waiting on them, wrist glowing like theirs, though I have just the one. I took a deep breath, waited for a word to come from one of them. Bells, Razor, and Eighty looked at me. The Eraser boys blinked at me. One of the three said, "Welcome to the rest of your life." The other two laughed.

Bells cut her voice over their laughter. "What's your name?"

I looked at her and could see she wanted me to know I was being judged.

"Hendrix Young," I said.

The name didn't impress her or the others. They stood near each other even then, looking out toward the heart of the Camp, where their supplies were packed away. I was standing right among their belongings. The warm of the fire licking my shins, a thin cold around everything else. We were in a clearing framed by the sound of water.

"Why you here?" she asked.

Sawyer told me that these first few moments was where a lot of Links' journeys ended. Use your personality, he said. They'll love you.

"Couldn't stay where I was," I said.

"You kill somebody?" she said.

"Yes," I said. "And now that I've been to the BattleGround it's more true." I struggled to keep my head up at her. She didn't ask me what else I done, but I guess she thought my crime was what it was and not some other evil beyond that. Her brown eyes shined even in the dying light. She nodded at me. I am one of many.

Razor looked at me hard. Eighty looked at me easy. LouBob wasn't arrived to the Chain yet, but had he been there he wouldn't't've said anything.

I watched them take me in. Saw them notice my gone arm.

"How you lose your arm?" Razor asked. It was healed enough that it couldn't have been from my proving-ground bout. Those kind of injuries don't usually make for survivors in this game.

"A saw," I say.

The Erasers lost interest and walked past me toward where they'd plant for the night. One Eraser said to his brothers, but loud enough I knew he wanted to show me he could say what he pleased, "Another nigger, hallelujah." They laughed. "That's most of them doing the crime so it's the way it's gonna be," another said. I turned to them. My spear waited on the ground at my feet. I picked it up. They must've seen it before, but it's a different thing to see a weapon and then to see a weapon in the hands of its master, and another thing again to see a weapon in the hands of its master after it has taken life. One of the Erasers had a coiled whip that sat on his hip. Another held a hoe like a farmer. The third, I couldn't see his weapon. I looked at farmer Eraser because that's the one who spoke.

"You think I made it here by letting y'all call me nigger?" I said.

I felt Bells, Razor, and Eighty watching. I held Spinifer Black ready, its edge low but pointed at the white men.

"Slipped out, Hendrix," said hoe-carrying Eraser.

"Keep steady, then," I said, and he smiled at me. Walked away to sit. I had no tent, but a space in the world where I could roam and a place to keep things of mine if I had things. I sat on the trunk. Ready then and forever.

The rest of them continued in their groups, me outside the both of them. A peanut butter sandwich dropped out of the sky to me. For me. I thought of how the world can be anything and how sad it is that it's this. With my teeth gummed from my dinner sandwich, Razor came to speak to me. He stood as I sat. I resisted the urge to stand as it would feel I was welcoming some challenge when truly I wanted to rest and do nothing.

"How'd you get cut by a saw?" he asked.

"Working a meat mill. Tried to do something for somebody."

Razor looked at me straight. He held his katana in its bright red sheath and pressed the thumb of the hilt up so I could see a bit of steel sleeping in the sheath. Real-life samurai shit.

"That's a bad break. I here for the same reason as you. But these people on my side. That's my family. I'm telling you welcome, and to remember a lot of things can cut. So it's good to be careful," he said.

"Sure is," I said. Then he left me to swallow my crusts.

The first test was to see how I took the Erasers. Out here it is those who will kill you, those who might kill you, and the family you choose. Eighty, Razor, and Bells have become a family. For certain Razor asked Bells to allow me to stand and sit among them.

The destination is never known. And there might be a new Link appeared as if wrought from the earth at night in Camp. The March itself is usually not too difficult. Our bodies most valuable to them as something to slaughter; they rather not lose us to a fall off a mountainside or a snake bite. They don't mind that they kill us—it's how they kill us they particular about. So they find us moderate routes toward wherever it is they want us.

We still resting now. I lie down near enough to the others, fall on a bed of grass. The clothes I wear simple but clean. I used one of my murder points to have a brand I never heard of clean my clothes for me each week. Death becomes laundry. Death becomes food. Death the currency of everything if you let it. And they let it. But since it's there I use it and I have a black shirt and pants to train in and sneakers that fit me and socks and underwear that all smell like pine and soap and the sweat of the March.

We sit and rest between halves of the day's journey.

"You done with the singing for today?" Razor asks. "Don't quit 'cause me." I look at him, at Bells, who's looking at the sky.

"Didn't realize I wasn't. Had it going in my head."

"What?" asks Eighty, his voice hard and heavy. Matched to his broad set.

"I be so glad when the sun goes down," I sing.

"They messed you up where they kept you, huh, Singer?" Razor says. I look at Bells, who hasn't taken her eyes off the sky. I see Razor's head bob slowly against her as she stretches and relaxes her ribs. His eyes closed. Eighty is up watching me, the Erasers, everything. There's always somebody on watch.

"I be so glad," I sing. He who has not been messed up has not been.

"He's from Auburn. The experimental facility. Twenty-four-hour forced silence," LouBob says.

"Damn," Razor says, looking at the light on his wrists.

"Everybody has a story," Bells says, getting up, forcing Razor to get up too. "Nobody here is coming from some happy place."

"When the sun goes down," I sing.

"See, now he's broken," Eighty says, laughing some 'cause he can hear Bells is serious. "Broken music streamer."

Bells gets up to her feet, stretches. Leaves Razor's head for the earth. She guides her machete through the air, practicing.

Then she sings, "I ain't all that sleepy but I, I wanna lie down."

I follow her: "Ain't all that sleepy, but I, I wanna lie down."

Convene in one minute, the Anchor says.

We all get up. I keep singing. As we get back into line Bells comes toward me to help me rise from my place. On the ground. She grips my hand. I feel the hard-callused wear.

"Everybody came through the shit. Nobody has to be sorry for you for anything, Singer." She speaks so her words are for me and me alone. "You're here now."

"I wanna lie down," I sing. A joke that's not a joke. A beg that's not a beg. I am grateful to her. She pulls me up. She looks at me with a straight face. We get spread and close at once and we March.

Vacation

After Staxxx's first year on the Circuit the night terrors had not stopped, but they had calmed. They'd shifted to a droning anxiety that she learned to acknowledge and accept as a fact of her life. Tonight, lying in a small cot, Randy Mac's heavy snoring and piney musk were the only things to ground her as she felt herself unspooling. Disassociating from herself. She tried to remember that she, Staxxx, was the one holding the man. It was her chest that his back was pressed into as he slept. She thought of LoveGuile so calmly resting just beneath her. What if she killed him? What if she just did it today? She had days where it seemed like all she could think of was killing the people around her. Those intrusive thoughts had been a part of her life since before she'd killed Sunset, but when he'd asked her to kill him, it was as if one of those thoughts had finally come to pass. It had hurt to lose a friend, and it had hurt to have to help him do it. But in some hard way, she was proud she had been there for Sunset at his end.

He'd said, "I will not force anyone else to have to consider forgiving me either. I'm not sure what I deserve." Those words spun around her nightmares. She had done the exact opposite. Forced so many to forgive. Forced it to show them they had it in them.

She had killed, so she was a killer. She was that before all else.

That's what her darkest thoughts said to her. Even the first time, when a teacher at her high school had tried to force himself on her and she'd gotten hold of a knife and split apart his jugular and somehow, also, her life. How many times since had she been in that same space? Been asked to accept some other's violence. So many like her had lived that same nightmare.* This was another part of her purpose. To live loud and be epic despite what had happened to her. Despite the world that had asked her to be hurt and be silent about it. The world knew her story, how she'd earned her first murder. How her family had abandoned her, like they were afraid of her. They hated visiting her in prison, then they stopped, moved away. They left her behind. It was the perfect storm, swept her into a breakdown. Her life, a hurricane.

But where did the Hurricane end and Hamara begin? It scared her that she understood the Hurricane more than the person she had been before she was in the games. The Hurricane fought, the Hurricane could rise to any challenge. The Hurricane could shoulder the burdens of others thrown on top of her own. The Hurricane held people it loved. Hamara, though. Hamara was something of a stranger.

What if she could just sleep forever?

She was one intrusive thought after another. Her mind scared her most in the quiet moments. When she was asked to kill, or lead, she could be present. She could thrive. In the times when there was nothing, when all she had to do was exist—

You are a murderer.

She let the thought float by. She did not resist it. She was a vessel of love. She was not defined by the men who had violated her or the family that had abandoned her or the millions who locked her in chains and watched her from the comfort of their own homes. She closed her eyes but still could see the bluish glow of the HMCs like a ghost behind her eyelids.

What if all she was good for was killing and everything that she said was just decoration? What if the exact opposite of what she hoped was true, that rather than everyone being a diamond at their core, what

---

* Cyntoia Brown was forced into prostitution and was initially given a life sentence at age sixteen for killing a man aged forty-three while defending herself. Cyntoia, Cyntoia, Cyntoia.

All across the world, women regularly serve prison time for killing their rapists.

if they were shit in a pretty container? What if they were shit in a diamond coat? What if she disappeared Randy from the earth? She loved
who he was. But what if her life was all about killing people she loved?
Who loved her. That was what it sometimes seemed like.

She let out a laugh that shook the cot they slept on. It squeaked and
gave. They'd almost broken it many times already. It was a shitty cot.
Especially compared to what Thurwar slept on, or compared to what
was in her own tent.

Randy rolled over. Staxxx could feel his breath against her neck.

Half-asleep, he asked, "What's so funny?" His deep voice, deeper in
the thrall of sleep, made her feel more tethered to herself.

"I was thinking, like, if I killed you, I'd have to explain it was an
accident, and it'd be like, *So it happened again, guys, don't be mad at me.
My bad for killing the homies.*"

Randy pulled in closer as if her skin held a richer oxygen, as if in
her he found fresh air.

"Funny." And with that he was back asleep.

Staxxx kissed the top of his forehead, a gentle gratitude washing
over her as she felt the binds of her anxiety easing.

"You hate me for killing Sun?" she asked Randy, but knew she was
really asking the world as he slept. "Do you think I'm broken? Do you
think I'm a person that can be in the world? Like, actually? Would I
be okay out there?"

She watched his body rise and fall, his muscles limp but still defined
in his skin.

"I think they're gonna put you on a muthafucking cereal box."

She said nothing. Even against the chorus of cicadas and grass-
hoppers, the depth of her quiet made Randy scrunch himself up just
enough that his eyes were even with hers. His eyelids pulled themselves open. He looked at her and she met his gaze. She wanted to be
in her body, felt herself floating away.

"You are broken. But you've handled everything that's been put in
front of you. So you're perfect too, and a badass bitch on top of that.
In a sick world, healthy is strange. So yeah, you're broken some. But
there's none of us on the Circuit that will do better on the other side.
And I say that as a selfish Link who views you as a messiah, but also as
a person who knows bullshit from the real deal."

"I'm floating a little bit." Her eyes were wet.

"I know you are. I'm here. What do you want to talk about? You want to talk about a before thing or now?"

Staxxx considered this, thought about what she felt up for. What her mind would be receptive to. "Before," she said.

"Well, that's a problem," Randy said. "My life really wasn't worth talking about before I met you." He closed his eyes, nestled back into her, and fell asleep with his lips on her collarbone.

She laughed and the cot chuckled in squeaks too. She laughed more. "Stupid."

She found Mac lovely.

Staxxx didn't know if it was some lingering desire from civilian life, to have a man trying too hard always, but she enjoyed it in the brutal context of her life now.

She enjoyed this time, this once or twice a week she'd spend with Randy. Months ago it seemed as though it would bring an intense instability to want more than one thing. To be with Thurwar and also have the freedom to share time and body with Randy Mac. The reporters certainly tried to instigate a war. They'd expected it to end with at least one person's dying. But it had not, thanks to Thurwar's maturity and decency and Randy's begrudging loyalty to Thurwar. It was an agreement that, at least in this way, allowed her to do what she wanted. Each one of them gave her different things, satisfied distinct needs. Thurwar was home. Randy Mac was a vacation. Another place. A variety that kept her even, in her body, stable.

She felt a pride at being able to be herself in this way, in front of the whole world. She was born for this. Despite all the intrusive thoughts, despite how hard it was, she wasn't afraid with love. She knew how to wield it, how to grow it, and how to receive it.

What if all she was good for was death?

She let the thought pass.

What if all the love she tried to be was a lie?

She saw the thought. Let it ride her breath. Yes, in some ways, she'd discovered herself on the Circuit, but that was inevitable. What she'd learned was that life, any life, was death and rebirth, death and rebirth. Everything always changed.

Hours before dawn she was up and staring at the tent. She could see the sky leaking dark through the netting that let air in and kept mosquitoes out. Randy rubbed her side and squeezed as if trying to keep her there a little bit longer. He was still asleep but coming out of it. She tried to start the day with Thurwar, even if she'd spent the night with Randy; he knew she'd be gone soon. In the past, she and the whole country had seen him cry, begging for more time in the morning. And she'd been strict but kind as she'd held firm, kissed him on the forehead, and disappeared to Thurwar. Now he often kept his eyes closed until she left. But today she waited with him.

She watched the morning settle over the Camp. Soon Thurwar would be Freed. Soon Staxxx would be a Colossal. Life was death and rebirth, death and rebirth. Staxxx was not the same person she'd been before the night she had killed Sunset. She was still learning this new self.

Thurwar would be Freed soon. They'd made so much love and so much death together. There was obviously no one on the planet who could be her match the way Loretta Thurwar was. She thought this as she traced her finger around Randy Mac's brow. His jaw was clenched, and he seemed to be dreaming through a harshness. She pressed softly on his thick eyebrows, which grew smoother after they passed under her thumb. She wondered where he was. She'd wait with him till he woke up. This man who was not Thurwar but was still a part of her. She decided she'd ask him what he'd been dreaming. She closed her eyes for a little longer and waited.

Staxxx was watching him when he floated up from sleep. He looked around with confusion, as if he'd woken up in a place he'd never been before. This was, of course, true every single day on the Circuit.

"What were you dreaming about?" Staxxx asked softly. She could smell his morning breath as he reached up beyond the cot and stretched his muscles.

He rolled up in bed, moving quickly. Watching any man move suddenly made Staxxx want to rush for LoveGuile. She let it lie and waited. He picked something up from the ground bedside the bed.

Randy swung back down, holding a notebook. He quickly jotted something down.

"What did you dream about?" Staxxx asked again. She climbed on top of him, locking his abdomen between her thighs, resting his notebook on her middle.

"A goat," Mac said. "I was dreaming about a goat."

"I'm flattered. I didn't know you dreamed about me still."

"All I ever do."

She pulled forward and kissed him. He received it gladly.

"What's wrong?" he asked.

She smiled at him. "We make it to the Hub today. Tomorrow latest."

Links never knew when Marches would end. They'd go for days and then suddenly they'd reach a pickup point where their van was waiting for them. The not knowing, the hoping for the Hub City, caused many Links to crack, but so did the fear of reaching that destination. Hub Cities meant BattleGrounds, and BattleGrounds meant death.

"You mean the great Hurricane is also clairvoyant. Or are you guessing?"

"I don't guess. I know these things. I can feel it in the air. You can't?"

"I could be feeling it more," Randy said. He put his notebook down and brought his hands to her waist. She grabbed his wrists and pinned them back down beside his ears. She held him there for a while. Then she got off him. The HMC popped out of the way of her head as she put on her clothes.

"How come you're still here?" Randy asked.

"I'm everywhere," Staxxx said.

"You never stay this late."

"I'm not in a rush to start today." She pulled on her sweatpants. "And like I said, we get to the Hub City soon. What if . . . ?" She didn't speak the question she was always thinking aloud: What if this next one is the one that breaks me?

"Are you worried about the fight you two have?" he asked.

Thurwar and Staxxx would have a doubles match in the coming days. A match against two men billed as being stronger and more unpredictable than any they'd faced before.

She frowned.

"I didn't think that was it. I know you two have nothing to worry about in doubles. I just don't know what's so special to have you feel-ing a way today."

"Sometimes it's simple, Mac."

"So?"

"It's simple," she said, and then she left from his space for home.

Grounded

For the first time, Thurwar was genuinely happy that Staxxx had spent the night with Randy Mac. She wanted an evening to herself to lament. She'd taken an early leave of the group and practiced with her hammer, and though she and Staxxx were scheduled for a tag-team match next, it was Staxxx who popped up in her mind's eye as her adversary as she drove Hass Omaha through the air.

Thurwar had let her worst thoughts flood the Queen's Tent. That she had already waited too long. That Staxxx would never forgive her for not telling her about the rule change ahead. That she had no idea why Staxxx had killed Sunset. That everything she knew about Staxxx was a lie.

Maybe she was cracking before the fight came. Or worst of all, maybe she wasn't, and so would actually be forced to allow Staxxx to kill her on her freeing day. Because that was what she would have to do. She couldn't imagine any other way. The idea of bringing Hass Omaha to Staxxx—it was a nightmare that she'd had on more than one occasion. She was no longer the person who harmed the people she loved. She was not. She couldn't be. What she had done to Vanessa was the greatest mistake of her life. She was no longer the person who'd killed her, although she still believed that she'd forfeited her right to life for having done so.

She briefly indulged the idea that the information on the card wasn't true. A burst of salvation. There was no guarantee, after all, that the woman who'd given her the card with the season 33 rule change had given her anything other than a brutal rumor. Some unfounded wish.

But Thurwar knew it was true. It was exactly the way the people who made these games thought. Once season 33 began, which would be right after their upcoming doubles match, Staxxx would become a Colossal. And as such, this new, brutal protocol would be triggered and a week later the season would launch with the match the world had dreamed of: Thurwar vs. Hurricane Staxxx.

Who was she now that the person who kept her going was the person standing in her way? She would let herself be killed first, she resolved. Wasn't that the plan in the beginning, when she first joined? To die? She would finally show the courage that the man from the U-Blockers had. She would win with Staxxx in their next match. They would win and then Thurwar would go to her freeing day. She'd end up Melancholia after all.

Thurwar watched Staxxx's shadow. The morning was still young.

Thurwar made space to feel proud of how jealousy no longer shaped her life. A certain petty part of her did sometimes wish bad on Randy, but after all they'd seen together, Randy was one of the few people who understood her. He would have been a good friend of hers if not for the way he shared in her destiny.

But he helped Staxxx be herself. Helped keep her together. And Thurwar was, in that sense, grateful to Randy Mac for sharing the load.

But Staxxx never stayed with Randy for breakfast. Thurwar listened to the Links gathering their food and felt a wave of relief to a tension she hadn't yet acknowledged when Staxxx's figure was there just outside the tent, hauling their customized morning meals, LoveGuile tucked into her armpit.

"Hey there, beautiful," Staxxx said.

Thurwar looked at her, her smiling mouth.

"What's wrong?" Thurwar asked, and made room beside her on

the bed. Thurwar tried not to think of season 33, as if Staxxx could hear the bleak thoughts that rattled in her head. Staxxx carefully put the two large food crates on the ground and then, in one fluid motion, slipped the pack off her back. Thurwar wiped her left hand against her thigh and continued to rub the spot next to her. Staxxx dropped her head into Thurwar's lap.

"Today is the last day of the March," Staxxx said.

"Okay. That's okay," Thurwar said as she wiped the tears falling sideways on Staxxx's face. "It's me and you."

"It's you and me," Staxxx said. "I'm not worried about the grounds."

Staxxx and Thurwar had trained together carefully for the last few days since the Melee. Their coming battle was against a pair who had shot up through the ranks in a way that had not been seen since Thurwar herself. Two men, two different styles. They would be prepared. Staxxx wasn't worried, but that was because she was Staxxx. Thurwar was extremely worried. This would be their greatest challenge on the grounds yet.

"I feel like I'm—like I'm a peregrine falcon. The ground is a different thing for a bird," Staxxx said.

There was a very specific kind of survival the Links sometimes grabbed for, a way of speaking in codes and puzzles to one another, to obscure what they were really saying from the audience. It wasn't a game, but it felt like one sometimes. Fans had picked up on the habit and tried to crack their codes, even though their exclusion was the very purpose of it.

"It's me and you," Thurwar said. She could smell Randy Mac on Staxxx's skin. "Tell me." And as the HMCs floated closer, Thurwar thought of the psychological burden she carried. Even without knowing that they would be forced to fight should they survive what came next, Staxxx was distraught. No. She could not tell Staxxx the truth. Keeping the secret of their fate was another way that Thurwar would protect her.

"The peregrine falcon can dive faster than two hundred miles per hour. I'm like that. I come to the ground to eat, to snatch things up before I come back to sky." Staxxx picked her head up, wiped her eyes. "When winter ends you hear it from the birds first."

Thurwar pulled Staxxx into her so she could kiss her forehead.

"I'll be flying with you."

Staxxx felt so much so loudly. She spoke in songs and poems and codes that Thurwar usually understood because she felt so many of the same things. But sometimes Thurwar wished Staxxx would say exactly what she meant, let the people know whatever she was thinking. Fuck the people, just pretend it was them alone.

But Thurwar also worried that the time on the Circuit had made it so some of Staxxx existed in a jumble that she herself could not parse. They called it "cracking," and Thurwar wasn't always sure that she was capable of keeping Staxxx together.

"Wanna run some weaponless drills?" Thurwar asked.

Staxxx looked at her, confident. "Sure," she said.

This was her way of being there for people. With her body. Thurwar knew one way to ground Staxxx and that was to get her to use her body.

Staxxx was already in good training gear: compression tights under shorts and a T-shirt. Thurwar put on some tights of her own and a long-sleeve compression shirt. They went outside and picked a spot hidden behind the tent to spar.

"Best of three takedowns?" Thurwar circled Staxxx, trying to have fun. She was having a good knee day.

Staxxx stretched her neck. "Sounds good." She looked to be considering a moment before saying, "Ey, Bad Water, come set us up."

Thurwar raised an eyebrow and Staxxx smiled back.

"Huh?" Bad Water said from somewhere on the other side of the Queen's Tent.

"Get over here, Walter," Staxxx bellowed.

In moments Walter arrived at the two women standing beside each other in the grass. He looked at them, his pale skin reddening as he waited.

"Thanks, Bad Water," Staxxx said.

"We just need you to say 'go.' We're running some drills," Thurwar explained. "Weaponless takedowns. You've seen us do this before, right?"

"I have," Bad Water said.

"Good, come on and learn something then," Staxxx said. "You just say 'go,' and try not to make Thurwar feel bad after I drop her, okay?"

"We're going to three," Thurwar said. "It's not going to be hard to keep score, though." Thurwar winked at Bad Water and she watched him shudder. She chose very precise moments here and there to remind her Links that she was a person like them, that she could joke too.

"No out of bounds?" Bad Water said. "My son used to wrestle."

"You have a son?" Thurwar said.

"I didn't know that," Staxxx said.

"You don't talk to me," Bad Water said.

"And that's not going to change now," Staxxx said, grinning. "All you got to do is say 'go' when we're crouched in position."

"Okay," Bad Water said, his mood lifting a bit, clearly pleased to be a part of something.

"Let's go," Thurwar said. She and Staxxx had done wrestling drills hundreds of times. Thurwar had incorporated weaponless training into the Links' practice rotation because she knew from experience that understanding your body as a weapon first was to be more fully lethal. She'd been disarmed more than once in the BattleGround, a fact that had become an epic statistic as usually disarmament meant death.

Now she and Staxxx crouched in front of each other. Thurwar looked into Staxxx's brown eyes, focused, sharp, grounded. Staxxx was all there.

"Wrestlers ready," Bad Water said.

He stood a few feet away from them, his back to the tent and the other Links, vulnerable. Everything about the man screamed newbie, Thurwar thought, but then she focused on Staxxx, who was a competitor's competitor and had never beaten Thurwar when they'd sparred best of three or five or seven or nine. The numbers always rose as Staxxx insisted she get another shot.

Thurwar crouched low but not too low, let her thighs feel strong, as Staxxx did the same.

"Ready," they each said.

"Go."

Both their arms shot up. Crouched, they held each other at the shoulder. Thurwar knew the force Staxxx could produce and considered both her options and her opponent's. She aimed to widen her neutral stance, and as she did Staxxx pulled hard on her left side and dropped down, crouched still with her arms wrapped around Thurwar's leg. Staxxx's head was pressed into her side and Thurwar knew the point had been taken from her. Staxxx held the inside of her thigh and guided her down to the ground. Thurwar fell on her butt and Staxxx gleefully collapsed on top of her.

"One takedown awarded to thee Hurricane Staxxx," Bad Water said.

"You only have to say 'go,'" Thurwar said as she got up. She brushed herself off, shaken not by the takedown but by how precisely and directly Staxxx had gone for her bad knee. Her knee was, in her mind, another secret that she didn't want to burden Staxxx with, but as she lowered into a crouch again she wondered which of those secrets Staxxx was already privy to. Staxxx, for example, didn't know Vanessa's name. She didn't know the whole story. She hadn't told Staxxx that she regularly had been physical with Vanessa, or what had happened when Vanessa had tried to fight back. She had never told Staxxx how every night she hoped for a forgiveness she didn't believe she was worthy of. And she loved Staxxx for never asking.

"Look at that. Grand Colossal and a sore loser," Staxxx said.

"Oh shit," said Rico Muerte; he and Sai and Randy were all watching the sparring now.

"I didn't lose," Thurwar said. "It's not over till it's over."

"Wrestlers ready," Bad Water said. "Go!"

And again their hands shot up. Thurwar immediately exerted a downward force on Staxxx's shoulders, imagined dunking her forehead into the ground, crushing her there. Staxxx resisted, as Thurwar knew she would, and without warning released all her force. Staxxx's head popped up just enough. Thurwar dropped low and drove her head into Staxxx's solar plexus and wrapped both hands around her knees. She could feel Staxxx's core as she pressed into it with her skull. She drove farther into Staxxx with her head as she stood up and Staxxx fell backward. She looked down at Staxxx on the ground. Her palms called for Hass Omaha and she hated herself for the instinct.

"Damn!" Rico said.

"The double-leg takedown," Sai said. "A classic."

"Thanks, guys, glad you don't have anything better to do right now," Staxxx said as she got up.

"Let's fucking go," Thurwar said. Her Links cheered her.

Thurwar wished she could say the truth. They looked into each other's eyes and lowered, at the ready. Sometimes being a leader meant carrying things alone. And she was the greatest leader in the history of the games. Or maybe she was just afraid of sharing a burden, sharing responsibility. She couldn't believe that there were people who thought she wasn't afraid of anything.

"Ready . . . Go."

They were wrong.

Staxxx rushed forward. Thurwar was ready. She absorbed the contact, then faked a low inside step before coming over the top and dragging Staxxx down with her hand collared around her neck. She pulled Staxxx down and pressed her chest over her back. Staxxx tried to stand and Thurwar circled her to get good purchase on her thigh. Once she had that grip, she pressed and flipped Staxxx onto her back again.

The small party clapped.

"GOAT shit," Muerte said.

"Exactly," Thurwar said. This was who she was.

"Can't win 'em all," Sai said.

"Can't win them ever," Thurwar said. Trying, trying to enjoy just this and forget for one moment what was to come.

"Lucky for me the BattleGrounds aren't weaponless," Staxxx said, sitting cross-legged on the ground.

Thurwar almost let out, *What did you say?* Instead, she lifted her arms in the air to the cheers of her spectators.

"Love you too, babe," Thurwar said. Salting the wound and watching close. What could Staxxx know?

"Fuck you," Staxxx said, and Thurwar thought, This woman is perfect. And all the joy evaporated in her chest.

Simon J. Craft

Just jump, Jay. Just jump.

Sung

We take steps heavy with loss. Both sides of the Chain depleted by one in the BattleGround. The Eraser triplets reduced to twins, their third dispatched by the great Raven Ways. Ain't have no chance. The brothers had been confined together in the womb, in the cell, and finally in this open world of the killing games. Now they're separate for the first time. The two that are left wet the swastikas on their necks with tears. And their third killed by a Black man at that.

On our side we lost Eighty. A good man that done bad long time ago. Big jovial man somehow, despite the blood on everything. Not a bad fight, but it wasn't a good one either. Eighty hesitated for just a moment and in that moment he found himself punctured, in a way that would never be patched.

Out on the Circuit, after the loss, Razor looks at me as we step through, crunching the evidence of spring's relent on our feet. He asking for a song.

"I don't got many remembrances memorized," I say.

"What you mean?" Razor says. "All the shit you sing sound like memorial shit, so go ahead."

I look to Bells, who walks head-up, crying and quiet.

"I'll sing one if you ain't got one. All this gah-damn singing this whole year and now Singer ain't got a song in 'im. Imagine that. That's fucked, bro. Gimme a tune at least. I'll freestyle one time for my bro," Razor says.

A tune to hum comes to me immediately. *Hmmm, hmmm, hmmm.* I go, "Hmmm, hmmm, hmmm."

I see Razor taking it in, closing his eyes, gripping the hilt of his weapon. He calls it Sansupuritā. When he was here in the living, Eighty and Razor and Bells would rhyme the miles away, passing the bars back and forth between them. More than a few times they formed their rhymes around my songs. Today, Razor takes my sound in, breathes it through his body as we follow the Anchor down a river I'll never know the name of.

Hmm, hmmm, hmmmm. Hmm, hmmm, hmmmm

I loved my boy a fat man

Right away Bells laughs. Another story of the name is, Eighty was first called Eight Hundred. But the way he thrust himself into working his body after barely winning his first two fights, the story is he lost two humans' worth. Changed his name to fit his size. Eighty.

I loved him when he got thin

Hmm, hmmm, hmmm

I know he done some wrong, but, Lord, he gone

So please go on let him in.

Hmmm, hmmm, hmmm

Hmmm, hmmm, hmmm

And Bells take it from him to the same tune.

Reggie was a legend

Ride or die, sink or swim

He stood with me, and now he's free

So please, God, let him in.

Hmm hmmm, hmmm hmmm

I feel it passing through me and I do not deny the spirit.

His mama named him a king's name

'Cause she knew what he had within

His only sin, was too human

So please, God, let him in

So please, Lord, let him in

For the next several miles the story of Eighty is told in song and the floating eyes swirl the air capturing it. Good TV, somebody somewhere is thinking. And they right. Part of me hopes the kin Eighty keeps is watching. Part of me hopes they find the strength not to.

"They don't call us Sing for nothing, you feel me, muthafuckers?" Razor says, looking straight up into the floating eye. "We earn that name on this side." He laughs the last of his tears away.

The Eraser Twins don't bother making a word. They listen silently through the March; surely their hearts sing songs in praise of the piece of themselves they've lost.

A faraway light in the brush greets us and so this sad March is coming to a close. I can feel that Bells and Razor aren't quite ready to settle in, can tell from their gait, their eyes. The dark leaving nothing but the hurt clear.

The Anchor pulls us to its stopping place above the fire pit. As if to show its power it always rests above the fire. A witch that cannot be burned. And though the Anchor pulls constantly, we slow our walk. The killing games like this. When someone is lost to the grounds, often another is received.

Eighty and LouBob and Eraser was lost at the last arena. LouBob forgotten as is so many that go inside. I try to remember to hold him in my singing in the morning.

Though Sing-Attica-Sing lost three, a single man is standing at the campfire. We watch him. The Chain slows, forms a smile of bodies around him. There's a chorus of insect life and wind. The crackle of fire is the sound of nothing if you've heard it long enough. This fire crackles different, its flames darker than what seems natural. The wrists in the Camp glow green and finally we stop. The lot of us stand not six feet from the new member of the Chain, who stands in front of the fire with a smile so huge it doesn't feel right. His teeth are a dull tan and his body stands strong. It's the kind of body that has carried itself up and down, up and down, many, many times. He is lean muscle; his skin looks tight on him. His linen pants are tucked into high-top sneakers and his shirt is elastic and compressed to his skin so that we can all see the shadows dancing up and down his muscles.

"Hello," he says, smiling and waving. And as he does we all grip a little harder onto the hurt we keep, because on each of his hands is a long double blade that is strapped to just below the knuckle, so it looks as if the metal were a part of him. He has two gold blades on his right hand, and on his left, one gold and one obsidian.

Razor steps to him first.

"What up, bro? What they call you?"

We watch, and the unsilenced of the nature around us gets real loud and clear. Bells takes a step forward. "You good, bro? What they call you where you from?"

"My name is Simon J. Craft," he says, and then he swipes his right-bladed hand at Razor's neck.

Razor jumps back and Sansupurittā is up and flashing before anybody that ain't seen the BattleGround a few times would have even had time to blink. Razor pulls the blade from the sheath and already Bells is running up to assist. Razor cuts through the low light at Mr. Craft's head and Craft sways back at the waist.

"My name is Simon J. Craft," he says as he twists in some impossible way to avoid Bells's crashing machete. Then next I know Bells's blood flooding the ground, she doesn't even get to pull her blade back for a second go.* Razor screams and raises his sword forward as I move to tend to Bells.

"It's Simon J.—" The blades clash. The sound of killing metal explodes as they swipe at each other. Then Razor's razor on the ground and his body follows.† A slash across the neck so deep he isn't on the ground a minute before his eyes close the last time.

I hold Bells. And she looks at me, disappointed, before her eyes flutter and she gurgles to her end. I see the blood on my hands and look up at the twins, who don't know what to make of what they just seen.

---

* Georgina "Ring Ya Bells" Hickory. Seen a lot. Done a lot. Found a home in the hell. She never sold poison to kids, but the poison found the kids anyways, so what was the difference? If you don't have a code you have nothing, and Bells had a code. You swing for your family, you hold your head high, you try to do right when you can. She didn't think she was the love type. She was wrong about that. She found it in hell, a home with love and singing.

† Edgerrin "Razor" Boateng was bound to lose one. He hurt muthafuckers who tried him. He had a family, he was smart. But sometimes you have to do what you have to do. Blood asks for blood. He didn't make the rules, they made him. But he counted his blessings; he was home again, in her. He'd gone all this way to find a peace he'd never felt before. Bells, he'd had her, she'd had him. He wished he could hold her forever.

Everybody in the Circuit seen some horror. But Razor and Bells famous worldwide. Razor and Bells some of the hardest in the games, both called Reapers, and both now still.

"You one of us, brother?" Eraser One says as he approaches, holding his whip in one hand, his other extended as if to shake. Hoping that the pinch of color in the man's skin is the shadows, or a tan, anything but heritage.

Simon J. Craft walks with his own hand extended, suddenly calm. Docile and in agreement. A warmth passes over Eraser One's face as he believes God has delivered him anew where he had taken. As though he's been vindicated. But before they can shake, Eraser's hand is on the ground, severed in another flash of violence.

"Fucking—" he gets out before Simon J. Craft slices his face and neck up good.

The last Eraser turns to run. Sprints pretty good, holding the hoe. Bells still warm in my arm. The brother once a triplet, then briefly a twin, runs and runs. I lay Bells down and because I don't know how much time I have left myself, I quickly pull Razor's body beside hers, put her hand in his so that at least if it's my last moments I gave them something close to a rest they might tolerate. Finally, far off, Eraser hits the invisible thick made up of his own wrists' pull to the Anchor. He struggles against it, running slower and slower, not because he tired but because the hold of the machine is stronger than his body ever could be. He doesn't stop struggling. He's still slowly clamoring when Simon J. Craft leaps into the air. They move together as if through sand. Movement sullied by their bondage. And even in those slow movements, hoe Eraser is stabbed, again and again, in the back. He dies with his face in the earth and blood pouring from his back. The triplets reunited sooner than they ever would have imagined.

And Simon J. Craft walks back slowly to me.

There is no song that comes to me, only the throb I feel in my long-gone hand. The feeling is more pronounced than any I felt when that hand was actually there.

I look at the dead beside me. The best friends I had left in life. And I wonder, Where is the fury? Where is the bloodlust? What part of me is gone now? If not now, when?

I sit on a log and watch the fire. Simon J. Craft returns, his shadow long behind him. I hold my spear up, its tip pointed to the sky. I feel my gone arm stretching toward this man, pulling to his neck as if to choke him, or maybe to his shoulder as if to try and coax him to peace. I feel it as if it were happening there in life before us.

"Simon J. Craft," I say. "Stop this."

And Simon J. Craft smiles as he says, "Yes, sir."

Babe?

"What the fuck just happened, babe? What the fuck just fucking happened. Oh my fucking God." Emily had been bingeing recorded streams again. Wil had wanted to be there when she saw this part so she'd watched with him.

He'd already picked up his holophone, trying to record her reaction. The shock she was feeling had rippled through the rest of the world with the same intensity, apparently.

She watched her husband and then turned her eyes back to the screen, where Hendrix was watching this new man, this new Link she'd watched kill four people in just a few moments, move into Bells's tent and get comfortable in a cot.

"I guess he's fucking tired!" she said. Because she knew her husband would appreciate her saying something.

"Babe. They're gone. This happened like a year ago."

"I know," she said, not having to embellish her shock at all. She knew what she was watching had happened in the past, was long gone, but it was unfolding for her then and there. She was alive with fresh sorrow. "I know," she said.

And the sound of her own voice made her cry.

She'd enjoyed watching the backlog Sing-Attica-Sing streamcasts even more than the current Angola-Hammond casts. She'd gone back and binged, watched the highlights of the streams and the Battle-Grounds. She'd come to know the different members and loved, in particular, the way Razor and Bells had loved each other. And the tag-team match when they'd both established themselves as legitimate Reapers, the way Bells had dropped her machete and pressed her lips to Razor's mouth as Plenty Pain Percy and Herc Miss Wonder bled out at their feet. It was beautiful in the horrible way that everything about Chain-Gang was.

Wil had said he felt the same way, and she hated to agree about something like this. She also hated to admit that part of the draw for her was that Sing didn't have the same pact of nonviolence that A-Hamm had now, and she had become addicted to the threat of violence, the sense that death could be around any corner for the Links. The Eraser boys, for instance, had dispatched a lot of weak Links without much thought or remorse. The other week Razor and Eighty had gotten in an argument with two of the Erasers and it had come to blows, but it had stopped because Bells had creeped behind the third Nazi and threatened to push her machete into his back. Both pairs of men had disengaged and they'd continued on the next day same as usual. It was absolutely thrilling to watch.

She was proud to boo at them, though she knew in her heart that she loved that they offered her a clear and obvious bad guy. A problem to be solved for the heroes, Razor and Bells, and their partners, Eighty and the one-armed Black man Singer. The Eraser boys were racist murderers and it was easy to feel that they deserved this punishment, deserved to be on a Chain. In some way their presence, what she appreciated as an obvious, simple evil, justified the whole thing.

"I know, babe, I know."

And Wil was crying now too. She saw this and loved him fiercely. It was as if their own friends had been taken from them. Murderers, yes, but somehow they'd gotten to know these people, and now where were they?

"He's a fucking lunatic. Simon J. Craft."

"Simon Craft," she said. "Simon J. Craft." She couldn't imagine forgetting the name. She didn't think she'd ever forget it. She watched the screen where he slept and studied his face as the camera closed in on him. "He's fucking sleeping. Christ. What is he?"

She scanned the cast and saw Hendrix Singer, the only remaining member of the group she'd grown to love, and felt a deep anger growing in her gut.

"He should slit his fucking throat right now," she said. "If he wants to just fall asleep like that, fucking slit his throat."

Wil looked up from his phone. He'd stopped recording. She wasn't sure what he was thinking about until it dawned on her that, in the time she'd been watching Chain-Gang, she'd never called out for a Link's death. Thus far, she'd feigned the role of moral overseer, interested, maybe even addicted, but rarely partial in that final way. She was passing through Chain-Gang, lingering perhaps, but always just passing through. And yet, here she was, tears in her eyes, her voice shaking as she screamed for the murder of a man she'd only discovered existed moments before.

"Right on, babe."

And in her thirst for retribution the shame that usually accompanied watching people die in this circus of justice faded away completely. She brushed the hair from her face so she could watch more closely. And to her dismay there was no more death. The equation was unbalanced and this coward Singer wasn't even trying to fix it. She felt a savory new desire. She inhaled and exhaled and felt her breath hot with rage. She realized that she was having trouble breathing.

"What is he doing! Fuck. He has to do it now."

"I know, babe, relax."

"Don't tell me to relax, I—I—" She wanted badly to throw something. "You don't get it, it's—" She couldn't breathe.

"It's okay, babe. That's how I felt when I saw it." His arms were around her. She smelled oak and vinegar and a perfume that was unfamiliar.

"Don't touch me," she said, and twisted out of his grasp. He held tighter and her hands were fists and she was pressed up against him, her arms folded so that her forearms were sandwiched between their chests. She wanted to pull back and punch him, and each time she tried and couldn't she wanted to hurt him more.

"You okay?" he asked. An insane question. These people she'd spent so much time with had been killed, basically in her own living room.

"Am I okay?" she said, willing her shaking to stop. She felt his hold soften and she allowed her voice to do the same. "Let go," she said.

He released her, and before his hands could even find his sides she pulled back and punched him as hard as she could in the chest. He coughed and took a half step back. He coughed again. The room was still filled with the same sound that coated the woods in that blood-soaked nowhere where what remained of the Sing-Attica-Sing Chain waited—just two men. Emily stood, a violence seething through her. Wil took a careful step toward her and grabbed her by the wrists, her hands still in fists. She let him for a moment before pulling away and snatching his wrists herself. She pulled him down to their floor and kissed him on the nub of his collarbone, kissed him again, then bit hard into his salt-slick neck. He made a growling sound that grew to something gentler. She bit harder into his flesh, feeling glee even through the fresh despair and rage. A rage so big it swallowed completely what would have been an awkward fumbling of Wil's belt before she pulled his pants down just enough.

"I l—" Wil started to say.

But she covered his mouth with her hands.

"You shut the fuck up," she said. Her own shorts were beside them at the base of the couch. She never took her eyes off the cast and never was the death made whole. Singer sat as Craft slept in a cot that had once been Bells's. She cried anew and fucked Wil to the sounds of crickets in some faraway night.

The Ride

The sounds of going and coming always preceded the March's end. They'd arrived. They'd found road. A hyper-highway of humans napping or catching up on news as their vehicles charioted them where they hoped to be.

On the shoulder the van was waiting for them. The Anchor stopped just ahead of the Angola-Hammond Chain and adhered to the air, where it waited near their ride.

"Fuck yes," Randy Mac said.

"Drop your weapons, convicts," Jerry said, an unfamiliar disdain glowing on him. He held a Slate in his hands like a threat, showing them the black mirror, their lives in his hands.

"Everything okay, Jerry?" Staxxx asked.

"I said drop your weapons. No trouble."

They dropped the weapons and stood together as the HMCs scanned across their bodies. The end-of-March Lineup was the end of the weekly *LinkLyfe* stream. It was the last thing viewers saw for free. The people who would see them next, on the BattleGround or at whatever Hub City attraction they were headed to, would have to pay.

"Well, I'll be happy to hear about whatever's bothering you once we get on the road," Staxxx said.

"You don't worry about me. I'm just fine," Jerry said as the cameras finished scanning the Links' bodies and flew into the head of the Anchor.

"Okay, I'm just saying, 'cause you don't seem fine. Yo—"

"Shut it, convict, or I'll have you eat Taser for the first half mile," Jerry snapped.

Staxxx looked wide-eyed at Jerry, then smiled and zipped her lips before tucking the invisible key into her sports bra.

The Anchor floated slowly and precisely toward Jerry and the van. The HMCs latched into the Anchor and then it rotated in the air, as if going to bed, tucking itself into a space near the bottom of the vehicle. Jerry would load the Links' weapons into the same compartment.

Once the HMCs were away and the Anchor had tucked itself in, Jerry seemed to relax. Which was strange, Thurwar thought, as it was then, in those moments between March and city, in the boring but necessary transport, that they were the most dangerous. How easy would it be to pluck Jerry from his life out there. He could only do so much on the Slate before his neck snapped, should they wish it.

"Sorry to be short with y'all. Just under a lot of stress right now and the bosses are watching. 'Cause of the protests and whatnot. Let's get in quick," he said, and Thurwar stopped thinking about the man's death. It was too easy. "I'm gonna go ahead and blue y'all, okay?"

"More than okay, Jerry. That'd be swell," said Randy Mac, his voice saccharine.

"We know the drill," Bad Water said. "I'd like to sit down." He did not move but he shifted his shoulders in the direction of the van.

Thurwar forgot about Bad Water constantly. She guessed he was speaking up now because he'd been included earlier. Socialization has an inertia.

"That's right, hurry it up, busman," Gunny Puddles said. Thurwar knew he was likely angry that Bad Water had spent time with her and Staxxx.

"Okay, quiet game starts now," Jerry said. He tapped a screen quickly and then her wrists glowed blue in the early sun.

"All right, load up," Jerry said. "I'll put everything in the compartment after y'all get settled." And the Links obeyed, shuffled in, all still following Thurwar. Thurwar looked back at Hass Omaha once before stepping forward and into the van. She took the far-left corner and pressed her shoulder blades into the back of the seat. They all faced one another in the back of the van. It was just a rectangle of space, benches along the walls, except for where the door opened and then finally closed once Bad Water had waddled in.

Thurwar felt the artificial cool humming in through vents near her ankles, felt its contrast to the natural cool of the morning. She looked over at Staxxx, who was still now, drawn into herself. Staring straight into nothing. Thurwar rubbed Staxxx with her shoulder, felt her warm. Staxxx kept looking ahead.

Thurwar rubbed again. Staxxx rocked gently to the side, then returned to center, her back to the metal separating the Links from the driver's seat. The door of the van was still open; Jerry was loading their weapons into an under-compartment. She didn't like to think about people handling Hass Omaha and knew it was an abomination for someone like Jerry even to touch Hass's handle. Then she heard the clang and settle, felt the compartment close. Staxxx still stared out at the road, less grounded than she had been. She was a person elsewhere.

She watched Staxxx's chest, saw the pair of Xs there, one for Dame Killowat and another for Herder Yurt, both kills she'd made with Thurwar at her side in a doubles match. She'd gotten the marks to commemorate the fallen that she'd felled with Thurwar there by her side. "Close to my heart," she'd said when she'd returned to Thurwar's arms, marked with fresh blood ink.

Thurwar poked at Staxxx's stomach, then again, hard between the ribs, as Jerry appeared at the van's rear. "Should be a short ride. There's some ruckus and crowds gathered, so don't do anything stupid," he said. Then, "Sorry."

He didn't tap the Slate in his front pocket, but he said the words in a way that made it seem like he had. Thurwar wanted him to leave, so she didn't move again until he'd slammed the door shut.

She waited until she felt him enter the driver's seat, then she squeezed and tickled Staxxx's side. Staxxx had always contained both hot and cold. Two fronts meeting. But Thurwar felt committed to bringing the present, jovial Staxxx back to the space. Arriving in a Hub City after the March was always jarring, with the press and all that followed. It was best to be sharp leading into it. She gently brought a finger to Staxxx's chin and tapped twice before quickly sticking a finger up Staxxx's nose. She was in and out, fast and efficient. Thurwar could see Sai was holding back a laugh. Randy watched, jaw clenched. Gunny Puddles stared, angry or sad as he always was. She moved a little farther away from Staxxx so they weren't touching at all. Staxxx looked at Thurwar, confused, almost as though she was surprised to be there. Her eyes were wide and wonderful.

"I love y——" Thurwar said as quickly as possible, and then she was electric with pain. She felt the shock as a hot squeeze that made her breathless. She dropped in a heap to the floor of the van and the pain moved efficiently, snapped itself closed once it was done. She let herself lie there for a moment, breathing in until her body returned to her control. Then she sat next to Staxxx again and Staxxx laid her head on her lap for the rest of the ride.

McCleskey

The thing I hate is a whiny bitch. And as a student of history, I know that the Blacks are the whiniest bitches there is. My father screamed that into me as a boy, and I'm glad he did 'cause I ain't ever forget.

"Know your history!" Daddy Frederick Puddlelow would scold me if I told him I had Blacks as friends in school. Would slap a textbook across my mouth to make sure I'd learned. He gave me his name and tools to get by in this world: He taught me history and he taught me young and good how to fight.

Outside the van, I can already hear them chanting for us. Not us. For Miss Hammer and Miss Hurricane. The Juliet and Juliet Supreme. Already loud as hell outside. My father would roll over in his grave he saw this shit. People screaming and hollering for murder women. Same women I seen drive a hammer through men's and women's and kids' faces. Same that carve men like hogs. They treat them like saints. That's the Blacks' gift. No matter how bad they is they get treated as the salt of the earth.

Thurwar came into the games gifted with a hammer and the riches of that Bishop woman. Can't admit she's been coddled the whole way. And then Hurricane Crazy Ass wants to tell me how to live when the whole reason I chose this life was so I'd be free of any of that shit ever again. I spent sixteen years straight not getting nothing except a hand to the face for moving too loudly through the home, for eating my fill, for not eating enough. I chose these games 'cause I told myself I was done with rules long time ago.

We slow down and the sound just outside the van is something different. Hub Cities are what make this life a life. The time between the March, getting pushed and pulled up and down the whole gah-damn broken country. The Hub is where the choice to be out here gets its worth. Where we get to rest in soft beds. Air set to temperatures of our liking. Eat hot food. See the cities in the greatest country in the world. Imagine complaining while living the fruits of this choice. And it is a choice.

A choice we all made. A fact you wouldn't know if you looked at the two Black Shebas, murderers just the same as me, but still sweethearts for themselves and America. The worst part is they have the audacity to think they have it worst. One of them is too good to speak to paying crowds. The other talks about love like she's the cure to something. They haven't seen worst, wouldn't know real shit if it punched them square in the titty. Daddy Puddlelow, he wasn't with no bullshit. From me or Mama Puddlelow. He was a cop and that's how that goes.* Mama disappeared; don't blame her though. She woulda got a bullet in the head eventually. He told her enough times. But then again he told me he'd put a bullet in my head too, and I'm still here, so maybe I do blame her some.

As the chants get louder they perk up, pepped and prepared to greet their adoring fans. If Queen T didn't have skin like dirt, would they love her still? If Miss Hurricane didn't have dreadful locs sweeping down her head, would her crazy be so cool? I think not. It's easier to be a Black in all this and it's been that way for years. Imagine being given all the gah-damn freedom the world has to offer and still thinking you weren't getting a fair shake. Imagine being called queen and

---

* It has been found that police officers' families suffer from domestic abuse at a higher rate than non-police-officers' families. The Domestic Violence Offender Gun Ban law passed in 1996, and it required that those convicted of a domestic violence misdemeanor be prohibited from purchasing guns. And yet, this ban does not exempt police officers or members of the military.

still sitting there, looking at me with eyes that say that I'm the one who should hate myself.

The fact is, there are some people who ain't right enough for the rest of the world, and that's all of us here in these Chains. I don't complain about none of it. I don't add some dumb-ass pretend love to the mix either. I know the history is right, it's all square. They've tried it with McCleskey and the courts told them to fuck off.* Nine honorable Supreme Court justices made it clear and still, wah, wah, wah.† All the fucking time. My father was an officer, but he wanted to be a historian. I wanted to be a historian, before I said fuck the rules. But I know my history.

The van slows and the sound of people gets louder. Not the usual rah rah and holler. This feels like a stadium, a chorus of people. Like they reading from a script. Can't quite make it out but it sends a feeling through you like a crawler passing over your neck. The rest of 'em feel it too. Miss Hurricane sitting straight as an arrow. I smile and give her a wink. Surely it's her people making the noise. History will remember her, and damn it, that's a blessing we don't all share.

---

* In 1978, Warren McCleskey, a Black man, was sentenced to death for the murder of a white police officer. He'd robbed a furniture store along with three accomplices. He was given the death sentence, that bloody promise.

   He appealed his sentence, citing both the Eighth Amendment (cruel and unusual) and the Fourteenth (equal protection), and used a study conducted by Dr. David C. Baldus that found that people who killed white people were over four times more likely to receive the death penalty.

   Warren McCleskey lost the case. It established in America the precedent that even solid statistical evidence of racial bias did not offend the Constitution.

† In a 5–4 majority decision the Supreme Court ruled against McCleskey, saying the data produced was best presented to legislative bodies, not the courts. The majority decision was authored by Justice Lewis F. Powell, Jr.

   All five of the majority justices were white.

   After Justice Powell retired, he was asked if there were any decisions he would change, if given the chance. He said yes, and cited *McCleskey v. Kemp*.

Hamara

The shock of being there pressed all around her. She was there but also slipping away from herself.

"Okay, I'm taking y'all's muzzles off in here because there's a rowdy group out there."

A place is a pin. A space-time specific. A drawing on a map.

"There you go, all free—I mean not fr— Well, you get what I mean."

A home is an origin story. A home is a thing to carry. A home is a wild field of energy that floods floods floods. Call me. Call me home.

Jerry read from his tablet.

"All right. Welcome to Old Taperville, your Hub City host. Here you'll complete required Civic Service obligations prior to participation in the BattleGround matches you may or may not have scheduled three days from now. Your schedule is fixed and, uh"—Jerry scrolled through, squinting at the words in front of him—"there it is, any intentional substantial deviations from your Civic Service obligations will result in your immediate termination from the CAPE program. I know y'all have heard this before but they're pushing on all this so just sit tight." Jerry looked through the rearview camera displays lodged into the front of the van. "Your Civic Service work will begin the moment you exit the transport vehicle. You will immediately be escorted to a press conference in a predetermined, accessible community venue."

Jerry looked up briefly—"It's a nice setup they got for y'all here, at a high school"—then went back to reading ". . . Um, following the end of the press conference you will be immediately escorted to your Civic Service locations. Today you will be working alongside members of the community at the local farmers market in Old Taperville Parkside Square.

"Following the Civic Service you will be escorted to your designated Hub City Lodging, which will act as primary holding. In Hub City Lodging spaces you will be given a perimeter within which movement is accepted. Movement outside of that perimeter will result in immediate termination. You will also have access to the full network of Link Market goods, purchasable via BP. You will be given access to training materials and there will be a personal computation terminal available in your assigned Lodging room. Following a forty-eight-hour period, those Links scheduled for the BattleGround, and those who choose to use allotted BP to spectate, will be transported to the predetermined BattleGround Arena and taken into fight custody. Noncompliance with, uh, any of the directives stated therein can result in immediate termination."

Staxxx heard all this and listened to almost none of it.

She thought, Home is another person, a half you find.

"You and me," Thurwar said.

Another half, whole. It's one, you find.

"You and me," Thurwar said again. And it brought Staxxx back to herself.

"You and me," Staxxx said. She looked up and saw Gunny Puddles staring at her. He smiled and his sharp teeth showed a contempt that helped ground Staxxx further. She held his gaze and smiled back.

"Can I get a confirmation that you understand?" Jerry asked. The Links said yes.

Staxxx looked down at her wrists, which were joined together now, bound to each other as if they were in standard handcuffs. There were people just outside the van and they were chanting her name.

"Okay, thanks, you guys. I'm gonna open the door and then y'all

are on your own. I don't wanna hang around for all this. A lot going
on out there today."

Staxxx's eyes had to adjust to the light of the day. The Links shuffled their way out of the van. Thurwar, usually the last to come out, got
up too. Living as a Link, they internalized a kind of showmanship. It
was understood that the people were waiting for a specific one of them,
who should be the grand finale of this small event that was getting out
of the vehicle.

Staxxx was alone in the van. The light poured in. They were screaming, not the name the world had pressed to her body, but the one she
was gifted when she became a body in the world.

Hamara

Hamara

Hamara

STACKER

The chant was deafening. She felt the people screaming energy and
clarity into her being. She took breaths. Looked at her fingers aching to
join together in some sudden urge toward prayer. She kept them apart.

Hamara

Hamara

Hamara

STACKER

When Staxxx was a child, her mother, when she was still clear-
minded, would say, "Be careful who you give your name to, girl. You
don't know how they gonna use it." Staxxx had been taught that when
someone said your name, what they said next had energy. What was
said about you had power.

And now her name had been disseminated around the country in
ways she could not control. To hear these people carry it so powerfully,
to hear her name this way. It was nothing like the screams for thee
Hurricane Staxxx. This was something different entirely.

"Damn," Staxxx said aloud. She sat there, the rest of the Links waiting for her.

"C'mon now," said a soldier-police guard as he poked his head into
the van. "Your subjects are waiting, convict."

"They are," Staxxx said, and she moved forward, felt the syn-
thetic cool bleed into the natural, warm open air. She stood on the

van step and let the people see her. They screamed as if now, finally, they were getting what they'd always wanted. As if seeing her there, standing with her hands bound together, was the home they'd always been searching for. She raised her arms above her head and the people screamed more. The shock of sound almost made Staxxx lose her balance and so she leapt into the air, down to the ground. She kept her hands up, and though the magcuffs gave nothing she was able to make a tiny X with two index fingers and lifted them as high as she could. A sea of Xs, made of arms and fists, flooded the crowd. They were less than one hundred meters from Xavier, her high school, the place where people had first screamed her name. Her stomach was warm with a nostalgia tinged with the sharpness of being a human in captivity; she felt as if she were being pulled apart and stuck back together every other second. She wept as she walked.

HAMARA

HAMARA

HAMARA

STACKER

She kept her hands up as she walked behind the rest of A-Hamm, just behind the armored soldier-police, who swung their batons at the crowd with a gleeful, swift, and casual energy.

A woman stood on the concrete base of the flagpole. She held a megaphone. The American flag hung above her, limp.

"And we won't stop until my sister is freed! I see you, Hammy, and we are with you. We won't rest until you are out of this."

The people screamed at this.

"We are all with you!" the woman yelled.

Staxxx had stopped walking as soon as she heard the voice. The voice of one of her best friends in a different life.

"Tracy," Staxxx said, though there was no chance that Tracy could actually hear her. Staxxx kept her hands high and looked Tracy in the eye. Tracy held her gaze and nodded before screaming back into her megaphone:

Hamara

Hamara

Hamara

Presser

The air was hot with day and the breath of thousands screaming. The Links stepped onto the pavement and then onto the small lawn that sat just before the stretch of road spanning the school's front, presumably where buses pulled up every day to unload and pick up the community's most precious cargo.

The Links walked in the space cleared by men in uniform. Apparently, the producers and GameMasters, those invisible orchestrators of their lives, had not quite anticipated that the crowds in Old Taperville would be so motivated. The protestors far outnumbered the fans, the black they wore distinguishing them from the people who were just there to be entertained. But still, in the middle of it, if you didn't know what was what, it would've been hard to tell the people who were there because they wanted to see Staxxx from the people who were there because they wanted to see her free.

Hamara

Hamara

Hamara

Thurwar looked back at Staxxx, who was smiling and nodding her head, her hands raised up. They'd worked on strength, adding extra push-ups to their daily regimen the last several weeks, and it showed in the lines of her triceps.

Thurwar was glad to be walking. The way they were forced to sit in the van made the pain in her knee scream more quickly than any of the Marching they'd done through the week. She avoided stretching her leg or otherwise tending to it in front of anyone. Thurwar's pain was her own. Sometimes they'd be stuck in the van for hours, but no matter how long, Thurwar would carefully give herself no more than one leg movement per hour. She considered the possibility that Staxxx knew about her knee and decided that she was probably just being paranoid. She wondered too if it was paranoia that had kept her from telling Staxxx about her knee in the first place. As if on some level she'd always known, somewhere in her being, what was coming. Whenever the pain in her knee became unbearable, she'd dive deep into herself and the silence and remind herself that she'd faced worse when she was inside. The specter of the pain of Influencing was a touchpoint in her mind of how bad things could be. She suppressed the memory to survive but she would always have the reference. As long as she was not being shot with the Influencer Rods, things could always be worse.

STACKER

It was the first time since her fight with Melancholia Bishop that a crowd was so decidedly favoring someone who wasn't her. Thurwar smiled at the thought and slowed a bit so she was shoulder to shoulder with Staxxx and rubbed into her side, her shoulder poking into Staxxx's exposed armpit. The crowd, seeing this, screamed anew. A few screamed "LT." It had been months since she'd tried to earn the esteem of any crowd, and yet now she felt a wanting that was hard to locate amid the raw intensity of so many people screaming for the person she loved.

They made it to tall glass doors. Staxxx put her hands down.

"How's it feel to be home?" Thurwar asked.

"It feels like a wild field of energy flooding everywhere."

"A very Staxxx answer," Thurwar said. And there was energy, thick in the air, on their skin.

The building was all hard tile, tan patterns on the floor. Inside. Inside was a thing to hold. They were underneath the sky so much she noticed every time a ceiling was above her head. This building smelled of settled dust and the acidic sharpness of cleaning products. It was pleasantly cooler in the space than it had been outside and seemed to get cooler the farther they walked into the building.

Two soldier-police held open the large wooden doors at the end of the hall, and they entered a room simmering with chatter that quieted as they walked in, then exploded into the flashing lights of cameras.

Thurwar was grateful. For all she'd suffered, and all the suffering she'd caused, she'd never had to return to her hometown as a Link, never had to feel whatever the complicated stew of feelings was that had drawn a large smile all over Staxxx's face.

In front of them, as they approached a stage with a long table, Rico Muerte bumped fists with the reporters and officials, and the locals who had been able to get tickets to the presser.

"We out here!" Muerte said.

Sai raised their hands up in the air for a few moments before lowering them as they walked down the aisles. Thurwar took in the sight of grown people stuffed into the small auditorium seats. Staxxx blew kisses at the flashing cameras.

Thurwar chose not to look down on the celebratory nature of moments like this. Everything you did in Chain-Gang could be the last thing you did. So each time you made it back to a press conference, it was essential to be remembered. It was a time to remind them, a calling out to the world, I'm still here.

"Damn straight!" Gunny Puddles said loudly, screaming up at the high ceiling.

"I love you," Staxxx yelled out to the room.

Some of the A-Hamm Links were already getting seated and Thurwar had just reached the stage steps herself. There were soldier-police at every entrance and four of them stood at either side of the stage.

She stepped up. The house lights flashed awake. She went to the table and found the seat with the card that read *Loretta Thurwar*. It was to the right of the center seat, where Staxxx had just situated herself. As she sat down she felt her hands release from each other. The green was a relief. Under the table, behind the tan tablecloth, she rubbed her sore knee so no one could see. She massaged her patella gently, then worked her way to the meniscus, the most problematic area. With her other hand she took a drink of water. Gunny Puddles sat to her right and she could feel his eyes on her.

"Nice crowd for your lady," Gunny said.

"Yeah," Thurwar replied between gulps. She stopped rubbing her knee. A set of larger cameras in the back of the room caught her attention. And then the press conference began.

"Hi, Staxxx, Kyle Robertson, H2 Sports. Obviously, it must be a wild feeling to see the crowd gathered here for you. What's it like for you right now?"

"Home is an electric field. I feel all of it. I saw some old friends outside and I'm grateful. This building is where I first became an athlete."

Pull back for wide shot of entire table. Back in close to Staxxx and LT.

"I have a long history here. It's where I became a criminal, as you all know."*

Zoom in on big smile. Staxxx in frame pointing to . . . pointing to X on her wrist. Get the X.

"Quick follow-up, does that mean you're especially motivated for this week's deathmatch? Considering the criminal history of one of your opponents."

Reframe to capture her laughing mouth. Stay as laugh settles, dies completely.

"You're asking if I want to kill a rapist? I do not. I'm about love. It's y'all that are about killing."

Pull back, upper body and the Xs.

"I've Low Freed rapists before. Didn't do anything for me. Didn't save me at all. But you already know that too. If it was that easy, this world would be a different place."

"Meghan Melendez, Channel Plex, Thurwar."

Pull and press to Thurwar.

"How are you feeling without your running mate Sunset Harkless, and how do you feel about the fact that he was killed by your very own Hurricane Staxxx and she refuses to say why?"

Tighten on Thurwar. Tighten further. Pause as she looks at Staxxx. Hold. Hold. Pull back. Frame Staxxx's fading smile and glance back at Thurwar.

---

* Eighty-six percent of women in jail have experienced sexual violence. A staggering reality. Most woman in jail have experienced sexual violence.

"First of all, Staxxx is her own person."

"I just meant—"

"We discussed it as a Chain and we won't be discussing it further."

"Do you have any words for those who watched you and Sunset over the years, or maybe Sunset's family?"

Pull back for shot of entire table looking at Thurwar. Hold.

"Sunset was the best friend I had. He was killed by a lot of things. He was offered a hole instead of help. So this was the last of many deaths for him. That's all I'll say about that. I have a lot of other things to think about in the next few weeks."

"Vihaan Patel, Old Taperville Streamlite. So what are you thinking about?"

Pan through right side of table before refocusing on Thurwar's face. Keep there. Thurwar, center frame.

"If you had three days before two incredible warriors tried to kill you and this beautiful woman beside me, what would you be thinking about?"

"Fair enough."

"Efa Teland, Crosshair Capital. This is the last fight together for the two of you. You have more doubles wins than any team in the history of Chain-Gang. How are you feeling leading up to this fight? How do you like your chances?"

Crop to Gunny Puddles, Thurwar, Staxxx, and Randy Mac. Slowly come in to just Staxxx and Thurwar.

"You come this far, it's not about chance anymore, honey. A Hurricane doesn't meet the Mother of Blood by accident."

"We've prepared and we'll be ready."

"And, Staxxx, after this fight you'll also make it to Colossal. Are you excited about that?"

Thurwar's face. Press in on her strained look. Reverse focal length back, reframing to both women.

"I'm Colossal already. After this Sunday, you'll all agree with what's been true for a long time now. Just because the truth is too bright for you to see"—*Hard close-up on Staxxx's face*—"doesn't mean it wasn't there the whole time."

"So you're feeling good about it?"

"I feel like a peregrine falcon mid-dive."

Staxxx's face: The frame. The whole of it. Stay there. Sit there. Let them see her. The tattoos creeping up jawline. Eyes staring, sharp. Press even tighter. Her eyes. Sharp resolution. Stay. Stay.

"You know what that's like? No, you couldn't ever."

Pull back. Her head, the smile returned there. Eyes softened.

"So yeah. I feel good. We'll be ready. We happen to be the best to have ever done these games. And that has nothing to do with chance."

"Thurwar, how does that sound to you?"

"I think she said it all."

"Gretchen Ebb, Ox News, and this is for Thurwar, or really anyone. This past week we've watched as you've fundamentally changed the Chain by unilaterally dictating that no A-Hamm Link can feed for Blood Points on another A-Hamm Link, or otherwise use force to deter potential future aggression. Why now? And do you think there's potential for some kind of blowback? Like maybe A-Hamm won't have as much of an edge on the BattleGrounds now that it's family time on the Circuit?"

Slide across the face of each Link. Linger on Gunny's grin. Sai Eye's raised eyebrows. Staxxx's frown, disappeared up into a smile. Settle tightly on Thurwar's straight face.

"Why now? Because it had to be now. I'm leaving soon, and this is the way it should be."

"But—"

"And understand that when you say 'feed for Blood Points,' you're talking about the underhanded shit that's gone on for too long on Chains all over the Circuit. You're talking about Links getting stabbed in the back. That's over for us and it's a good thing. The world deserved to see Helicopter Quinn go out fighting. So many great Links never make it to the BattleGround for their biggest fights because other, weaker Links do something cowardly on the Circuit. But to answer your question, I did it because it was right. And no, I am not worried about how it will affect us on the grounds."

"It's bullshit but that's all right."

Whip to Gunny Puddles. Pull back to include both.

"I know what I am and what everybody at this table is. We ain't no saints or whatever the people hollering outside think we is. I'm here to eat and get mine and that's it. But for now Her Majesty makes the rules."

"So." *Find a standing Gretchen Ebb in the crowd, second row, far right, pale green blazer.* "Is it that you were afraid for yourself and the other Links? Is that why you've forced a new way of life on the Chain? Or is it because of some idea of civility? It seems it can't be both to me."

"Of course it can be both. But I don't have to be afraid for myself. I'm freed very soon."

Back to Staxxx, leaning forward. Almost standing up. Then to her leaning back in her chair, laughing a big laugh. Scale aperture up, blur everything behind her. Make her a painting in this moment. Lock focus on eyes. Brown. Glowing.

"Come join us in A-Hamm, Gretchen, and see how you feel about it."

Slowly flatten out picture and pull back.

"To be fair, I'm not a criminal accused of—"

"So then leave it to the criminals to sort out themselves."

Thurwar's face, straight, even.

"Gina Preian, Megavolt Streams 3. Thurwar, as your illustrious career as a Link begins to wind down, what are you most proud of, looking back? And what do you think the families of your victims will think about your possible freeing?"

Thurwar appears confused. Her eyes, shine on them. See the light they reflect.

"There are a bunch of other people on this Chain who have been working very hard prepping for this weekend. Do you want to ask any of them about what they think?" Thurwar sits back, drinks a gulp of water.

"Yeah," says Rico Muerte.

Find him.

"I'm getting ready to whoop"—*Find Rico Muerte near table's end*— "some real ass. This weekend gonna be historic. What do you wanna know about that?"

Reporters' hands fly up through the dark.

We the Enslaved

When they asked her what she was most proud of, what she always thought about was hunger. She'd helped organize it, the hunger strike when she was still in prison. She'd stopped eating. Stopped working her busywork because conditions in her own prison were beneath human decency and beneath human dignity. And she'd gone on strike not just for those around her, but for those in other prisons like hers—there were so many—and those in the immigration detention camps too, who were being held for no crime at all except trying to live. Prisons have a way of speaking to one another, and when they'd learned about the horrors elsewhere, they took action. She'd written a draft of her statement and slipped it on a piece of paper to a reporter who had taken an interest in the lives of women in prison.

To all with a conscience and a sense of justice:

We the enslaved of the GEOD system facility known as the Forthwright Detention Center stand imprisoned but in power and solidarity with the imprisoned located at New Holly, and we reject the separation of families and the inhumane violence set against innocent refugees. We reject the notion that so-called aliens, because of their non-citizenship, must be subject to inhumane conditions in poorly organized *detention centers. We further condemn the rape and sexual assault that is and has been prevalent in these facilities as well as the trading and bartering of children into any number of horrors.* We demand that these so-called immigration detention centers be abolished and ask for a more humane method of accepting those in need into our country. We demand an end to neo-slavery in GEOD systems and all American detainment institutions, which have long kept the harsh flame of slavery alive in this country. We find abhorrent the ease with which humans subject other humans to torture in the name of righteousness and justice, and we are ready to put our lives on the line to ensure our demands are met.*

Signed,

Dr. Patricia St. Jean
Marsha Banwitten
Loretta Thurwar
Lacie Kolare
and all members of the Forthwright Rights Collective

They had been her words, but the small group of women who had identified as part of the collective on her block believed in the words and had given the okay. They had starved together.

They had been on day six of their hunger strike when the guards had thrown her into isolation and told her she would be Influenced. She'd seen the smiles on some, heard stories of eyes ripped from skulls, had begged them not to do it. They'd said, "Let's see how ready you are," and stabbed a black rod connected to a wire and finally a controller into her thigh.

She'd eaten her fill that night. The Influencing had shown her that her life, already a blight, could fit so much more pain than she had imagined. And she was not willing to see how much of that pain they could pull out of her. The following day she'd signed the papers to join the CAPE program.

---

* About 14,700 complaints alleging sexual and physical abuse were lodged against Immigration and Customs Enforcement (ICE) between 2010 and 2016. Thousands and thousands. ICE was created in 2003 as part of the government's response to the September 11 attacks.

Interview

There was a man in a white shirt, a bass drum harnessed to his front, probably in his sixties. He swung a deep hit every third syllable. He was a grand unifier for them all, a battery. One of many. By the time Nile saw him, as they walked toward the school where the Links were waiting, the back of the man's shirt was translucent with sweat.

The people united will never be defeated.

Twenty-four members of the Coalition to End Neo-Slavery had made the trip. They'd arrived later than they'd wanted, but they were there. They'd come wearing black, as had most people at the protest. They were in the hometown of the Hurricane, just days before Thurwar's penultimate BattleGround match. They'd long planned to be here to protest, just as they had at Vroom Vroom. They hadn't planned on being joined by thousands. But the energy of the movement was different now.

Nile felt like a drop in a tidal wave. They were doing something, there was no question. He looked at Mari, who wore a black shirt that read *ABOLITION NOW* in thick red block letters. She was staring straight ahead at the masses around them, but she didn't seem to be seeing anything at all.

The people united will never be defeated.

There was space to move but only forward. They filled the road and the roadside with bodies. There was a couple, two women in black dresses, burning sage that smoked up and added a savory warmth to the air, which was electric with purpose. Just the fact of them, this mass of people, was a statement. And yet there was so much more to say. There they all were, on a westbound road to a farmers market of all places. Mari thought of the ridiculousness of the world and the hard beauty of what she was a part of. She didn't want to be there. She was tired. Or rather she was exhausted by the brutality that was so ubiquitous in American culture. A reporter trailed by a cameraman holding a small rig on his shoulder pushed past the women in black; their bundle of sage fell to the ground. Both women disappeared into the mass to retrieve it, and when they came back up, Mari saw they were both smiling. One grabbed a lighter from a pocket, the other held the herb.

The people united will never be defeated.

A reporter, a woman with a shaved head, approached Mari.

Before she realized it, she had agreed to be interviewed. She cursed herself for doing something so stupid, considering her plan.

"Can you spell your entire name out for me?"

Mari stared at the woman. She decided to herself, Fine.

Marissa Roleenda spelled her name.

The woman smiled at her and asked, "How do you justify calling for the freeing of rapists and murderers?" And wasn't that what it always came down to? Fear.

The people united will never be defeated.

Mari looked at the woman and took a breath.

"I'm an abolitionist, which means I'm interested in investing in communities to address problems rather than carceral answers that don't serve communities at all. Murderers and rapists do great harm," Mari said, "but the carceral institutions in this country do little to mitigate that harm. In fact, they do more harm to individuals and communities. The carceral state depends on a dichotomy between innocent and guilty, or good and bad, so that they can then define harm on their terms, in the name of justice, and administer it on a massive scale to support a capitalistic, violent, and inherently inequitable system." And though this was what she said, and had said so many times, a part of her even then understood what this reporter was getting at. There were some people who she did not think should be released. Her father had been one of them.

"It seems like you've done your homework. But the fact remains that these systems protect communities from violence. Are you saying you aren't worried about killers and rapists walking free on the streets?" the woman asked, dropping her tone as if they were just now starting to speak about something serious.

"I'm saying that the death penalty has always been an abomination, even before the CAPE program. Prison as it exists is an abomination. Right now, the fact is, people are doing the exact kinds of harm you're describing. Prisons haven't deterred the harm they're meant to deter. They're a failed experiment."

"What does that mean? Aren't there fewer criminals on our streets?"

"I mean that all those issues that you're talking about are symptoms of our current system. Rampant poverty, a lack of resources for people suffering from addiction and mental health issues—those are difficult problems, but ones that can be addressed. But they aren't. Because criminalization dehumanizes individuals and implicates them rather than a society that abandons them in times of need."

"And what about the jobs Chain-Gang All-Stars and the prisons you hate so much create? Have you considered those positive aspects of our carceral system?"

Here Mari smiled weakly, an automatic response to an absurd idea, that this was about employment or that employment might justify these deaths. The woman's face snapped from a sinister but inviting warmth to a slate of cool anger.

"Is that funny to you?"

What do we want?

"It isn't."

Justice!

"There has never been a time when men didn't prey on women. When the strong didn't prey on the weak. As an abolitionist, how do you answer to those who fear for their lives, for their children and their families? Would you release people who have victimized others onto the streets?" The woman's voice shook. "You want them out so they can do it again?"

Mari hadn't wanted her father released to her, but she wished he'd grown up in a world that had loved him better. She'd feared what her life would be with him in the world but knew that he didn't deserve what he'd been given. She'd been angry for such a long time about how his decisions had shaped her life, and she was afraid of what her life would have become with him. She had not wanted him released to her, but she had wanted him freed to the world at least. When he'd died, at least a small part of her had felt settled, that a long journey had concluded. Another, louder part felt renewed in her desire to dismantle it all.

The woman looked straight at Mari, and the cameraman peeked out from behind the viewfinder and turned to his coworker with wide eyes.

Mari looked at the woman, who was angry, who was upset, but who was not her enemy.

When do we want it?

Now!

"Do you not have an answer? My sister was— I want to know what you'd tell her if she was still alive."

Nile watched Mari speaking with the woman as they marched. He got closer so he could hear.

"I'm sorry you lost your sister. I'm sorry she was robbed of a chance to live and I'm sorry you have to suffer that loss."

"It seems like you'd like to reduce our justice system to a series of 'I'm sorry's.'"

Mari paused as if trying to find words that hadn't been invented yet. "We aren't asking for an erasure. We aren't trying to forget the pain of victims. For us, abolition is a positive process. It means creating new infrastructure, new ways of thinking about reducing harm. That's what we're saying. I'm not saying there isn't something to be afraid of. We're saying the thing we fear is already here, so it's wrong not to try to do better. And I can't say that any one of us has the perfect answer of what to do, but we might be able to figure something out if we consider it together."

What do we want?

Justice!

The cameraman recording them took steps backward as the interview followed the flow of the protest.

"And besides that, Chain-Gang has only deepened an already incredible indifference to human suffering. That's what we're protesting today."

"And yet, you don't have any answers for the actual people who won't ever get to be who they were again. For the people whose trauma will shape their whole lives," the reporter said.

"I—"

When do we want it?

Kai stepped forward. "That's enough, I think."

Now!

"Maybe," Mari said, still to the reporter. "But I don't think so."

"That's enough, Mari," Kai said.

"I'm sorry about your sister," Mari said. "And I'm sorry for you." Nile tried to move even closer.

"You're sorry," the journalist spat. "But my sister's still in the ground. So what does your sorry do?"

When do we want it?

Now!

"Let's go," Kai said. She put a hand on Mari's shoulder.

Kai

What do we want?

"You didn't have to speak to her," Kai said. There were so many reporters scattered through the masses. Kai wasn't sure who many of them represented. And though she trusted Mari with the message, she wasn't sure she wanted Mari's face so clearly presented for the public. *Justice!*

"I know," Mari said. "I wanted to." Kai saw her retreating back into the faraway place she'd been in for the last several weeks. *When do we want it?*

Kai had tried to see if she could understand. *Now!* She'd made some of Mari's favorite meals to try to draw her out, but Mari had eaten them in a reclusive silence in her room. She'd holed herself up in a solitude that was unlike her. Even Nile—a boy who was clearly in love with Kai's daughter—hadn't been around much. Mari had lost her father, a man she had hardly known but who was known to the world. In the years since Mari's graduation Kai had tried to keep her as close as possible. She'd sensed Mari's struggles with anxiety when she was away even though Mari rarely spoke about them. She'd wanted to make her feel safe. *What do we want?* And yet the only answer she could come up with, the only thing that felt right, was to continue pushing, to continue keeping her close under her wing. *Justice.*

So now she decided not to say anything to her daughter. Because that's what she was. For Mari's whole life, Kai had been the one Mari could depend on. Not Kai's sister, who was incarcerated, or the man they'd called Sunset. She was the one who had been there for Mari. She watched her as she chanted with all of the many people who walked down that small road with them, completely blocking one side of it. *When do we want it?*

Already there were thousands of people and they hadn't even gotten to the high school, the meeting point, which was only a short walk from the farmers market, their ultimate destination. It was a beautiful thing to be a part of. A beautiful thing to get to do with her daughter. To walk with thousands, to show up and be a drop in a great waterfall. And still she had a feeling—she had a feeling that was keeping her from taking part fully. She felt the need to protect. She was worried for Mari and the coalition, as she always was in big demonstrations, but especially following Vroom Vroom; it kept her from being present. *Now!*

She watched as Nile shifted past Marta until he was shoulder to shoulder with Mari. He smiled at her, and when she smiled back it seemed the smile on her mouth was for him rather than from her. *What do we want?*

Kai thought about Mari's father, Shareef, and all that might have been had he been in her life. It was a spiral of a thought experiment that she had been explicitly told by her therapist to curb, and yet it was that possibility that she was thinking about as they continued walking toward the school. She glanced at the drummer, who was several yards ahead of them. His arms were at his sides, his head held high in the air. A woman with green strands braided into her hair carried his stick and beat the drum for him while he rested. *Justice.*

It was clear they were approaching their initial destination. Megaphoned voices were giving out directions and commands and encouragement and leading chants. *When do we want it?* An energy that had been thrumming began to pulse and grow as the people became more concentrated. Chants bled into one another as different parties yelled, announcing their hopes with their voices. There was a feeling of community that could not easily be captured. To pound the ground, to show up with one's body. *Now!* It was a special and necessary thing. It was not always the most effective action, and for some it was tiresome. But for Kai it was rejuvenating. To remember that they were not alone, that they were legion. It made her feel a power that she didn't feel anywhere else. *What do we want?* To be among all those different people from different shades of life, to be there with her daughter, who had grown into a brilliant and focused young woman despite the early trauma, in spite of her anxieties. Kai was the one the steering committee of the Coalition to End Neo-Slavery looked to for most things, but Mari, very clearly, was the organization's heart. *Justice.* Mari was so often the one offering up readings for them, the one willing to engage with the hard question of freedom and all of its implications, even the most obvious and unpleasant, the question of the incarcerated who were violent and would continue to be violent if given the chance. And Kai got to do what she cared about best with her daughter. *When do we want it?* She hadn't pushed Mari into the life of caring, of actively advocating, of abolition, but she had welcomed her enthusiastically. *Justice.* But she wondered, sometimes, if welcoming and pushing weren't the same thing for a child like Mari, who had two parents who'd spent most of her life incarcerated.

Now!

Nile bumped gently into the person in front of him. The people had come to a sudden stop.

"Sorry, sorry," Nile said.

"No worries," the woman said. *What do we want?*

And when Kai looked up she looked first at her daughter and then at what her daughter was looking at. *Justice.* They were late—or were they right on time? *When do we want it?* The women who had become the crux of the movement were walking right in front of them. *Now!* Passing them on the same crosswalk, the soldier-police surrounding them and the other poor souls forced to play in those insidious murder games.

They were leaving the school, heading to the market. The protestors cheered them on. Mari was watching Thurwar closely, and Kai could swear that Thurwar had not only caught Mari's gaze but was staring right back. *What do we want?*

Balloon Archway

They were used to crowds, though not usually this size. But it was the energy, the way they screamed the names out, that made Thurwar remember what her life was. That was, there had never been a time when so many people, who cared sincerely for them, were around in these numbers. It made it impossible to forget they were the subject of a great and incredible evil. There were so many people there, and in their presence Thurwar felt a part of something massive, something terrible that could unearth something good.

Soldier-police pushed and swatted a path clear for them to walk toward the market. The people in black clothing did not aim to touch her and most did not take pictures. But they called her name, Staxxx's name, the names of everyone on the Chain, with a tenderness that hurt to hear. It made her remember who she'd been before all this. When her name had meant she was being recognized for who she was, not the commodity she had become. And that reminder brought with it a deep understanding of Bishop and all the other Links who had made to end their lives in battle. Thurwar usually, when she thought of her own death, thought of it as a deserved punishment. But these people, these people screamed so loudly not only that she didn't deserve to die, but that she didn't deserve any aspect of what her life had become.

Suicide was a part of the CAPE culture, though it wasn't publicly called that.* It was almost never on the March, out in the open with at least the potential for a sunny day and a bit of peace, or in the adrenalized mayhem of the deathmatches that Links killed themselves. Although that did happen. There were the Arson Johnsons, the Melancholia Bishops. Arson Johnson was famous for being Melancholia's first BattleGround kill. He'd kneeled and taken Hass Omaha's blow almost gleefully. And years later Melancholia had all but done the same in front of Thurwar.

But despite the brutality of the March, it was in the more domestic stays in the Hub Cities prior to the BattleGround matches that most Links chose to separate themselves from themselves. It was when they returned to a life most like a civilian's. When survival is difficult something in you begs the attempt. When it's easy, it's a different thing entirely. Thurwar thought of this as she walked from the school, careful to let Staxxx lead the way, though she stayed just behind her.

Free Hamara, free Loretta! the crowd screamed.

Thurwar, overcome by a spirit she did not dare smother, punched a fist into the air and the crowd screamed louder. A further affirmation of a truth Thurwar tried not to let too close: She was a human being tortured. That had been true before she'd joined CAPE and it had grown truer every moment of her life the past three years. It hurt to admit this, although it was something she couldn't ever forget. But she had never had the truth she lived affirmed so brightly by people outside the Chains.

And now, to complete their torture, they were going to ask her to destroy her favorite person. The person who had kept her on earth. Thurwar let the people's voices carry her. She let their hope seep into her veins.

The eight soldier-police around them, four in front and four in back, stepped quickly and precisely. Another blessing of the Hub Cities was the sweet semblance of privacy. In the cities, the HMCs were seldom seen. The exclusivity of being a Hub City depended on a "you

---

* Suicide is the leading cause of preventable death among prisoners. From 2001 to 2019 suicide exploded in prisons. In that span of time the number of suicides increased 85 percent in state prisons, 61 percent in federal prisons, and 13 percent in local jails.

had to be there" energy, and so, in these times between the Circuit and before the BattleGround, the Links were not on-screen.

They were walking toward a park in the middle of town. She wanted Staxxx to enjoy being loved, she wanted Staxxx to love her, she wanted to keep loving Staxxx, and she wanted to tell her they would soon be asked to kill each other. She couldn't decide which of these she wanted most.

Then Thurwar saw her. In the middle of all this feeling and energy. It was the girl. As if summoned by the force in the air. As if the truth had appeared physically to move her to action. As if the raw energy of the people around Thurwar had manifested in the presence of the young woman. She was standing on the white lines of the crosswalk. The same woman who'd given Thurwar the card that had thrown her life into this new lonely terror. She stood there like an omen. Thurwar kept pace and nodded to her. A woman she was grateful for but also hated, for stealing from her the bliss of ignorance.

She made sure not to turn around or to indicate otherwise that she'd seen someone important to her. Someone she knew in some strange and delicate way. There were eyes everywhere, even without the HMCs floating around. People were always watching.

She considered the woman, the truth-bringer, and noticed that her brightness, which had peppered Thurwar's dreams for the past week, was gone. And she decided that maybe even if she did hate her, she also loved her. There was a reason she'd appeared again now. Thurwar was a curator of truth herself. She staged it, gave it light, made it available to herself when needed, and sometimes shelved it altogether. Stashed it hard into the recesses of her mind. But there was no destroying what was true. Still she curated, and she was good at it. The proof was her life. She continued to continue, had not removed herself from herself as so many in her position had when given the chance.

There was a concentrated and still-growing mass of people at the town's center, where they had a farmers market. There was a balloon archway so tall and welcoming it made Thurwar a little sick to see it. Pastel blues and greens and whites and golds swayed in the breeze as a DJ played a song that the world knew as Staxxx's intro song. Electronic and bright but also melodic and deep.

They continued on a sidewalk in a space that people might have described as quaint. She focused on Staxxx, who seemed to be trying to squeeze everything around her into her mind at once. She looked this way, then at a tree, giggled at a squirrel moving up a trunk as if that squirrel had been her squirrel and she was tickled to find it. Behind the two of them Randy and Sai walked, both smiling, the ripples of Staxxx's energy washing through them. Bad Water smiled too, excited to be around other people. And behind all of them was a huge congregation, a black wave following, chanting so loudly that they could never be ignored.

Their lives were always strange. Every day they lived the cruel and unusual, but as the screams for their liberation shook behind them and the smell of popcorn wafted in from the approaching market, Thurwar felt a new flavor of dread. The end of what had been her life was right in front of them.

"Inmate Thurwar, Inmate Stacker, you two will be at station one, Deane's Creams," one of the men in armor plates said. As usual, the police had equipment that suggested war and not cotton-candy stands. Equipment that would only make sense if they were expecting other similarly armed police officers suddenly to revolt and turn against them. Four of the other remaining soldier-police had moved back to the metal barricade that had been erected around the entire farmers market. The protestors, upon realizing that they would not be let into the farmers market—the official price for entry that morning was significant and had to have been paid in advance—flooded the perimeter. Now, behind the metal barricade, there was a second wall, this one of people all dressed in black. Meanwhile the Chain-Gang fans inside the farmers market were studiously buying cotton candy or perusing the tomatoes, going out of their way to pretend that this was all normal and that there weren't an extra thousand people there, protesting just a few yards away.

"Got it," Thurwar said, and she looked at Staxxx.

"Us," Staxxx said, and it made Thurwar's heart dance a little bit. Then Staxxx looked at the soldier-police officer and said, "Do you think they have any vegan flavors? I'm lactose intolerant."

"I know," the officer said with a grin. "Literally everybody knows you're a lactose-free pescatarian."

"I'm just saying, 'cause that would be a pretty fucked up Civic Service to have me at an ice-cream stand all day knowing I can't eat any of it," Staxxx said.

"You might just have to owe your stomach one. I bet they got that fresh straight-from-a-cow shit," Rico said.

"Never 'owe your stomach one' before the grounds," Staxxx said, and she might as well have been chatting about the weather. "That's a pro tip." And then, with a vicious speed, she turned around and punched Rico's stomach. Just before she made contact, though, she erased her fist's velocity to nothing, so she barely pressed into him before turning back to the armored men. "Bad Water got lucky that one time, isn't that right, day-old-tuna man?"

"That's right," Bad Water said, his cheeks glowing.

Thurwar drank in the moment. The little moments of Staxxx. The way she carried herself. When she was feeling good, there was no one like her. When she was feeling bad, she was just as special. A person so unchained despite it all. Staxxx reminded anyone lucky enough to see her that there were parts of a human that could never be chained.

"Okay, enough." The officer made his voice big to try to remind them that he was in charge, though his having to try made it feel exactly the opposite. Under the scrutiny of the protestors, who were still flooding the surrounding area, the officers seemed keen on proving they were good men, that they weren't the enemy, and yet there could be no enemy but them. They were the ones with guns. On the opposite road two more soldier-police tanks rolled down the road. The sound of them smoothed the head officer's mouth into a calm line.

"Stacker and Thurwar, down that way to station one now. Or do you need an escort?"

"We can make it, I think," Thurwar said. They left the group and walked in the direction of a table covered with cloth and six tubs of ice cream. There was a large sandwich board out front that read DEANE'S CREAMS in extravagant red script. A man and a woman and two kids were waiting in front of the table already.

B3 IS NOT FOR ME. B3 IS NOT FOR ME. B3 IS NOT FOR ME.

The chants were everywhere in the air.

Thurwar was alone with Staxxx, or as close to alone as she could ask for. She grabbed Staxxx's hand into hers for just a moment before letting go.

They walked in the soft grass, and once they were a few feet from the officers it was as if the spell had been broken and the gravity their bodies had become accustomed to was reengaged. A stricter perimeter for their movement had been established, although their wrists still showed green.

A small boy stomped toward them, trailed closely by his parents, who smiled warm and shy.

"You're the greatest of all time," he said definitively to Thurwar. Then he turned, just so, to Staxxx and said, "And you're the third-greatest of all time."

"Jimmi," the boy's father said.

"Wow, in my own hometown?" Staxxx said, winking up at the parents. More people had gathered around them. The feeling of being closed in on was familiar to them both. Staxxx let out a too-huge sigh. "You know what, that's okay. Everyone's entitled to their opinions," Staxxx laughed. The parents looked at her gratefully.

"We—we really are huge fans of yours. We always have been. We remember when you ran at Xavier. We support you completely," the mother said. And Thurwar considered this familiar absurdity. How it was punctuated so strongly by the massive crowds all around them.

"Can you sign my hammer?" the little boy asked Thurwar. He offered up a LifeDepot™-brand hammer, the kind that might be in any toolbox. The suggestion that this might somehow be like Hass Omaha was insulting, but the insult was received with a smile. She had signed so many rubber grips before.

"Sure, you got a marker?"

"I do!" a different person, not in the first family, said, and it was clear that this large crowd would make the short walk to the ice-cream stand a journey. "But why don't we let these ladies get to doing what they came here for, y'all," the man said. He wore a maroon apron that read DEANE'S across the front. "Why don't you sign little Jimmi's and then we'll let the rest flow through the stand?"

"Sounds good," Thurwar replied. She took his marker, wrote "LT" on the grip, and followed him through the crowd.

The Farmers Market

Randy Mac stood at the register of an organic cheese stand associated with a farm owned by an Amish family.

"Seems like partaking in this would be a little against the code or something?" Mac said. He sniffed cheeses. A line had formed in front of the stand, the people's holophones out and ready to record. Randy knew the reason they were participating: money.

"It is," the bearded man said, and then he smiled.

"Say it. Say the thing you say," said the first man in line, who had to be Randy's father's age. He pointed a holophone.

EVERY DAY A DEVASTATION

"No," Randy said, and he handed the man a circle of cheese.

"Fuck you," the man said, smiling as he took a video anyway.

The farmer's wife appeared from behind the stand with a goat that had apparently been sleeping.

"You kidding me?" Randy asked, taking the goat in with his eyes.

EVERY DAY A DEVASTATION

The goat was a regular beauty. He kneeled down and petted her head. "She's beautiful."

Sai Eye made lemonade. They worked in front of a pile of lemons and limes that climbed up to their waist. The owners of the lemonade stand were a youngish couple with pale skin and brown hair. They looked like they could be siblings.

"I have to know what I'm selling," Sai Eye said, taking a drink from a paper cup. "Okay, okay. That's good shit."

"Thank you," the couple said in tandem.

EVERY DAY A DEVASTATION

There was already a line twenty people deep. Having done a lot of so-called Civic Service before, Sai Eye knew what was to come. People telling them what they thought or didn't think about their identity. So many opinions that were never asked for. Civilians offered their opinions like gifts to Sai Eye Aye. They'd gotten used to it. Sai Eye had long before decided to accept their harshness with a laugh.*

"Before we get started, we just wanted to say thank you for being here. We totally support you and, like, your whole thing," the woman said.

"So you guys wanna help me escape today? Is that what you're saying?" Sai said, straight-faced.

"No, no." The man literally hopped forward in the soft grass. "We just meant we're totally supportive of you and your identity."

"So no escape, then?" Sai asked, then laughed, letting them off the hook. "I'm just joking. Let's sell some lemonade."

The people never stopped chanting and it made the whole thing, the farmers market and the Links' presence there, even more ridiculous. Sai Eye could lean into the joke.

Sai put their hand in the middle of the group and gestured for the other two to do the same, as if they were a high school basketball team. "'Lemonade' on three," Sai said.

Walter "Bad Water" Crousey was, as usual, surprised to be alive. But life was a thing that seemed to stick to him despite all the bad luck that found him too.

---

* Trans Americans are more than twice as likely to be incarcerated as cisgender Americans. More than twice. And trans people of color are more likely to be incarcerated than white trans people. The vulnerable are targeted, again, always.

He gulped a sip from a water bottle. "I get it, 'cause I'm Bad Water," he said.

"Exactly, except our water is good," the young man who owned the stand said.

Good water, a rarity for so many. His name was a reminder that some places, like where he was born, still had to struggle to find drinkable sips of the most basic necessity. That and Wright had liked the ring of it.

"Right," he said. And waited. For now no one was at the water stand but him and the stand owner, who was probably eighteen. Around the same age Crousey had been when he'd been thrown in.

Ten years ago he'd been innocent.* And now he wasn't in the same way. Now he'd killed. Funny how things went. He tried to forget that he'd been thrown in for nothing. Thrown in for being poor, lawyerless, and dumb. He went in for murder and was sure that they'd see he wasn't like that, couldn't be like that. And yet here he was.

The soldier-police walked Rico to his stand. Bunches of shining tomatoes of many sizes and colors. In a few minutes, customers would start asking him for pictures. Could they see that he was terrified? This was a question that had run through his mind from the beginning. So much of his life had been spent wondering exactly this. He looked at Randy, who was petting a goat and laughing. Sai was sipping lemonade. Even Bad Water was—well, he wasn't doing anything, but he didn't look terrified. Just lost, or surprised.

Why the fuck am I such a bitch? Rico thought as he wiped his hands against his gray sweatshirt. There was an energy summoned by the collective that surrounded them, and it scared the shit out of him. Each of them might know how terrified he was if he could not prove otherwise.

Rico smiled. "What's poppin'?" he asked an old white lady and her daughter.

They looked at him.

---

* It is estimated that between 2.3 percent and 5 percent of incarcerated people in America are innocent. That number represents potentially over 100,000 people. George Stinney, Jr., again and again.

"How's it going?" he tried again.

EVERY DAY A DEVASTATION

The crowds screamed, pressing and punctuating each syllable into the air. Rico looked past the tomato hustler and her daughter, out at the masses. The people closest to the gate were watching him, carrying signs. The dissonance between the protestors and the people in the farmers market made him want to jump out of his own body. It was a dissonance that he felt in his core. They were all humans, and yet they had completely different ideas about what humanity meant.

"We're doing well," the mother said.

"We got some great tomatoes today," the girl said. And when they spoke, their eyes brightened, and their almost trembling voices caused a great wave of calm to rush through his body.

EVERY DAY A DEVASTATION

They did not know he was terrified; in fact, they feared him.

"Lemme see how great" is what he said. And he smiled but hoped they knew he knew.

.   .   .

EVERY DAY A DEVASTATION

Ice Ice the Elephant. Was a man, a warrior, a great gladiator, and a wise ally. He was a Link in Chain-Gang All-Stars. These things were true.

"It's an easy day," he told himself as he held a paper cone to the machine spinning fresh pink sugar.

"Ice Ice over here with the cotton candy," a young man said to his phone, presumably to the five people who cared that he was livestreaming.

"Hey," Ice Ice said to the boy.

"Oh shit, Ice Ice the fucking Elephant just spoke to me, y'all. Insane," the boy said, still mostly just glancing at Ice Ice occasionally while he talked into his holophone and its electric reflection.

Ice Ice gave a cotton candy to a woman who grazed his hand unnecessarily.

"Thanks," she said. "Wish you and me could get outta here after this."

She didn't, but it was a delusion, an offering, and a joke all in one.

Ice said nothing.

He looked over his shoulder to the woman who ran the cotton-candy stand. The woman who handled the register.

"You're doing great," she said.

If that's how they felt, he didn't see why they were pussyfooting with the signs and the screaming.

"That's a lot of horseshit, isn't it?" Gunny said to the old man, who was angling a rocking chair so it could better catch the leaves of light that poked though the sugar maple just behind the woodcrafts stand Gunny had been assigned to.

"Sorry?" the man said, looking up at him. He had a thick white beard and sharp blue eyes. He was almost comically comparable to Santa Claus.

"It's horseshit that all these people are trying to ruin the good time y'all are trying to have this afternoon."

Gunny gestured to the protestors, the closest of which were about thirty feet to his left.

"Fuck off!" Gunny screamed at them.

EVERY DAY A DEVASTATION

Santa looked at Gunny and Gunny watched some slow math unfold in his blue eyes. Gunny saved him the trouble.

"I'm not fucking with you. I know where I'm supposed to be and I'm sorry that these people are causing so much trouble, thinking they know shit."

The man was silent as he stood up from the rocking chair.

"When we start selling, please keep the cussing to a zero."

Gunny regarded him. It was a little sickening how unafraid he was. The way he acted as if he were dealing with some intern and not a man who had gutted hard sonofabitches up and down the goddamn country.

Gunny threw his head back and laughed.

Then the black outside the gates began spilling in. The screaming and chanting changed. And Gunny Puddles thought, Finally. This at least was something.

"Oh dear," Santa said.

"Oh dear is fucking right."

Deane's Creams

He watched.

"You have any lactose-free stuff?" Staxxx asked as she offered herself in the form of a big hug to Melanie Deane, who smiled and hugged back. The tiny woman disappeared in Staxxx's arms. She was beaming when Staxxx released her. Next, Staxxx kneeled down to shake the hand of their eight-year-old.

"I'm Jim," Jimmi said.

"Big Jim," Staxxx said immediately. "Who thinks I'm third place." Jimmi smiled with his whole body.

Thurwar greeted Jimmi's mother, then she and Staxxx addressed the other young man at the stand, who wasn't smiling at all. "Hi, handsome," Staxxx said, and Thurwar smiled at him and offered a hand, which he accepted without a trace of glee.

There were a lot of people watching this happen. In fact, his people had heard that there were over eight thousand unplanned guests outside the farmers market. And inside the farmers market, there were supposed to be nine hundred and thirty-one paying patrons cycling through over the course of four hours.

But now, at the start of this Civic Service sequence, fewer than four hundred had arrived. That was troubling, certainly. That was why he was there. There were a lot of people watching, yes. But none watched like him. His outfit was curated by the same stylist who had dressed their hosts for years now, though his clothes were far simpler, more mundane than anything a fight host would wear for a cast. The idea was to be just the opposite of television-ready. He smirked to himself, his eyes hidden behind the shining dark of his wraparound sunglasses. He'd already spotted three different patrons wearing just the same sort, with a fourth passing by now. "That's a win," he said to himself.

"What?" Rebecca, who was stationed in the back of one of the soldier-police vans, said.

"Nothing," he said, touching his glasses, which were also a two-way communication device the ArcTech people had thrown in during their last product demo. And that was when they'd expected a group a fourth of this size to show up. He had assured the board that things were fine and now he was here to see with his own concealed eyes how big a lie he'd told.

He felt the breeze against his calves. He'd paired his glasses with brown khaki shorts and a nicely ironed teal polo and a headband that said *ThurWAR!* to complete the ensemble. He was standing at the edge of the crowd watching Thurwar and Staxxx become acquainted with the rules and regulations of Deane's Creams and a single word came to mind. A single word was the foundational bedrock of his approach to the work he did, this art he manifested in real time all around the world: elegance.

His name was Mitchell Germin, and he was the director of content and broadcast management. That was his title, but to the people on his team, especially his assistant directors, like Rebecca, he was a master of creating elegant and sustainable entertainment ecosystems. And sometimes, like right then, as he watched two of his prized mares try to make nice with a frowning teen, thousands of unpaying lunatics yelling all around them, his job required him to become a freaking spy.

But when he wasn't doing ground-level reconnaissance, trying to get the temperature of a scene, to make sure the product wasn't being compromised, he was a man who helped orchestrate the most elegant sports program the world had ever seen. More than a sports program—it was the most real of the reality casts. There were stakes in this show so deep audiences were literally addicted to outcomes. But that always had been true. What he'd done was twofold: He'd introduced Blood Points, the currency that now had entire podcasts dedicated to its use, and he'd also realized that when you emphasized the fact that everybody involved in the Chain-Gang Circuit was a criminal, companies became more and more willing to advertise with the organization. Once they'd started identifying each Link by their crimes, their deaths no longer held the same weight to the viewers. The nut to crack in any criminal-justice sport was to separate the criminal from the human. When humans saw other humans, they felt "bad" for whoever had gotten sliced up that week. When humans saw a criminal die, well, that was different.

"That's really them! They're taller than I thought," a man standing next to Mitchell said, his voice drenched in awe. Mitchell shifted his weight a little, then spoke.

"Six foot one and five foot ten, but taller in their boots."

"It's really something," the man said. He was about Mitchell's height, meaning that both of them were significantly shorter than either Staxxx or Thurwar.

This man was one of so many. And here was another piece of elegance. He clearly felt awe and respect for these two women but also was not bothered by the fact that they lived a razor's edge from death. He knew it likely helped that they were Black women; market research found that the public generally cared less for their survival. In the center of the complicated nexus of adored and hated, desired but also easy to watch being destroyed, it had to be a Black woman. Thurwar, and Melancholia Bishop before her, had taught audiences the feelings that he wanted viewers to have for all of the Links.

"We can teach our audiences who to view as important," he'd said five years ago, in his first official meeting with the board, the subject of which had been the mounting protests against action-sports. They'd been common then. But since he'd been hired they'd all but disappeared. That was, of course, before last month, when that bitch newscaster undid so much of what he'd worked for.

But every problem could be fixed. All she'd done was shat in a room he'd kept clean for years. Now he was in the process of power-washing her stench away. Getting things back to how they were, to the new truth he'd nurtured and grown.

He focused back on the stand, where William and Melanie Deane were frowning at their eldest kid. When they'd done the family background check he'd noted that the eldest son, William Jr., was not actively participating in or subscribed to any official Chain-Gang content, which all but guaranteed that he, and by extension his entire family, was an undesirable in terms of Civic Service placement. But the letter William Sr. had attached to the application stating just how much it would mean to his family, how he couldn't afford tuition for his son and having Links to help out would certainly mean he'd make the month and then some in sales with the rest going toward furthering his son's potential—Mitchell had always considered himself a man with a good heart, so he'd allowed Staxxx and Thurwar to be placed with the family. This was how he was being rewarded.

"You don't have to help us. This is bullshit that you're being forced like this," Bill Jr. said, just loud enough that Mitchell could hear. The crowd of protestors was churning near a barricade about twelve feet behind the Deane family.

Staxxx and Thurwar looked at each other and then at the kid. Thurwar leaned in and said something Mitchell could not hear. He cursed the GameMaster Board's collective decision not to record during Civic Service. He touched his glasses on the right side.

"Hey, Rebecca," he said.

"What's up?"

"Make a note to reconsider Link audio/visual isolation during Civic Service."

"Copy. Anything else?"

"I'll keep you posted." He let his hand casually drop to his pocket.

"Junior, please don't make this harder for them. They're working to pay their debts and I think you should be mindful of that," William Deane said. He looked at Thurwar apologetically and Thurwar met his eyes. It was hard to tell what she thought of him. But all these interactions, undesirable though they might have been, reminded Mitchell of the nuanced ecosystem he had installed and the synergetic pulse of a program that now was a cultural mainstay.

The next few minutes felt calm as Thurwar and Staxxx were shown the flavors and given aprons of their own. A line had formed at the table, the longest of any in the market.

Hamara matters! Loretta Thurwar matters!

Thurwar was his symbol. Thurwar had elevated the entire landscape of the games. He'd known from the beginning that people had to know that a win was possible. There was no joy quite like conquering, and he knew that viewers needed to believe it was possible for their favorite Link to win, to achieve High Freedom. So he'd created a golden boy, a former killer turned better killer turned freed member of society. Enter Nova Kane Walker. He'd gone from murderer to number seven on the "America's hottest men" list. But Thurwar was about to do it on her own. She was believable because she was real.

Elegance was the game.

Because that was the last part of it. Being invisible. Prison wasn't sexy or cool. Chain-Gang was both of those things. Chain-Gang was adventure, openness. It was beautiful women who sometimes killed people handing out ice cream. It was compelling, easy watching or the most visceral viewing experience ever conceived. And so here he was. One of the conductors, invisible to all, watching as the people gathered to see what he had made and maybe get some ice cream.

"I won't be a part of this," Bill Jr. said. His parents got red at the ears and cheeks. Bill Jr. walked away from the family and Mitchell thought, Fine. Still a win.

But then Bill Jr. turned toward the barricade behind him and walked forward. Loud boos and fuck-yous rained down on him. He accepted them without pause. He screamed out into the crowd of black, filled his chest and let his voice loose: "B THREE IS NOT FOR ME!"

The protestors exploded into cheers.

He climbed and was pulled over the barricade. William Deane, Sr., looked sick.

"Fuck," Mitchell said.

"What is it?" Rebecca said into his ear.

"Fuck."

This

The Deane boy had leapt over the barricade. He'd yelled some-thing to the people closest to him and they'd pulled him over. This was the work happening in real time.

The father Deane ran to his son, his face awash with anger. He knocked over a cylinder of hand-spun Dreamcream and lunged for his eldest son, who jumped out of the way of the first grab, his ribs leaning over the metal, pressing into the barricade.

Neither father nor son made much noise except for grunts of move-ment. The father tried again to reach for his son. The boy pressed him-self out into the crowd, a hand stretched, saying, "Help me." And the protestors pulled him over, right in front of his father, who watched him with dread that swiftly morphed into a palpable rage. His whole body clenched as he screamed at his son, holding one of the boy's sneakers in his hands.

"If you don't get back here right now—"

"Fuck that!" the son yelled back, on the other side of the barricade. The crowd screamed with him with a new victorious energy, but there was also a new tension radiating through the rest of the protestors and marketgoers. A ruckus was always a concern, especially when it wasn't clear exactly what was happening.

"Get your ass back here now," the owner of the ice-cream establishment said, and in his anger, his frustration, his embarrassment, he pulled back and swung his fist over the barricade, hitting a woman holding sage directly in the temple. The punch snapped through the general noise, a sudden, singular pulse. A trigger.

There is a space in time when violence tears through from imagined to physical—and if that physical is met with more physical, then the violence can become both the vehicle and driver for all that comes after, and what has escaped can be incredibly difficult to contain.

Hands got thrown. The barricade of linked metal fences fell as a woman leapt forward and met the father Deane's chin with her fist. Protestors flooded into the farmers market. Some grappled with Deane, some moved on so as not to be trampled. The patrons inside the farmers market, out of either fear or anger or some sense of purpose, began to throw punches, and of course, the violence grew and spread. The truest human virus multiplied through the masses. The violence took control.

Parents ran their children away to the edges, to the exit, which was no longer an exit but just another space for people to flood through. Where there had been order, now there were bodies running, flailing, standing, blocking. The protestors tried to help their comrades. The patrons of the market fought whoever was in front of them as they tried to escape. Some people urged calm, for the others to resist the violence, but the unified chanting was over; no one voice cut above the rest. Now all that could be heard over the chaos was the commands of the soldier-police, who called from their tanks' speakers, "All agitators will be arrested. Evacuate peacefully."

Inside the market, caught in the scrum, a soldier-police guard kicked down a man, who screamed, "What the fuck are you doing? I work for CAPE."

The officer helped the man up and he scrambled to find an exit as the same officer pointed his weapon at a woman in black and fired a round of rubber bullets that exploded into her clavicle.* The ammuni-

---

* Kinetic impact projectiles, or rubber bullets or rubber baton rounds, typically have a metal core. Rubber is a minor component. "Rubber bullets," which are used in "crowd-control situations," often result in permanent disability or death.

tion broke her bone; she shrieked and fell and several of the protestors pulled her into their cave of bodies. "Protect our family!" they screamed. This was just one of many huddles that had formed, each of them holding an A-Hamm Link, as if the Links were captains of teams about to take the field. The woman with the shattered clavicle screamed at Sai Eye's feet and Sai Eye kneeled in the circular wall of arms and legs around both of them.

"Hey, mama, breathe through it, you'll be okay," they said, although they had no idea at all if that was true.

In a different huddle of protection, a forced reprieve from the chaos and a pocket of resistance against the chaos, Thurwar and Staxxx crouched in the few feet of space carved out by the people around them, who'd linked arms in a circle, protecting them. Nile, Mari, Kai, two other members of the coalition, and a few more men and women. Thurwar tried to stand every couple of seconds to look about, to find her family, A-Hamm.

"You two get down. You'll get to everyone after it clears out." The sound of weapons firing poked holes in any calm that might have been had, but still Kai's words to the two women had been heard. Thurwar kneeled down. Staxxx sat cross-legged.

"So, what are you guys doing after this?" Staxxx said. She had to scream the words to be heard over the chaos outside.

Thurwar watched the nervous smiles form. To be surrounded by brutality and possibly death and have Staxxx at your side trying to crack a joke. That was what it was to be a Link on A-Hamm. These people were getting an exclusive experience. Thurwar would have laughed, had she not been distracted by the young woman from Vroom Vroom. She stared at the truth-bringer.

"Just chilling, maybe protesting some more, you know. What about you?" Nile said, holding a wide smile. His smile: a lie they all accepted gratefully. Thurwar realized then that this was the young man who had been in Vroom Vroom as well. She could tell, looking at him and the others, that none of them knew about the information the young woman had given her.

"Sounds good," Staxxx said. "Probably hanging out with this beautiful lady. Fight planning and whatnot. Got to check in with the gear guys, do some fine-tuning. You know, the usual."

"Right," Nile said. There was a loud bang. The huddle shifted harshly to the right before correcting itself, leaving Thurwar and Staxxx in the middle, untouched. Mari looked over her shoulder. Plumes of white smoke were tracing through the air toward them.

"For now, we're here," Mari said, and the group agreed in nods. Thurwar looked at the young woman and then at Staxxx and wondered how long it had been since she'd felt protected by anyone other than herself and Hass Omaha, or Staxxx and LoveGuile, or Sunset and that lucky sword of his. She realized that if Mari hadn't been there in front of her, she would not have said anything. She would have chosen to pretend. She knew that had the world not forced this meeting she would have let the days play out as if she had never learned what was coming. But watching the young woman, a terror deeper than any desire radiated through Thurwar's body. She could not let another woman tell Staxxx that they would meet in the BattleGround. She pulled Staxxx's ear to her lips. She felt herself cleaving open. She gripped the ridiculous apron on the grass because she had to hold something and she spoke to Staxxx and only Staxxx, knowing that she was ending the part of her life she enjoyed best.

"Next fight, after our double. They're going to make us kill each other. They're changing the rules," Thurwar said. "Once you make Colossal, it will be over. They're going to do it. Any two Colossals on the same Chain have to see the BattleGround against each other. It's coming season thirty-three."

She was grateful the people huddled around her couldn't hear the words she was tucking into Staxxx's ear, but she imagined the girl who had given her the truth to tell knew exactly what she was saying.

Thurwar was crying now, harder than she'd known was still possible. She was crying not just because something was ending, but because she was throwing this harsh new world on the woman she loved. And so she felt a thrill of confusion when Staxxx looked at her, not harshly or cynically, but honestly, with her eyes and lips, and cupped her hands around Thurwar's ear so only she would hear this story, and she said, "Let me tell you what happened to Sunset."

PART
III

Sunset Harkless

The day Sunset Harkless left his life behind, he looked up and watched the HMCs float into their compartment in the Anchor.

BlackOut initiated, the Anchor said. And A-Hamm cheered. It had been their tradition to enjoy the BlackOuts, to tell stories around the fire with a different vigor. To try to remind one another of who they were. And that's what they did that night. They sat around the fire for a long time; it was almost certainly the last BlackOut Night of Sunset's career as a Link and they knew he'd leave them with some kind of speech. Sunset Harkless was a talker. He always had been.

"It's getting late now," he said finally. Sunset smiled with his teeth. The shots of gray in his thick sideburns shined against his brown skin. He wore no bolt leather, only a shirt and a brown leather vest, and the cargo pants he called his everything pants because of all the pockets. All the Angola-Hammond Links were gathered around him.

"It's about my time," Gunny Puddles said, and began to get up.

"Hold on a second, sit tight," Harkless said. And Gunny did.

The night was fresh with dark and the glow of the fire and being unwatched.

"Y'all know I'm getting ready for what's next."

"High Freed," Thurwar said loudly.

"High Freed," the Chain echoed.

"Freed at last," Sunset laughed. "I been here a long time. I'm remembering now the first time I met my good friend over here, who happens to be the baddest motherfucker ever to carry a hammer. Including Miss Bishop, in my opinion." Thurwar looked straight at Sunset and nodded appreciation.

"Some of y'all ain't ever seen a merger, but I'll tell you, back in my day it was not some easy thing."

Staxxx saw Thurwar's eyes hold their lock, watched Thurwar's grin flatten. Sunset held his sword in his hands, appreciated the blade, let the light of the fire bounce off it, then stabbed it into the dirt beneath him.

"We came here—me, thee Hurricane, Randy—to a Chain that already had an order. Even a few Peanuts can disrupt an order like that, but a group like us, shit. I was almost Reaper myself then. It was meant to be an explosion and it was. 'Cause it wasn't just me and Randy and the Hurricane. You remember there was also Joey Daze."

The Chain settled into a deeper quiet. Sunset smiled but did not laugh.

"Joey Daze was a Rookie if you ever saw one. More green than my young boul right here." Sunset pointed at Rico, who sat up straighter at having been acknowledged. "Skinnier too. Y'all remember Joey Daze? You know Micky ain't give him that name. I gave him that name. 'Cause he had that look over his face. Confused to still be alive, confused all the time. Joey Daze—y'all remember him?"

The Links were quiet. Staxxx watched Thurwar. Thurwar's eyes were on the ground.

"Y'all remember him? I know y'all ain't forget him."

"I remember," Randy Mac said.

"Good," Sunset said. "He came over with us. A Rook for sure and damn dumb look on his face almost all the time. That was Daze. Y'all know I'm a talker, so I knew him a little bit. Found out his parents in Undrowned Lanier, a Southern boy. He had an accent on some of his words, but I think he tried to tuck that part of him away. Thought he sounded tougher without it. Anyways Joey Daze was another one who was there on the merger. Do any of you remember what happened to him? Not all of you was there, but I'm asking if you remember."

The fire danced. No one said anything, but Staxxx remembered.

Sunset laughed up into the air. "Nobody can remember, huh? He had a flat, confused-looking face."

The Links were still waiting.

"Joey Daze, Joey Daze, y'all don't re—"

"I killed him," Thurwar said. Staxxx watched Thurwar pick her head up. "I killed him."

Sunset jumped up. His sword was pierced into the earth at his feet. "You did. You did. You did. Do you remember why?"

Thurwar looked up at Sunset, her eyes glistening with hurt. Hass Omaha was pressed into the ground beside her. Angola-Hammond for so long had depended on these two forces, Thurwar and Sunset, existing in an easy friendship. A calm back-and-forth.

"Do you remember why, Loretta?"

"I wanted—" Thurwar began. Staxxx touched her knee, but Thurwar removed her hand as if to say, *This I will do on my own.* "I killed him because, four."

"Because four," Sunset laughed, and Rico Muerte and Gunny followed weakly. Ice and Sai and Randy and the rest were silent. "What is four?"

"Because four was too much," Thurwar said, her voice loud though wavering. "When you came I thought four people was too much. So I said I'll take three."

"You did. And what did I say?"

"You said that can't happen, not on my watch."

"And what happened next?"

"And then—and then I ran up and hit him. In the temple, while he was standing. He was dead already. But I hit him again on the ground in the same spot."

"And then you said . . ."

" 'There ain't any watch here but mine.' "

"So is 'four' the reason you did it?"

"I did it because I could and because I had worked for something and I didn't want you all to come destroy it. I wanted you to know who I was. I think I did it because I wanted you to see who I was and how things were here."

"What else?"

"I did it because I didn't want to be afraid," Thurwar said. "I didn't want my Chain to be afraid of anyone but me."

"So because you were afraid. And that wasn't the first time you'd done something like that. Just blasted someone from this earth because you felt like you needed to."

"No."

Thurwar stood up but did not move.

"It's the Circuit, so people turn up dead all the time. We're used to it. If it's not us, then we move on."

"Relax, Retta, I'm just talking. But the reason I bring this up, the reason I'm remembering that today on my last BlackOut is—look at who is in front of you now. That story sounds like it's about somebody else. Sounds like you can't believe Loretta could be the one I'm talking about. But I seen it with my own eyes. Daze died before he could even wipe the confusion off his face. And now she's about to be the Grand Colossal and she would never do nothing like it. And I ain't change her. Shit, I was scared as shit. But she changed and I changed and I'm proud as shit."

Sunset Harkless walked from his place opposite Thurwar and they stood face-to-face.

"Loretta, you done some terrible things, but I'm proud of who you are right now. What I want for you is to see what you've done and forgive yourself." Sunset wrapped her up in a hug; her arms were limp. She squeezed her eyes shut. "If you can forgive yourself, you'll do what you need to do, here and after High Freed." He let Thurwar go.

"That's the real High Freed, goddammit. If I ain't take what I've taken and kill who I've killed, goddammit, I'd be a preacher." Sunset chuckled and looked at the rest of the Chain. "You forgive yourself, you're High Freed. That's what I want for y'all. Forgive yourself, then you can start working on everybody else. Do that for me while I'm gone, okay?"

The Links said nothing. They sat there quietly for a long while then.

"I'm heading to bed," Randy Mac finally said. He looked at Staxxx, who nodded at him, silently saying she would join him soon. Thurwar saw this and left for her own tent, which she disappeared into quickly.

The rest of the Links tucked into their tents or sleeping bags, found sleep. Sunset waited at the fire with Staxxx.

"Follow me, Hamara," Sunset said as he got up, pulling his sword out of the ground. He kicked a bucket of water on the fire, unleashing the dark more fully, and then he walked away from the Camp.

Staxxx picked up her scythe. They walked in the dark, Staxxx just a step or two behind Sunset. Sun, who had protected her in the games until it had become time to protect him. Sun, whose crimes were supposed to be unforgivable and yet here she was, his friend. They got to the edge of their range. The place where their confinement became a physical pull. Staxxx leaned back against the invisible wall, which slowly angled her toward the ground until she caught herself by stepping back. Sunset smiled.

"Don't lose that, the fun part."

"I am the fun part," Staxxx said, and she meant it, but also she was afraid. The look in Sunset's eyes made her feel as though she was seeing a part of him she'd never seen before. A real raw calm. He was jovial and animated usually, but it always felt to her like it was something he had to summon. She gripped the shaft of LoveGuile, then released. She laid the weapon on the ground.

"I have something I want to tell you. Something important. You know I have my ways of getting info."

"What ways?" It was true that Sunset always seemed to know a little more than everyone else.

"It doesn't matter now, but the driver we've had the last couple months used to be my in-law. He told me something I think you'd want to know."

"What is it?" Staxxx wasn't sure she wanted to know, but she knew that she had to.

"I can tell you, but only if you do something for me," Sunset said.

"I have too much anxiety for this, Sun, what's—"

"I'm serious, Hamara. It's important. It's about you and Loretta. I just need you to do something for me. Will you do it?"

Staxxx and Sunset stood on the edge of their containment in a wildness that the world did not have the privilege of watching.

"Yes, I will."

"I'll tell you and I can't untell you, you understand?"

"Tell me."

Sunset put one of his large, callused hands on Staxxx's shoulder. "I'm sorry for this." Staxxx was already crying. "After you make Colossal, they're going to change the rules. Next season, after your and Retta's next doubles match, it's gonna be only one Colossal allowed per Chain."

Finally. Finally, the worst thing was here. Finally they'd found a suffering they'd never top. She listened.

"Any exceptions have to meet on the BattleGround. I'm telling you because, crazy as you is, I know you can hold it. Loretta, I don't know what she'll do. She holds all of it in and I don't know how much room she has for this."

And even with her life shattered in front of her, Staxxx felt the calm terror of separating from herself, of watching herself unfold.

Sunset put a hand on her head; his fingers slipped through her locs and touched her scalp as he brought her into a hug.

"Thank you for letting me know," Staxxx said. She tried to push him away. She wanted to find Thurwar, but he would not let her go.

"Wait, Hamara. Please. I need you right now."

Staxxx swirled. Her new life born of this sudden truth strangled her. "I can't. I won't."

"I know it's impossible but also it's obvious. The way they are. They wouldn't let it be. You two have already done something so special. You've shown them we are just like them. You reminded them we're all just people, so they had to snuff it out. And now you have to decide what you'll do."

"Fuck you."

"I'm sorry to do it. It's a bit more selfish from me. I've been selfish a long time."

"You two are the only family I have," Staxxx said, wanting to disappear. She could do it. She could bring the long sleep. That's what she would do.

Sunset spoke her thoughts but claimed them for himself. "Now I want you to kill me," he said.

Staxxx pushed him away again.

He let her go, stood there with his hands at his sides, a small smile, his eyes on the ground.

"I'm asking here. I need the help. If you say it was Gunny they won't protest."

"I refuse," Staxxx said.

"I know you wouldn't do that. I'm sorry. I don't know, Ham, I'm desperate here. My freeing day is this coming BattleGround. I won't see the new season. And I ain't going out to the world."

"What do you want me to tell the group? How do I explain it? I refuse," Staxxx said.

"I need you, I—I just need some help. All this killing, but somehow I don't have it in me."

"What about forgive yourself? What about all that you was just saying?" She understood completely but still she needed to hear him say it. "Why are you asking this now?"

"Because I've done what I was supposed to do. I'm done with this life."

Staxxx was not satisfied and her dissatisfaction was loud on her face.

"'Do as I say, not as I do'?" Sunset laughed. Sunset could always laugh. "I'm not going back out there. You know what I've done. I've hurt so many. I'm not the man they remember. But I don't have it in me to prove that. I just cannot speak to my daughter about who I was. I can't explain to her who I am now. I'm sorry. I do not forgive myself. I will not. And I will not force anyone else to have to consider forgiving me either. I'm not sure what I deserve. But I can't go back outside. I want better for y'all. But I know my limit. So I want you to take this sword and help guide my hand. I'll help you, but I need some help too."

"Why not let it happen on the grounds?" Staxxx begged.

"I ain't brave enough for that," Sunset said. "I know it's not right to ask, but I'm not sure I'll have this brave with me on those grounds. I'm scared I'll do what I always do, kill as I always have. Please, Hamara. I've thought on this."

This was her life. Her purpose. To sow a hard kind of love into the world. She was there to help people do the things they couldn't do themselves.

"You just have to help guide my hand," Sunset said. "I'm not asking anyone for grace. I don't want them to have to think any kind of good of me. Tell them I did something to deserve it. I just ain't going back out there." He smiled again and began to weep. "I ain't upset. I'm tired. I'm happy to get to rest."

He brought his sword to his neck.

"Please guide my hand," Sunset said.

And Staxxx walked behind him. He dropped to his knees. The blade was pressed to his throat. "I love you," he said to the world and to Staxxx and to his daughter, to everyone he had ever hurt and all those who had hurt him.

Sunset Harkless held the blade and Staxxx held his tough knuckles. As Sunset pulled, Staxxx let him go. He pulled through and across and his life flowed, flowed out of him. And Staxxx held him, at his chest, as it happened, rather than the blade, because she knew what he wanted and needed was to be held.

Tear Gas

So you didn't kill him?" Thurwar said. Staxxx squeezed Thurwar's hand, which was limp, then Thurwar squeezed hard back. The truth hurt her but also it felt, to Thurwar, like she was being told a story she'd forgotten. One she'd always known.

"Didn't I? I didn't save him," Staxxx said. "But maybe I saved someone else. If I didn't own it someone would have died for it. He knew what he represented to people. He didn't want them to know what he'd chosen. I was keeping a secret for him."

"What I don't understand"—Thurwar tried to breathe and struggled—"is why you—what do I have to be for you to trust me? Why wouldn't you trust me with this?"

There were the sounds of bullets being fired into droves of protestors, the men shooting them urging calm. Everyone was crying because of the tear gas that the soldier-police had thrown all over the farmers market.* It had settled into their huddle and now it was difficult to see; to breathe was to hurt.

---

* Protocol for the Prohibition of the Use in War of Asphyxiating, Poisonous or Other Gases, and of Bacteriological Methods of Warfare
  Signed at Geneva June 17, 1925
  Entered into force February 8, 1928

"I wanted to put our new way of being into practice. To tell you and everybody, 'Look what I did,' and ask you to forgive me. And you have. I wanted them to see that."

Thurwar knew by "them" she meant the viewers. The people who ate popcorn while Links died.

"I want you to care about me and not them," Thurwar said, crying, as most everyone left in the market was.

"I care about all of it," Staxxx said.

She wanted to be upset but the tears and the moment made her feel something much greater than anger. She brought a hand to Staxxx's neck and pulled her closer so she could kiss her forehead.

"I'm sorry you had to do that. I'm sorry he asked you to. I'm sorry he asked you and not me."

Staxxx heard this and tried to breathe and squeezed Thurwar's hand.

"Us," she said.

The crowds had largely dispersed. All that remained was a few small groups huddled together, protecting the Links, and the soldier-police and the especially excited fans, who were happy to hit someone under the cloak of chaos. The protestors around Staxxx and Thurwar coughed but stood firmly together. The police begged again for peace as they rolled their tanks forward.

Staxxx righted herself and surveyed the scene. She felt hurt but also revived in telling Thurwar the truth. She felt relieved to know that

---

Ratification advised by the U.S. Senate December 16, 1974
Ratified by U.S. President January 22, 1975
U.S. ratification deposited with the
Government of France April 10, 1975
Proclaimed by U.S. President April 29, 1975

The Undersigned Plenipotentiaries, in the name of their respective Governments:

Whereas the use in war of asphyxiating, poisonous or other gases, and of all analogous liquids, materials or devices, has been justly condemned by the general opinion of the civilized world; and

Whereas the prohibition of such use has been declared in Treaties to which the majority of Powers of the World are Parties; and

To the end that this prohibition shall be universally accepted as a part of International Law, binding alike the conscience and the practice of nations.

Tear gas has been deemed a "riot control agent," which exempts it from chemical weapons law. As such, it is regularly used by police on citizens in city streets, while still being prohibited from war zones.

Thurwar had known what was coming and that their end was not a secret she'd have to carry alone, hadn't carried alone. It was still them even then. As a pair, they were full of destiny; that they could never deny.

People were fleeing west and it seemed the police were letting them. A few they shot with their rubber bullets in the back, but they were far more concerned with clearing the space and retrieving the Links. The wail of approaching paramedics almost drowned out the sound of the fading chaos.

"Probably a good idea for all of you to get going, huh?" Staxxx said. She touched Kai at the shoulder. "You all get home okay, all right?"

Kai nodded and the huddle quickly collapsed. Staxxx coughed loudly, then smiled. "Thank you," she said.

Mari extended an arm down and saw the lines on Thurwar's wrists. The control installed into her body. Thurwar took her arm, tearing up and coughing. Standing, she towered over Mari, looked down at her warmly, holding her hand in hers, the girl's small but not very soft.

"Thank you," Thurwar said. "It means a lot."

Mari looked her in the eye and said, "Thank you. You knew my father. Sha—Sunset. Thank you for helping him." Thurwar heard the woman, this young woman whom Sunset had imagined and hoped over and dreamed about and cried over. "We're all with you. My name is—"

"Marissa," Thurwar said. "He talked about you all the time."

"I know," Mari said. Staxxx watched and listened.

Then they released each other.

Staxxx and Mari shared a gaze, their eyes each full of tears. Mari and the woman who she believed had killed her father.

Staxxx began, "I—"

But Mari lunged at Staxxx before she could continue.

"Whatever it is, it's okay." And Mari hugged into Staxxx and Staxxx hugged her back and they cried, and though it was hard to breathe they tried to breathe each other in.

The sounds of gunfire got closer and additional canisters of gas exploded near the group.

"Time for y'all to head out," Thurwar said.

"Okay," Mari said as Kai watched.

"Thank you," Kai said to Thurwar. She nodded at Staxxx but said nothing to her.

Then the sudden family dissolved. Mari and the coalition left, moved in the direction that the soldier-police were ushering them in. Thurwar looked at her wrists, the glowing lines, thought of the anguish she had held. Thought of how Staxxx had lied and lied again and how she loved her the same, or more.

"Wanna make a run for it?" Thurwar said.

"Wherever you go, I'll go," Staxxx said.

They walked several yards to a place where the air seemed a little clearer and sat on the grass to watch the soldier-police beat and restrain and beat again anyone who had not evacuated. Their wrists soon flashed a blinking triple red, which meant they couldn't move much if they wanted to.

Their eyes and lungs burned.

"All this?" Thurwar said, surveying the wreckage. She saw that a few soldier-police had ID'd them and were coming their way.

"We're a big deal, you know?" Staxxx said. She rested her head on Thurwar's shoulder. "I've been here before. I thought being back would make me feel something. And it does, but not like I thought."

"What's it feel like?" Thurwar asked, her eyes closed.

"I feel like this place isn't my home. You know, my family, they don't think of me. They're not here anymore. One died when I was inside."

"I remember."

"The other left, was never seen again here, in the town that knew her daughter was a murderer."

"What else?" Thurwar said, her body frozen.

Staxxx waited, then said, "I'm scared, but also kind of proud? Look at all this. They heard me. They heard us."

Thurwar took in the chaos with their names on it. Maybe they had.

She laughed. "Wait a second, isn't that your mom right there?" Thurwar asked, pointing across the market.

Staxxx picked her head up, looked out at the wild field of people.

"Fuck you," she said, smiling.

Thurwar was glad to know that even in that moment she could still bring a smile to Staxxx's face.

"But what if she was here? What would you say?" Thurwar asked.

"I'd say, 'Mama, these people love me. I wish you did too.'" Thurwar watched Staxxx thinking. "I'd say I did what I did because that man tried to take something from my body. I'd say, 'Mama, they're gonna make me kill this woman I love 'cause they think it will be the greatest entertainment event in the history of mankind.'"

The police tased anyone still left in the market. Their bodies fell, writhed. Some got up, some lay still.*

"Why didn't you tell me?" Thurwar asked.

"Because after Sun was gone, I wanted to enjoy you the old way. Just like you wanted. And because a part of us maybe already knew this was coming. Nothing as good as us could exist here."

The soldier-police had wrangled most of the people they wanted and headed toward Staxxx and Thurwar.

"I want you to say you're terrified. Because I'm terrified. I want you to tell me what to do," Thurwar cried, and she felt so much at once she was already trying to bottle the feeling, because to survive she had to curate. Curate everything. But this she delivered raw.

"You know what we have to do. You're going to live. And I will too."

"No. Say exactly what you mean." Thurwar was desperate. They would only have a few more seconds before they were pulled into some van. "What are we going to do?"

"You know what you're going to do. You're not going to get destroyed by them. I'm not going to let you get Influenced again," Staxxx said. "You know the answer, so you tell me what we're going to do."

Thurwar let the feeling of being crushed be her body.

"We're going to fight each other. We're going to try."

"Exactly that," Staxxx said. "Also, T, if my mother were here, I would tell her to go to hell. And that I'm an electric field and I was the one who killed Sunset. And he was one of the best men I ever knew. And I love this lady here and I am the Hurricane."

---

* Tasers can kill. On January 4, 2020, in Spring Valley, Rockland County, New York, Tina Davis was killed by police. They tased her and she died because of it. Her name was Tina Davis.

And then the soldier-police pulled them up from the ground and there was purple glowing on Thurwar's wrist again, and her hands were forced to clasp together. She wished she had Hass Omaha just so she could have something to hold on to besides herself. They were led to a transport van, and she rubbed her shoulder into Staxxx's side as they walked and Staxxx rubbed back.

The Legend of One-Arm Scorpion Singer Hendrix and the Unkillable Jungle Craft

He waited in a van and he thought about the legend they had become. The time they'd spent. "Singer, you ready?" the driver said. Singer, you ready. Singer been ready. Singer not ready at all. Wasn't all that always true. He heard that man but he wasn't done remembering and so he sat and thought of where'd they come through to get there.

On that first night Scorpion Singer did a peculiar thing. He pulled the far-off body of one Nazi back toward the body of the second Nazi so that the two could rest together forever. He offered them some mangled dignity they would surely not have afforded him had they been given the chance. Soon the producers would retrieve the bodies, so there was no need to bury.

The sun was learning the sky once more when Singer turned toward the man who had massacred most of Sing-Attica-Sing. He was asleep in Bells and Razor's tent, a symbol of their strength. Hendrix stepped in tentatively, Spinifer Black, the long, sharp obsidian death that he'd made famous, in his hands. The blade saw the room before he did. He pointed the sharp end down by Craft's neck, near the Adam's apple.

"You can't sleep here," Singer said. He kicked at the man's shoulder and pulled the blade back to keep Craft from impaling himself as he shot up. The three eyes of the HMCs cast a glow on the scene, each helping the other better take in what was unfolding. Singer kept his voice calm and low. "You can sleep over there across the way or outside, but not here. It's only a few hours left till we have to March, but this ain't yours to sleep in."

Craft blinked what small sleep was in him away. "Yes, sir," he said. Then he pulled his body up and made his way out into the young dawn. He found a tent that belonged to an Eraser and disappeared inside. Hendrix stood a few minutes more in the big tent space, thought of Bells and Razor, of Eighty. They'd been a good family of bad people, as Eighty liked to put it. He missed them so soon and he missed them hard.

"Lord, why?" he said, and went outside to the smaller tent just a few steps off.

Later that morning, Hendrix Singer walked back out into the young sun and the dew-splashed grass and looked to the sky. The blue/white made his mouth water, as if his body were craving a bite of cumulus. Soon, though, the drones appeared with their boxes of meals. He looked across to the long-dead fire in the center of the Camp. Craft was there, sitting up, his legs sprawled out. A wide smile flashed on his face when he saw Singer, then disappeared. Hendrix stepped back into his tent to retrieve Spinifer Black and watched as Craft straightened. Singer walked toward him and sat on the opposite end of the central ashes.

"Do you know where you are?" he asked.

Craft's face was bare, clean-shaven. The light changed his eyes from gray to blue. His pale skin seemed depleted and dull, as if it had been a long time since he'd offered himself to the sun. He wore the blades he'd killed Bells and Razor and the Erasers with on his hands.

"Yes, sir," Craft said.

"You do, huh? You know what this is? Where is this?" Singer asked.

"This is hell," Craft said. And at this Singer, despite himself, smiled. And Craft smiled too, though his eyes were dead, and soon the smile was as well.

"I know you said it before, but who are you? Who do you think you are?"

"I'm a son-of-a-bitch rapist motherfucker."

Singer stared at the man, and when it was clear to Craft that he was not satisfied, the other man spoke again.

"I'm Simon J. Craft."

"Simon J. Craft. What the J got behind it?" Singer asked. He blocked his eyes from the sun and saw the fleet of foodstuffs floating still farther down. When Craft didn't answer the question Singer tried again: "What the J stand for?" He looked back at the man and saw that his gaze was scattered, searching. His pupils darted back and forth; he got up, then quietly sat back down. Singer shifted his feet just so and tightened his grip on his spear. "Don't worry about it. It can be Jungle, or whatever you like." An ease washed over Craft's face. An ease that was broken by a harsh smile that disappeared as quickly as it came. "Jungle good name for a wild man anyways," Singer said, and then the first of the drones dropped a box behind Craft. In a snap of movement Craft had turned his back to Singer and was stabbing down into the box.

"Ey, wild boy," Singer said. "Stop that." And Craft stopped moving. Hendrix watched and considered what was what. There were beads of orange juice on Craft's exposed chest and a glaze of grits on the blades over the back of his hands.

"Look at me, jungle boy," Singer said. "My name is Hendrix Singer, and in this level of hell, I'll be your overseer. You understand that?"

"Yes, sir," Craft said. He glanced at the black spear, then back to Singer. But he seemed always to bring his eyes back to the spear.

More boxes dropped around them.

"First lesson is about how to eat and not slaughter your breakfast, which out here on the Circuit comes every morning 'round this time." Hendrix waited for a laugh that would not come. He imagined the ghosts of his friends, who he hoped understood why he was helping this man. He hoped that on their side they were somewhere beyond hate. That they'd know Singer hated the man in front of him but also knew that the man was his charge. Hendrix didn't understand himself. He just knew that despite his strength, this man seemed helpless.

"You understand that, jungle man?"

Craft said nothing.

"Don't worry. You will."

They were expected to lose their first fight.

"There will be two men on that far side," Hendrix explained as they waited for the gate to the arena to open. "Follow me, then when you're unlocked, you attack. Here, it's okay to kill. Here, you must. There will be two of them. It's us two against them." The roaring sound of the crowds usually made Singer's stomach bubble, but the project of coaching this man into survival somehow calmed him. Craft smiled, then didn't, then smiled, then didn't, and it was clear that even he was nervous. Even the jungle man held fear.

"You listen to me," Singer said. "Anybody out there that isn't me, once you see them, you kill them. You understand? Me, you never attack. Them, you kill."

"I understand."

"Okay, you'll do fine."

When asked for last words by the host of the BattleGround, Singer said, "I hope you're proud of what you've made of this man beside me." Then he sang, *"It's a long John—"* before his mic cut away to Craft.

"Do you know they're calling you Jungle Craft, sir?" the blond man in the sky asked.

"My name is Simon J. Craft," Craft said.

"So I've heard," the announcer said with a laugh that was shared by thousands. Then they released them from their locks.

Singer and Craft moved in tandem, as if they were communicating telepathically. They ran toward the huge men, the Boulder Brothers, swinging their chains on the other side of the arena. As soon as they got close, a chain shot out at Singer, which he deflected with his spear, stomping down on the chain so that the Boulder Brother couldn't pull it back. He grunted and tried to retrieve his weapon as the other Boulder Brother shot a chain at Craft. Craft tumbled forward, the chain missing him completely, and then he swiped through the first Boulder Brother's arm, almost severing it from his side entirely. The brother screamed until his neck was taken. He thudded down. The other managed to pull his chain from beneath Singer's foot and swing it above his head, an attempt at keeping his opponents away. Craft watched and waited, crouched low for an opening. The Boulder kept his eyes on him and Singer closed the gap between them, ducking under the chain and stabbing up into the crescent below the man's chin.

The crowd screamed and the Legend of One-Arm Hendrix Singer and Jungle Craft was born.

On a long March, many months into the pairing, Hendrix Singer, it seemed, was tired of singing. People across the country knew their names. They'd been to many different arenas together.

"You know how I got this asymmetrical life?" Singer asked as they stepped across hard baked earth. It was a hot day. Singer had made sure that Craft was prepared for each March. Before the arena matches he managed his Blood Points for him, helping him with guards and weapon maintenance and food. The routine had settled around them, and though he was still prone to a fit of sudden weeping or laughter, Craft was mostly silent and mostly did what he was supposed to. But at Singer's question, Craft looked at his Chain-mate and said nothing.

"Jungle, I'm asking you if you wanna know how I lost my arm. You wanna know?"

"You lost an arm?" Craft said.

And Hendrix laughed for the next two miles.

That same night they sat sweating together in the heat of wherever they were. Hendrix swung at mosquitoes as Craft dismantled a turkey burger in hard chews.

"What kind of crazy are you?" Hendrix asked. "I known a few that seen the Influencer b—"

Craft dropped his burger and began to beg. "Please, I'm sorry. I am sorry."

Hendrix looked at Craft, who wept. He watched him for a long few moments.

"All right, all right, Jungle. You keep it up, you won't have to worry much about that, okay?"

"Yes, sir," Craft said, and he picked his burger off the dusty earth and continued eating it.

"Okay, dammit, ask me a question now. I got a voice, so dammit, go on."

"How'd you lose your arm?" Craft said through a mouthful.

Singer threw his head back and laughed anew at the emerging moon, at the Anchor above him, at his life, at this country, this world that had made the two of them what they were.

This is how he came to be known as "Unkillable."

They'd been Marching for not even an hour when Hendrix Singer heard the chatter of voices. Out on the Circuit, unfamiliar human voices meant death was only a few moments away. He'd been through two Melees, but he'd mostly stood to the side, as on both occasions Bells had hacked through a man right at the start, ending them immediately.

"Jungle," Singer said. "Stop moving a second." Craft stopped. "I want you to go in your pack and wrap that bolt leather around your arms." The Anchor began to move more quickly in front of them. Craft obeyed. "Tie your hair back some so it's not in your eyes." Singer held Spinifer with his armpit, then used his mouth to pull a sweatband from his own wrist and gave it to Craft. "Move quick, keep up with this thing. Don't let it drag you." They shuffled forward, readying themselves. When he was satisfied that Craft was set, Singer spoke again, but quietly; the Largesse State Pen Chain was already looking at them. Their Chain was a healthy eight members deep.

The two Anchors of the Chains met in the sky.

Melee initiating in thirty seconds.

"J, I want you to fight as hard as you've ever fought today. Everybody that isn't me is about to try to kill you. You understand that?"

"I do," Craft said.

"Well then, let's see if this is our last day in hell."

"It is not," Craft said.

Yolker StashCash, who was the high rank in the LSP Chain, held a claymore in one hand and a shield that bore a rising sun and dollar signs in the other.

"How you wanna do this, bruh?" StashCash said. He was bald at the head and muscled through his body. The rest of his Chain looked strong as well.

Melee in ten, nine, eight—

"I'll take a one-on-one with whoever y'all choose," Singer said.

"Nah, we pass on that fair one shit," StashCash said. "Let us take the wild man."

Melee initiated.

"We can stop talking if it ain't about nothing," Singer yelled across the way.

Melee initiated.

"Let us take the wild man, we fuck with you, Singer, my people fuck with you," StashCash said. And Hendrix looked over the eight men and women. They weren't well armored, but they had bats and claymores, lances and hammers and knives.

"We pass," Hendrix said. Then he looked at Craft and whispered, "Get them, Jungle Man." And Craft took off running, with Hendrix right behind him.

The rules of Melee required only one life be lost to end it. When it was all over Simon Craft had a flesh wound on his right abdomen and Hendrix Singer had sprained something, so he had to limp the rest of the way to Camp. He was also bleeding from a shallow cut on the shoulder connected to his gone arm. But the two men walked away from the battlefield having left not a single member of the Largesse State Pen Chain alive.

Not a single new Link had joined Sing-Attica-Sing since Craft had. Months passed. It felt as though they were destined to journey the world alone. Singer had no idea that it was because of an ongoing legal action brought against the Sing-Attica-Sing CAPE program division, which asserted that Simon Jeremiah Craft's mental state through his time on the Chain called into question the institution's claim that he'd been of sound mind when he'd signed on to be a part of the program. The case was waiting to be heard, and until it was resolved, no new Links could be added to the Chain. So the legend of two remained theirs.

They sat at the fire after a day's March. For over a year it had been One-Arm Scorpion Singer Hendrix Young and the Unkillable Simon Jungle Craft. As they sat across from each other, so far from where they had once met, or maybe not that far at all—the Circuit was a path to nowhere and sometimes it was a loop—Singer told Craft to come sit in front of him.

"Take one of your Wolverines off for me, okay? Sit down right here." And Craft did. He sat on stony earth. The March had taken them to some stretch of land close enough to the water that they heard the night tide, though they could not see any waves. "Give that to me," Hendrix said, and he held the long double blade in his fingers. Craft's skin had grown tan through their travels, but the thick bands on his hands from where he wore his weapons were as pale as they'd been that bloody day he'd appeared.

Hendrix stared at the weapon and then laid the blade on his thigh so he could put his hand through the grip and wear it as Craft did. Craft sat between his legs, looking into the fire, and Singer sat up on a stump.

"You ready?" Hendrix asked.

"Yes, sir," Craft said, and Hendrix pulled the wild hair on Craft's neck so that his head bent gently and his neck pressed forward. Hendrix brought the blade to Craft's neck and carefully began to shave the spiraling, crazy hair. As he did it he sang a tune.

"I got big money on you two," the driver said. They slowed, their wrists still blue. Man talking to himself feel godly among the silenced. "I'll be rooting for you," driver says. He want us to know that we looking pretty dead from where he sitting, but he hoping we shock the world. One Arm and the Unkillable. We shocked before, no reason we can't do it again.

"A lot of folks rooting for y'all, remember that."

The van slows and already I've forgotten because what I remember heavy and I ain't got the space.

Bad Water

🐟

Thurwar was forced into the back of a cramped space with Bad Water. The soldier-police were punishing her, it seemed, for the chaos that had erupted, and so had pulled her away from Staxxx. Now her knees pressed against Plexiglas in the backseat of a police vehicle and Walter Bad Water was staring at her.

"I'm not crying," Thurwar said as she wept.

"I know you're not," Bad Water said. And he looked out the window as the rest of A-Hamm got shoved into similar cars.

Thurwar couldn't see exactly where Staxxx was. She thought about how soon the time would come when they'd be apart forever. She cried so hard her body shuddered as the car began to roll onto the road.

"I'm not supposed to be here," Bad Water said, speaking over the muffled sound of Thurwar's sorrow. "My M is a lie. Never killed nobody until all this."

Thurwar felt her mind jump away from the bleeding sorrow in her chest. She said nothing for some time, then, "Why'd you sign?"

It was a question with an obvious answer, but she needed to escape into the distraction.

"I signed because I was innocent, and I was tired." They were all so tired.

Thurwar looked at Bad Water. He would surely die soon. Had been a little bit killed already. She'd ignored him because he'd become friendly with Puddles and because he didn't carry the will necessary to survive in this space. She was repulsed by how completely unfit he was to be there. She also admired how resolute he was in his unfitness. But the fact that he had somehow stumbled his way into four wins on the BattleGround was an insult to everything she was.

"I'm different," Thurwar said. "My M is the truth. I killed somebody. A woman named Vanessa. She was beautiful, sweet. I destroyed that."

After they were quiet for a while Bad Water said, "I saw Staxxx do it. On BlackOut. They were far off but I could see."

Thurwar said nothing.

"Sunset wanted it. I could tell. He did it, just seemed like he wanted her help. Staxxx didn't do anything, not really."

"Thank you," Thurwar said. The world ran past their windows.

"Why'd you sign?" Bad Water asked. This was the most they'd ever spoken.

"Because, I—" Thurwar thought of all the lies she'd told in regard to this question and how everybody's true answer was some version of the same thing. "I was in a lot of pain," Thurwar said. She stared at Bad Water as Staxxx's hometown slid behind him. She looked at his face, his stubbled jaw, clear eyes, and watched as his crusting lips curled into a smile. He began to laugh, harder and harder.

Thurwar watched him, then smiled and coughed some small laughs herself.

"Right," she said.

And they rode the rest of the way, sometimes laughing, sometimes silent.

The Regional

Thurwar washed the tear gas off her skin in her room at the Regional. She showered and then let her muscles relax in the heat of a short soak in the tub. Then she changed into her pajamas, silk and branded with hammers, and turned to the Compstreaming console to watch old fights and prep, as was her ritual.

First she watched the men she and Staxxx would face together in two days, their old matches, spent time studying them as she had been since the battle had been announced. She'd never seen anything like them. She needed a more concrete strategy, she knew, and turned to her old match with Unicorn Racine as she considered. She watched as she murdered Unicorn Racine, how she'd sucked in the fervor the crowds gave her after. She sat in her master suite and remembered what it had been like to be the person she was watching on the archived streamcast. She hardly limped then, the glory an incredible anesthetic.

She was watching a memory of a person who had been her. A person who was her. A person whom she had shed because they no longer suited her. A person who had gotten her to the place where she was now and whom she often hated.

"I love you," Thurwar said to the memory. Then she turned the stream off. The words had felt flat coming from her mouth. The resentment for herself was there as ever.

"See yourself and who you were and think about how you view that person. You have to be kind to yourself and . . ." That was from the doctor she'd befriended back when she was inside. She'd been blessed to have a woman like that as a cellmate. Patty, with all her softness, was tough enough that she hadn't been broken down by the other prisoners, and many of them respected her. She taught classes on basic science and offered tutoring sessions that Thurwar would sit in on even though she had no desire to learn science. It intrigued her, though, to see just how much a single woman could know about the world, the body, about what made them go. Years before, Doc Patty had burned down her own lab, the story was. Inside, Patty had been gentle, someone many of the other women had looked to for guidance. Thurwar had not explicitly sought out Patty in that way, but their friendship had changed when the doctor spoke to Thurwar one evening in their cell as Thurwar cried on the bunk above.

"Thank you, Loretta," Doc Patty said.

Thurwar said nothing.

"You've been very kind to me, and I know how you've been making sure I'm kept well. Thank you. You're a good one, Loretta."

"I'm not," Thurwar said. She quieted her tears.

Thurwar held her breath, hoping for anything to hear besides the chaotic, messy, constant noise of the prison.

"Sure you are," Doc said in a voice that promised the Caribbean. "And if you can, you should look back to those people you have been, those people got you crying over yaself each night, and remember they some ones that need love too. Ya understand me?"

Thurwar did not understand then. She felt so alone, so completely removed from any kind of good.

"Ya un—"

"She's a killer," Thurwar said. "That me, she killed my favorite person. I don't love her, and I shouldn't."

"And I'm telling you, you have to, my friend. Loretta. And that li'l baby girl that came before the person you crying over so much. Love her too. Love all the way through it. I learned that's the only way."

"And here we are."

"Yes we are. And you spending your time going back to hate your own self. It's a fool's errand. I know."

"Right."

"Look down at this."

Thurwar looked but she couldn't see anything, except for the doctor's leg stretched out over her bedside.

"Ya looking?"

"Yeah," Thurwar said.

"This my cutting leg." And Thurwar could see. She had noticed before in glances but not thought much of it. A mosaic of scars and cuts decorated her leg so completely, it was an entirely different color from the woman's kneecap and the sliver of thigh Thurwar could see. In that gray, cold cell Thurwar took in the proof of the doctor's pain.

"Whatcha think I did this for?"

Thurwar said nothing.

"I was hating myself for things that I couldn't control. I was hating myself for not being better. Hating myself for—"

"We're not the same. I did have control. I had choices," Thurwar said.

"And so what?" Doc said. "I learned a long time ago. On this one thing you don't negotiate. You love through all the people you've been and hope you have a chance at being better." The doctor pulled her leg back onto her bunk. "What I'm telling you is you can curse yourself to the moon and back and what will it have you feeling like? But try to look at yourself and say 'I love you' and see what happens."

"It would be a lie."

"Ya done worse than that before."

Later, when the doctor had heard that Thurwar was to be Influenced, she'd cried herself. And she'd been so vigilant once Thurwar had returned to the cell. She'd asked Thurwar to move her eyes, to stretch this way and that. To smile, to frown. "What are you feeling right now, Loretta?" the doctor asked.

"I'm—" Thurwar began, but she was lost in herself. What she'd thought was pain was just a cheap imitation. In that six-by-six cell they called the Hole, she'd discovered the real thing, and it was still hot inside her. A terror she had to escape.

"They told me they'd do it again," Thurwar said.

"Loretta, I'm so sorry. I'm so sorry," the doctor cried, even as she continued to examine her patient. She told Thurwar to let her know if she felt any cognitive changes. If her mood shifted. And it did. She felt a new hopelessness, a desire to end.

"I'm leaving," Thurwar told the doctor the next morning. And the doctor did not fight her, though Thurwar heard her muffled weeping through that night and the next.

The hotel was called the Regional and it was closer to the city they'd actually be fighting in than it was to Old Taperville. The first nights in Hub Cities were nights of leisure and relaxation. The Links stayed in a heavily guarded wing. Thurwar and Staxxx, because of their position, were generally allowed to spend their nights together, and their rooms were always adjacent, Thurwar in a corner room and Staxxx in the very next available.

When they'd pulled up into the Regional their cuffs were disengaged to green, and the Links were led individually to their rooms. Thurwar had taken in hers, the king-size bed, a bottle of champagne on ice with a nice note from the manager.

After watching her old match, she'd decided to log into her messages folder at the Holo Computing terminal. She'd been actively neglecting them for several months.

Dear LT,

I just want to say that every day you're what keeps me going. I think about you when I have to deal with bitches at work, when I'm pounding at the gym, literally all the time you inspire me. I can't wait for the day you're High Freed. It should be a holiday. I wish I could spend time with you and Staxxx. Looking forward to your next everything. This is how I get when I watch you do anything.

[1 image attached]

Love,
W

Hey Ms. Thurwar,

I saw your last fight and am glad it was an easy one. Some people were angry but I was not at all. You are my absolute favorite Link ever, after Melancholia Bishop. I am probably one of your biggest fans. I argue in school about you and I don't lose the arguments because if you and Raven Ways and Hurricane Staxxx and Plyrolla Happs and Quest Quest the Source and even UJC and Singer all had a fight, I think you would win. That's how good I think you are. Thanks for reading. (Even though I know you don't read most of the letters because people send weird stuff.)

> You are dope,
> Randy L

Dear Thurwar,

I'm sure you get this a lot, but you're a legend. Truly your existence has brightened this earth. Sending my support, love, and energy to you. And I know it's not your thing, but I figured maybe you'd like me to send you this as well. Hehe;)

[1 image attached]

> Yours,
> A. Grower

Dear Loretta,

My favorite fight of yours of all time was the Unicorn fight. I think that's where you turned the corner. Were you scared? I bet you were. And that's what's cool about everything you do. Even though it's scary you make it work. You push through. I miss that Thurwar. The Rah-Rah Blood Mother. You're getting a little boring now. You're fun when you fight but that's it. You only have a couple more kills before High Freed. Don't you want to make them special?

> From,
> Concerned Fan

Miss Loretta Thurwar,

The heart of wickedness is shrewd and cunning. I implore you to take a step toward righteousness and forsake your sinner's heart that you might be made anew. It is one thing to have taken life. Life that was crafted perfectly by GOD himself, but to continue to live as a whore and jezebel?! It is an affront to GOD himself. GOD himself weeps watching you use your considerable celebrity to advance the agenda of the homosexuals of the world who mean to spend their tyranny on us all. You seem a reasonable enough woman, despite your insidious past, and I, as a fan of athletic competition, have seen that you are an athlete of some caliber. And perhaps GOD himself has blessed you with the power to rid the world of the very same evil that resides in your own heart. You have chosen to be Sodom when you might have been Samson! GOD himself will throw you to an eternal fire. You might have found grace and yet you choose this! You work so hard on your body, I have seen. You are shaped and strong, but your heart is weak. Your thighs are cut and ready. But your mind is easily persuaded. You choose women. I fear for your eternal soul. I watch and pray that you might find a nice man on the Circuit to lie with instead of the lunatic Hamara. Seek the light, be a vessel for GOD, and GOD himself will set you free.

> SEEK SALVATION,
> —Righteous Virtue

LT,

I wanna fuck the fight out of you. I think you'd like it. Let me know?
> [1 image attached]
> —PJ

Dear Loretta,

I hope this finds you well. I feel sick imagining what's in the other letters coming in with this batch, but I just wanted to send love and light. This is my second message to you. Good things come in threes. You knew my father. You are supported. You are loved.

> From,
> A friend.

LT,

You're a fucking bitch. Nigger bitch slut. I bet you want this. You're welcome.
[1 image attached]
BigD Bandit

Dear Blood Mama,

Hey there. Hope you're doing well still. Fucking crazy week it's been for both of us! The UnMelee? What the fuck? I told my wife, "Thurwar's thinking, 'What the fuck?' right now." I'm sure you were. Cause at the end of the day you're a fighter. I want you to make High Freed. I've already picked out an outfit to wear the day you do it. I just feel like I want them to respect you enough to understand you are Thurwar, not Sunset (RIP to him, I know that was your boy) or Nova (fuck that guy). You are the real deal. At this rate the Melanchoniacs will never stop with it. Fucking pricks. I watched Bishop. She was great, but you are better.

Anyways. Keep on with it.

Since the last letter, I imagine you've actually read a lot more of these than you let on. The wife, as I said, has been watching with me. She fucking loves it. And that's a blessing. Thank you. I want her to open up to me, you know? I want her to try things. I like that, with all due respect, we get to watch you and Staxxx cause I think it's opening her up to the idea of what else we might do to spice things up. I think you might be the key. Just wanted to say thanks. And since I have an old stream on anyways you can see how thankful I am. HAHA:)
[1 image attached]

Best,
iLL Willy Wil

Thurwar,

Murderers deserve to die. YOU deserve to die.
—Kep

Yo,

[1 image attached]

How's this

[1 image attached]

You Like?,

[1 image attached]

Thurwar had finished with the messages. She tried not to think about their contents, let them roll off her like water. She also knew that her engagement with the messages was monitored and recorded, so even though she'd seen a message that was almost definitely from Sunset's daughter, she logged out of the fan mail and clicked through to the pages dedicated to weapons and armor upgrades. She tried to receive the love Marissa had sent, tried not to wonder what she might have been alluding to. Instead she focused on the coming matches. She used a hefty portion of BP to acquire a katana that would be delivered to Rico Muerte by the morning. She needed him to have it as they did their final day of fight planning before any individual work and prep. She also upgraded Rico's meal plan to a basic level that would keep him from complaining about peanut butter and jelly.

She looked through her weapons and gear, and when she was satisfied with all the Links in her Chain, she stepped from the computer terminal and sat at the end of her bed. There was a knock at the door.

"Rico Muerte here to see you," one of the guards said from beyond the door.

"What is it?" Thurwar yelled back.

"I just wanted to say, um, thank you. I confirmed the shit you sent and I want you to know that it means a lot to me and I got you forever." The sound of Rico's voice made Thurwar get up from where she was sitting.

She opened the door.

Rico was staring at the floor. His shoulders heaved up and down.

"It's called Sansupurittā," Thurwar said. "It belonged to a strong Link. It's a good weapon. Make it yours."

"Yes, ma'am," Rico said. "Imma make you proud." Then he lifted his head and looked at her, letting the tears fall. "On God I will," he said. And Thurwar nodded before she closed the door.

Ten minutes later, there was another knock. Staxxx.

Thurwar stood up quickly. Her knee protested with a spasm of pain.

"I need some time by myself right now," Thurwar called.

"Really?" Staxxx said.

Thurwar was quiet.

"Just kidding," Thurwar said. She opened the door.

"Bitch," Staxxx said, and then she joined Thurwar on the bed.

Preparation

Their assigned preparation space was a soccer field that belonged to "the fucking Turnwain Titans," Staxxx screamed when their van pulled in. Jerry, still in the same bad mood, didn't speak much to them, but he opened the van's storage so they could retrieve their weapons and a bundle of wooden practice staves.

Staxxx showed no sign of being tired although she and Thurwar had kept each other up into the early morning, as if they didn't know they would soon be forced against each other. They'd loved each other deeply through the night, savored the taste of each other's sweat. They'd woken up and tried to feel as though they were not afraid.

"Old rivals," Staxxx explained now. She made an effort, as she always did, to keep the Chain's morale up for the three hours of physical practice they had here before tomorrow's fights. She and Thurwar knew what was coming, and the performance of normalcy was a welcome distraction. A perimeter had been set up and a smattering of reporters lined the outer edges of the soccer field, but the space was dominated by the soldier-police, at least thirty of them, all armored and ready.

"Rico, grab somebody else's wood for once," Staxxx said as Rico stared at the men. "But before that," she continued as they pulled the weapons from the open compartment, "we have a special reveal today." The Links—Sai, Randy, Ice Ice, and Thurwar—all waited as Staxxx pulled a sword in a gleaming red sheath from the van. Bad Water watched a little farther off and Gunny Puddles acted disinterested, though he was watching too.

"Rico, please step forward." And Rico stepped up.

"Let it be known on this day, Rico Muerte graduated in the hearts and minds of the people from that guy with a golf club to the wielder of—I can't pronounce the name, but this cool-ass blade." The Links, even Gunny, gave a quick applause. "Get on your knees, Peanut."

"Not a Peanut anymore!" Rico said. He got down on one knee.

"So as a member of the illustrious and renowned Angola-Hammond Chain, do you accept the responsibility to forever hold it down for the squad?"

"Yes, ma'am."

"I'm not an old lady, but okay."

She pulled the blade from the sheath; it shined in the morning sun.

"Do you accept the Chain-Gang as family and promise to do your best not to harm another member of the gang?" She brought the blade down and let it rest on his right shoulder.

"Yes, m— I do?"

"Damn right you do. And do you vow to go out swinging, to do everything in your power to see High Freed?"

She brought the blade to his left shoulder.

"Fuck yes!"

"Then on this day I bestow upon thee, here in the land of the vile Titans, the blade called . . ."

"Sansupurittā," Thurwar finished.

"Yes, that. I bestow it upon you, Vanier Rico Muerte Reyes. Do you accept?"

"I do," Rico said.

Staxxx sheathed the blade and presented it with two hands to a still-kneeling Rico. All the Links cheered; most of them had had a similar moment, and they knew what it meant to be given a proper chance to survive.

Rico stood up. "Let's fucking go!"

"All right, three cheers for the boy getting some hair on his chest,"

Gunny Puddles said. "Now I'd like to get some work in before the sun goes down."

A-Hamm walked into the sun-swept soccer field holding their hammers and scythes and blades and tridents and all types of ways to kill. They stretched and then did a few weaponed laps around the field. Thurwar had made sure that all of the A-Hamm Links understood the weight of their weapons, the literal weight of them, as they exercised, to simulate as close an approximation of the BattleGround as possible.

"Let's go," Thurwar said. And they all followed. Thurwar had created a work plan for each Link. She used BP to buy video clips of their opponents and scrutinized the film, for the ways they left their bodies vulnerable. The night before, she and Staxxx had also strategized about how to help Rico make it through the weekend against Rainfall Lolli, a Cusp who definitely had Reaper potential, and they tried to game-plan Randy Mac's next bout, against Raven Ways.

They all made sure to treat Mac just as they always had during training that day, to laugh or sometimes not laugh at his jokes, to respect him casually and easily, as it was understood that these were the last days of his life.

And even as they knew that, Thurwar and Staxxx worked with each other because their next match would be as trying as any they'd seen. They could only spend so much worry on Mac.

The Drive

Nile knew Mari's mother would never forgive him. He wasn't sure if he would be able to forgive himself. But they were already on the road, hurtling toward an arena where no good could come.

"How did you get this ticket again?" he asked. The streetlights shined. He backed away from the steering wheel, let the autonomous movement have the reins. Mari stared out her window; he could see her reflection in the sweeping black of the outside world. She didn't answer, which wasn't a surprise. She had been reluctant to tell him anything, but he had a car and she didn't, so now they were on the road.

"What did you tell Kai again?"

He felt a pressure at his throat and chest. He wanted more than anything to serve Mari in whatever way she wanted him to. And yet, right now he also wanted to turn around and leave her back at her home and pretend he had never heard her plan.

"Why does it matter what I told her?" she said, still not looking at him.

He pushed on the brakes, engaged manual control, pulled to the roadside, then turned the car off.

"Mari," he said. He turned on the overhead light.

Finally she looked at him, her eyes shimmering.

"I told her I love her and good night," Mari said.

"She doesn't know?"

"Correct."

The dread he felt from the Old Taperville protest was still a hard stone in his body, and here he was carrying Mari into something much worse.

"And you have a ticket for the front row?"

"I do. They're from my uncle."

"And it's even possible?"

"It is. I've done my homework." She wiped her eyes and let him see she was still ready. "Let's go."

"I don't want to do this."

"Let the car do it then. Just sit back and be here with me. Let the car drive us."

Nile winced as the light from a passing car flooded them, then disappeared.

"You understand how I feel about you, right?" Nile reached over and took her hand, rubbed her thumb with his.

Mari took a deep breath. "Yes," she said. "That's why I asked you."

"Because you know I care?"

"Because I knew you wouldn't say no."

Nile smiled, hoping the shape of his lips would make the pressure he felt in his chest fade.

"And?" he asked.

"And so, I have to do this. Tracy Lasser is one person. Look what happened. If I can inject some of that energy into the actual space, it will do something. Look what she was able to do. Look at what we did with her."

"There's no reason to believe it will do anything."

"And you can go ahead and believe that."

"I'm just saying that—"

"If you aren't going to take me, just say so."

"Mari, I—"

But before he could finish Mari leaned over and kissed him. She pressed hard into him and he leaned back at the force. She pulled away and looked ahead. They were quiet.

"Put this fucking car on and let it take us there," she finally said.

And Nile understood that with him or without him, Mari was going.

"No," Nile said. "I'll drive us."

The Morning Of

The morning of her last doubles match Thurwar woke up in a king-size bed with the woman she loved in her arms.

Staxxx bristled as Thurwar woke.

"Not yet," Staxxx said.

"No, get up," Thurwar said, sitting up.

Staxxx grabbed a pillow and swung for Thurwar's head, but Thurwar caught her wrist and pinned her down before she could strike.

"Oh no, you're so strong," Staxxx said.

Thurwar reared her head back and played as if she were going to crash her skull into Staxxx's, but slowed to kiss her forehead.

"I am," Thurwar said. She rolled over and lay back down next to Staxxx. Her readiness to start on time was gone. All she wanted was to close her eyes and stay exactly as they were forever.

The morning of the doubles match, Staxxx woke up having hardly slept. She'd consoled Mac for a few hours in his room before leaving him and trying to sleep in Thurwar's bed, but she had a strange dream, more feeling than anything she could easily express in words. Shadows and light and mirror images. She felt the beginnings of her pre-match last words. She wanted to tell the world something they would remember. She wanted to call them to their higher selves.

Thurwar was up and ready early as usual and Staxxx tried to get her to sleep in. To her surprise, Thurwar reclined back into the bed for at least a few extra moments. She reached over and touched Staxxx.

"You know about my knee, right?" Thurwar asked.

"What about it?" Staxxx said, though of course she knew. But she wanted to be sure of what Thurwar was saying.

"It's weaker now. I can move on it. But it's a weakness. A vulnerability. I don't know if it's been ID'd yet."

The light was pale and soft, filtered further through the thin hotel shades.

Staxxx turned so she was looking at the side of Thurwar's face on the bed, and then Thurwar turned so they could look straight into each other.

"Are you telling me this for me, or for us, or for you?" Staxxx asked.

"For us," Thurwar said. "Or for you? I don't know."

Staxxx frowned.

The morning of the doubles match, Hendrix Singer felt a pain in his gone arm so deep and real he slipped from the bed to pray for forgiveness. He prayed for the man he had killed just for loving a woman whom he had also loved. He prayed for the woman whose great misfortune had been knowing him. He prayed for each soul he'd loosed the Jungle on and each soul he'd Freed with his black scorpion. He prayed for the silent at Auburn and the silent in cages all around the world. All those smothered by other men's fear. He prayed for all those suits who had no idea what they were a part of and all those who understood it perfectly. He prayed for Simon J. Craft, who had almost been erased entirely but was still there, flickering but bright. He prayed for himself, for an answer to all he had done. He prayed to understand his purpose. He thanked God for showing him his life had not been for nothing. He did not know what it was for, but he knew it was not for nothing. He thanked God for the gift of knowing he deserved his life.

The morning of the doubles match, Simon Craft woke from a dream of a young man. A man who was angry from hurt. Who leapt from salve to salve to quiet the pain that troubled him. He saw the man breaking things, breaking women and children, men. He hated the man, wanted to kill him.

He woke up in tears in a room he couldn't remember ever having been in before. He was scared. The walls were screaming at him. He was afraid, pain waiting everywhere like a shadow. But he remembered his name.

Thurwar wondered why she'd told Staxxx what she'd told her. Maybe the truth felt more necessary now that they were so close to the place they'd imagined for so long, even if Thurwar hadn't imagined it like this.

"You're so cute, baby," Staxxx said. "You really think you have to help me. You want me to kill you?"

"I just don't wanna hide anything. You know about my knee. You know how I got here, how it was my fault. You know about Vanessa and you know about my knee. I want you to know exactly who I am."

"Lo, I already know everything. How could I not? It's us."

Staxxx still felt the charge of her dream and somehow it helped her say exactly what she meant.

"But you're cute, though," she finished. "Let's eat."

And she smiled. She relished the moment, the gift of her and Thurwar existing in the same time and space, no matter how briefly.

"Okay," Thurwar said. It seemed as if something in her had been healed, for now. They knew each other so well, the idea that Staxxx needed to know anything more was absurd.

Hendrix Singer Young and the Unkillable Jungle Craft arrived in the arena and found their armor and weapons waiting for them in a locker room that belonged to the away team. It had been a long while since they hadn't been the ones the people would cheer best. Singer smiled at Craft, who sat and waited for direction.

"These two ain't got no weaknesses," he said to Craft, "but they also ain't unkillable. You got that honor alone."

They sat in the cold room. The sound of gathering already started to make his stomach shake. Singer unrolled a length of bolt leather. Craft had his fight pants on, his back exposed so the huge letter R stood against four Ms.

"Let me get you ready," Singer said.

Craft gave his arms to Singer, the good angel, who wrapped him in the protection.

"You ready to do what you was put on this earth to do?"

"Yes, sir," Craft said.

"You Jungle Man, right? You the Unkillable?" Bolt leather on his arms and around his neck. A chest guard, plates for legs. The good angel draped him with his safety.

"You ready for this?" Thurwar asked. She spoke earnestly to Randy Mac, who was up on the undercard, as were Rico and Gunny. Randy was to face Raven Ways and Thurwar was almost certain it was Randy's last day on earth. She felt a deep pity that as a final gift she kept to herself.

"I think my number's up, Blood Mama," Mac said quietly as they stepped into the van.

She did not argue with him, out of respect. He was a good Link, maybe great. But Raven Ways was Raven Ways.

"You know his distances, though," Staxxx said.

She'd sparred with Mac the last few weeks and used LoveGuile to help him imagine the length and precision of Raven's halberd. Still, she knew that it was very unlikely she would see Mac again.

"I'm happy I got to be a part of your story," he said.

"You're a legend all your own," she told him.

Singer remembered the early days when he got his voice back. Tried to think what his life might have been had he never signed the devils' papers, and he had trouble seeing it clear.

"Either way I cut up meat," he said, and laughed grimly.

"Me too," Craft said.

Hendrix smiled.

> *It's a long John,*
> *He's a long gone.*

Good Angel sings and it means fight is coming. He shows me who and I do it. I am Simon J. Craft. All the time I am. The task is kill. I do it. I sing with him.

> *Like a turkey through the corn,*
> *Through the long corn*

They wrapped bolt leather around their arms.

And midsection. Touch the seven Xs there first. The one M a commander among a legion of marks on her body. Can you miss the people you never knew except to kill?

Protect the neck.

We dress for big loud hell.

There was music. Randy's, then Raven's. Then a whole three minutes. Thurwar tried to think about what was in front of her, not what was in front of Mac. Another two minutes. Then Raven's music, and the pain.* Wanting to hear something, trying not to hope but hoping anyway.

"I'm sorry," Thurwar said to Staxxx.

"He was a legend already. They won't forget him," Staxxx said. She pledged to have him remembered. "May he enjoy his freedom. Suck my dick, America." And Thurwar echoed her.

Staxxx would mark him along with the two whom they would see soon. Three Xs. She was running out of skin.

––––––––––

* Randall "Randy Mac" McMorrison, age thirty-two. Low Freed.
    What I'm saying is, that's a whole lotta prisoners for a land that claims free. Whole lot of animal slaughtering. I seen the best I've seen in the hole you keep the decrepit, so suck my dick.

A fight before us clashing up above. Today we a main card for the ages. The best of all, word is. They would have us wait in the hall. I explain to the men that Craft doesn't do great around people that ain't me. So we sit in the locker room.

Well, my John said,
In the chap ten,
"If a man die,
He will live again."

Just a jaunt, Jay.

Just jump.

"My name is Simon Jeremiah Craft."

"You don't say," Good Angel says.

We walk out to the screaming angels. Screaming for us. Asking us to kill. I will protect the Good Angel.

We walk.

We kneel.

We wait for the chance to jump.

The sound of the people is heavy. It changes something inside you, Thurwar thought, to know so many expect something of you. She wondered how much she'd changed these three years, how much she'd stayed the same. No part of her wanted to kill today, and she could admit that to herself. She ran through the gate and entered what looked like a rodeo space. The fans circled above them, the closest not six feet up. Micky Wright chatted from his BattleBox. Thurwar walked to the Keep. She kneeled into it and waited. Across the way the two men sat quiet. Expectant, not scared. What a group we are, Thurwar thought. She took a deep breath.

"Suck my dick, America!" Staxxx screamed. She stomped around the dirt, tied her hair back, and picked LoveGuile up again. "Suck my dick, America!" A catchphrase of catchphrases. The crowd blew up. "Love you, Mac." A sudden gale, the storm together. "You guys wanna hear about a dream I had?" she asked. Her voice, the voice of a young god. "I was in a world of pure dark. I could see nothing else. I stumbled around for ages, hoping for something." She stopped and the HMC in front of her sailed the air at her lips. "Then after a long while I saw a little pinprick of light, so I ran to it. I ran and I ran and when I tried to touch it my shadow swallowed it whole.

"But then I closed my eyes and tried again, and I was in a space where the light was endless and there was a pinprick of dark and I knew I was in the same place I'd been before."

"Okay, Ms. Stacker, please, we'd like to get to the good part." Micky Wright, the MC of the evening, stood on top of the announcer's box.

"That is the good part!" Staxxx laughed as she kneeled beside Thurwar. She couldn't just give the answers away. The magic came from sitting with the puzzle, as she had. Letting it seep into you. One day they'd understand.

And then the crowd gasped.

Out of thin air, it seemed, a new woman had appeared. Not a Link, but a woman in the unmistakable clothes of a civilian. Thurwar stared at her along with the entire rest of the country.

The woman was Sunset's daughter, Marissa. And there she was on the BattleGround, holding a sign that read:

WHERE LIFE IS PRECIOUS.

Shareef

Mari had walked through security carrying nothing but her wallet, a marker, and a neon-green poster board.

The security guard at the C-gate entrance smiled at her, gold caps shining, and asked, "What's on the sign?" She'd thought she'd feel a radical terror but instead she felt an instinctual understanding of what to do next. She unraveled the poster board, which had been rolled into a loose cylinder, and displayed the plane of blank green without resistance. He looked at her, confused, and she dug into the left pocket of her pants and pulled out a thick black marker. She waved the marker between her fingers, summoned a smile. "Was in a rush," she said.

Her smile was reciprocated. "I get you," he said. "And now maybe you have a little more time to decide who to root for?" he said, laughing. And Mari laughed too as she was allowed through the barrier to find her seats.

Mari found the people sitting in the seats nearest to her. The men and women who had presumably paid hundreds of dollars to witness this circus of death firsthand were, more or less, regular people. They were communal and chatty, asking Mari several questions she answered as though she was trying to expend as little energy as possible engaging with them, which she was.

"First time up this close?" a woman with red hair asked.

"Yes," Mari said. She was seated in the front row, and had they been at a baseball game, which was what the stadium had been designed for, she would have been near third base.

For the BattleGround, though, a short clear wall had been erected in front of the seats as if it were a hockey match. It was only about five feet high, but while sitting down they peered through it as they watched. And she did watch. She saw Randy Mac get impaled by a halberd, and the people around her screamed in a complicated jubilation and sorrow. Many people, including the woman with the red hair, wept.

Mari bent into her sign. Drew the letters thick. She realized she was crying too and she tried not to wet the fresh black.

"Who you got in the main event?" the man to her left asked. He was there with several other men, who might have been his brothers or cousins. They were loud and all had the same face, the same way of speaking. They were analytical and precise with their observations and assessments of both the murder happening in front of them and Thurwar, whose likeness was projected from their phones, which they passed around, each man assessing her as if they were a board scrutinizing a dissertation.

"Thurwar," Mari said, looking into the man's blue eyes briefly before returning to her sign.

"Ladies have to stick together, I guess." He smiled and Mari did not. "We put money on the other side." Mari continued writing. She looked at her board. It gave her a place to put her eyes, gave her fear a place to rest. "Good news is, one of us is right. Right?" he offered with a laugh.

"Sure," Mari said.

She tried to escape into herself. There was a tremendous energy in the space, and she was ashamed to feel it so clearly. Gunny Puddles killed a man. Rico Muerte killed a man. There was a feeling of grand worship, a power and excitement. She was ashamed at how familiar it was. Mari's secret was she'd watched *LinkLyfe* regularly. She'd watched to get to know her father, a man who'd hardly known her. She'd watched as he'd done good, as he and Thurwar had shaped the A-Hamm Chain into something different. She'd felt the rush of being wanted every time he said her name. She'd found a way to love him through the horrific show and now it was right in front of her. She'd watched the man they called Sunset because even though he was gone, even though he'd lived a life away from her, he was hers.

She finished and put her marker onto the floor near her sneakers.

Thurwar emerged with no music and Mari stood with everyone else to see the icon, hammer in hand. Staxxx's music sounded and the roar of the people made the hairs on her arms rise. The energy was unmissable. Their bodies were gleaming in their armor. If it weren't real it would have been beautiful. As it was, it was awe-inspiring, an opening that came from the chest and spread through the rest of you.

Thur-WAR, Thur-WAR

Hurricane Hurricane Hurricane Staxxx

"First things first," Staxxx said. "Suck my dick, America!" Staxxx screamed. The people screamed too. The red-haired woman burst into tears again.

"Love you, Mac," Staxxx said.

Mari watched and listened, but also finally felt the terror she'd expected much earlier. Now that it was time to do what she'd said she was going to do. Now that the rest of her life was before her.

She couldn't move. Suddenly she was cemented in place. She turned to the red-haired woman, who was screaming, thrilled with life even in sorrow. She clearly was a fan of Staxxx and Thurwar as well.

"My father was a Link," Mari said, yelling into the woman's left ear. The woman glanced at her, clearly surprised at the sudden offering of such juicy information.

"Yeah?" she asked, still up and mostly focused on the BattleGround. "What was his name?"

"I'm going to hop this wall in a second," Mari said. "I'm going to go on the BattleGround to remind us all that we're better than this."

"What?" the woman said, confused, still cautiously friendly.

Mari stood on her seat.

"His name was—is—Shareef Harkin Roleenda," Mari said, and then she leapt and pulled and kicked her way over the wall and onto the BattleGround, the green poster in her hands.

She landed hard and was there on the grounds for at least three seconds before she could feel people noticing. She walked a few steps toward the middle before realizing that she'd hurt her ankle. No matter. She raised her sign above her head, took slow steps. The eruptions of applause shifted to smatterings of sound, clear confusion. The contrast was stark.

"We seem to have somebody who's a little lost," the announcer said. Mari watched as he retreated into his small room on the field.

Had she not been completely enthralled by the heat she felt, the power of her steps, she would have laughed at him. Lost.

Staxxx still had not been locked into her position and now she was walking toward Mari, scythe in hand.

Mari smiled at her and Staxxx smiled back. Beyond her Thurwar looked with eyes that reminded Mari of Kai's: worried, concerned.

"It's okay," Mari said. She held the sign up for all to see, slowly rotated it so everyone in the arena could see both sides. It was then that she noticed the soldier-police flooding from both gates in her direction. First they pulled Staxxx back to the Keep and locked her in. Then the armored men ran at Mari.

Mari kneeled down and kept the sign high in the air, proudly speaking the truth. You didn't get to have it both ways. Either we loved one another or we did not.

The front of the sign read: WHERE LIFE IS PRECIOUS

And the back, which fell facedown when Mari dropped it, read: LIFE IS PRECIOUS. And even though the men circled her, the entire stadium could see the message. And for a moment, before the producers had forced the Jumbotron cameras to black, the message had been magnified for all to see. *Where life is precious, life is precious,* and it dawned on the crowd, rapt and ready though they were for the doubles BattleGround match of the year, that life might not be precious here.

And the entire stadium could see when one of the officers pulled a weapon that looked like a gun from his side and shot a black rod into Mari's neck. And the entire stadium saw as Mari was Influenced.

The Feeling

A tearing and opening. A need to end. A way in with no way out.
What she felt was all the hurt her body and brain could summon at once. It started from her ankle, which felt as though it had exploded, and then, when the man grabbed her, as she writhed with the black rod in her neck, the feeling blossomed further and further and Mari was sure she would die and she welcomed it, hoped for it, begged for it.

As Mari was being Influenced, as she felt her rolled ankle, as an explosion erupted again and again inside of her, every other millisecond, she understood the illusion of time. She understood that she could easily be thrown into a space beyond time, that suffering could stretch and re-form what she had known as seconds and mangle them into years.

This was no epiphany, this was pain, and yet, she felt more than understood that she would do anything, anything, to end the pain she was feeling. It seemed her eyes had shut off, or maybe she had just closed them. Either way the space she generally remembered to have eyes was a wrenching, a pulling that made her feel as though maybe her eyes had been pulled out.

She was suffering. And she would do anything to end it. And yet she could do nothing because she was afraid to move. Her everything was—

And then it ended and she was floating, being carried, and she could feel her body, her body and her breath.

Yes

Thurwar looked across the way, out in the far-right field, where the two men were waiting. She was trying to forget what had just happened. Trying to forget it even as it continued in front of her.

They pulled away Marissa, who had finally stopped convulsing, by her legs and shoulders. They were quick with her body, trying to get her away from the cameras and all those eyes, as if once she was out of sight, she would be forgotten. It hurt for Thurwar to see it happen, to know what being Influenced would do. Her attachment to life had been completely different since she'd learned that kind of pain was possible.

She had to forget Marissa right now, though. She couldn't believe she was trying to remember her battle strategy now instead of thinking about what had just happened, one of the most courageous things she'd ever seen. But there she was.

She looked at Staxxx.

"She'll be okay," Staxxx said.

"Maybe," Thurwar said.

"She will."

"Yes," Thurwar said. Staxxx smiled.

"Wanna hear a joke?" Staxxx asked.

They were close, but still they had to yell to hear each other over the ruckus of the crowd.

Thurwar waited.

"This," Staxxx said.

"That's not funny," Thurwar said, laughing. That was the joke. The joke was everything. That they'd been thrown into evil and discovered it was a land they could master.

The people in the crowds were restless. They didn't know who or what to boo and cheer and it made them uneasy.

Micky Wright spoke clearly.

"That's one way to get attention. But might I suggest to all the rest of you that you not do that ever."

The audience didn't laugh. Made a collective mutter that conveyed, *We don't know if we believe in laughter right now.*

"I'm getting noise from the bosses. They say give the people what they want! And didn't you come here for some BattleGround mayhem!"

Yes, they said.

"Did you come here for a doubles match for the ages?"

Yes, they yelled.

"Did you come tonight because the baddest in Chain-Gang All-Stars history are here for what will be, for at least one team, their very last doubles match ever?"

Hell yes! the people screamed.

Thurwar closed her eyes, drank the energy in. She looked at Hass Omaha, which was directly to her left. LoveGuile was stabbed into the ground just to the right of Staxxx.

"Then if you're ready for a classic, why don't you make some noise!"

And they did. They screamed, pushed what had troubled them just a moment before deep into their minds. A seed that was buried for the moment. There was a sourness in their bodies; the word "precious" rang somewhere inside them, and it would be there forever, but in the moment, they pretended to forget.

"RELEASE!" Micky Wright screamed.

The empty sound of the BattleGround release flushed through the arena. Thurwar pulled her hammer from the ground. Staxxx held Love-Guile in her hands and they waited for the men, who were calmly walking their way.

Through the Door

F our martyrs step into a rodeo. It's a joke. The killing kind. The kind where you ain't laughing much but see something a little different after the punch has lined. Where life is precious, life is precious. And surely that's not here. Type of courage most ain't lucky enough to see. It's a full crowd that seen it. And it's more protesting outside the arena than cheering in. Maybe something right coming, maybe we'll see something different, but for now, we forget all that ain't the ladies' death.

We walk, released into what the world has been waiting for. The woman that wears the crown in the killing games, Thurwar, carries a hammer and jogs behind her lady, the scythe holder, the one they call Hurricane, a fine picture of death waiting to reduce us to Xs on her skin.

"I'll meet the hammer. You go scythe," I say. I yell 'cause the crowds are louder than they've ever been. I feel their voices in my bones.

I hope I am not commanding him to his death. Simon J. Craft, who has been reduced to the Unkillable. Simon, who deserves no sympathy but won't ever be undeserving of love.

"Yes, sir," he says, and he runs.

I hope I am not sprinting to a ruin.

Thurwar knew well the man called Singer, the unlikely Colossal. Was he crazy or holy? And the Unkillable, surely he was crazy, though a different kind. The kind born of Influence.

She watched Singer, his eyes sharp and sad. He wore a shoulder guard that punched down and protected his arm. He wore bolt leather and had an embroidered air horn on his shirt, the emblem of a popular music-streaming service. Singer ran toward Thurwar. She knew he liked to open with a long thrust, so she watched the black tip of the spear. She did not want to kill him, but she would as soon as she had the chance.

Long nights I've wondered about this woman. This woman who's seen more death even than me. Wish I could know her well. What does this fourth door offer her? What has she discovered? I tell Craft to run toward the Hurricane woman. And although I tell him I will seek the hammer, I veer and sprint to the woman they named after wind and thunder. I push to fly off the ground. A one-arm and an Unkillable might smother a storm. My gone arm points me to a change of plans. The Grand Colossal notices my approach, as does the scythe. We run toward the storm.

It's not an uncommon tactic, to try to dispatch quickly one opponent on a double team. Watching the men sprint toward Staxxx, Thurwar felt a panic like falling from solid ground to harsh waters. She pushed as hard as she could toward the men. She didn't feel a huge pain, she was too adrenalized, but her knee said be gentle. Her leg buckled under the sudden strain and change of direction. Thurwar was on her knees in the dirt. She watched as the man called Unkillable leapt into the air. Staxxx stopped to engage him. She shot LoveGuile out like a poker into the man's face. In the air he received the blow from the blunt side and continued to fall toward her as if he had not felt a thing.

Thurwar picked herself up off the ground. Her knee hurt, but it was still hers. She rushed.

Craft dances with the stormy god. Swinging his arms to kill, he slices and breaks the tie keeping her hair from whipping about and her dreads fly free as I approach them. She spins, using the scythe to keep

Craft away. He leaps, ducks it, moves like the precise human animal he is. I want her eyes on him. She is focused for her life. The scythe moves like a kind of magic that Craft has not seen before. But she must watch him too. The Grand Colossal has stumbled and I will have the lunge. She's just getting back to her feet and I reach out with my gone arm, imagine it stretching out to aid Craft, who is swinging and dodging, the sound of metal singing as the scythe repels his claws. A special thing, a wild dance between two forms of death incarnate. Pain and love trying, trying to kill each other. I know the hammer will soon be upon me. I stretch. The one called Staxxx stumbles as if tripping. I thank my gone arm. Even as she falls back she repels the angry swipe of the Jungle. On one leg she swings and Craft is forced back.

But in the position, off-balance, she is vulnerable. I am close enough. Spinifer, bring this beautiful woman to ruin. Bless her to Freedom. I run and pull back.

On my side my gone arm tries to repel something.

On my side my gone arm tries to deflect.

The hammer rips through my arm that is no longer there. On the side of my head I feel the hammer, thrown through the air. A brutal release, an abrupt song. It's a long John.

I thank the world, unsure no longer. Worthy of life, I'm sure as it leaves. In the end, surely we are blessed. The royal and low, the queen and the singer. Surely we are blessed. The hammer welcomes me, Hendrix Young, to the unbound.[*]

It isn't a good idea, but in the arena, when death is coming you find ways to redirect it. Thurwar got up off the ground and, after running three paces, saw she would not make it in time to help Staxxx. She turned her run into a spin, held Hass at its end, and then spun once more. As she rotated, her eyes tracked Singer and her body did the critical math. She let the hammer fly, threw it and it flew, and it met Singer at the side of his head. He erupted into stillness. The crowd screamed for the kill. They screamed for Thurwar.

---

[*] Hendrix Young, Colossal. 1M. A love that kills like he did is not a love at all. Learned that lesson some years ago. Sing when you want. Give the grace you can to what you can. Pray the redeemer accepts you, grants you grace. You are the redeemer.

This is why we love you, they said.

They screamed because the man they called Unkillable noticed that his companion was dead on the ground, even in wild pursuit, and he stopped suddenly. The Unkillable Jungle Craft's arms went limp and he ran toward the man who had guided him from hell to a kinder, easier hell. Thurwar watched as Simon J. Craft ran past her to the body of Hendrix Scorpion Singer Young.

Simon kneeled there, held Hendrix, what was left of his human suppleness, in his arms and did not move. The crowd stood silent. Their hearts opened; some resisted, some gave in. Eyes found tears. Simon Craft held Singer's body, squeezed it to him, then laid the body on the ground.

Staxxx walked up to the man, who was unmoving except for his heaving breath. Craft took his fist and gently punched Singer's knuckles.

Thurwar watched this. Staxxx approached and rested the scythe on Craft's shoulder.

"Sorry, baby. I love you," Staxxx said, and then she pulled Love-Guile across his neck.

He dropped forward. The Unkillable Simon J. Craft was killed.* Staxxx walked away from the scene, dropped her weapon to the ground, as did Thurwar. They returned to their Keep and held each other's hands for what was next, and the people wondered if this feeling was salvation.

---

* Simon J. Craft, Harsh Reaper. 4M 1R. Jungle Jungle Jeremiah. Just Jump. Just a Jaunt. The J stands for. Those that cause suffering. What of them? What of me? Simon asked of himself. He was a murderer, a rapist. He was. He had not always been. What of that person that had been? What of what could have been? Because he was ruined he ruined and was ruined further.

There was a light. He jumped to it.

Season 33

The men were dead on the floor. He'd been hoping it'd be the women dead on the floor because as much as he didn't love Thurwar, the Blood Mother, the most famous woman in sports, he certainly didn't want to be the guy who had to announce what he was about to announce.

"Great fight," he said with the enthusiasm of a deflated soccer ball. The field workers bagged the men's bodies.

"A shocking conclusion for the great Singer and Jungle Man, who was killable after all. Almost certainly some of the very best these games had to offer. They had a great run. Let's clap it up for them."

The thing he did not like was happening: He was seeing what he was. The bodies were not cold and he was about to announce an atrocity worse even than the one they had all just witnessed. This was who he was. He just didn't know how he'd gotten there. He'd watched the news, seen the clips of Tracy Lasser quitting, and thought, Huh. Good for her. And it was not until days later that he woke up in the night terrified for himself, for what he had become, what he was. In the board meetings he had done all he could. That was what he told himself.

The people in the stands were clapping for the mangled dead. He chuckled, because what else was there to do. We all allowed it. We all voted for it. We all knew it was happening, so why suddenly be out-raged? Why now did he feel that sinking? Something long growing. Something with jaws ready to eat inside him.

"And of course the most dynamic duo, the bloody lady love bunnies themselves, have conquered the mountains in front of them once again to close out season thirty-two of Chain-Gang All-Stars.

"What's more, the Beautiful Bard, the Hurricane called Staxxx, has finally, finally reached Colossal. Making her and her love bunny the first-ever pair of women to achieve Colossal rank on the same Chain." The last bit was unscripted. He wanted to paint the picture clearly so even the idiots in the stands, the people who loved him or hated him or watched him with greedy expectant eyes, would understand exactly what was happening next.

He was on top of his little stage and he saw the two of them, Staxxx and Thurwar, holding hands, turning their heads to look at him as soldier-police led them back into the tunnel. A season had ended, which meant a new season had begun. And because of what was being announced they would not offer any post-fight commentary.

He looked up at the Jumbotron, so he could see himself, but that made him feel a little sick, so he looked out at the crowds of people who had come to see something legendary, had been satisfied, but still wanted more.

"I'm getting word now of some stunning new rules from the Game-Masters." He said this and touched his ear, although there was no mes-sage being relayed. He had already been given the script, had rehearsed it in the week leading up. But he wanted to put some distance between himself and the invisible hand that controlled the Chain-Gang. He was on the board, but the big-money owners were the ones who controlled everything, really. This was what he told himself. He was a hire, not a legacy. He wanted Thurwar, that impossible bitch, and that lunatic Staxxx to know that, despite all their differences, he would not do this to them.

"Uh-huh. Oh my. What wild minds," he said to no one, to himself and to the world. Then he took a breath. "I've just got word that we'll finally have an answer to the question on all of your bloody beating hearts. Who is the strongest? Who is the baddest? Who is the greatest Link of all time?" He spoke, but his words held no light or flair. He spoke with a disinterest he knew would get him fired. He wondered if his agent knew Tracy Lasser's people.

"The new rule, which I've been told will be effective immediately, as season thirty-three of Chain-Gang All-Stars has just begun, is that no single Chain may contain two Colossal-ranking Links. In the event that a Chain does have two Colossal-ranking Links, they will meet in the BattleGround. And so, in a week's time, for the most coveted treasure of High Freed, Loretta Thurwar will battle Hamara 'Hurricane Staxxx' Stacker. Until then!" he said, leaving out the sponsors completely. He climbed down into the BattleBox and sank to the ground.

The people were shocked. They were quiet. And in silence, Micky Wright thought, Maybe there is hope yet.

Suck My Dick, America

Y'all had a rough night. I'm not setting y'all to blue. Don't tell anyone, okay?" Jerry said. This was his kindness.

"Suck my dick, America," Sai Eye Aye said, and broke the silence that had shaped the space of the van for so long. Randy Mac's absence was a splinter in their hearts, but it was also a clear and present pain for them to dive into with their whole bodies, to avoid the terrifying future that season 33 had brought their leaders. Thurwar sat in her usual corner and Staxxx, instead of sitting beside Thurwar, sat across from her, in the space Randy Mac would have occupied had he not lost his life.

"Suck my dick, America," Ice Ice the Elephant, Rico Muerte, and Staxxx said in return.

Thurwar, lonely already. Without the weight of Staxxx on her shoulder, she felt lost. She let the absence be. She tried to ignore her knee and the way it screamed. Whatever had been wrong for so long was worse.

"That's the spirit," Jerry said.

And the Links were unified in their hatred of him but said nothing.

Gunny Puddles said, "There's plenty other countries out there."

And the rest of the Links, even Bad Water, looked at him with disdain.

Rico leaned over from his bench to Gunny's right and said, "SUCK MY DICK, AMERICA," as loudly as he could in Gunny's face.

Gunny smiled and leaned back.

Why couldn't she just kill him there? Thurwar thought. Why, if none of it mattered anyway, couldn't she ensure the peace and safety of the group just a little bit by removing Gunny Puddles?

"You can say that all you want, but don't make a change of nothi—"

"Anyways my guy did good. He did what he could," Rico said.

"What they say the count was, almost five minutes?" Ice Ice said. "That's a legendary match if ever there was one."

"Still ended the same," Gunny said.

Thurwar remembered that Randy had come from a rural facility, where he'd worked as a goat farmer. He was one of the few who discovered something he truly loved in prison. If only he'd had the chance before. Who might he have been? Thurwar tried to look at anything, anyone but Staxxx. Did this mean they were already opponents?

Yes. The fight began the second it was assigned. The second you knew it was coming, you were preparing. In her mind Thurwar tried to dissect Staxxx the way she dissected all her opponents: cataloging her tendencies, predicting her first strikes, imagining her death. Staxxx had started off a counterstriker, known for turning an opponent's aggression into their death. But in the Hurricane Era, Staxxx had come to be more of a lead. She hit first and she hit last.

Sai said, "I'll beat your ass right here if you want it."

"You'll what?" Gunny said, still smiling.

Thurwar realized as they rolled on that it wasn't as difficult as she would have hoped: Staxxx liked to end matches quickly, as did all great Links, but she almost always opened with a horizontal spin slash that could—if she missed—be leveraged for momentum for a second or third attack.

She tended to be flashy, but without sacrificing much precision. LoveGuile was much longer than Hass Omaha. These were all thoughts, Thurwar realized, she'd had before. She told herself it was because they'd fought together so many times and she'd needed to understand her as a fighter and partner. But also, to be a Colossal, to be the Grand Colossal, one had to have imagined winning in the Battle-Ground against any and every Link. Out of force of habit, every time Thurwar watched Staxxx, she'd give her feedback on her performance. Most of it stemming from the idea that if Thurwar had been on the grounds against her, hypothetically, she'd have won because of Staxxx's tendency to do whatever it was Thurwar had noticed while watching her fight. But to strategize was one thing; to know it was coming was another.

"I will beat the brakes off your ass right now," Sai said.

"And I'll be there for seconds," Rico added.

Thurwar looked at Staxxx, then Rico, Sai, Ice Ice, Bad Water, and Gunny. In them she saw herself reflected. She had imagined Staxxx dead. In fact it was something she imagined every day. She'd trained herself for the feeling. And the thought of Staxxx dead, her body cold, unmoving, caused an electric adrenaline that started in Thurwar's chest and spread through each and every one of her muscles, turning into a warm hatred of everything around her. That hatred was a powerful motivation. A desire. Staxxx gone from this earth, the idea of it, had carried her to Grand Colossal. A hatred of the cruelty of a world that had allowed Staxxx to be in a system like CAPE in the first place—that had carried her as well. But Thurwar didn't know what would happen now that Staxxx was to be the object of her violence. It seemed impossible to use Staxxx's death to motivate her to kill Staxxx, but there the feeling was.

She was tired. So tired. Thurwar stretched her knee out in front of her in the van and rubbed it the way she did when no one was watching. She rubbed her knee and felt the relief she so often denied herself. She rubbed her knee and Angola-Hammond watched.

"No, you won't," Thurwar said, kneading around her meniscus.

"Randy isn't eve—" Rico started. His voice shook. Rico's own match, his own murder, still fresh on his voice and in his eyes. He was still young, hadn't learned yet to hide the hurt, the blowback of killing.

"I'm already not having a great night," Staxxx said. "You aren't going to do anything to anybody."

"Randy would."

"I said shut it!" Staxxx screamed.

Thurwar looked at Staxxx and Staxxx glared back hard. Thurwar felt the greatest pain of her life. A not knowing if Staxxx still felt how she had, if Staxxx might have killed the part of her that loved Thurwar in order to survive.

"That's right," Gunny Puddles said, laughing so hard spittle escaped from his throat. "Chain-Gang is family."

"Exactly," Staxxx said, smiling too.

Sai deflated into their seat.

"Suck my dick, America," Rico said.

"That's the spirit," Jerry the driver said again.

And they continued down whichever road they were on, to wherever it was they'd begin this Circuit March.

BlackOut

They arrived. Tired from their lives and their truths more than from walking.

The Camp was some meters away from a canyon. At their feet was red earth, redder in the firelight, darker and darker toward the wide chasm of earth that contained the last remnants of a dying river.

They'd walked along the canyon for some time before reaching Camp. Staxxx had held her same place at six o'clock as they'd Marched, and it felt the same, although Thurwar told herself it was different.

It was a massive, sad relief to hear the Anchor announce:

BLACKOUT. *March will initiate in fourteen hours.*

"Well shit," Ice Ice the Elephant said. "I'm glad for that at least." He put one of his large hands on Thurwar's shoulder and turned and walked to Staxxx, whom he hugged.

Thurwar found her dinner and, rather than bring it into the tent, opened the box of crispy broccoli, an organic roast chicken, and a brioche bun with truffle butter and aged Parmesan. She pulled the meal out and set the tray on her lap. She bit into the bun first before she twisted open a bottle of still water.

"BlackOut dinner," Thurwar said. "Cheers." She raised the bottle

up and it shined as the light in her wrist split, reflected and refracted
against the clear.

Staxxx sat down on an actual chair, across the way from Thurwar, a
fire between them. A-Hamm together, they could speak and be heard
only by themselves.

Thurwar drank her water, balancing her tray on her thighs.

The rest of the Chain stood around them, unsure, uneasy.

"Relax," Thurwar said. "Have a seat. It's BlackOut."

Then Staxxx said, "Did something happen? You guys are stressing
me out."

And at this Gunny Puddles began to chuckle. He sat down and
opened the box with his name on it. The others followed suit.

Thurwar tried to remember the men they'd killed just earlier in the
day. How they'd seemed to find peace. She knew it was a convenient
illusion, but it felt real. She hoped they would forgive her. She hoped
whatever she did with Staxxx, there'd be forgiveness waiting for her.

She could feel herself shedding something. This resistance that had
once defined her. A persistence, a hardness. She felt it slipping away.
She was grateful.

"So what's the plan?" Sai asked.

"You guys aren't going to eat, huh?" Thurwar said.

She thought of what she'd seen and done with the humans around
her and felt lighter than she had in a long time. The worst that could
happen was here, and so she was taking a moment to be relieved. She
stretched her knee out. Rubbed it some while balancing the tray. Let
the taste of chicken fill her up.

"It's not fair," Sai said.

"It's fucked," Rico said.

"That's the game," Gunny said.

"It's not right, but it already wasn't," Thurwar said.

"But this is—" Rico started, and Staxxx interrupted him.

"It's a BlackOut, and you all are killing the vibes. Mac didn't say
suck my dick for no reason. This is what is here. This is what it is. And
so for now, today, all I wanna know is"—here Staxxx leaned in toward
the fire—"who y'all got?"

"Whatchu mean?" Rico said, though they all understood.

"It's a simple question. And are you gonna spend the BP to watch us?" Staxxx pushed.

A-Hamm looked to Thurwar, as they did for so much.

"Answer her," Thurwar said. She smiled, though some part of her felt a bleed. Already they were doing a kind of consoling. They were helping the Chain, releasing some pressure for them. Giving them the space to know with certainty that change was coming.

They were across the circle from each other but at least in this they were unified. Another performance. Something to make okay what never could be okay.

"You a great one, Miss Thurwar, but that one is the right kinda crazy with the reaper stick. I'll watch and I'll be in the premium seats for it," Ice Ice said.

"I am pretty good with this thing," Staxxx said. She petted Love-Guile's head.

"I watched your first match in the E-block rec room when I was inside," Sai Eye Aye said. "I've never seen anything like that. I knew from then Loretta Thurwar was seeing High Freed. Respectfully," Sai added.

Staxxx laughed and Thurwar nodded.

Rico, who had actually gone from glassy-eyed to quietly crying, laughed at himself.

"It's—it's hard to beat Staxxx if she's focused. I don't even feel comfortable saying it. Fuck. Staxxx is tough if she's serious." He looked at the ground as he spoke.

"When am I ever not serious?" Staxxx asked.

The whole Chain laughed now.

"Exactly. I think Thurwar a year ago wins it. Right now, I can't call it."

Ice Ice the Elephant said, "Inside thirty seconds, Staxxx. Anything longer, Blood Mama reigns."

"You guys sound like the ReVegas people. Sheesh," Staxxx said.

"Thurwar," Bad Water said.

"And Mac says Staxxx," Staxxx said. "He just told me in my ear."

"I've been an underdog before," Thurwar said. The other Links began to eat, and they let their minds wander about the kinds of deaths that would unfold around them in a week's time and in the weeks after.

They stayed there in the warmth and light of the fire and Thurwar didn't have to wonder if she'd done something good.

"I'm definitely gonna be up in the close boxes," Sai said.

"Me too, if you spot me some BP," Rico said to Thurwar.

"Ask Staxxx to front you since she's so tough," Thurwar said. Her laughter made the Chain relax further. So they laughed too.

"I'm saying, she's just really a bad matchup for anybody."

"Whatever," Thurwar said. And they enjoyed her. They were proud to be led by the woman named Loretta Thurwar.

The night moved through itself, and when the feeling was that sleep was the only thing left to do, Gunny Puddles asked a question.

"While we're all kumbaya, I've been meaning to ask: Why did you kill Sun? He was a sonofabitch, but he treated you like royalty. Why'd you do that to somebody of that kinda cut?"

Thurwar's eyes found Staxxx. The night was cool and held the sharp sound of wind moving through the canyon like a low breath. A constant call to remind them it was there.

"He asked me to. I had to help him."

The Chain heard this. The air held the sound of openness.

Gunny nodded. He didn't challenge her further.

Here Staxxx got up and walked slowly toward the chasm, slowly in the dark toward the split in the earth. She left LoveGuile by the fire and walked away from the Chain.

Thurwar sat with the rest of them. She loved them, didn't want to disappoint them. She hoped they knew it. When she looked up to where Staxxx had gone she could not see her.

Thurwar got up, her knee gently throbbing.

She couldn't see Staxxx, so she walked faster in her direction.

She needed to see Staxxx that moment. She needed to.

And she did.

The glow of Staxxx's wrists led Thurwar back to her. She was waiting at the canyon's edge, the light coming off her body like a prayer.

"I made this, you know," Staxxx said. She looked down, and the way she hovered over death made Thurwar's heart seize.

"Made what?" Thurwar asked. She wanted to reach out and pull Staxxx back. But she could have just as easily pushed her over.

"This canyon. I was practicing one day and got a little excited and *wham* . . . went and cut a hole right in the world." Staxxx leaned over the edge. Thurwar closed her eyes. Tried to let what would happen happen. Maybe this was the easiest way.

They were two of the greatest warriors the world had ever seen.

Thurwar reached her hand to the small of Staxxx's back.

She grabbed the edge of her sweatpants and pulled her back toward her. They turned to face each other.

"I believe it," Thurwar said.

"I don't like thinking about either one of us without the other," Staxxx said.

Thurwar brought Staxxx in closer, felt the look in her eyes and hoped Staxxx could feel her too.

"I don't know why we have to do this. Let's just leave together. Both of us." Thurwar said the words and felt weary as she heard them in the air. "Why are you making us do this? It's supposed to be us. Why are we going to the grounds?"

Thurwar had asked before; she knew she would not get to ask again.

"If I jumped right now, what would you do?" Staxxx said.

"I'd follow you," Thurwar answered.

"And if you did I'd do the same thing," Staxxx said. "And if Puddles came over and tossed a knife in my neck?"

The thought sent a hot wave through Thurwar's body.

"I'd turn him to dust," Thurwar said.

"And then what?"

Thurwar imagined standing over the mush she'd make of Puddles. "I don't know," Thurwar said, but she knew there'd be a fire, a hatred in her that would continue to swell, something that would need something else to eat.

"You'd kinda wanna go find his family, or at least his dog or something, right?" Staxxx said. Her voice smiled, but her face was mournful there in the dark.

Thurwar listened.

"I know we've sent a message in all this. And if we go to the grounds it gets to live in a different way."

"How will it? I can't—"

"Well, I can," Staxxx said. "If they make me kill you, I know that

I'll spend the rest of my time trying to destroy them. You get it. I know you feel it."

"I don't. I won't do it."

"If you won on the grounds then at least I'd be—"

"If I killed you, then what? What would that do?" Thurwar had stepped even closer to Staxxx. She could almost feel the heat of her skin.

"It would make you stay. You'd find a way to turn them to dust. Or you'd try. You'd find Tracy, you'd become a part of something, and you'd work and work and work and maybe somewhere in that you'd forget me at least a little and live a little bit for yourself. I want you to have something to keep you here so that all you are can be out there for just a little longer. And you shouldn't have to do anything, you've done so much, but I know you. You'll try because that is what you do, and that will be something. That will be everything."

"So I'm a messenger for you? What if I don't want that?"

"You're my message and I'm yours," Staxxx said. "Whoever wins, it will be the same."

Thurwar brought her hands up past Staxxx's shoulders, held her head in her palms.

"Us," Staxxx said.

"But what's the message then? What message is worth all this?"

Staxxx took Thurwar's wrists, squeezed them. Thurwar let herself cry.

"You're right," Thurwar said, "I know." And she kissed her to let her know she was the best thing in her life and she wanted all the time they had left.

Game

The sound was everywhere. The roar of thousands, joined. The two warriors had been separated for the first time in a week. North Gate. South Gate. They would emerge onto a field of grass, a lush span of green inspired by the cotton fields of the Angola plantation/prison. Shrubs here and there. But mostly clean, even grass. The GameMasters knew this was not a match that needed distraction. This was what the people wanted. This was a perfect match. This was a finale, but also a beginning.

They watched. They believed in their mission, which was to serve themselves and then the world. Whatever they did, whatever outcome, they could own and sell and forge into a new kind of life. They were artists of the highest order.

The full range of human possibility was there on this one night. This was it. The promise that all the games had implied. This was it.

The GameMasters watched. They were the board of directors but also, they were more; they were dealmakers and wardens and politicians and owners, and they lived in a rarefied version of the world, a space above, for them alone. They sat and drank champagne to their philanthropic hearts' content. They watched a game they'd won already, many times over. The seats near the bottom were the most expensive; they got cheaper and cheaper as you rose up. And yet, the closed-off sky lounges they sat in cost a price most could never imagine paying.

They drank and did not think about the philosophical. The girl with her sign had made them sick to their stomachs. The questions made them sick to their stomachs. The thousands of protestors outside made them sick to their stomachs. And yet, they still were unsure, would not acknowledge, what those people were so offended by. What was the great evil? Couldn't they, those people who did not have the wit or gumption or grace to sit in these high-up lounges, understand that they, the GameMasters, were transforming this terrifying world into something beautiful?

They watched on a live cast as Tracy Lasser handed the microphone to the adopted mother of that foolish girl, who was recovering still from her Influencing, but who had shown up tonight like a mascot. "And we will not be moved. We will never be silenced. My daughter's message will be heard. We will not stop until the system is reimagined completely. Until the state works to disappear problems and not individuals. Until the courage of people like my daughter is met with change, we will not stop." The woman turned and looked at the girl, this Mari, and handed her the microphone.

"They could not stop me. Never forget that they cannot stop you," Mari said. Her voice shook, but it was loud and had a weight to it. She had recovered, had become an ad for the lunacy these people were selling. There, dressed in black, she could say anything and people would eat it up. She had trespassed and now millions of people viewed her as some kind of hero. She was alive and yet still she'd become a martyr, born in holophone recordings of her Influencing. "We are many, we are united, we are—"

They cut the cast.

Couldn't they see they'd taken horror and hidden it away?

Couldn't they see that they'd taken that same horror and put it out in the world to remind the people that they, the GameMasters, had saved them?

A knife is only ever so far from your neck.

A man of ill intent is only ever so far from your children, your daughters, your sons.

Couldn't they see that? How blind must they be if they couldn't see the beauty the GameMasters had built.

There were two ways to think about it.

You could believe there were good people and bad people. And that the good deserved glory and the bad deserved punishment.

Or, you could believe that no one deserved to be punished, but that the punishment was a necessary fallout. An unavoidable sacrifice to serve the greatest good: humanity. And so they, the GameMasters, shouldered that burden as well. Always for the ultimate good. The difficult good. The goddamned world of good that was only possible because they were willing to build the infrastructure to facilitate the salvation. Remove a cancer. A justice of effort performed for the people by the best of them. An effort to incapacitate an ever-present evil, to perform the retribution necessary to honor the many victims of the world's great pain, to deter the seeds of evil growing in the masses and rehabilitate, when possible, those who sought redemption.

Those who they believed deserved it.

This is the world. This is the fact. A service as necessary as life itself. And they, we, you, them—everyone agreed to the arrangement.

The people in the sky lounge raised their glasses.

"Cheers," they called, and then they turned their attention to the green fields they'd designed.

Colossal

You call me Colossal.
　　Come call me what you call me, come, come call me to life,
call me now.
　STAXXX
　Call me criminal. Cold heart catastrophe
　Call me uncalled, call me king
　Call me crazy, even as you kill me, you call me killer
　Call me, hear my name, call me now
　STAXXX
　Call me culled, call me kite
　Call me candlelight kept
　Call me Kane, call me Christ
　Call me church of the Creator
　Call me what you call me
　STAXXX
　Call it as it is
　The life you give is death
　The death I give is life. Is love at least
　So call me Colossal
　Call me corrupt, call me clean

Call me cure, call me Hurricane

STAXXX

Hurricane

STAXXX

Hurricane

STAXXX

Come call, come call, come call me complete.

Freeing Day

And then she emerged onto the grounds with her scythe in her hands. And the people called her name so loudly they shook the earth.

They announced her.

Micky Wright was absent, as if it were too much of a day, too epic a meeting, for even a single other soul to be on the grounds.

Staxxx's words were still racing through Thurwar when she stepped out from the tunnel into the light. Adoration exploded. She punched a hammered fist into the sky as her eyes adjusted and she took in the magnitude all around her. A sea of men and women shimmering in the stands, screaming and crying and breathing for her. She could hear the chants of protestors outside. She raised her fist for them.

She took her breaths as she walked through the grass, tried not to look at Staxxx, who was, of course, locked into the Keep opposite her. Thurwar turned to the stands. She saw her Chain, locked into their seats but screaming their throats sore. They were there, close to it all. She could see Sai's neck muscles bulging as they screamed, saw Rico and Ice screaming the same. She saw Bad Water cheering, and even Gunny, watching all of them, there for all of them.

She listened, felt it all. Closed her eyes and let it spill over her.

THUR-WAR

THUR-WAR

THUR-WAR

Thurwar noticed the HMC floating in front of her. She looked at A-Hamm and winked. They had begged her to do this and so she would.

"Here we are!" Thurwar screamed. And the people were in shock. They had not heard from their queen before a fight in so long.

"Here we are again, the same place I started," Thurwar said. Her words were hers, but she spoke for all of them, all those Freed and un-Freed, High and Low. "A freeing ground."

She felt the hammer in her hand, thought of its weight, how carrying it had damaged her, how she'd used it to damage others. How she needed it, like she needed this. How sometimes what hurts you is also what you need.

She dropped Hass Omaha down beside the Keep.

"The bad news is, I forgive you," Thurwar said, and the people screamed. "The good news is, I forgive you."

Who was she speaking to?

The whole world.

"You should never forget that we are phenomena you have not seen before. Isn't that true?"

The whole world said yes.

Thurwar smiled to herself and allowed herself Staxxx's eyes. Their gazes met. Thurwar's saying, *How am I doing?* Staxxx's saying, *I'm in awe.*

"This is something you have not seen before, I'm glad we agree. You've never seen a Blood Mother before."

We have not! they screamed.

"You've never seen the Loud Theater Terror, the Low-Tide Titan, Lord Thunder herself!" she screamed back. Let herself fall into the old self, the character the world had called its own. "The Lion Tamer, the one who sang the last melody. The one who trained you all!"

Thurwar looked again at Staxxx, who kneeled and laughed. Because it was true; Thurwar, long ago, had shown these crowds the power of call-and-response.

"Who taught you who you are?" Thurwar said, jumping into the air.

THUR-WAR

"Who is your favorite Colossal's favorite *Grand* Colossal?"

THUR-WAR

"And if all that is true, I want you to remember this too." Thurwar spun slowly, so that each of the thousands might feel as if she were looking specifically at them.

"We are something you have never seen before." And before she kneeled into the Keep, she said, "When you think of us, remember that just because something is, doesn't mean it can't change, and just because you haven't seen something before, that doesn't mean it's impossible. They call this a freeing ground. So who's going to be freed: me or you?"

Then she kneeled into the bay and the crowd went quiet. This was what they were born for.

A voice that was no one's, a machine made human or a human-feigning machine, said, "LOCK-IN," and Thurwar felt that hold for the last time in her life.

Loretta Thurwar

An HMC floated toward each of their lips.

Locked, they were still. They held the stillness, felt their power. Staxxx thought, How embarrassing for you. All these chains and look at me, free as all wind. "I've said it all," Staxxx said. "Pay attention."

Thurwar looked across to Staxxx and into the HMC. "I love you," Thurwar said. And they were released to the sounds of thousands.

Thurwar ran. And so did Staxxx. They moved in quick, leaping steps over the grass that sprung them to each other. They ran just as fast as they could into each other's arms. Her knee, she did not care, it hurt but this was it. She'd give everything her knee had. They arrived at each other.

They held each other. The people were quiet. They held each other, and each knew she was holding a part of herself in her arms.

"Us, okay?" Thurwar said.

"You and me," Staxxx said.

When she pulled her lips away from Staxxx's the people were stunned to silence.

They let go of each other and Thurwar looked one last time at Staxxx, this warrior who had shocked the world by being herself.

The killing time was here.

"You ready?" Thurwar said.

"Swing through," Staxxx said.

"What?" Thurwar said.

"I love you."

"Wait," Thurwar said.

But Staxxx had already pulled away.

"You and me," Thurwar said.

"Us," Staxxx said. And they turned away from each other. Thurwar wiped her eyes and jogged to retrieve Hass Omaha. When she turned Staxxx had pulled up LoveGuile from the ground and the people were elated once more.

The world roared and rumbled as Thurwar felt her hammer's weight. She imagined its force and all it had stripped from its world. Hammer in hand, she ran.

They met each other not far from Thurwar's Keep. Staxxx was faster, and for the first time in Thurwar's life LoveGuile's head was rocketing toward her.

Thurwar's body took control. The thought that drowned was: I should just lie here, I can't do this. But her body said, This one thing I will do for you, let me hold this endless hurt, here you need not think, just move.

Staxxx's body was in the air, and she threw her momentum into a downward slash of incredible speed, which Thurwar knew she'd be able to adjust even midswing.

Thurwar took a hard sidestep and before LoveGuile could poke its nose into the grass, it was whipping around a crouched Staxxx as she spun her body again and sliced it through the air. Many Links had tried to sway at the waist against this attack and found their intestines on their boots soon after. Thurwar jumped back and felt the vicious trail of air left behind by the blade.

Again, Thurwar's body said.

And again it came. Staxxx's feet angled themselves for another rotation, and her waist and arms followed as LoveGuile came again through the air, horizontally, the slash that cut Links in half. Thurwar waited for it and Hass Omaha begged for release; it was tired of watching LoveGuile dance alone. Following the feeling, Thurwar jumped back again, but as she did, she loosed her grip on Hass Omaha so that she held the very end of his handle and swung up into the air.

The clang of metal on hammer made the people explode to new life. LoveGuile shot straight up into the air. Thurwar saw the opening. The way to crush, the path to freedom straight through a heart that had kept her alive for so—she thought too long, and even as she moved forward to deliver a blow, Staxxx, in her strength and grace, was able to end LoveGuile's ascent and charm it into a nosedive toward Thurwar's head. Thurwar stopped her swing and shrugged up as she swayed. LoveGuile slashed through the Hammer logo on her shoulder guard and Thurwar felt a tingle that rattled from her shoulder to her hands.

Leave thought behind, her body said. Trust me. I can do this.

LoveGuile bounced off her armor and was rearing back to cut through her face when Thurwar pressed forward. More thought drowned. She was there, completely. Fully in a moment unlike any before, there with Staxxx. All she could ever do was press forward. Thurwar and Staxxx. Their eyes met: grateful and destroyed.

Thurwar tossed Hass Omaha to her left hand, then grabbed the scythe's shaft below the head with her right. For the first time that evening, LoveGuile, the weapon that women and men the world over feared, was still. Thurwar turned her body while holding on to the scythe and swung hard and down toward Staxxx's crown. To survive, Staxxx had to let go of LoveGuile completely, and Hass Omaha came crashing to the floor as Staxxx's boot crashed into Thurwar's face.

The first strike to land.

They stood in their seats. She had missed but she'd swung through, and knowing she could made Thurwar feel something worse than anything she'd ever felt. She took a breath. She was still there, breathing. Her body, the feeling said, I know it hurts, see the hurt, feel it, then move.

The people roared and roared. An appetite that would never be satisfied sharpened and stretched. Thurwar held LoveGuile and stumbled, the weight of Hass and the blow to the head unsteadying her. Staxxx grabbed her weapon with two hands before drop-kicking Thurwar in the chest and stomach. Thurwar released LoveGuile as she was blown back and rolled. When she looked up, Staxxx was running toward her. A body running forward, a hurricane in the flesh. Staxxx swiped hard at Thurwar and Thurwar got to her feet and began to jump back, and even as she did, she knew it would not be enough, so she collapsed to her back and watched the blade rend the air above her face. She kicked forward, and heard Staxxx gasp, and the sound of it made her want to split herself open. But she got to her feet. Tired but ready. She could see Staxxx's breathing was heavy.

They pressed off the grass toward each other. Staxxx leapt into a tight sideswipe and again Thurwar saw the world slowly as Hass pressed LoveGuile away: a second impossible deflection.

LoveGuile recoiled and already Hass was back and ready to eat. Poised to devour the Hurricane Hamara Staxxx. With her hammer back in her dominant hand she swung up toward the sky, toward the jaw, up to break. Thurwar swung as if to crush the dark clouds above. Her body helped her summon a velocity both devastating and absolute. She swung knowing that when she connected, Staxxx would be remembered, multiplied, forever.

But as the hammer moved, she realized that Staxxx had taken the deflection and used it for her own devices. She was already spinning, bringing LoveGuile back around toward Thurwar's neck. She could not stop, she could not move; all she could do was see what was waiting for her on the other side. As she swung up, Thurwar was ready to be freed.

What hit the side of Thurwar's head was LoveGuile's blunt back. Staxxx was turned back around and her face was once again in the path of Hass's murderous rush.

"Gotcha," Staxxx said, and she dropped LoveGuile to the ground.

Before the scythe could find the earth, Hass Omaha rose and blew Staxxx away. The two were freed, and Loretta Thurwar stood among the people, who'd been thrown to a rapturous, rapturous silence.

Acknowledgments

This book is possible because of so many thinkers, activists, writers, and advocates who helped grow my point of view and guide research that deepened my understanding of our carceral world and country. This understanding was the inspiration for so much of this book. Teachings and essays by Ruth Wilson Gilmore, Angela Davis, and Mariame Kaba were incredibly important over the years I worked on this book. I am extremely grateful to the Rockland Coalition to End the New Jim Crow, a group of passionate community members who have helped me learn in practice how we can change our systems to better reflect the world we want to live in. The Unity Collective, and working on that project, also helped me feel in community with people who were thinking through these issues.

I'd like to acknowledge and send love to the family of Tina Davis.

For contextual information on many of the statistics and facts cited in this book, I referred to the American Constitution and its amendments. For legal citations dealing with criminal law, I referred to Title 18 of the United States Code.

The resources provided by the Prison Policy Initiative were a great help in researching incarceration in America, as was ProPublica. The

Institute for Transparent Policing made me aware of the Law Enforcement Support Office. I also drew a lot from TransEquality.org.

Albert Woodfox's *Solitary* has been an essential inspiration for me in the process of drafting this book. The *New York Times* coverage, particularly that done by Campbell Robertson, of Woodfox's, as well as Herman Wallace's and Robert King's, time in solitary confinement was also extremely generative for me.

Reporting in *The Guardian,* and several other news outlets, made me aware of Cyntoia Brown and her imprisonment.

E. Ann Carson, PhD, authored a report on suicide in prisons and jails, which I pulled harrowing statistics from.

A joint report by Reuters and the National Center for Women & Policing (November 5, 1999) provided history and context regarding police and domestic abuse that appear in this book. The report is based on data from "On the Front Lines: Police Stress and Family Well-Being" by the House of Representatives' Select Committee on Children, Youth, and Families and "Interspousal Aggression in Law Enforcement Families" by Peter Neidig, Harold Russell, and Albert Seng.

The *New York Times* piece "A Vast Racial Gap in Death Penalty Cases, New Study Finds" by Adam Liptak, and that paper's coverage of Warren McCleskey's pivotal case, was extremely valuable background material, as was NPR's coverage of the overturning of George Stinney, Jr.'s conviction. Alan Lomax recorded the Black prisoners of Darrington State Prison Farm, whose work songs appear in this book. Love to those prisoners and all the incarcerated and formerly incarcerated. Your voices are essential.

I'd also like to thank Peyton Shining Fox Powell for the incredible love and support without which this book would not have been possible. I'd like to thank Dana Spiotta, Arthur Flowers, and George Saunders for their mentorship and guidance through these years. Many thanks to the Syracuse MFA program as a whole, especially Sarah Harwell and Terri Zollo for creating a space for so many of us.

Eternal gratitude to Lynne Tillman for setting me properly on this path. Big thanks to Walker Rutter-Bowman for reading an earlier version of this book. And another huge thank-you to Ingrid Rojas Contreras for her guidance in all things novel. Thank you to the Hermitage in Sarasota for the time to focus on this project.

Thanks to the entire FAM for keeping me grounded and making everything jokes. Thanks to the Rensselaer/Greenridge/Plimpton team for everything.

Forever gratitude to the incredible Meredith Kaffel Simonoff for all the different ways she makes this possible, and to Naomi Gibbs for working in the trenches through this long process of getting a book into the world.

Massive thanks to Lisa Lucas, Natalia Berry, Josie Kals, Julianne Clancy, Asharee Peters, Altie Karper, and Kathleen Cook, and everyone at Pantheon whose work was integral to this book's existing in this form.

Thanks to my sister Afua, who is an inspiration to all those looking for how to be themselves. Thanks to my sister Adoma, who is another person who makes so much of this possible. Thank you, Mom; this book and everything I ever do is yours. And thank you, Dad; it hasn't always been easy, but thank you for all of it. This book is dedicated to you, I think you would have liked it.

A NOTE ABOUT THE AUTHOR

Nana Kwame Adjei-Brenyah is the *New York Times* best-selling author of *Friday Black*. His work has appeared in *The New York Times Book Review, Esquire, The Paris Review, Guernica,* and elsewhere. He is a National Book Founda-tion "5 Under 35" honoree, a winner of the PEN/Jean Stein Book Award and the Saroyan Prize, and a finalist for the National Book Critics Circle's John Leonard Prize for Best First Book, the Aspen Words Literary Prize, and the Dylan Thomas Prize, along with many other honors. Originally from Spring Valley, New York, he now lives in the Bronx.

A NOTE ON THE TYPE

This book was set in Garamond, a typeface originally designed by the Parisian type cutter Claude Garamond (c. 1500–61). This version of Garamond was modeled on a 1592 specimen sheet from the Egenolff-Berner foundry, which was produced from types assumed to have been brought to Frankfurt by the punch cutter Jacques Sabon (c. 1520–80).

Typeset by Scribe, Philadelphia, Pennsylvania

Printed and bound by Berryville Graphics,
Berryville, Virginia

Designed by Jo Anne Metsch

DA   'F